INTRODUCT

A Contest of Wills by Becky Melby
Minutes after braving frigid waters in
near Cedarburg, free-spirited, forty-
literally grabs the nearest man to solv
able Wilson Woodworth offers Willow and her children a ride—simple kindness that plunges both into uncharted waters. When a contest to win retail space in the coveted historic district draws the unlikely pair into some outlandish schemes, will they find that opposites attract?

In Tune with You by Rachael Phillips
Twenty-five-year-old Chesca Appel, part-time choirmaster and music box shop manager, plans a magnificent cantata to celebrate Easter. Then her pastor requests two unexpected additions: drama and children, neither of which she feels capable of handling. Enter Seth Amundsen, a tone-deaf football coach who loves both. He, the rowdy children, his alluring ex-fiancée, her vengeful mother, and a basketful of trouble all join to make a cantata more memorable than Chesca ever imagined.

Silvery Summer by Eileen Key
With art, culture, the scent of strawberries, summer at its finest, and love in the air, newly retired Claire Parsons can't resist wondering if she misjudged Cedarburg's—and Eli Mueller's—influence over her. They both broke her heart once. Does she dare let them work their magic on her at this stage of life? Will love come full circle in Cedarburg?

Maybe Us by Cynthia Ruchti
With college five years behind her, Beth Schurmer can't afford to invest in a love interest. . .plus her Yarn Shop and caring for her grandfather. Love has threatened to bankrupt her more times than she can count. It's a good thing her neighbor, chocolatier Derrick Hofferman, feels the same way. But as autumn comes to Cedarburg, Beth considers that wool of three strands might have merit after all.

CEDAR CREEK SEASONS

FOUR-IN-ONE COLLECTION

EILEEN KEY, BECKY MELBY,
RACHAEL PHILLIPS,
& CYNTHIA RUCHTI

Print ISBN 978-1-61626-645-5

eBook Editions:
Adobe Digital Edition (.epub) 978-1-62029-074-3
Kindle and MobiPocket Edition (.prc) 978-1-62029-075-0

Cover design: Kirk DouPonce, DogEared Design

Published by Barbour Publishing, Inc., P.O. Box 719, Uhrichsville, Ohio 44683, www.barbourbooks.com

Our mission is to publish and distribute inspirational products offering exceptional value and biblical encouragement to the masses.

ecpa Member of the Evangelical Christian Publishers Association

Printed in the United States of America.

On behalf of Eileen, Rachael, and Becky, Cynthia writes:

My first Cedarburg experience was a quick drive-through on my way to someplace else. I caught only a glimpse of its charm, only a hint of its untold stories. I've returned several times since, intent on soaking up all the details that make Cedarburg such a surprising and embraceable community.

Special thinks to those who helped stir our appreciation for the unique natural and handcrafted beauty, the irrepressible celebration of art and culture, and the history in Cedarburg's buildings, its bridges, and its society. Thank you to Arlene, Deb, Lori, the incomparable Jim Coutts; to Kristine and the staff and volunteers at the Chamber of Commerce and General Store Museum, the Cedar Creek Trading Post and its sweet music, and to the proprietors and hostesses at the Stagecoach Inn and the Washington House Inn. Thank you, too, to Herman, for getting my (Cynthia's) car back on the road when it collapsed under the mid-February cold.

Many other Cedarburg residents and self-appointed tourism volunteers shared their stories and enthusiasm with us. We appreciate you all, named or unnamed.

A CONTEST OF WILLS

by Becky Melby

Dedication

To Bob and Dianne,
for your example of finding balance at this
stage of life. You two live with equal doses of
purpose and pleasure—and we're taking notes!
Love you both.

Thank you to my agent, Mary G. Keeley,
of Books & Such Agency.
Special thanks to Rachael, Eileen, and Cynthia
for making collaboration so much fun.

And thank you to Toni and her kids for losing their van door
and giving us a memory to laugh (and write) about. And to
Cole, for sticking a bean in his ear and sparking an idea.

As always, thank you to Bill for patiently holding my
kite string and reminding me to take time to "be still."
I love you, Dr. Snuggles.

This is the day the LORD has made;
let us rejoice and be glad in it.
PSALM 118:24

"Be still, and know that I am God."
PSALM 46:10

Chapter 1

Winter

Willow Miles planted her hands on her ample hips covered in a red-and-black-striped vintage bathing suit. Her teeth chattered as she glared at the winter whitecaps whipping the gray surface of Lake Michigan. The woman who owned this getup during the Roaring Twenties probably had more sense than to wear it on New Year's Day in Wisconsin.

A sign for the Polar Bear Dip marked the gathering spot for a motley crowd of *un*sensibly dressed crazies waiting out the count. "Ten. Nine. Eight. . ." Bundled onlookers joined the chant.

"Seven. Six. Five. . ."

Digging the toes of her argyle kneesocks into snow-laced sand, Willow stuttered, "This is ins–sane." She was all about spontaneity, but there were times a woman on the brink of forty should say no. When Crystal and Elsa, about to become her best friends for never, each grabbed an elbow and began a pathetic rendition of "Happy Birthday to Willi," she knew it was too late.

The trio stumbled into the frigid surf off America's Third

Coast. The water stung her feet and burned her calves, but by the time it reached her flapping thighs, she couldn't feel much of anything.

"Go under! Go under!" The voices of people she once thought cared about her screamed from the safety of parkas and scarves.

"Fine!" Grabbing the hands closest to her, she yanked hard and leaned backward into water so cold her breath solidified in her lungs. As she surfaced, the hand she held in her right tore out of her grip, accompanied by a string of fiery words. Fiery *male* words. A dripping gray-haired man in plaid trunks stomped toward shore amid her shower of apologies.

Elsa, soaked from head to toe and laughing with a wheeze that sounded like an ailing vacuum cleaner, pulled Willow to her feet. "What were you *thinking*?"

"I was thinking it was Crystal." With that, she grabbed the hand of her half-dry friend and dunked again. Lifting pasty-white arms to a cloudless sky, Willow rose out of the water. "This is awesome! *Hap*-py New Year!"

Wrapping her arms around her best friends till death—which, considering the windchill, could be any moment—she splashed to shore and the waiting bathrobe held by her adopted daughter. "Th–thank you." Willow slid into the paisley chenille robe, knotted the belt, and planted a loud smack on Star's expertly blushed cheek. Water dripped from Willow's flower-studded bathing cap onto Star's coat. "That was a blast!"

Try as the poor girl might, Star couldn't, under the circumstances, pull off the bored teen look. An embryo of a smile curved one side of her mouth. "So. Check this off the bucket list, huh?"

"No way!" Willow looked to her friends for nods of confirmation. "We have to do this every year until we're old, old ladies."

"You *are* o—" Star clamped her hand over her mouth, but her eyes gleamed.

Willow curled a fist and popped it lightly on the girl's nose. She would gladly be the brunt of a million jokes if it would keep a smile on Star's face. "Take me home."

The gleam ramped to a genuine glow. "I can drive?"

Hopping on one foot, Willow pulled off a wet sock and slipped her blanched foot into an Indian-print mukluk. "You have to. I'd get arrested on a DWH."

"What's that?"

"Driving while hypothermic." She wiggled her eyebrows and blew a stream of condensed air at Star.

"You're not changing clothes first?" This followed by a look informing Willow she was exponentially dumber than a toadstool.

"We'll be home in fifteen minutes. I'd have to stand in line at the restroom longer than that. Get the boys and let's boogie."

"Ralphy! Del!" Star screamed then coughed with the rush of cold air into her lungs.

Willow covered her ears. "I could have hollered myself."

Star shrugged and went off to find the boys who failed to respond to her yell. Willow made her rounds with hugs and shivered a prayer all the way to her van. "P–please let it start."

In a parking lot of rust-free cars, the ancient maroon van stuck out as much as a short, pudgy woman running through the snow in a purple paisley robe. Willow smiled at her usually faithful four-wheeled soul mate that had once been her home.

"Willi! Wait!" A duet of voices slowed her steps. She grinned at the boys she'd done a passable job of raising for eight years. Reddened cheeks peeked from matching Green Bay Packer jackets.

"Let's go, troops."

"Can we go home with Elsa? *Puh*-lease?" Ralphy blasted her with bionic nine-year-old charm. "They're going for pizza."

"Sorry. Family night. New Year's Eve was all the fun you're getting for the weekend." Willow kept walking, chunky knees stiffening with each chill-wracked step. Rigor mortis setting in. Would people pay to gawk when she became an ice sculpture? What would they call her? The Chunky Chilly Chick?

Chili. She turned to the pouters. "I have chili on the stove, and after a three-hour hot bath, I'm not going out again to pick you up."

"But after pizza they're going to the Chocolate Factory for brownie fudge sundaes."

Of course they were. "Elsa has money. Elsa has a real job and a husband with a job." *Elsa started life with a plan she's actually following. Elsa didn't wake up one morning to a sheriff telling her she had three kids.*

"But. . ." This from Del, whose monosyllabic vocabulary foreshadowed the approaching teen years.

"The only 'but' I want to hear is the one sliding into your seat. Go."

Heads down, they ran to the van.

"I love you guys more than peanut butter cups!" she yelled, adding humiliation to disappointment.

A man in a floor-length fur coat with a beanie copter on his head gawked at her.

That'll be two dollars, mister.

She waved. The man looked away. Star reached the van just ahead of the boys. In seconds, the engine sputtered to life. Willow pointed her index finger heavenward as she angled her approach toward the passenger side. "Thank You, Je—" A shriek from the direction of her van split the air, followed by giggles, followed by another shriek.

Willow ran around the back bumper and stopped, now frozen figuratively as well as literally.

The boys balanced, arms outstretched like gangly surfers, on top of the van's sliding side door. . .which lay flat on the snow-covered ground.

ଓଃ

A shrill scream drew Wilson Woodhaus's attention to a battered burgundy van. He waved good-bye to his vintage-dressed buddies and walked around the front of his '85 Camaro. He rubbed a splotch of road salt off the canary-yellow hood as he craned his neck to determine the source of the scream. From this angle, he couldn't see anything other than the lady in the purple robe and old-fashioned yellow bathing cap sloshing through the wet snow in striped boots.

A peculiar sight. Possibly not significantly stranger than his 1920s frat house garb, but at least he wasn't running, drawing attention to himself, like the woman in the robe.

Whatever caused the commotion, there was now an adult presence. Sidestepping a patch of ice, he opened his car door, slid, beaver skin coat and all, into the bucket seat, and removed the ridiculous beanie from his head. At the push of a button, the subwoofers vibrated and the Temptations belted out "Treat Her Like a Lady." With a swift twist, he stilled the song. Breathing a sigh as a Mendelssohn concerto calmed the air, he put the car in reverse.

A pounding on the back window made him slam on the brake. The robe lady waved at him in the rearview mirror.

"Stop! Please!"

Wilson rolled down the window as she spun across the ice and grabbed onto his side mirror. He cringed, experiencing her chokehold on the chrome of the only car he'd ever owned as acutely as if her fingers gripped his throat. "Something wrong?" It was a rather banal comment, considering the scream.

"I need a man!"

He arched his brows.

"A hand. I need a *hand*. With my van door."

He got out of the car.

Purple Lady laughed. "Look at us! We're a matched set." She pointed to his grandfather's coat then whipped open the robe, gesturing to her vintage swimsuit.

Wilson blinked and felt his face warm. "Is the door frozen?"

"Could be." She closed the robe and hopped on one foot, then the other. "Frozen to the *ground*."

"What?"

"Come see." She led the way between two rows of cars. "My son yanked it open, and it slid off the track and plunked into the snow. See?"

Interior side up, the van door rocked on its back in a snowbank like a disabled turtle.

"Can you help us get it back on?" She rubbed her arms as expectant eyes pleaded from under the dripping bathing cap.

The woman was wet. His chivalry hadn't gotten much practice lately, but the realization spurred him to action. "Here." He unbuttoned Grossvater's coat. "Put this on and get in the van. On second thought, go get in my car." *And please don't drip.*

"Th–thank you s–so much." She turned and ran to the Camaro.

Wilson eyed the Packer-jacketed pair. Not a lot of muscle

power there. "Well, men, are you with me? Let's extricate this thing." A confident demeanor could mask a lot of ignorance.

His green-and-gold crew gaped. The older one narrowed hazel eyes. "Let's *what*?"

"Extri—lift this thing."

"Oh. . .yeah."

His helpers put their backs into it, but after three futile attempts to reattach the door, the girl with her forehead resting on the steering wheel let out an annoyed sigh. "It's not gonna work. Just stick it behind the seat and let's go."

The older boy looked at her as if he'd just discovered a new species of maggot. "Are you crazy? Willi would freeze to death on the way home and you'd lose your license."

"I would not."

"Yeah. . .um. . .I think there's safety laws against driving cars without things like. . .um. . .*doors*."

"Duh. You'll have your seat belt on."

Wilson planted the door in a snowbank. "Where do you live?"

"Cedarburg," the little one answered. "On Sheboygan Road right by the creek."

"Go ask your mom if she wants—"

A car door opened and closed. Wilson recognized the timbre of the slam and turned to see Grossvater's coat barreling toward him.

"Chili!" the lady yelled.

Wilson looked over her bathing cap at his yellow wheels. "Wasn't the heater on in my car?"

"No! I mean yes, it was nice and warm, but I've got chili on the stove! Star, grab my phone and call Elsa and tell her to come back and get us. Quick!"

For a millisecond, Wilson considered leaving them to work things out on their own, but words he'd just read that morning came inconveniently to mind. " '*Whatever you did not do for one of the least of these, you did not do for Me.*' "

Were women in paisley bathrobes part of "the least"? He looked down at the boys' snow-crusted boots. "I live in Cedarburg." At times, chivalry felt like a curse. "I'll give you a ride."

The woman lowered her frantic arms. "You'd do that? For complete strangers? Then you'll join us for chili. No arguments. Star, grab my purse. Boys, get in that scrumptious yellow Camaro. Hurry."

Whooping with joy, the boys ran. The girl slammed the driver's door of the van with a force that probably wasn't joy. Her footsteps crushed the snow as she rounded the front of the sad-looking vehicle. Five feet from Wilson, the girl stopped. Her mouth opened. The ring in her nose kept swinging. "Willi!" Her face blanched, leaving only spots of unnatural pink. "You can't invite him to our house. Do you know who this is? It's Wilson Woodhaus. He's like the best, most amazing artist in the whole town. The whole state. The world, maybe."

The woman folded her purple arms. "We'd appreciate the ride, Mr. Woodhaus, but I guess I'll have to rescind my chili offer." She tipped her head to one side. "Apparently, you're too good to eat."

Chapter 2

Chaos in the midst of order.

Wilson fiddled with wheat-colored fringe on the place mat Ralphy, the younger boy, set in front of him. None of the five woven plate rugs matched, and the chairs were a hodgepodge of decade and design. Living in this conglomeration of style and color would make him nervous, yet the decor worked. It had a unique charm—fitting for a kitchen with "This is the day the Lord has made; let us rejoice and be glad in it" lettered above vermillion cupboards.

Del approached with a stack of plates. In keeping with the theme, each one appeared orphaned from a different set.

"You like variety," he observed to the back of Willow or Willy—what was he supposed to call the woman, anyway? "Mrs. Miles" seemed a bit formal and also made the assumption she was currently married. *Married!* Was she? Would she have invited him if she were? Of course she would. This was a thank-you, not a date. But would her husband get that? He scanned the pictures on the fridge, searching for a likely face to attach to the man who might stomp in at any moment and kick him out of the greatly distressed Queen Anne chair.

Two of the many plastic frameless frames smothering the

fridge featured Willow and a man. He appeared too old to have a strong right hook. If that was her husband, she'd married into another generation.

"I like garage sales." Willow/Willy lifted a spoon from a pot of something that smelled tantalizing, though unchili-like. She set a bowl of grated cheese on the table. "And flea markets and antique stores and hand-me-downs. Or ups." Her mouth curved as she tapped the knobby white cheese bowl.

The woman had one of those fascinating faces that appeared instantly younger when she smiled. Her eyes, blue with hints of turquoise, glinted as if she were harboring a delicious secret.

Wilson shifted his gaze to the stove. How long had he been staring? Would she realize that analyzing facial features was an integral part of an artist's job? He nodded toward the simmering concoction. "That smells intriguing." He cleared his throat. "Do you go by Willow or Willy or—"

"Willi. With an *I*." She ran the backs of her fingertips along her roundish torso, ending with a finger flare at her hips. "My parents obviously envisioned a leggy, long-waisted daughter. Who knew they'd have one without a waist at all." She grinned and turned back to the stove.

Oh, how he hated these verbal setups. Did women know what torture they put a man through when they made self-deprecating statements designed to garner a compliment out of a clueless—

"Hot or not?"

Wilson gulped and shifted his eyes back to his place mat and Jamaican-flag-striped plate. She definitely wasn't what he'd call "hot," but how do you let someone down easily? He took in the whole picture, from fur-lined moccasins and dark jeans to the blue-and-red-plaid shirt that hung loosely from a. . .a *generous* upper body. She was short, but not what anyone would label petite. An artistic flare was evident in her makeup and jewelry. He liked her pendant and matching earrings—blue stones snaked by gold wire. "Well. . ."

"Maybe I'll just put the habaneros on the table and everyone can add what they want." She set two spice jars in front of him. "It's Cedar Creek Chocoffee Chicken Chili."

"Choc-*what*?"

"Chocoffee. The secret is a cup of strong coffee and two squares of Baker's chocolate."

That would explain the indefinable aroma. Why, again, had he said yes to this?

Star, his one-girl teen fan club, sauntered in, took a spoon out of a drawer, and dipped it into the pot. "It's easier if you just call it Number Twenty-Four."

"I take it you're entering the chili contest at the Winter Festival."

"Always have, always will. Haven't won yet."

Star licked the coated spoon, raised an eyebrow, and lifted a calendar from a nail on the wall. "Last week we tried Pumpkin Pineapple Chili. The week before, Black Bean Beet." She tapped a lime-green fingernail on the page. "Three weeks ago, it was Hot Hungarian Jalapeño, and last month she made us eat Sweet Potato Salmon Chili and by midnight we all had the—"

"Star!" Willi snatched the calendar. "I bet Mr. Woodhaus would like something to drink while he's waiting."

"Water would be fine." And safe. Best not chance whatever weird concoctions lurked behind the picture gallery on the fridge. Ginger Peach Garlic Tea, maybe, or Raspberry Cayenne Carrot Juice.

"Speaking of the Winter Festival, you should enter the bed race with us." Willi-with-an-*I* turned from him to the girl. "That fur coat and copter hat would be perfect, wouldn't it?"

Star nodded as she poured what appeared to be water embellished with lemon slices from a pitcher, handed him the glass, and left the room. Wilson settled against the back of his chair.

Clunk! Something hit the floor above the kitchen. The Tiffany lamp over the kitchen table shimmied. *Thwack!* A picture slipped cockeyed on the wall. Wilson sat up straight, muscles taut. "What was that?"

"Boys." Willow chopped onions and scraped them from the cutting board into a boat-shaped bowl. "You don't have any, do you?"

Onions? No, she must mean boys. "Never been married."

"Me neither."

She seemed to enjoy the surprise that must be registering on his face. She nodded toward the fridge. "That's my dad." Had she caught him staring at the pictures of the older man? She looked up at the swaying lamp. "Kids! Come and get it!"

A stampede descended unseen stairs. Were there more than three? And all without a husband? What had he gotten himself into?

"They don't seem to be afraid of your chili."

"They get only bread and water in between chili experiments." She set a sour cream carton on the table. "Makes anything yummy."

Wilson laughed—a startle reaction. Her deadpan statements followed by that sudden smile were disorienting.

The boys landed, breathless, in the chairs across from him. Star walked coolly and gracefully into the room with a large portfolio under her arm. *Oh no.*

"Good." Willow pulled a loaf of savory-smelling bread from the oven. "I was hoping you'd bring your sketches down."

Oh *no*. Wilson swallowed hard, forcing down the dread. "You draw?"

Star shrugged. "I paint a little, too." Her cheeks pinked. "I love your work. I go to every one of your shows at the Cultural Center and I took crazy notes when you spoke on pigment washes."

"Huh?" Ralphy's freckled face scrunched like a wrinkly shar-pei. "How do you wash a pig tent? *Why* would you wash a pig tent? Pigs don't sleep in tents anyway."

Star launched a straw at him. Del dropped his head back, mouth wide open. "I don't be*lieve*. How can you be my brother and still be so stu—"

"Del." Willi slid into a Shaker chair. "Would you give thanks for this food and our guest *and* your little brother, please?"

"I guess." Tangled curls bounced as his head rebounded, chin to chest. "Lord, thank You for whatever it is we are going to eat and thank You for a real, live artist in our house, and thank You for taking such good care of us all the time. Amen."

Willi cleared her throat.

"And thank you for Ralphy even though sometimes he can be a real—"

"Del!"

☙

Willow held her breath and poured a second cup of coffee for the man who sat on her plaid couch leafing mutely through her daughter's sketchbook. Star sat across from him, twirling her thumb ring like she was winding an alarm clock. Streaked and choppy blond hair tousled over her shoulders, half shielding her face.

Please, please say something positive.

He wasn't a very talkative person. Granted, when the talk at the table turned to the video game she'd found on eBay, Wilson Woodhaus was a bit out of his element. The boys had done their best to explain Flobgobbers IV to the poor clueless man, but the more they laid out strategies of Whipplestops versus Pollyworgs, the gigglier they got. She'd finally had to step in and distract them with do-it-yourself sundaes.

Apparently, professional artists weren't all that into food fights.

She eyed the chocolate smear above his right knee and the strawberry sprinkle clinging to the collar of a shirt with creases that had to have been ironed in. People still did that? If the guy could iron, he probably knew how to pretreat chocolate stains. To be on the safe side, she'd tuck a stain stick in the bag with the chili she'd send home with him.

His lips puckered. His mouth squinched to the left. What was going on in that handsome head?

How did that adjective squeeze in? She scurried the coffeepot back to the kitchen and analyzed from the safety of her butcher's block. He was tall, but not muscular. There was a softness about him she supposed some women would see as teddy-bearish. A slight paunch. Smaller than hers. A few grays mingled with a full head of thick black hair. So what, out of all of that, made "handsome" enter the picture?

The eyes. Did God use that shade just this once and then throw out the formula? She'd never seen such a startling combination of ocean blue and. . .what? Silver, maybe. The color of moonlight, if moonlight had a color.

Heat surged from a furnace in her chest. *Happy forty to me*. But what had triggered this one? Up to now, she'd only experienced spontaneous combustion while drinking hot tea or blow-drying her hair. She glared at the artist on her couch. No, it couldn't be.

Wilson Woodhaus closed the book. He raised his eyes to Star, face devoid of hints. Willow padded into the living room. His head turned slightly right, slightly left, then back to center. Star ceased winding her thumb.

"You have. . .an exceptional gift."

Star stared. Tears gathered. Willow gasped.

"What are your career goals?"

Career goals? He was talking to a girl who, most days, had to be rolled out of bed like a felled log. A girl who listened to death metal and wrote poetry so dark it sucked the light out of a room.

"I'm planning on going to the Art Institute in Milwaukee for advertising."

You are? Since when?

Wilson shook his head. "Don't."

Say what? The girl verbalizes her first-ever life goal and the guy says "Don't"? Willow bit her knuckle and waited for him to squirm out of the hole he'd dug.

"Don't go for advertising. You have something extraordinary, Star." He opened the book to a pencil-and-watercolor picture of Cedarburg's covered bridge at sunset. "You understand light."

His voice, hushed yet infused with passion, loosened the tendons in Willow's knees. She sank onto the deacon's bench.

Tears, the happy kind Willow hadn't seen in years, eroded riverbeds in Star's makeup. "Thank you."

"I'd love to take you on as a student."

Star's face elongated. All ten ringed fingers flew to her mouth. "You would?"

The teddy bear artist nodded.

"How. . .much would it cost?"

"It doesn't matter." Willow rose on unsteady legs and sat next to Star. "I'll paint a few more chairs and clean a few more houses. Just say yes."

Half laugh, half sob, the sound engulfing Star's "Yes" processed in Willow's brain as a sweet melody.

"Thank you, thank you, thank you. Both." Star gripped Willow in a magic-filled hug. "I love you. I have to call Shel."

Willow swiped a shirt cuff under her nose. "Go. Call."

Star danced out of the room. And Willow locked eyes on the hole digger who now stood on a snowcapped mountain. "You have no idea what you just did for that girl. I don't know how to thank you."

"She's very talented. And very poised for her age. You've raised her well."

Poised? The girl who called me an evil despot six hours ago? "I can only take credit for half of it."

"Of course, I didn't mean to slight your. . .her. . .father."

Willow flicked her fingertips. "Her father was, *is*, a bum."

"I'm sorry."

"Me, too. Sorry for the kids. They're not mine." Tucking her legs under her, she nestled into the chair and traced a cabbage rose on the overstuffed arm with her fingertip. "They were a gift." She smiled at the confusion that did intriguing things to his face. "It's a long story."

Wilson picked up his coffee mug, cradled it in both hands, and leaned back on the couch. "I have no pressing engagements."

Except ironing tomorrow's shirt. Willow licked away a smile.

A CONTEST OF WILLS

"I made a lot of bad choices in my twenties, ended up in debt and living in my van. And then I got a job working for a single mom who'd made even bigger mistakes. She'd been given a second chance, so she gave me one. She invited me to live with her and her three kids. . .right after I got arrested for spending the night in her furniture store."

Chapter 3

Willow blew a flake of sawdust off the seat of the stubby-legged chartreuse "child chair" on her workbench. It had to be perfect. She was raising the price by two dollars a chair.

She reached for a foam sheet. "Two dollars times approximately three bazillion should just about do it." She scanned the twenty-by-twenty cement block room, tallying her Popsicle-colored inventory. A dozen child tables, thirty-six chairs, ten potty step-up stools, eight rocking chairs, and body parts for a dozen rocking horses. If she sold out at each of the seven craft fairs scheduled for spring, replenished her stock in between, sold out at the Strawberry Festival, and repeated the process until her cardiac arrest at the Wine and Harvest Festival, she'd just about have enough to cover Star's art lessons.

No prob. Easy-peasy. After nine years using a scroll saw, she could cut round holes in playhouse cubes in her sleep. Bound to come in handy.

"Lord, didn't I hear You say 'Yes' before I told Star to say 'Yes'?"

She hadn't signed anything or scheduled the first lesson or handed over any money yet. She could still get out of it. *Right.*

And watch that rare smile disappear? A smile which had lasted a day and a half already and was even peeking out at seven a.m. as Star walked out the door for school? Not a chance.

Willow wrapped the chair and its sherbet-orange twin, did a half back bend into her shipping department, and retrieved a box. Climbing onto a stepladder that swayed like a rope bridge, she stood on tiptoes and stretched toward a stack of unfinished stools. A wave of seasickness swept over her as she wobbled back down. It had dawned on her more than once that a person who worked with wood for a living could make herself a new ladder. It would be the first thing on her to-do list if she survived the cardiac event.

That, and updating the electric. She unplugged the space heater, making it safe to plug in her branding iron without blowing a circuit. She calculated the time by the slant of the light filtering through the ice-glazed window well cover. A good three hours had passed without a blown circuit.

The branding iron smelled hot enough. She tipped a stool and pressed the iron into its naked underbelly as slick and accurately as a seasoned cowpoke. No one would rustle this four-legged creature away from her at Strawberry Fest. Unless, of course, they bribed her with twenty-one—*make that twenty-three*—dollars. She inspected the burnt words and her rocking chair logo.

TLC

TENDER LOVING CHAIR CO.

CHILD-SIZED FURNITURE MADE

BY TENDER LOVING HANDS.

As smoke wafted from the second stool, her phone dinged, announcing an incoming text. She set the branding iron down and wriggled her thumb and forefinger into the back pocket of jeans that had had far more phone room before she'd started training for the Great Chili Cook-Off. Her imagination added a cork-popping sound effect as it sprung free.

A three-word message banished a morning's worth of worry.

LUNCH. ANVIL. NOON.

Sleep she would sacrifice for the sake of the cause. This, she would not.

Spinning on her heel in the single square foot of open floor space, she grabbed the tape dispenser, spun back, teetered, and toppled backside-first into a bin of packing peanuts.

Her hips stuck, wedging her like a glass slipper on an ugly stepsister. Her feet didn't touch the ground.

Rocking back and forth between her shipping department and her sanding area catapulted her body and her pride face-down into a pile of wood shavings.

Her business and her backside were outgrowing the space.

☙

The icicles hanging from the Washington House roof were too blue. Not enough snow crowned the gold letters above the door of the B&B.

Wilson laid his paintbrush in the tray and walked away from the easel. The timer on his watch had beeped lunchtime minutes ago anyway. He maneuvered around canvases and easels, silently calculating the dwindling number of days he'd have to struggle with this crowded mess. In the bathroom, he washed his hands, wiped the splashes from the sink, and refolded the towel.

The dish drainer in his galley kitchen held four items. He set his plate, glass, knife, and fork on the counter. From the freezer compartment of the refrigerator, he pulled out two zipper bags labeled "Monday."

But today was Tuesday.

Chocoffee Chicken Chili had tampered with his system. And not just the one for weekly menus. He glanced at the counter and the bottle of Tums he'd raided at two a.m.

Willow had sent home enough leftovers for four meals, but it was so good he'd scarfed down half for Monday's lunch and half for supper. He put the Monday bags back and pulled out Tuesday's bags.

Burritos, or his sister's stuffed peppers for lunch? Neither would be very kind to his gastrointestinal system, but eating Monday's chicken soup today would throw his whole week off kilter. He set the peppers on the counter to thaw for supper.

Burritos in hand, he stared at the blank canvas of the refrigerator door. One lone magnet broke the stark whiteness—a souvenir of his sister and brother-in-law's summer visit to Door County. Charlotte and Harvey traveled three hours north and brought him a lighthouse magnet. Wilson traveled to France and Italy and brought them original works of art. Yet he was the one eternally indebted to their generosity.

He picked up the goldenrod flyer that had come in the morning mail and secured it with the magnet. A spot of needed color.

As he waited for the microwave to call him to lunch, he studied the icicles hanging from the eaves trough, blocking his view of Charlotte and Harvey's century-old farmhouse. How to capture the light that glistened at the tip of the ice?

The microwave dinged. He carried his plate and glass of milk to the table in the alcove, set them next to his day planner, and slipped into the sweater hanging on the back of the chair.

A hug of hand-knit merino wool warmed him. He bowed his head and thanked God for frozen burritos and a sister who gave him magnets, knit sweaters, and a barn.

As he ate, he looked over the next day's schedule. He had a group lesson at four, a class at seven, and two hours in between to fill with a frozen meal labeled "Wednesday" and C. S. Lewis. Only one white space interrupted tomorrow's flow of back-to-back classes.

He put his finger on the five-thirty slot he hoped to fill. Would his offer offend Willow? How should he word it? He pulled his phone out of his shirt pocket, found the number he'd added to his contacts list on Sunday. . .and set the phone down.

☙

"You could have had a serial killer sitting right in your kitchen!"

An unflattering grimace showcased Elsa's capped teeth. Crystal's curls bobbed in agreement like a bouncing Slinky toy.

Willow arced her gaze up one side of the eight-foot blacksmith billows mounted on the restaurant wall behind Elsa. "In my kitchen"—her gaze slid down the other side—"Ralphy's the only cereal killer. This morning he went through three bowls of—"

"Be serious!" Crystal jabbed the air with a half-peeled straw. "Why didn't you call one of us? We were right there. When the kids told me how you got in the car with a complete stranger, I just—"

"Now he knows you never lock your doors," Elsa added.

"And he knows the layout of your house."

"And he knows your *children*."

"Whoa." Willow lifted her purse. "Did my children happen to tell you the man wasn't really a stranger?"

"You knew him?"

"No." Amid stereo questions, she pulled out a postcard. She set the watercolor picture of Advent Lutheran Church on the table.

Crystal's brow ridged like a potato chip. "He's a pastor?"

Their waitress refilled coffee cups then tapped a pink-painted nail on the postcard. "I love his work."

Elsa flipped the card over. "Wilson Woodhaus. *He's* your knight in shining armor?"

Crystal giggled. "Did you see him at the Polar Dip? He was wearing a hat with a propeller on top."

"So he could *fly* to her rescue."

They giggled in harmony.

"He has a booth at all the festivals. I've stopped and talked to him a few times. He's a nice man. One of those still-waters types."

Elsa nodded. Neither looked at Willow. "I sat in on one of his lectures once. Fascinating guy. He's traveled all over the world. He's nice. And single. And not bad looking."

"He's not exactly hunky, but I'd call him handsome." Crystal aimed her critique at Elsa, not Willow. "Definitely worth pursuing."

"Definitely. And just the fact that he accepted a supper invitation means he wasn't repulsed, you know? I mean, *she's* not bad looking, either. For her age. But a girl would have to know what to talk about to engage a guy like that in conversation."

"Right. Might take a little studying to develop some common ground, but if the girl were already kind of artsy. . ."

Of all the times she'd wished she could be a fly on the wall, this really wasn't one of them. *Hey guys, look! My antennae are still wiggling. I can hear you.* She cleared her throat.

Crystal stopped her monologue. "Did you want to get in on this?"

Willow grabbed the partially naked straw and blew through the end of it, slamming a paper projectile into the freshly waxed space between Crystal's eyebrows. "Yes, if you don't mind."

"So what do you think a girl would have to do to sustain the interest of a wealthy, witty, world-savvy artist?"

"Well, for starters, for their first dinner together she would fix him something other than Project Chili Number Twenty-Four."

"Nooo." Crystal stretched out the *O* on a shocked sigh. "You didn't. The guy probably has his own gourmet chef and you fed him a chili experiment?"

"I did." Willow took a slurp of water. "And then, a girl in pursuit of the rich painter probably wouldn't blurt out her entire life story within two hours of meeting him."

Gasps echoed off the high stone walls of the converted blacksmith shop. Crystal cringed. Elsa's eyes protruded like a bullfrog in a breath-holding contest. "How can I say this delicately, sweetie? I'm afraid you—"

"Botched it?"

"Blew it?"

"Messed up big-time?"

Willow stacked the stainless steel saltshaker on top of the pepper. "There was a moment, though, after I told him about getting arrested for literally sleeping on the job, when he said he should take me to Real Chili in Milwaukee sometime."

"Really?"

Two pairs of eyes lit like coals in a blacksmith's furnace.

"I think maybe he was saying I should go somewhere and taste what chili's supposed to taste like." The salt toppled off the pepper. "This is silly. I have no business entertaining such a crazy thought even for a minute. I have a good life. I'm totally content being single. And forty. And chunky and poor and—"

Her phone rang. She looked down at an unfamiliar number. Probably a sales call. She shut the ringer off. "And dateless and pathetic and. . ."

*

Wilson set his phone down without leaving a message. The words he'd rehearsed needed a human voice on the other end. He had to read her tone, to know if she interpreted his suggestion as pity.

Her story had touched him in a way he hadn't fully processed. She'd gotten teary eyed as she told about the woman who had invited her in, mentored her, and introduced her to Jesus, then died suddenly of a prescription drug reaction. "Raising her kids was the least I could do," she'd said, as matter-of-factly as if she'd agreed to water the woman's plants.

He'd never met anyone quite like her. When he worked up the courage to call her again he just might add something to his proposition.

Wilson washed his plate, silverware, and glass and set them in the dish drainer. He turned toward the gold flyer, asking himself if forty-two was too old to start a new life chapter. He smoothed the paper and ran his fingertip under the largest font then pulled the paper out from under the lighthouse magnet. Did he really want to clutter his life with people who weren't assigned to slots in his day planner? "Should I do this?"

The refrigerator stared blankly and offered not a single word of wisdom.

Chapter 4

He waited three more days then called again, pacing a sawdust-covered floor while he waited for her to answer.

"Hello?" Willow sounded completely out of breath. Had she run up the stairs to answer the phone, or did she have some kind of problem? Asthma? A heart condition?

"Hello. Willow." He was supposed to call her Willi-with-an-*I*, but that was silly. His uncle Gus had called him Willy instead of Wilson until he turned thirty. He absolutely hated the name. "This is Wilson Woodhaus."

"Oh. Hi. Wil. . .son."

"Are you all right?"

"Yes. Sorry. Kickboxing."

His well-honed imagination failed him. He couldn't make the picture come together in his head. "You're a kickboxer?"

She laughed. It was a sound he couldn't quite describe. It made him uncomfortable, as if she knew something he should be privy to, but wasn't.

"Kickboxing is what Del calls my shipping method. I haul the boxes up from the basement, line them up like a choo-choo train, and shove them to the door with my feet."

Choo-choo train? "What do you ship?"

"I didn't tell you? How is it I told you about my homeless days but never got around to what I do for a living?"

"You said you clean houses."

"I do. But I also make children's furniture."

"Really?"

"Really. Not the most feminine job, but I love it."

Wilson stopped pacing in front of an unframed painting of the not-covered footbridge at Covered Bridge Park. Purple foxglove graced the banks of Cedar Creek. She was a carpenter. He painted flowers. Weird. "I was wondering if you were free tomorrow night at five thirty and if we could—"

"Oh! The UPS guy is here. Can I call you back in just a couple of minutes?"

"Yes. Of course."

The phone went dead. And so did his nerve.

CS

Willow shivered in the open door as Frank hauled her boxes into his brown truck.

"It's freezing out here, Ms. Miles."

"I know. Just w–wanted a l–little fresh air." *And a whole lot of stalling.* What was she going to say to Wilson Woodhaus? And why was he asking her out after all she'd told him? "How's your wife, Frank? Is she done with her chemo yet?"

"Yup. Last tests showed the tumor was gone."

"I'm so happy to hear that. You tell her hello for me."

"I sure will." He talked over his shoulder. "She feels like she knows you after all the cards you've sent with me."

"Oh! That reminds me. I made something for her." Willow ran down the basement stairs and retrieved a box about a foot long. She ran back up and handed it to Frank. "It's a wig stand."

"Ms. Miles, you are about the most thoughtful person I've ever met. Erma will love this." He handed her a metal clipboard.

She signed the form, said good-bye, and went back inside. Leaning against the door, she hugged her thin blouse to her goose-bumped belly. "You're acting like a child."

Saying it out loud didn't end the polka party in her gut.

Wilson Woodhaus was just a man. A rich, famous, worldly-wise man, but nevertheless, he was still human. And if, after all she'd told him, he was still calling to ask her out, the least she could do was give him a courteous answer. And a chance.

She let her fingers do the walking across the kitchen table to her phone. As she picked it up, the string from a black Mylar balloon drifted across her ear. She looked up at the annoying reminder of yesterday's milestone and set the phone down.

"This is ridiculous. Fair, fat, and forty people get gallstones, not dates."

Snagging the black orb hovering over her head, she headed for the basement stairs. There were potty step-ups to be painted and rocking horses waiting for tails. As she passed the fridge, the Polar Bear Dip picture slid out of its frame and sailed to her feet. Elsa and Crystal glared up at her. "Fair, fat, forty, and *afraid*," they yelled.

"I am not." She lifted her chin. Both of them. And marched back to the phone.

One date. She didn't want to offend him. After all, he might be the key to Star's future. "I can do this. I can be scintillating for one date." It probably wouldn't go anywhere anyway. What did it matter if she exhausted her entire repertoire of social brilliance in one evening? He'd move on after one night. He probably had women tucked away in Mediterranean villas and artsy East Coast brownstones. That would explain the never-been-married part. She pushed the little green icon next to his name.

"Hello," he said. "Willow?"

"Hi. Sorry to be rude like that." She stared at her reflection in the microwave and fluffed her hair. "What was it you wanted to ask?"

"Yes, well. I hope you don't consider me impertinent."

Honey, at forty impertinent might be a compliment. She plucked a stray eyebrow hair and waited.

"Something you said the other day got me thinking, and I was wondering if maybe the two of us could talk about an arrangement that would be mutually beneficial."

An arrangement?

"My house isn't large, but there are times when it's just a bit too much for me to handle alone."

It sounded like dialogue from a prairie romance. Only it was usually a father left with a passel of kids who offered the woman a roof over her head in exchange for raising his kids, running his house, and warming his bed. The back of her neck prickled. She opened her mouth but didn't know what should come out of it.

"And I'm sure with all those kids you could use a little extra help."

Prickles turned to the feel of fiberglass insulation against her skin. The man's audacity was triggering the mother of all hot flashes. In four strides she reached the front door and opened it wide.

"So I thought maybe we could barter."

Barter. The word had a few meanings. Trade. Swap. Negotiate. What was the man saying? His house was small, but he'd help her raise her kids if. . .if *what?* "Mr. Woodhaus"—*Wilson* was way too personal—"I'm afraid I'm not interested in that kind of arrangement."

Silence. A sigh. "I didn't mean to offend you. When you mentioned you cleaned houses, I just thought maybe it would help us both if you came and cleaned for me in exchange for—"

As her finger zeroed in on the red button, she heard him say "art lessons."

଼

Willow sat in the van and stared at the old stone barn. Snow dusted the red roof and gathered in the crevices between the round fieldstones. Ancient trees surrounded the building. An artist's haven. She pictured the interior. Scandinavian, maybe. She'd once met a woman in Door County who'd turned the farm her father had built into an artists' retreat, complete with a round fireplace room at the base of the silo. She could envision one huge, airy, vault-ceilinged loft space, filled with paintings and sculptures from all over the world, all lit with multifaceted LED lights hanging from invisible cords. On one end would be an efficient but lush studio apartment. If his car was any indication, it would be ripe with color. Wilson wasn't home and she couldn't wait to explore his digs.

She turned off the car and the music that had turned her thoughts heavenward. The wipers stopped. Icy beads scudded across the windshield. The wind had picked up and leaden clouds promised more snow. She zipped her jacket to the top, flipped up her hood, and grabbed her cleaning bucket. Head down, she walked up the flight of stone steps leading to a red-painted door. A wrought iron handle creaked as she turned it and stepped in—to a galley kitchen the size of her laundry room.

He'd said his place wasn't big, but she'd assumed, when he said he owned a barn, that he meant not big compared to the Milwaukee Art Museum or the Louvre. She took in white walls, off-white cupboards, and almond-colored appliances. Efficient, yes. Lush, not so much. She walked toward the next doorway, prepared to gasp.

She did.

The room was about the same size as Del and Ralphy's. Nice for a bedroom—nowhere near big enough for a living room that doubled as a studio. Paintings took up every available nook, but nothing decorated the walls except a framed Bible verse. The room did have one redeeming feature. A drab, blue curtain hung on the far end, but no window coverings blocked a wall of tall windows framing an art-inspiring view of heavily wooded hilly acres divided by a creek.

Three medium steps took her to a stark neutral-walled bathroom where a person could do one's business while simultaneously washing hands in the sink and soaking feet in the tub. *Efficient.*

In the bedroom, a high antique bed was pushed against one wall. A carved highboy dresser and a ladder-backed chair left just enough room for one person to walk sideways to the head of the bed. Very cozy. But then, she'd never been claustrophobic. Put Elsa in this room and she'd jump out the window.

And that was that. It would take her all of about twenty-eight minutes for a thorough cleaning. She took off her jacket and rolled up her sleeves as she walked back to the kitchen.

A bold font on a neon gold flyer balancing precariously on a stack of magazines caught her eye.

WIN ONE YEAR'S FREE RENT—
PRIME RETAIL LOCATION

"Sponsored by the shopkeepers of Cedar Creek Settlement." If anyone needed business space, it was Wilson Woodhaus.

She scanned the fine print. A committee would narrow entries down to four. The winner would be decided by the public. Whoever got the most votes would have a twelve-hundred-square-foot shop rent-free for a year.

Twelve hundred square feet? Cedar Creek Settlement? *Are you kidding?* "Forget him. *I* want this."

Chapter 5

The old stone building, webbed with dormant ivy vines, rose before her like a promise. *Your future awaits,* it whispered. The wrought iron arch over Willow's head proclaimed CEDAR CREEK WINERY. On a snow-blanketed second-story sill, three pudgy earthen crocks huddled beneath a weathered board announcing CEDAR CREEK POTTERY.

And what will I call my shop? She opened the right side of the bright blue double doors. "Cedar Creek Children's Chair Company" had a nice alliterative ring to it. "Five Cs" for short. She'd have to order a new branding iron.

The old plank floor groaned as she walked through the winery and up a half flight of stairs. Elsa's shop was straight across the hall. The store was void of customers but filled with rack upon rack of clothes from days gone by. Willow fingered a beaded lace collar on a wasp-waist red velvet gown with leg-of-mutton sleeves.

"Isn't it gorgeous?" Elsa peered from between two scantily clad mannequins, a corset and a pair of nylon stockings in one hand and a poofy rainbow-colored slip in the other. "Try it on."

"The red dress with the twelve-inch waist? Sure. I'll slip right into that little number."

Elsa stuck two open safety pins in her mouth and garbled, "You don't have to zip it."

"I couldn't get one thigh into that thing."

Elsa pinned the corset. "The mirror in your head is warped. You know that, don't you?" She handed Willow the slip made of layers of tulle. "Put this on."

"I'm not the cancan type. Now, if you have a size forty poodle skirt. . ."

"Put it on the dummy."

"I am the dummy." Willow lifted the cotton-candy mass over the head and shoulders of the svelte but armless giant Barbie. "I agreed to clean Wilson Woodhaus's house." On the last word, her mouth filled with pink netting.

"You agreed to what?"

Pressing her lips together to stop the tickle, Willow straightened the elastic waistband on the plastic, hipless mockery of real womanhood. "I'll explain all that over crepes. How come you didn't tell me about the shop space contest?"

"I didn't think of it. You never said you wanted to open a store." Elsa handed her a stocking and crouched to put the other one on a stiff celluloid leg.

"I never did, but I never saw the words *free* and *rent* used in the same sentence before."

Elsa nodded toward the glass-sided counter. "Over there."

Willow hung the stocking on her shoulder and picked up a bright gold flyer like the one on Wilson's counter. Next to it sat a stack of applications. She scanned the rules. "I have to write an essay? I can't write an essay."

"You just have to tell people why your stuff is amazing and why the Settlement needs what you have to offer. Crystal and I can help. It'll be fun."

"Where's the shop space?"

"Upstairs on that end." Elsa looked up, red-faced from the exertion of straightening a stocking seam, and pointed. "Go look at it. Jan will be here in five minutes and then I can go for lunch."

The stairs greeted Willow with delightful old-building creaks as she ascended to the third floor. Hand-painted signs on the risers of several steps advertised the upstairs shops. Her logo would fit nicely just above EYELASH ART or right below BROTHER JOHN'S ART WORLD. "Come to Five Cs, Citizens, for the Comfiest Children's Chairs and Necessities in Cedar Creek Settlement." Her hand pivoted on the newel post at the top. Her steps echoed as she walked through another doorway, down the hall, and turned right. Maybe she'd have her own tongue-twister contest after she opened shop. A free potty chair to anyone who could say— "*Wilson?*"

ଔ

Wilson jumped at the sound of his name, dislodging the end of the tape measure he'd wedged into the mopboard. With a slithering whine it recoiled, slicing along the web between his thumb and forefinger. "Flabberdaster!" He flung the metal snail. It clamored across the hardwood floor. His hand whipped to his mouth, and he tasted the rusty tinge of blood.

The woman to blame stood two feet away with hands upturned and mouth agape. "I'm so sorry. Are you bleeding? Here." She took a flesh-colored snake off her shoulder and reached for his hand. "Wait." She dug a tissue out of her pocket without bothering to check it for the obvious and pressed it to his wound.

"I've got it." He tried to pull his hand free.

"Just be patient." She wound what he now realized was an old nylon stocking around. . .and around. . .and around his hand. "That should do it."

"Thank you." *I think.*

"What are you doing in here? Wait. . .I know what you're doing here. The same thing I'm doing, only I didn't know I could actually get into this space to actually do it, but now that. . ." Her lips blurred as her words picked up speed. "Look at this. It's way bigger than I dreamed." She paced off the wood floor. "And light! Look at these win—" She came to a dead stop. Slowly she turned. *Inch by inch.* She lasered him with a burning look that suddenly cooled in a fit of laughter. "We're enemies!"

"Say what?"

"You're entering the contest, right?"

"Yes."

"So am I, so we're fighting over the same plot of land—like the French and the Indians or the Mexicans and Americans. You and I are in mortal combat." Hands balled into raised fists, she grinned. "Is that going to create a problem with you giving my daughter art lessons?"

He refrained from correcting her misconception about the French being at war with the Indians. Afraid of encouraging her absurdity, he covered an unexplainable smile with his stockinged hand. "I'll do my utmost to remain neutral when it comes to your daughter. However. . ." Now where was that lead-in leading to? His mouth seemed intent on engaging without consulting his brain. "I make no concessions when it comes to my students' mothers. The gloves are off, so to speak."

"Fun. What are you doing for supper tomorrow night?"

"I thought we were enemies."

"We are. Romans 12, you know. If your enemy is hungry, give him chili. Extra spicy. Pardon the paraphrasing. So, are you busy?"

"N–no."

"It's strawberry chili night at Miles's Mansion." One eyebrow wiggled. Her voice undulated as if she were luring him into something lascivious. "You know you want to."

He cleared his throat and tried to loosen his tie. He wasn't wearing one. "Will the children be home?"

"My kids, my friends' kids, and an odd assortment of other Cedarburgians."

"Well, that sounds delightfu—did you say *strawberry* chili?"

ଓ

Wilson closed the basement door. Star had just given him the five-second tour of the TLC shop. He looked at Willow with a knowing nod. "I understand your motivation."

Crystal pulled her away from the sympathetic eyes with a hand on her arm. "Willi, this is incredible." She took another bite and pulled the plastic spoon slowly out of her mouth.

"I'll second that." Wilson filled another cup with chili. His third helping.

"Thank you. This might just be it."

"It? Ah. . .your entry for the Winterfest chili cook-off. You do have a thirst for competition, don't you? What's in it?"

"It's pretty basic. I just substituted pureed strawberries for half the tomatoes."

The back door banged open. Ralphy stomped in, splattering a six-foot radius with wet snow. His grin lifted blotchy cheeks framed by snow-crusted hair. "Hill's ready! Come on!"

The pile of boots by the back door dwindled in the ensuing

scramble until only one pair remained. Wilson's. Willow knew that because he was the only man left. "Well?" She nodded toward the boots.

"I thought sledding was optional."

"This is Wisconsin. How could sledding be optional?"

He stared out the kitchen window in the direction of the iced-over creek and the newly glazed path leading to it, his face as tight as the canvases he was famous for.

"When's the last time you were on a sled?"

His Adam's apple rose and fell. "Thirty years ago."

She repressed the "Seeeeeriously?" rising in her throat. "Guess we'd better fix that ASAP."

"It's dark out there."

"Look at that moon. Besides, once we start moving it's best to close your eyes and just go with it." She gave an uncomforting laugh.

"Are you sure the creek's solid enough?"

"Only one way to find out."

Wilson gave a curt nod and put on boots and a well-broken-in leather jacket. "Lead the way."

As she walked through the door ahead of him, she looked over her shoulder. "I'll go down with you."

"Do you doubt my skill or my courage, Ms. Miles?"

"Neither. I intend to shove you off when we catch air off the ramp." She chose a yellow plastic sled from the pile just off the deck and stepped in line. When Wilson hesitated, she grabbed his hand. "The gloves are off, as you say."

It wasn't until she'd positioned herself in the center of the sled that it dawned on her how much of a contact sport this was. Wilson would need to wrap not only his arms, but also his legs around her. Were his arms long enough? Did the thought repel him? She glanced up jean-clad legs, past the leather jacket, all the way to scared-looking eyes. "If you'd rather grab your own sled that's fine with—"

Plunk. The plastic skiff quaked as he sat behind her. She squeezed her thighs, but there was no way she could diminish their girth. His legs overlapped hers. His hands laced over her middle.

"Ready?" Star appeared beside them. "I'll give you a push."

For a brief, suspended-in-time moment, Willow closed her eyes and let herself feel small in the circle of his arms.

And then they flew as one down the bank, up the ramp, into the air, and onto the glassy surface of Cedar Creek.

Sideways.

The sled stopped. They didn't. In slow motion it might have been pretty. Wilson's arms remained clamped at Willow's waist as they slid on their sides, spoon-fashion, across the ice and into a snowbank. By the time they stopped, his fingers were still laced—this time around her neck. "Are you all right?" she gasped.

Seconds passed. His fingers didn't move. She felt a rumble but couldn't identify it until a gut-level laugh erupted from the man who held her life in his hands. "I'm fine." He released his hold on her neck and tipped her chin so she had no choice but to look up at the man silhouetted against a moonlit sky. "In fact, I haven't been this fine in a very long time." He shifted and helped her sit up. "Ms. Miles, I'm going to thoroughly enjoy being at war with you."

Chapter 6

"Don't get all *star*struck, Star." Willow parked her repaired van in front of the Cultural Center and wrinkled her nose at the girl clinging to the inside handle of the passenger door. "Just have fun with it, honey."

"I make mistakes when I get nervous. I'll squirt him with lead-based paint. I'll drown him in eraser crumbs. He'll inhale art gum and die of COPD." Star gave a sigh worthy of a standing ovation. "He's just so, so good."

"Don't put him on too high a pedestal. Good is a relative thing. Look, you'd go down the thousand-foot toboggan slide at Whitnall Park blindfolded and not flinch, right?"

"Yeah. But what does that—"

"Mr. So So Good was scared to death to get on a little plastic sled in our backyard."

"Seriously?" The ever-elusive expression bent the corners of Star's mouth heavenward. "He was scared?"

"Terrified. I had to hold his hand the whole way." The heat sneaking under Willow's sweater had nothing to do with the vents pointed her way.

"Yeah. About that. You do know people were laughing at you, right? All cuddled up like sardines at the bottom of the hill.

Speaking of *star*struck."

Willow cleared her throat. "It's 5:28."

The van door opened, and Star's laugh escaped on an icy breeze. The wind fluttered the to-do list clamped to the dashboard.

Star—lesson—5:30
Clean—WW's
Finish order for preschool
Work on essay for contest
Update website—add Adirondacks
Hire somebody!

The last item was in Crystal's neat, scrolling cursive. An item Willow would have to ignore—unless she ended up in a lovely well-lit shop of her own with orders flying in faster than she could process them.

She crossed the first thing off the list and moved on to the second. Tackling Wilson's kitchen. Their deal was dusting and vacuuming in exchange for art lessons, but if Wilson did anything to crack the pedestal he balanced on, an hour with Star could end up feeling like twelve rounds with Apollo Creed. It would take more than sucking lint off his carpet to get him to stick to his end of the deal. Willow had every intention of cleaning and organizing her way into Wilson Woodhaus's good graces.

And she'd start with the cupboards. As she drove out of town and along the tree-lined lane to his quirky old barn, she tried to remember the configuration of cupboards in his miniscule kitchen. She'd come equipped with trash bags and a laundry basket full of dollar store drawer organizers, plastic containers, and lazy Susans. A person could never have too many lazy Susans.

She parked at the foot of the red-painted stairs. As she wrestled the laundry basket up all twelve of them, she pictured Wilson shoveling the rough-hewn steps every time it snowed. A man with his talent ought to have a nicer place. At the very least, an indoor stairway. She balanced the basket on one hip as she turned the doorknob. The door flew open and dollar store plastic skittered across white vinyl. Willow got down on her knees. Chasing a runaway lid, she crawled under Wilson's sad little excuse for a kitchen table. Her caboose banged a chair, sending a pile of papers snowing down onto the plastic jungle.

Smack-dab in front of her lay a single-spaced document.

Why the Shops at Cedar Creek Settlement Need Wilson Woodhaus.

Wilson's essay for the contest. The essay she hadn't a clue how to write. Was this a gift from heaven or a temptation from the other realm? She tried to avert her eyes.

Could she help it if the paper happened to land, faceup, at her knees?

ଓ

Wilson sat across the table from the girl who simultaneously jiggled her leg and tapped a pencil on her knee. "Tell me a little about yourself and where you hope to go with your art."

"I've always loved to draw. It's like an obsession. My mother used to say I was born with a pencil in my fist. After she died, art was kind of my therapy, you know? Willow bought me gobs of paper."

"Speaking of Willow, how is she doing with preparing for the contest?"

"Great. All because of you."

"Me?" He couldn't remember anything he'd said that would have helped Willow with the application process.

"Yeah. She figured if you liked it, it had to be good."

Ah. She was referring to the shop space. "It was quite warm and inviting."

"You should tell her that."

"I think she understood that I found it more than adequate for my needs."

Star blinked. "Stick with the warm and inviting thing. She could use that as a slogan."

"Or *I* could." He lifted his left eyebrow and smiled at her. "I'm a fierce competitor and I have every intention of winning."

"You're entering?"

"Of course. That's why I was there the other day when she—"

"*What?*" Star's posture turned rigid. "What were you doing? Spying on her? Trying to steal her secrets?"

"Spying? I was there first. What are you—?"

Her chair scraped the floor as she stood. "How could you do that to her? Willow is the kindest, most giving person I've ever met in my whole life. She gave up all her hopes and dreams for me and my brothers and she's always doing nice things for other people and I can tell she really likes you and when you two were sledding together it sure looked like you liked her, too, and—"

"I *do* like her!" Wilson stood and planted his hands on his hips. He was not taking on this wildcat as a student. And where had that profession of *like* come from? He took a calming breath. "Star, this isn't personal. It would be a wise business move for either of us to get exposure like this."

"*Exposure?* So you'd expose the most kindhearted person in the whole world to heartbreak on the off chance that your stupid chili is better than—"

"*Chili?* What in the world does chili have to do with the price of tea in China?"

Star's ringed fingers clutched her hips, mocking his pose. "How could chili not have something to do with a chili contest?"

Wilson closed his eyes and sank back into his chair. As the irate girl stared, he dissolved into a belly laugh the likes of which he hadn't experienced in more years than he could count. What had happened to his boring, well-ordered life? "Sit down, Star. Please."

He was thoroughly going to enjoy the unpredictability of being at war with Willow Miles. And her daughter.

ᴥ

Depictions of the charm and serenity of historic Cedarburg. . .from the covered bridge dusted with snow in winter to the familiar silhouette of Cream City brick buildings on Washington Avenue. . .the gallery of world-renowned watercolor and ink artist Wilson Woodhaus will draw tourists. . .uniting with the residents of Cedarburg to support our mission: Preserving Yesterday's Heritage Today. . .

The lyrical lines of Wilson's essay jammed her brain as Willow arranged trash bags, rags, disinfectant, and a roll of self-adhesive paper on the kitchen floor. She could never in a million years write like that. *Cushy chairs for children's bottoms. . .tiny tables for tea with Tigger. . .rocking horses in rainbow colors. . .* Anything she came up with sounded more like a television script for Wonder Pets. She didn't stand a chance against Mr. So So Good.

Don't put him on too high a pedestal. He was, after all, just a human like anyone else. With flaws and weaknesses—unarmored spots in the soft underbelly of his competitive psyche. She dropped to her knees and sneered at the handle of the cupboard under his kitchen sink. "We'll see just how perfect you are, mister."

This was the housecleaning polygraph, the spot in every house that told the truth about a person's character. After years of cleaning houses she'd come to see this spot as symbolic of the inner life of the owner of the house. Here she would find tulip bulbs stashed for transplant a decade ago, newspapers dating back to the Vietnam War, and half-empty, disillusioned cans of petrified Miracle-Gro.

But here she would exercise grace. Here she would ensure Star's lessons continued. And here, just maybe, she'd give Wilson Woodhaus a hint of what it would be like to have a woman in his life.

"Here goes." She yanked the handle. And gasped.

Red-and-white-checked shelf paper covered the bottom of the cupboard, and on the paper sat a bottle of dish detergent and an empty wastebasket lined with a plastic grocery bag.

Nothing else.

Wilson Woodhaus was not a stuffer nor a stasher nor a keeper of secrets. He was who he appeared to be.

Twenty minutes later, after giving each cupboard and drawer an inside and outside wipe-down it didn't really need, she realized something else. Crystal had described Wilson as wealthy, witty, and world savvy. Willow had seen a bit of the wit and she had no clue about the world-savvy part, but one thing she knew as she peered into a nearly bare refrigerator.

Wilson Woodhaus was anything but wealthy.

In the dim glow from the appliance bulb filament, she made a decision.

The man who lived on generic hot dogs and off-brand ketchup didn't need another competitor. He needed a champion, a person who loved to talk and loved to sell, who knew every person in Cedarburg and had once sold a black-and-white-spotted rocking-cow and a hot-pink potty chair to an eighty-one-year-old bachelor.

She closed the refrigerator door. "Willow Miles, image consultant and PR manager, at your service."

Chapter 7

"A tad more cocoa?"

Willow leaned against the refrigerator as her three biggest critics slurped her latest experiment. "Star?"

"I thought you'd decided on the strawberry one."

"I had, but Crystal said that one of the chili cook-off judges has diverticulitis and she can't eat seeds so—"

"What's a diver's tickle eye dish?" Ralphy's nose crinkled.

Star gave an eye-roll performance deserving a 9.8 for creativity and opened the cupboard next to the sink.

"It's when you get little pockets in your. . .it's a stomach problem."

"Eeewww."

Star turned around, holding a bag of semisweet chocolate chips. "I think it could handle a few of these. Chocolate makes everything better."

"Oh yeah?" Del opened the refrigerator. "Chocolate-covered green olives, anyone? How about chocolate herring or—"

"Chores." Willow defused the gross-out session. "We have an insane two days ahead of us. Right after supper, we have to put the banners on the bed. I want everything done so we can all turn in early. Go lay out your regular clothes and your costumes.

Tomorrow I have to get the chili over to the community center by ten forty-five, and before that Wilson's coming over to help get the bed down to the—"

"He didn't chicken out yet?" Del popped a green olive in his mouth.

"No. Why would he?"

Willow's phone rang. She picked it up. "Hello?"

"Willow?" An unfamiliar voice spoke her name. "This is Sharon. We close at five, and we're still waiting on your display."

Sharon. Sharon who? Willow looked at the clock. Four forty. *Close what at five? Display? What display?* She looked at the list on the fridge. Only two things remained un-crossed-out for Friday—*make chili* and *finish decorating bed*. "I'm sorry. Who is this?"

"Sharon Goldman."

"I'm so sorry." *Again.* "I just can't place you."

"I'm the one who sent the letters about your display."

"Display?" A cold finger of dread drew a meandering line down her back. Alzheimer's. This is exactly how it happened to old Mrs. Westerforce at church. The blank stare, the brow wrinkled in confusion. "What display?"

"For the contest."

"I'm supposed to have a display? All the form said was bring your pot by ten forty-five."

"*Pot?* Ms. Miles, this is not Madison, you know. Just what kind of store are you—"

"Store?" Willow kneaded the expanding muscle bundle at the base of her neck.

"This is Willow Miles, isn't it?"

"Of course."

"And you are planning on participating in the Settlement

Shops' competition, correct?"

"Oh!" An off-key combination of sigh and laugh burst from deep in Willow's lungs. "No. I thought about it, but I changed my mind."

"Without letting us know?"

Willow stared at the phone then set it back on her ear. "Why would I let you know I'd changed my mind?"

A huff ricocheted off her eardrum. "You're one of only four chosen to compete out of more than—"

"Chosen? How could I be chosen if I never entered?"

"Excuse me? I have your application and essay right here. Are you feeling all right? Is there someone else I could speak to? A family member, maybe?"

Family member. As in the girl who'd stuck the stupid application form in Willow's face every day for two weeks. She thought of the unopened envelopes from the Settlement she'd pitched at the wastebasket with all the other unsolicited mail in the past week.

Willow made a slow turn, narrowing her eyes at the girl who stood in front of the stove shielding herself with a plastic colander.

Star was grinning.

"We'll be there in fifteen minutes, Sharon. You'll recognize our van. It will be the one with a teenager duct taped to the front as a hood ornament."

ↃS

Wilson studied his exhibit then sized up the competition in the room that would soon be his. Two women arranged handmade dolls and stuffed animals. In the opposite corner, tables overflowed with candles. Cinnamon, bayberry, lily, lemon, pine.

If he closed his eyes he could imagine walking through an open-air market in Paris. Or a compost heap—not all of the scents mingled well. The earthy girl who'd made the candles didn't look like much of a fighter.

And then there was Willow. And Star. Arranging a veritable explosion of miniature nursery-colored furniture. From where he stood, the vermillion, chartreuse, and aquamarine paint on her pieces brought out pops of color on his canvases. New leaves in a springtime picture of the covered bridge matched a lime-green chair. Pink roses in pots outside the Stagecoach Inn seemed to suddenly bloom brighter with a raspberry-colored rocking horse as backdrop.

We look good together, Willow. She wouldn't regret this. No matter who won, they'd all gain from it—business *and* personal gain. He sauntered over to her. "Nice setup."

"Can't imagine how it could be with only fifteen minutes warning."

"Wha—?" He looked at Star, who shrugged. "How did that"—he cleared his throat—"come about?"

"My daughter seemed to think that when I said no I really meant yes and took it upon herself to enter me. Which reminds me. . .Sharon?" She waved at the woman setting up the voting table. "Do you happen to have my essay handy?"

"Of course. I've made two hundred copies of each one." She reached into a box and handed her a piece of paper.

Willow arched an eyebrow as she read. "Tender Loving Chair Company—child-sized furniture made by tender loving hands. The perfect complement to the Shops at Cedar Creek Settlement." She eyed Star with more than a little suspicion. "Statistics show that 56 percent of the visitors to Cedarburg are over sixty. We can assume that the vast majority of them are grandparents, and what grandmother could possibly resist a bright pink rocking chair or an exquisitely crafted rocking horse?" Willow tipped her head to one side. "You wrote this?"

Star hesitated. Her eyes darted toward Wilson.

Willow whirled. "*You* wrote this?"

He took a step back. Her eyes looked exceptionally blue when they were open as wide as eyes can open. "It was a collaboration."

"Why?" The hurt on her face stabbed him. "You needed somebody easy to beat? Somebody who couldn't hold a candle to 'depictions of the charm and serenity of historic Cedarburg' or 'the covered bridge dusted with snow' or the 'nostalgic black-glass facade and lit marquis of the Rivoli. . .'" Her mouth opened. Her eyes closed.

"You read my essay?" He infused his words with indignation, though he felt not a twinge of it. "Why? You needed to find my weak points? To plan your strategy for beating me? Was this all a ruse, pretending to not be interested when all this time—"

"No! I didn't read it on purpose. I decided not to enter because I—never mind." Her face turned a delightful shade somewhere between dusty pink and ash rose.

"Any chance we could call us even?"

"Not until you explain why you entered me in this contest."

He held up his watch so she could look at it. "We need to let them lock up. If you insist on an explanation, I'm afraid it'll have to be over dinner."

Her face darkened to a color even he couldn't name. Not quite barn red, but close. "Well, I. . .thank you, but I have to get home for the boys and we need to finish decorating the bed for tomorrow—"

"One thing at a time." Star stood with a finger in the air.

"You two go eat and when you're done, you can both come and work on the bed." She held out an upturned palm. "Just fork over the keys and I'll take care of everything."

Willow sighed but fished her keys out of her purse and relinquished them. "I think you've taken care of enough for today, missy."

"Oh no." Star glanced at Wilson. "I've only just begun."

Wilson winked at her. He wasn't a winker, but it seemed the appropriate gesture for acknowledging an accomplice.

☙

Willow set her napkin on her plate. "And what about you? Kids are my excuse. Why is it you never married?"

"I was close once. Years—" His phone rang. He glanced at it. "Sorry. Another starving artist. This'll just take me a sec." He smiled as he answered it. "Hey, Mike. Yep. Thanks for the tip. Begging for their wood scraps was awkward, but who needs pride, right? Hey, I'm in the middle of something, can I call you tomorrow? Okay. Thanks again."

She couldn't make eye contact for a moment. The image of Wilson begging for wood froze her.

He set the phone down. "Where was I? Oh yeah, marriage. I was close years ago. Emphasis on the *I*. Thought we had a thing, you know, but then I went and blew it all by proposing."

"And?"

"She said I was fun to hang out with, but I had an ego the size of Alaska and the only humans I was capable of loving were the ones I created on canvas."

Willow gasped. "That's horrible! What did you say to that?"

"I said, 'I do believe you're right. Have a nice life.'"

Eyes burning with tears of laughter, Willow shook her head.

"But you don't have a huge ego. I've never seen any evidence of it."

"Thank you. By the grace of God alone. I was quite the intellectual snob before the Lord got a hold of me. Had to go through some really rough times—clay in the hands of the Potter, and all that. You mentioned living in your van. I can relate to that." He ran his thumb along the edge of the table. "I rented a single room for years and lived on Spam and generic baked beans." His top lip curled.

She thought of the empty refrigerator and the bedroom closet with only two pairs of pants, five long-sleeved shirts and five short-sleeved. His starving artist days were not past tense. "But now? Are you content?" *To live in a barn?*

A smile that certainly appeared content eased across his face. "In many ways, yes. Most ways, actually. I have everything I need except. . ."

Someone to share it with?

His gaze rose to the Goliath-sized bellows. ". . .shop space on the third floor." He grinned and slid his hand over hers. "Which brings me to the real reason for this dinner."

Willow gulped. *Yes?*

"It was Star's idea to fill out the application for you, and I offered to write your essay because you do amazing work and people need to see it and you clearly need more space and"—he took a quick breath and his hand tightened on hers—"because I can't think of a more deserving, kind, wonderful person to lose to."

Her spine turned to jelly. "But you won't lose. Not a chance." Stealthily she took out one of the business cards she'd taken from his display and slid it under her saucer. *Not if I can help it.*

Chapter 8

She hadn't expected him to show up at the chili contest, but there he was standing next to her, appearing to hold his breath right along with her as the judges closed in on the Cedar Creek Chocoffee Chicken Chili.

What she really hadn't expected was his hand encasing her tight fist.

Did he even know what he was doing, or was it a reflexive action brought on by the suspense of the moment? She eased the pent-up tension in her right hand the way she used to lift one finger at a time from Ralphy's back when he was finally asleep. It took five judges tasting six pots of chili to completely relax. The moment she did, Wilson laced his fingers through hers.

Were her calloused hands irritating to a man who wielded an itty-bitty paintbrush all day? Was she gripping enough? Too much? Would he think she'd never held hands with a man before? She had. Eleven years ago, come Valentine's Day. Pitiful.

The small crowd clapped. What had she missed?

He dropped her hand.

What had she done? Had he finally realized his hand was interlocked with hers? "Go."

And now he was telling her to get away from him?

"Willow?" The head judge stared at her, head tipped to the side. "Do you want this or are you holding out for first?"

The room dissolved in laughter. She'd won second place.

Cheeks ablaze, she took the certificate and walked back to her spot next to the cheering man who painted pictures and framed canvases. . .and engulfed her in arms that apparently at times wielded more than a teensy paintbrush.

☙

The beaver coat hadn't had this much fun since Groundhog Day of 1925 when Grossvater and his frat buddies dressed a statue of Christopher Columbus in a chicken suit and got expelled for a week.

He and Willow had spent the morning tasting and voting on chili submitted by local restaurants then huddled together for warmth while they watched the parade. As they held hands and sipped hot chocolate spiked with cayenne pepper, Wilson had never been so grateful for the cold.

He blinked back into the here and now and secured a handhold behind the headboard of the rickety brass bed-on-skids. On the bed, dressed in a vintage paperboy outfit, Ralphy leaned on a pile of pillows, newspaper in hand, calling out, "Read all about it! Cedarvaudevillians performing live at Winter Festival Bed Race!"

Dressed in knickers, Del manned one side of the foot of the bed. On the opposite side, Star twirled knee-length pearls. Fringe jiggled on the way-too-big flapper dress flouncing over her jacket and jeans. To his right stood Willow in a yellow-and-black-striped suit topped off with a straw boater hat and cane. But the thing that undid him was the mustache painted on her top lip.

"Ready?" She reached out and spun the copter on his beanie cap and twitched her 'stache. Once again he was reduced to laughter the likes of which he'd never, before Willow, experienced. If he ever found the alien responsible for sucking the common sense out of his normally practical brain he'd have to . . .hug it. "Ready."

He'd attended many a bed race over the years—from the safety of the crowd lining the banks of Cedar Creek behind the old mill. Never from the frozen surface of the middle of the river. "One-two-three-*go*!" He pushed. The crowd cheered. The bed moved. To the left. Out of the corner of his eye, he saw the Green Bay Packer quilt on their rival's bed slide out of sight. "Come on, Del!" He moved closer to the boy's side of the bed. "Let's give it all we—"

Del's feet slid out from under him. As the bed slid past, Wilson snatched him in a football hold. "Grab on here!" He held him until the boy found his footing.

"Nice save!" Willow yelled as they rounded the barrel and got a full view of the Packer bed closing in on the finish line.

"We're losing."

"Are you having fun?" Willow panted out the words.

Wilson grinned. "Absolutely."

"Then we're not"—they slid over the yellow tape marking the finish line at a forty-five-degree angle three bed lengths behind their competition—"losing!"

This time, as the crowd cheered, it was Willow who initiated the hug.

☙

Hand in hand they walked past ice sculptures of Aaron Rodgers, Elvis, and a squat troll then climbed the worn steps to the shop space they were fighting over. Willow smiled up at Wilson's cold-pinked face. "I assume you have a game plan for working the crowd."

"I do."

Nice words. "Is it a secret?"

"Yes. You'll just have to watch me in action."

She did watch. As live music drifted through the corridors and tourists filtered in and out of the empty shop, gapers gathered around Wilson and his painting-in-progress. One woman commented on his "folksy realism." Many mentioned how wonderful it would be to see all of his work in one place.

Willow engaged a steady flow of oohers and aahers. She handed out brochures and business cards and took three orders in the first hour but ended each conversation with, "Are you familiar with Wilson Woodhaus's work?" and gestured toward his easels. Then she'd whisper, "Vote for him. I'm just here for the fun."

Around four o'clock Wilson took a break and walked over to her. "How's my favorite enemy? I didn't ask if *you* had a game plan."

"I do." *Nice words.* "But it's also top secret."

"Judging by the number of lingerers, I think you and I are way ahead of the others and just about tied with each other."

But not in the votes. She smiled. "Time will tell."

He straightened her business cards and opened one of her trifold pamphlets. She pointed to a cluster of potential voters gathering at his easels. "You have customers."

"I'll get to them. I was just wondering if maybe you'd like to come over to my place tonight. I thought we could sit by the fire and discuss strategies for winning."

"Does that mean you'll divulge secrets?"

His eyes held hers for a long, light-headed moment. "I think it's safe to say some secrets will be divulged."

Chapter 9

Willow curled up on one end of the overstuffed plaid couch and watched the fire in the potbellied stove through a clear glass cup of hot cherry cider. The flames seemed to dance to the music coming from tiny speakers on top of the antique buffet Wilson had turned into an entertainment center. "This music is so familiar. What is it?"

"Verdi. *The Force of Destiny*." Wilson sat about ten inches away from her, arm resting on the back of the couch, stocking feet sharing a leather ottoman with hers. "Are you a classical aficionado?"

"Um. No. I'm actually more of an oldies aficionado. I like music I can dance to."

His lips pinched, giving his profile a stern schoolteacher look. "I see."

"Opposites are supposed to attract, you know."

"That would explain it, then." He shifted so he was facing her. "You're spontaneous, I'm a planner. You cook, I microwave. You like playing in the snow and I like painting it." The heat from his smile rivaled the flames. "What's your favorite movie genre? I'm guessing romantic comedy."

She laughed. "My life is a comedy. Not the romantic variety, but I live with comedians. I don't need to pay to—" Her phone, sitting next to the tissue box, vibrated. She picked it up. "Hello."

"Willi!" Star's panic-filled voice brought every muscle to attention. "Ralphy stuck a bean up his nose!"

Willow closed her eyes for a second then held the phone out and pressed the SPEAKER button. "As I was saying. . ." she whispered then returned her volume to normal. "Cooked or uncooked?"

"Uncooked. From that bag you left open on the counter."

So now it's my fault? "Okay. Good. Well, not good he stuck a bean in his nose, but good it's uncooked and good it's one of those. They're small." She held up one finger to Wilson and mouthed "Listen to this." First, she had to swipe the smile from her face. "Put a tissue between your face and his nose then pinch the nostril without the bean in it shut. Now put your mouth on his like you're doing CPR and—"

"*What?* Are you craaaazy? I am not going to put my mouth on—"

"Okay, try this first. Have him pinch the clear nostril shut and blow his nose. Gently." As they listened to Star relaying instructions, she simply stared at Wilson's smile.

"I envy you," he whispered. "My life is so boring compared to—"

"Eeewww! Gross. It worked."

"Okay. Thanks for watching them, honey. Get them to bed so you can have a little time to yourself."

"How are things going with you? He kiss you yet?"

Willow's face warmed. She reached out for the SPEAKER button. Wilson caught her hand then leaned closer to the phone. "Not yet, Star. Do I have your permission?"

"Yes. You have my permission. Just remember everything I told you."

"I remem. . .ber." His answer slurred as his lips touched Willow's in a soft, tender, too-short kiss.

And Star laughed.

ଓ

The secret he'd intended to divulge was that he liked her. A lot. *Not* that he'd told her daughter he liked her. Or that her daughter had given her blessing and had warned him not to hurt the most important person in her life. But now he'd gone and said it all. And Willow sat with a growing pyramid of crumpled tissues on her lap.

"You really told her that and she really said that?"

"Yes." He ran the back of his hand along her soft, damp cheek. "All those thats."

"You have no idea what those thats mean to me. Star and I have always been close, but life is difficult for her. All these years since her mother died she's waffled between gratitude and being angry that I'm taking her mother's place. To hear her say I'm the m–most imp–portant person in her l–life is just so. . ." Her eyes gleamed. "You've brought out good things in my girl."

"Art can be amazing therapy, allowing someone to open up parts of themselves they've kept closed. But you and God and her mother put those things in her."

"Artists can be good therapy, too." Her lips tipped up at the corners and she glanced toward the little woodstove. "I'm not generally a relaxer, but you make me feel peaceful."

"And you"—his fingers slipped through her hair—"have brought laughter into my life. I wake up every morning now wondering what adventure Willow's going to drag me into. My life used to fit so neatly into the little boxes on my day planner. I thought I was happy that way."

She pointed at the framed scripture on the wall. BE STILL, AND KNOW THAT I AM GOD. She thought of the words circling her kitchen. *This is the day the Lord has made. Let us rejoice and be glad in it.* She'd made a conscious effort to fill her days with rejoicing. She needed to learn to be still. "We balance each other."

His arm tightened around her shoulders. "You are a beautiful woman, Willow Miles."

She jerked away. "Don't."

"Don't tell you you're beautiful?"

She nodded. A tear spilled onto his hand.

"Why?" He whispered it, knowing she felt the flutter of his breath on her cheek.

"Because I'm not. It's enough—no—it's way, way more than enough that you said you like me. I never in a million years thought I'd have a chance at something that feels this good. I gave up praying for it long ago and figured God had given me a family and that was more than I could have hoped for." She nodded toward the entertainment center. "I thought the true 'force of destiny' had planned for me to raise those kids, and I've tried so hard not to want more. So this"—she slid her hand over his—"*you* are an answer to prayers I never uttered. You don't need to say I'm—"

"Beautiful." He lifted her chin. He couldn't let her miss the sincerity of his next words. "I'm not a flatterer, Willow. I don't say things I don't mean. Your eyes, your skin, your hair, your generous heart and caring spirit, all combine into an exceedingly attractive package. You may have noticed I refuse to call you Willi."

She nodded. "Why?"

"Because, whether you believe it or not, you are as lovely

and free flowing as the tree you're named for."

"But I'm—"

He laid two fingers over her lips. "Don't insult my taste by saying negative things about the woman I'm about to ask to dance with me."

"To *this*?" She gestured toward a speaker.

Wilson picked up a remote and flipped to an oldies radio station. Bon Jovi sang "Livin' on a Prayer." He stood and reached for her hand. "To *this*."

☙

Valentine's Day began with an apple.

A Granny Smith apple. Dipped in thick, rich caramel. Smothered in Belgian dark chocolate. Garnished with a ribbon of pink. Pink *chocolate*.

Willow leaned her elbows on the table for three at the Vintage Café as she described each decadent layer and the pink bow tied to the stick with AMY'S GOURMET APPLES lettered in gold. Elsa appeared close to tears. Crystal sighed. "And tonight?"

"I don't know. It's a surprise. But I have orders to dress up."

"Isn't it awkward competing against the guy you're falling for?"

Elsa set her napkin on the table. "Which one of you is going to win the free rent? Are you workin' it, girl?"

"How can we help?"

"I'm telling everyone to vote for you."

"Don't." Willow stared up at gold and purple walls. How to explain?

"Huh?"

"Wilson needs it way more than I do."

"Willi! Are you kidding?" Crystal's coffee cup halted six

inches from her mouth. "You're overworked and underspaced. You need this. You deserve it. If the guy hasn't made any money on his work after all this time, he's not going to be able to support a store."

"I have as much business as I can handle through my website and craft fairs."

"That's just the point. You can't handle any more because you need to hire someone so you can grow, and you can't hire anyone because you work in a shoe box."

Willow looped the handle of her purse over her shoulder. "But you should see his work space. An artist needs a beautiful place to create and display his work and—"

"Stop!" Elsa held a spoon in each hand. "Look." She set one spoon on the table. "Love is here." The other spoon slammed down a foot and a half away. "And business is here. You have to keep them separate. Have. To. Keep. Them. Separate. Do you understand?"

"Yes. I. Un. Der. Stand." Willow copied Elsa's insulting cadence. "But I disagree. Now, if you'll excuse me, I'm going to clean Wilson's apartment. And if you two want to help me, you'll vote for Wilson. Daily." She shoved a two-dollar tip and Wilson's business card under her saucer and stood. "Happy Valentine's Day, ladies."

Their whispers followed her out the door. "If she doesn't figure out how to separate her business and her love life. . ."

ൽ

Even though Wilson wasn't home, just being in his living room banished all traces of her bad mood.

"Ohh-ohhh livin' on a prayer. . ." She waltzed across the wood floor with Wilson's dust mop and stopped at a painting on an easel in the corner. It hadn't been there last week.

It was a painting of the barn she stood in. She'd never seen it from this angle. Wilson must have sat out by the creek to capture it. She imagined sitting beside him while he painted this summer setting—reading a book or simply gazing at the riot of wild columbine and purple coneflower carpeting the hill that sloped up to the stone foundation.

She counted the tall windows in the painting. Nine. She stood back. There were only four in the living room. She looked at the dark blue curtain hanging on the south wall. No light seeped through, meaning it didn't cover a window. She touched the bottom with the dust mop, feeling like a six-year-old waiting for the bogeyman to jump out of the closet.

A tiny puff of sawdust landed on her clean floor. She pulled the heavy blue corduroy aside. And gasped.

Like Lucy walking through the back of the wardrobe, she stood in a completely different world. An enormous, light-filled, white-walled room. Old, hand-hewn timbers on the slanted walls met at a massive beam a good twenty feet over her head. On the far wall, a fieldstone chimney rose above a large open hearth.

Everything else in the unfinished and unfurnished room was brand spanking new. A black granite island, walnut flooring still with stickers on some of the boards, banks of cupboards and a whole wall of empty shelves all in walnut, just a shade darker than the floors. Recessed lighting everywhere, but hardly even needed at this time of day, not with sunlight pouring through giant west-facing windows.

Willow walked over to the island where the sparkling granite was partially concealed by blueprints with WOODHAUS STUDIO printed along the top in perfect block letters. An invoice lay to one side. An electrician's bill—in five figures. An ostentatious red PAID covered half of it.

"And all this time he's made me think he was poverty stricken!" Her fingers curled into her palms. New wood whined under her feet as she stomped toward the deceptive blue curtain and flung it open. Back in the tiny, dark living room, she pulled out her phone and made a call.

Voice mail.

She took a deep breath. "Elsa, I'm so sorry for everything I said and for not listening to you. I've changed my mind. I do need your help because I do want to win. Boy-oh-*boy* do I want to win!"

Chapter 10

Willow's dangly emerald earrings caught the light from the candle flickering on the white linen tablecloth between them as she bent over her open purse. She wore a dress of the same verdant shade. How was it that the green made her eyes bluer? Wilson had once thought he knew everything there was to know about color.

She fumbled the purse and two of her business cards sailed out. One landed at the feet of a well-dressed woman who retrieved the card and held it out.

"Please. Keep it," Willow answered with an adorable smile.

The lady examined the card. "Are you Willow?"

"In the flesh."

"My daughter's looking for a sixteen-inch shelf for my grand..."

The woman chattered on. Willow opened her trifold brochure, and Wilson took advantage of the opportunity to study the curve of her chin and the way her nose tilted up just the slightest bit. She'd been a little reserved all evening. She wasn't used to dressing up, she'd said, and there was something endearing about her self-consciousness.

"Thank you." Willow nodded to the lady who'd just

promised to vote for her.

Wilson gave her a thumbs-up. "You're good."

She shrugged and took a sip of coffee. Silence hung like a blank canvas, and he couldn't think of a thing to fill it. He'd already complimented everything green—and blue—at least twice. He swiped his hand to include all the interior of Galioto's Grille. "Don't you love what they've done to the place?"

Willow nodded. "You sound like you've had some experience with remodeling."

"I have, actually. My dad was a contractor. I learned at his knee—er—hammer, I guess."

"Must come in handy."

More than you know. He raised his cup. "Would you like more coffee?"

"No." She refolded her napkin and set it back on her lap.

He waited for her to resume eye contact. She didn't. "Did I say Happy Valentine's Day?"

"A few times." A hint of irritation tinged her voice.

The hostess approached. "How is everything?"

Willow squinted at the woman's uniform. "Gloria. Do you have children, Gloria?"

The woman grinned. "An eight-month-old girl. Tabatha."

"Beautiful name. Wouldn't you love to see it stenciled on a little chair. . ."The brochure reappeared as she launched into her spiel. Three minutes later, their hostess walked away promising to "Vote for Willow."

"Very. . .smooth." *And tacky. What part of romantic dinner for two don't you understand?*

"Thank you." She snapped her purse shut. "So. We never did discuss strategy last week."

Had she really taken him seriously on that one? They'd

discussed all the strategy he cared to. Lip to lip. "Okay, well, I've spent a few hours at the Shops every day." If she was doing the same, their paths hadn't crossed. "I've sent out e-mails, texts, and tweets and blogged about it on my site. How is it going for you?"

"Wonderful. Great. Yeah. Only two and half weeks left."

"Until we get the results, but voting ends next Friday."

"Right. Yes." He heard her swallow. "Ten days."

If he didn't know better, he'd swear that was fresh news to her. "No matter who wins, we celebrate together, okay? Something really special. If you win I'll send you to a spa for a day of pampering and then we can—"

Their waiter approached. "Can I tempt you with some dessert?"

Willow smiled. "Do you have children"—her chin jutted forward and she squinted—"Brian?"

"One, and one on the way." The young man's chest broadened.

"Do you know if it's a boy or a girl?"

"A boy. That makes two. We. . ."

Wilson excused himself and went to the men's room. He turned on the water. As he reached toward the soap dispenser, his gaze fell on a stack of business cards sitting on the sink.

Vote for Willow.

"Unbelievable." He yanked a paper towel and ripped it. The dispenser popped open, sending paper rolling across the floor. "If that's the way you want to play it, lady, you got yourself a fight." He slammed the wadded paper at the wastebasket, missed, and marched out the door.

Ꮳ

Her to-do list flapped in an ice-laden gust as Willow slammed her front door and stepped off the porch.

Print Vote for Willow cards. Check. *Print flyers.* Check. *Add blurb to brochure.* Check. *Bake and frost chair-shaped cookies.* Check. *Announcement on website.* Check. *Blog post.* Check. *E-mail announcement.* Check. *Twitter.* Not so much.

She'd slashed that last one with red pen. She'd never chirped or cheeped or whatever a person did on that thing and she didn't have time to start now. *Time.* It was not on her side. She hadn't paid attention to the fine print when certain people signed her up for this nonsense. But, nonsense or not, she was going to win.

She turned off Sheboygan Road and onto Washington Avenue. A snowflake landed on her nose and she glared up at low, snow-filled clouds. The forecast predicted up to ten inches, but it hadn't started yet and she had places to go and people to see before it got too deep.

The official Cedarburg website claimed there were eleven thousand, three hundred, and twelve people she needed to talk to in the next eight days. Taking off the three hundred plus on her TLC mailing list and dividing it by the U.S. average family size of 3.14 left approximately three thousand, three hundred, and thirty-five households to visit.

After she'd hit all the businesses in town. She shifted the strap on her canvas bag to a more comfortable position and headed east. She popped into the Old Mill Antiques and gave a cookie and her rehearsed plea for votes to the clerk. She passed the Settlement Shops, deciding to leave them for last. The Shops were half a block from home and the perfect place to schmooze indoors after the weather got bad.

Leaning into the wind, she charged ahead. At Goldsmith Jewelry Works she just left a brochure. She spent a moment soaking up sparkle and warmth in the pink-and-gray-walled

Bangles 'n' Bags. Downtown Dough was like her second home, but she pulled her gaze away from the solid wall of cookie cutters and handed two rocking-chair-shaped cookies to her longtime friends behind the counter. "Proof that your products work." The girls laughed and promised to vote for her.

She bought a cup of coffee at Cozy Cuppa and lingered just a moment over the music boxes at Sweet Sounds. She left cards at the Rivoli Theatre and Washington House Inn. The smell of wool at the Yarn Shop reminded her of the sweater hanging on Wilson's kitchen chair. She didn't stay long. At the Chocolate Factory she talked about her business and talked herself out of butterscotch marble ice cream. Massive caramel apples banked the windows at Amy's Candy Kitchen. Blinking hard, she walked in and gave her little speech.

The snow was up to her ankles when she finally trudged up to the doors of the Settlement Shops. The memory of Wilson's cold blue eyes and the knowledge that she'd ruined their Valentine's date was tampering with her zeal. She needed another look at the empty shop space to revive the sense of purpose she'd had while frosting cookies at three in the morning. She thought of Elsa's spoons. *Love is here. Business is here.*

Wilson's gorgeous studio was *not* her business. Nor was his income.

She had to apologize. Maybe she'd invite him over and he'd get snowed in and— *Willow!* Her conscience chastened. Her will argued back as she trudged the last few steps. The kids would be home. It's not like she'd be alone with—

"Wilson!"

The sight before her was as incongruous as picking fresh cherries in a snowstorm. Wilson Woodhaus, the *rich* and famous painter, sat on one of *her* stools, painting flowers on a little girl's cheek. He looked her way. His face held the expression of a man who'd just walked the required number of paces before turning his dueling pistol on her.

In front of his painting of the millpond with icicles hanging from the top of the dam, stood a woman with a stroller.

You thief! You use my *stool to lure* my *constituents!* She plunged her hand into her bag and pulled out her last six weapons. Frosted cookie chairs. *Look, little girl, come get a cookie from Willow. Orange orange, raspberry red, lemony lemon, grape-ity grape.* She grinned like the rabbit on a Trix commercial as she walked slowly past the cozy little face-painting scene, cookies spread like a hand of cards. A straight flush.

The little girl turned. A green stem streaked from her cheek to her nose. "Mom-mmmmy! Can I have a cookie?"

Yes! Round one goes to Willow Miles!

ᘓ

Drill in hand, arms folded across his chest, Wilson stared out the window. As it was supposed to, March roared in like a lion. On the other side of the glass, snow blew almost horizontally. Wind whistled around the corner of the barn. They'd had snow almost every day for the past week and a half, piling up to more than fourteen inches on the ground.

He turned away and looked up at the light fixture he'd just installed. He set the drill on the island. It was only noon. He could get in a few more hours of work before heading to the Settlement Shops, but his heart just wasn't in it. He hadn't quite recovered from long days of face painting, balloon tying, and hosting a coloring contest—all things that could have been fun if the woman strong-arming customers next to him hadn't turned into Attila the Hun. A week wasn't long enough to recover from her.

He shoved the curtain aside, walked into the kitchen, and opened the freezer. Two containers of Willow's chili called out to him. He ignored them and took out a zippered bag labeled "Saturday" and set it in the microwave. He had a backlog of Fridays and Saturdays, thanks to the woman who'd introduced him to spontaneity and weird chili. The woman who, at the moment, was treating him like he was a carrier of some flesh-eating disease.

He couldn't think of a thing he'd said wrong on Valentine's Day between the apple and dinner. They'd had one phone conversation that day—her side profusely sprinkled with words like *wonderful*, *amazing*, *special*, and *sweet*—describing him, not the caramel. By dinner you'd think Snow White's apple had arrived on her doorstep by mistake.

The microwave beeped. He didn't even know what was in the steaming bag. Whatever it was, he couldn't stomach it until they hashed this out. He wasn't going to stand across the room from her at the big reveal. If she won, he wanted to be at her side to pick her up and swing her around and celebrate over dinner. If he won, he wanted a big fat congratulatory kiss right there in front of God and everybody. If they both lost, he wanted to laugh with her. . .and share a consolation kiss right there in front of God and everybody. He picked up his phone and punched her number.

"Hello?"

"Listen, I don't know what I did, but I'm sorry." His words started fast and picked up speed, like hers often did. "If it's just that the competition got out of hand, it's over now and we—"

"Mr. Woodhaus, it's Star."

"Oh."

"Willi's getting her hair cut."

He looked at the snow plastering the kitchen window. "She's out? In this?"

"She walked. She's stubborn. I guess you know that by now."

"I've had some hints."

"I don't really know what's going on, but I've heard her talking to her friends. I think she's waiting for you to apologize for something."

He rubbed his hand across his eyes. "Wish I knew what."

"If it helps any, she's been a mess the past few days. I've never seen her like this." She paused. "She misses you. And so do the boys and me. We were kind of hoping. . .well, you know."

He looked at the wrapped package waiting by the door. "Yeah. I know. So was I."

Chapter 11

She didn't feel as good as she looked, but a new outfit and a new haircut never hurt. Willow took a final glance in the mirror in the restroom at the Settlement Shops. A few bold, blond highlights gave her hair a sun-kissed look. Her new stretch jeans sported rhinestones on the pockets and her raspberry-colored blouse was gathered in just the right places and hung loose where it should. Knee-high boots completed the look. Even her old leather jacket took on a classy, shabby chic look combined with everything else.

If only she hadn't been so nasty that the one person she wanted to care wouldn't.

She would have made things right a week ago, might even have been able to get beyond his deception if his blatant ploy to lure potential customers away from her hadn't flipped her ugly switch. But now, instead of satisfaction, all she was left with was regret.

She'd apologize today.

Right after she won.

She walked down the hall and turned left into the room filled with a surprisingly large crowd. She reclaimed her place with Star, Crystal, and Elsa. Against her will, her gaze landed on Wilson. The collar of a blue shirt stuck out of a black sweater she'd never seen on him. It looked soft.

Sharon Goldman stepped to the center of the room that would soon overflow with child-sized furniture. She held an envelope in her hand. The crowd quieted. "Ladies and gentlemen, it's been a fascinating few weeks. We've had some very creative competitors and I'd like to thank them all. This is generally a quieter time of year for all of us here at the Settlement Shops, but this competition has served to. . ."

"Get on with it already," Crystal muttered. "Just say Willow Miles won."

"And now, it is my pleasure to announce that the person who will be occupying this space rent-free for a year. . ."

Star sighed, long and loud. Willow tucked her hair behind her ear, smoothed her blouse, and cleared her throat.

". . . is. . .Wilson Woodhaus!"

Willow's breath lodged in her throat as if it had turned to ice.

The crowd, all but the tight knot gathered around her, cheered. All six arms of her support system attempted to hug her at once. She pushed her way through them. Amid a flurry of "I'm sorrys" and "It should have been yous," she put on her gloves and hat, zipped her jacket, and ran down the stairs.

☙

The snow had stopped. The sun peeked through a crack in the clouds. Willow sludged through slushy snow, walking across Sheboygan Road instead of turning, with no plan in mind other than getting away.

Three blocks from the Settlement, a car pulled to the curb beside her. Her peripheral vision picked up the yellow glow.

Wilson.

He slid across the seat and opened the passenger door. He didn't say a word.

Willow closed her eyes briefly, let out a tired sigh, and got in. As he drove, she kept her eyes on the rutted road. "Congratulations."

"Thank you." In silence, he headed out of town. Toward his house. Not a particularly good idea. A little far for an angry stomp home. He glanced her way. "Up for a walk?"

Was he eavesdropping on her synapses? "I suppose."

The covered bridge came into view. Wilson put on the turn signal and parked just off the road.

Snow blanketed the roof of the weathered gray bridge. Drifts formed meringue peaks at its entrance. They wouldn't be walking on the bridge. Just as well. She didn't want to be in a place covered with hearts and somebody-loves-somebodys when she was ticked at the somebody she was with.

Wilson got out then reached into the backseat for a bulky black trash bag. Maybe returning empty chili containers. Or full ones. That would make a memorable breakup scene. Willow stepped into a snowbank higher than the boots that complemented the new outfit she'd bought for the somebody who would no longer care. They walked toward the footbridge that arched across the river and made an idyllic place to hold hands and gaze at the covered bridge while whispering sweet nothings. In their case, they'd simply be whispering nothings.

Wilson stopped at the top of the curve, set the bag down, and leaned his elbows on the railing. "Care to tell me what I did wrong?" His voice was lukewarm.

As she opened her mouth to blast him, the irony suddenly smacked her like the heel of a hand on a forehead. A *duh* moment. *I'm so angry at you for not being poor!* "I saw your studio."

"Oh? What did you think?"

"Very nice."

"And that has what to do with you being mad at me?"

"Everything. You said your business wasn't doing well and mine is going okay so I decided not to enter the contest because I wanted you to have the shop space and then you went and—"

"Wait. When did I say my business wasn't going well?"

Um. When had he? "You don't have any food in the house and your closet's practically empty and you got that phone call from another starving artist and you talked about begging for wood."

A smile altered his profile. He pressed his lips together as if trying to restrain it. "That's what this is all about? Did you really think I put all my clothes and toys in storage just to give you the impression I was hard up so you wouldn't enter the contest I entered you in?"

Absurdity piled on top of irony. *Willow Miles, you're a moron.* "No. But. . ."

His smile widened. His fingertip trailed to the tip of her nose, lingering for a brief moment. He turned, folded his arms, and leaned against the railing. "About ten years ago at an artists' retreat, two buddies and I got to talking about our lean years and agreed the Lord had used that time to stretch us. Our careers were taking off and we were all afraid of losing our dependence on God. So we made a pact to live on a set percentage of our income and give the rest away. We still call ourselves starving artists. Now it's just kind of a reminder of where we've been."

He lifted his head and seemed to scan the silver-rimmed split in the clouds. "The challenge completely altered my priorities.

It wasn't easy at first, but the blessings were astronomical. As I started making more money and that percentage became a comfortable income, I was able to travel a bit, but I couldn't see the sense in changing my everyday lifestyle—even when it came to building my dream studio. I bartered for masonry and electrical work and I asked for leftovers at construction sites and did the carpentry work myself."

"Oh." Humiliation lowered her eyes to the snow under their feet.

"I've never told anyone about our pact. It's not something I talk about, but I never intended to deceive you. I didn't show you the studio, because I thought it would be more fun to let people see it after it was all done, and the main reason there's no food in my house is because my sister cooks for me."

Willow stared down at a narrow trickle of water cutting a path through the snow. "So I've spent the past two weeks thinking you were a con artist but you're really"—she wiped a tear before it had a chance to freeze—"just a *kind* artist." She sniffed and wrinkled her nose, wondering if he'd thawed enough to appreciate her corniness for the apology she meant it to be.

He reached out and cupped her face in his hand. "I'm really just a *con*fused-in-love artist."

A second tear fell, rolling over his glove.

"Do you want to hear about my plans for the store?"

She nodded.

"It's such a big room."

Her pulse tripped. She nodded again.

"So I thought I'd ask my starving artist buddies to help fill the walls."

"That's generous of you."

"But that still leaves a lot of empty space, so I started brainstorming. Would you like to see one of my ideas?"

"Yes."

He picked up the trash bag. "Reach in."

Her brow furrowed as she pulled out a lavender potty chair with her brand on the bottom. "What does this have to do with—"

"Turn it around."

Across the back and arms, butterflies in rainbow colors flitted around flowers like the ones he'd painted on the little girl's cheek.

He took the chair from her and set it down. "I thought maybe I could give you a hand with furniture making and you could help fill up some of the space in the shop"—he lifted her hand and placed it on his chest—"the way you have in here."

Her breath caught in a sob. "I'd l–love that."

"Just *that*?" He took her hand from his chest and wrapped it around his back. His lips hovered so close she felt the warmth of his breath.

"And you. I love that and you. Not in that order."

His eyelashes skimmed her face. "I thought of a name for the store."

"You did?"

"Yes. How does Willow Wood House sound?"

She bit down on her bottom lip. He'd paused between "Wood" and "House," hadn't he? Willow. Wood. House. Not Willow Woodhaus. "I. . ." *I don't know how to answer because I don't know what you're asking.*

Does it matter?

She gazed up at eyes the color of moonlight. *No, it doesn't matter.* The answer to either question was the same. "I like it."

"Good. I thought the dual meaning might"—his cold nose brushed her cheek—"you know"—his lips teased hers—"come in handy sometime."

Becky Melby is a Wisconsin resident. She and her husband Bill have four married sons and eleven grandchildren. Becky has coauthored nine Heartsong Presents titles and written two novellas for Barbour Publishing. In her spare time Becky loves riding on the back of her Honda Gold Wing or making trips to see grandkids in the RV.

IN TUNE WITH YOU

by Rachael Phillips

Dedication

To my parents, Betty and Aaron Oglesbee,
uniquely designed individuals who sing
beautifully in tune with God and each other.

*" 'Call to me and I will answer you and tell you great
and unsearchable things you do not know.' "*
Jeremiah 33:3

Chapter 1

Spring

Chesca Appel recognized the words to "Jingle Bells." But the flat, wandering tune—that was anybody's guess. Why would someone sing it in early spring? This sun-starved morning, she was trying to think Easter.

Stopping before Christ the King Church, she peered in every direction. No one.

"Oh, what fun it is to ride in a one-horse open sleigh—AAAY!"

She cringed. Torture for a choir director. Odd scraping sounds split Cedarburg's early-morning silence. The jolly, off-season, off-key elf was ice-skating?

Maybe if she closed her eyes, she'd find herself back in her apartment, swaddled in her quilt, with the alarm Saturday-silent. The raucous baritone now assaulting her ears would fade like a passing car's radio. She could sleep instead of facing this way-too-early meeting with her pastor.

Rounding bony forsythia bushes near the church's entrance, she saw a brawny young blond guy, still roaring "Jingle Bells," sliding on the icy parking lot. Suddenly he somersaulted, landing on his back.

No more singing. Or movement.

Dashing toward him, Chesca started to call 911 when a rumble rose from the motionless figure.

Laughing. The guy was laughing.

She stopped and checked her own vital signs. Heartbeat? A blimp above the flat line. Breathing? Sort of. Outrage levels? Spiking into the danger zone, because his eyes twinkled like a fourth grader's, as if he'd put a frog into her backpack, not caring if he was sent to the principal's office.

"I couldn't have done that if I'd practiced. What a rush." Grinning and grimacing, he sat up.

"You're bleeding." Concern replaced annoyance. She pulled a tissue from her bag. "Have you broken anything?"

"Nah. I've taken worse falls. Part of my job."

Was he a stuntman? The guy didn't grab the tissue. Should she dab the cut on his cheek? She wouldn't mind. He was the best-looking guy she'd met in a while. She reached toward him—

"Where are my glasses?" He patted the ground around him.

She retrieved them from a few feet away. "Here." She hoped if he were that blind, he couldn't notice her blushing.

He stuck them on his nose and stood. "Thanks for your help, Ms.—"

"Appel. Chesca Appel."

"Pretty name. Never heard it before." For the first time, he looked directly at her.

Wow, his smile seemed even bigger than his voice. *Fortissimo.* She took a step back and modulated her tone to friendly polite. "Chesca is short for Francesca. I was named after my ancestor, Princess Franciszka Urszula Radziwill."

What was wrong with her? She wasn't in the habit of

blurting out family tree facts to strangers.

Her embarrassment faded to disbelief when he removed his Green Bay Packers cap with a flourish and bowed low. "Please pardon my lack of polish, Your Highness. I've never met a real princess before. Seth Amundsen, at your service."

She stared, sure his surprise Shakespearean-accented speech was designed to deflate her apparent aristocracy complex. But the big jester turned prince's face held nothing but courtesy, even admiration.

Until he glanced at his cell. "Late for my meeting. Hope to see you again, Princess."

The man slid across the parking lot again, belting out a final awful chorus of "Jingle Bells" as he disappeared around the church.

Her mother always said she possessed an overactive imagination. But Chesca had never, in her oddest fairy-tale dreams, invented a Seth.

She sighed. Even if he was real and she encountered him again, a guy that handsome had to be attached. If not, every girl in Cedarburg was after him.

It was just as well. She didn't relish the prospect of wearing earplugs on a date. A choir director with sensitive ears—

Oops. She was also a choir director with an appointment to discuss. . .what? Pastor Hoke seemed uncharacteristically vague about their agenda. Something about Easter. She'd chosen a cantata, *Holy Lamb of God*, which the choir really liked. Had Pastor Hoke changed his mind? Had he also received complaints about the service music?

She was thinking the worst, as usual. How long had she been lost in la-la land? She glanced at the cell in her cold hand, still poised to rescue the irrepressible Seth. Ten minutes late for her meeting! She clumped through tired gray snow surrounding the parking lot. As she approached the church office door, her chilly bones ached for a hot cup of tea. Surely if Pastor Hoke, a fellow tea drinker, wanted her to face the music, he would put the kettle on first.

ꕥ

She cast a longing eye toward the sanctuary doors. If only she had time to pray in its stained-glass quiet. But Pastor Hoke's door creaked open.

"Morning, Chesca." His lined face beamed like the absent sun should have. He offered her a steaming black mug. "You like vanilla chai, right?"

"Good morning. Sorry I'm late." She sipped the velvety brew. This meeting was looking better already.

But as she entered Pastor's office, she almost dropped her mug.

There, holding a Windex-blue sport drink, sat a grinning Seth Amundsen. "Chesca! So you're the choir director!" He leaped up and took her hand in his huge ones. She noticed he didn't wear a wedding ring.

"You've met?" Pastor looked delighted. "Because the choir only sings for early service and Seth attends the later one, I assumed you might not have."

"Just this morning, out in the parking lot." Chesca took a chair. One part of her wanted to throw confetti. It wasn't every day a small-town girl met a churchgoing hottie like him. But why did Pastor Hoke call a joint meeting with her and the Jingle Bell Prince?

Pastor and Seth bantered about sports, which rated seven-billionth on her list of concerns. Then a thought occurred that almost sent her drink out her nose: Did Seth want to join the choir?

She choked. Seth, sitting nearest her, pounded her back as if she were a bass drum.

Pastor rescued her. "Seth, would you please get Chesca some water?"

Seth tore out the door.

"I'm okay." The possibility of Seth's choir membership still clogged her brain. By the time he returned, however, her Seth-insanity began to subside, especially as his eyes met hers in genuine concern. Still, why did he make her feel as if the laws of gravity had changed?

"I'll pull up the church calendar, and let's try this again." Pastor tapped his computer's keyboard. "I can't wait until your Easter program, Chesca. *Holy Lamb of God* promises to be even better than last year's cantata."

Relief swelled in her like a Bach organ piece. The music she'd prayed over and studied would not grow dusty in a closet.

"But I think our people need visuals that will help them really experience Christ's passion and resurrection."

"Visuals?" Okay. She had enjoyed excellent amateur photography at Cedarburg's Cultural Center. Surely someone in the church could help her. Colorful medieval pictures contrasted with black-and-white contemporary photos? She felt a tingle of excitement. "I could project photos and art on the sanctuary screens that would follow the cantata text and music. Or we could make a video—"

"Sounds imaginative, but I had in mind something more personal, more human." Pastor Hoke leaned forward. "Let's add drama to the cantata."

"Drama?" Her tingle tapped out. "I know very little about it—"

"Not a problem." Pastor Hoke turned to Seth as if introducing a star. "This incredible guy has a degree in theater, as well as elementary education. He teaches children's drama classes at the Cultural Center."

"Just started last spring," Seth grinned. "But they're going great."

"He's an assistant high school coach as well as a teacher, so we grabbed a meeting with him when we could." Pastor beamed.

I'm busy, too. She loved her church job, but no way could she manage without working at the music box store.

"Seth is starting a drama program here at Christ the King. We need more children's activities."

"Children?" She'd been an only child. Her classical music education hadn't admitted their existence. The few little ones who attended the traditional first service were cute, but—

"You like kids, don't you?" Pastor was willing her to say yes.

"I–I've never worked with them."

"They'll love you on sight." Seth's face reflected Pastor's enthusiasm.

You don't even know me. Yet the tingle returned at his words, spiraling up and down her spine.

Still, the men's twin excitement made her want to hibernate. She found herself participating in a blow-by-blow decimation of her carefully laid plans. Neither Pastor nor Seth knew anything about music. They didn't understand the complications their changes would bring. And when a bunch of kids invaded formerly sane cantata rehearsals, would her choir run screaming for cover?

Hottie or no hottie, she was going home to sort things out. Chesca surrendered her e-mail and cell number to Seth, agreeing to meet next week. She escaped to the drinking fountain to pop Tylenol, then outside. But her pounding head did not escape the thundering echoes of Seth's dissonant farewell from the parking lot.

"Oh, what fun it is to ride in a one-horse open sleigh—AAY!"

Chapter 2

Despite lack of an invitation, fluffy flakes turned Washington Avenue into a snow globe. But Wisconsinites never let snow interfere with their plans. Chesca kept busy in Sweet Sounds, the arbor-like music box boutique snuggled in the front of the Cozy Cuppa Coffeehouse. During a late-afternoon lull, she and her laptop retreated to the velvety patchwork sofa in its back corner to review accounts.

"Almond tea?" Charles, the owner, offered her favorite in an antique German china cup.

"You're spoiling me. But thanks." *Ah-h-h.*

The bells on the front door rang occasionally, but customers, intent on hot chocolate and lattes, did not wander toward Sweet Sounds. Chesca glanced at her computer. Five o'clock. Half an hour before closing.

Returning to the boutique, she slipped the laptop beneath the counter and retrieved the goose-feather duster. She brushed it gently over porcelain egg music boxes Mrs. Metzger, her boss and landlady, ordered for Easter. Some boasted exquisite spring murals, others miniature figurines. They featured tinkly songs such as "Younger Than Springtime" and "Easter Parade." Chesca's mother had taught her, even as a toddler, to handle beautiful things with care. As she dusted an Italian wooden music box and two triptych music boxes with their fragile foldout scenes of Jesus' life, she thanked God for the gift she'd never appreciated until she worked at Sweet Sounds. She wished she could give it to some customers—and their children—who apparently resided in Plastic World.

Chesca's protectiveness didn't change the fact she loved children's music boxes—especially Belle from *Beauty and the Beast*, the best of the Disney figures—and she enjoyed watching little girls' faces light up when she wound the pretty collectibles. Now she glanced around Cozy Cuppa. Almost empty. She tickled the bunnies' pink noses in the Beatrix Potter display. "Still sneaking carrots from Mr. McGregor's garden?" she whispered. Picking up Peter Rabbit, she shook her head in mock disapproval. "I could buy a bag for you at the Piggly Wiggly."

"Or I could."

"Aaaahhh!" She didn't mean to send Peter skyward. But if Seth, the owner of the deep voice in her ear, hadn't caught him midair, Peter would have gone to pieces.

"Hey, you want to reform the poor guy, not send him into the ionosphere."

That sideways grin. She wanted to wipe it off his face, but he looked so cute she couldn't bear the thought. Seth's big muscular frame filled Sweet Sounds—she almost felt his warm breath on her face. Chesca summoned a pardon-you smile. "Thank you for rescuing Peter. I was a little startled."

"You're welcome." He ignored her hint for an apology. "Thought I'd let you know several kids have volunteered for the cantata. So maybe we'd better get together and figure out what to do with them?"

"But you should listen to the cantata first—"

"Drop a CD by Parkview Elementary, okay? I teach fifth grade there. Or send me an MP3 file." He consulted his phone. "How about Saturday morning again?"

No way. "Maybe Sunday evening at seven?"

He winced. "That's football night."

"I thought the playoffs were over." Even she knew that much.

"We're coaches—we watch off-season film."

Great. Her Easter cantata rated below sports reruns.

"Monday at seven?" His eyebrows rose above those gorgeous Lake Michigan–blue eyes.

Chesca shook herself, ready to defend her laundry night. "Well—"

"Great! Meet you at the truck stop in Jackson." He disappeared like an L. L. Bean genie, leaving Chesca to fume about the affront dealt her hand-wash-only sweaters and the fact she'd never entered a truck stop in her life.

Chapter 3

Chesca often heard singers with unique talents. But none quite like these.

Hanging on the knotty-pine wall of the Buy-It-All Shop section of the Hi-De-Ho Truck Stop, a dozen plastic fish wiggled at her from their plaques. As she waited for Seth to arrive, two adolescents pushed buttons, and the finny creatures serenaded her with a song conglomeration her ears had never imagined. The truck stop's background country wail of lost love and beer competed with "Don't Worry, Be Happy," a shark's "Mack the Knife," a fish skeleton's "Bad to the Bone," and even one bass wearing a Santa Claus hat, belting out a soulful rendition of " 'Twas the Night before Christmas."

No wonder Seth likes it here. Any moment, she expected the holiday fish to bellow out "Jingle Bells" half a tone flat. Instead, Tommy Trout, wearing fuzzy bunny ears, began a merciless version of "The Bunny Hop."

She wasn't surprised to hear heavy hops behind her, accompanied by Seth's off-key "La-la-la-la-lala." She *was* surprised when large hands fastened onto her waist and propelled her forward.

"You can do it," Seth yelled in her ear. "Hop-hop-*hop*."

Her initial ire drowned in a river of giggles as her right foot obediently followed the movements her kindergarten teacher taught her. Seth danced her past the slack-jawed fish-music lovers, hopping through the restaurant's open door.

She fell into a cracked-vinyl booth, with a menu and glass of ice water at her elbow. The waitress also brought them large crockery cups of coffee, though Chesca didn't care for it.

"Seth, son, you need to learn a few things about women." The twang from the salt-and-pepper-haired server's lipsticked mouth bespoke a background far south of Wisconsin.

"Good thing you're here to teach me, Janet," Seth called as she bustled off, shaking her head. His eyes briefly fixed on Chesca in a way she imagined he might look if his team had just won a championship.

Why, oh why do you have to be so good-looking? Aloud she said, "Um. . .hi."

ଓ

Chesca hadn't walked out. At least, not yet. But she looked like a little girl who had just finished her first Ferris wheel ride—eyes round and dark as chocolate balls, black waves cascading down her back.

"Hey, Peter Rabbit would be proud of us." He watched her undecided mouth curl into a smile. "Maybe Pete would even want us to bunny hop on a music box next to his."

"Somehow I find that difficult to visualize." She chuckled, a husky woman sound he hadn't expected.

"I'm not the music-box type, unless you want one to play the Packers fight song." He leaned forward. "You, on the other hand. . ."

She propped her chin on a fragile hand. Long lashes rested

on a cheek turning as pink as the flowers that soon would cover trees in his folks' backyard.

He grabbed the menu to keep from touching her face. "The Hi-De-Ho isn't exactly posh—"

"It's not?" For the first time, her eyes twinkled. "We *could* have met in Cedarburg."

"True. The Cozy Cuppa serves up hot cinnamon scones and a butter pecan breve espresso that could warm the coldest heart and stomach in Wisconsin." He kissed his fingertips with a flourish, suddenly realizing why he had invited her here. His late grandpa made it Seth's favorite spot. He cleared his throat. "However, the Hi-De-Ho's Bellyful Burgers rate the best in the world."

"I already ate." She patted the portfolio. "We have lots of planning to do."

"Okay." He hoped to delay business as long as possible. "However, I skipped lunch to work out with some kids, so please indulge me. I'm much easier to get along with when I receive my daily allowance of cholesterol."

"He's right, honey." Janet, materializing beside them, poised pen and pad. "If you got to work with a man, make sure he's fed first. Of course, if you really want to get something done, do it without him."

Chesca's soft eyes blanked and her small hand clenched on the table.

Whoa, why did he feel as if she'd dumped her ice water on his head? Maybe she didn't like working with guys? He hurriedly consulted the menu. "I'll have the Bellyful Basket. Pistachio shake. The usual for dessert."

Janet winked. "You're in luck. Herb just took a cherry pie out of the oven."

"Cherry pie?" Chesca appeared to have lost interest in her portfolio. "À la mode?"

"Is there any other way to eat it?" Janet scratched an additional order on her pad. "Do you want me to bring your pie now, miss?"

"I'll wait until he has dessert."

"Then I'll eat dessert first." Seth slapped the menu shut.

"Gotcha." Janet zipped away.

Seth grinned at Chesca's I-can't-believe-you stare. "I tried my entire childhood to talk my mom into dessert first. I'd say, 'It's not like it would ruin my appetite.' She knew I was right, but she wouldn't budge." He raised a victory fist. "But today, Mom, I'm eating cherry pie first. And it's all Chesca's fault. Ooh-ooh-ooh-ooh!"

A toddler at a neighboring table let out an aboriginal scream, so her parents paid little attention. Two guys at the counter apparently decided their blue plate specials warranted more attention than Seth's dramatics. Chesca flushed Pepto-pink, but she was still laughing when Janet hustled over with their dessert.

"That was quick." He lowered fist and voice.

"Anything to shut you up."

☙

"The cantata begins with 'Joyful, Joyful, We Adore Thee'—perfect for the Triumphal Entry, don't you think?" Chesca sipped the coffee she hadn't ordered.

"You want the cantata to cover all of Holy Week?" He pulled a small clipboard from his coat pocket and made a note. "Including Palm Sunday?"

"Yes. Pastor Hoke surprised me when he said he hadn't

planned anything special for the actual Palm Sunday. I thought the children could wave palms, approaching the altar as the choir sings."

"We'll stick Jesus and some disciples in, too." He scrawled again.

"Who will play those parts?" She loved the idea of a flesh-and-blood Jesus, but this sounded complicated.

"I know a college student who'll do great. I'll draft my football friends for disciples."

"Do they attend Christ the King?"

"No." He ran a big hand through his hair. "We want guys who look and act like fishermen, right? Maybe a sleazy tax-collector type, too. Or a Simon the Zealot/mugger guy who slips knives under people's ribs—"

"More coffee?" Janet interrupted Seth's cast of thousands.

"Hey, you're a tea drinker, aren't you?"

He remembered. Chesca gestured toward her cup. "Yes. But this is extra good."

"Janet serves only the best."

A smile crept across the waitress's face as she filled their cups. Seth bent over his illegible list, muttering. Three deer heads eyed Chesca from the opposite wall as she reviewed her very traditional song list. What other surprises did Seth have in store?

The delicious coffee, her first in years, might present the least of the changes she would encounter this spring.

Chapter 4

Seth had tried to wiggle out of attending Chesca's choir practice, but no dice. She said no CD could substitute for a live performance.

Boy, she was right. Sitting in the balcony of the dimly lit sanctuary, Seth listened as his mechanic, a Walgreens clerk, his former pediatrician, and thirty more people he thought he knew sang as if they performed on a public TV station's opera night. He had no idea the choir sounded so professional. The church had hired Chesca right out of college, but she knew what she was doing. This evening she corrected her singers umpteen times, and their final rendition of "Joyful, Joyful, We Adore Thee" made him want to rise to his feet and praise God.

Their expressions, however, didn't match the incredible sound. More like "Wooden, Wooden, We Will Bore Thee." Several buried their heads in their music. They laughed and talked between songs, but when they began " 'Tis Midnight and on Olive's Brow," faces froze, and the singers looked as if they were about to play in a national poker tournament. Dare he suggest to Chesca that her choir could use a face-lift—the kind that had nothing to do with surgery?

He wished he could see her expression as she directed,

but he liked watching her hands. They moved like a potter's, shaping music like clay. Sometimes she seemed to pull songs from people, drawing them like water from thirty-five wells.

When the choir began "God So Loved the World," he *had* to see her face. He crept to the balcony's right side, hoping the dimness would prevent his distracting her or the choir.

She hadn't seen him. Her intensity made him wonder if she would see him if he fell over the rail. Her movements wrote a praise poem. Her eyes looked past the choir to heaven.

Worship.

Recently Seth had learned to worship God with a new heart. But this woman? Her very nerves seemed to touch His.

CS

"Welcome, Ms. Appel. Thanks for joining us here at the Cultural Center."

Seth's voice sounded uncharacteristically adult. Chesca quieted her giggle into a grown-up smile. Important, because half a dozen children turned toward her as one.

"Thank you, Mr. Amundsen. I'm looking forward to working together." She knew she sounded as if she addressed a committee, but her brain felt as trembly as her knees. Curious glances approached her, probed—all except the defiant stare from a girl wearing her stringy hair in four random ponytails. Where did she find those 1980s neon scrunchies? And those ill-fitting black lacy fingerless gloves?

"I just finished copying the cantata's first act." Seth half apologized in a whisper.

Great. He's behind schedule already.

He boomed out, "Introduce yourselves, please. Get to know Ms. Appel while I finish copying scripts." He zoomed out the door. Chesca gulped.

To her surprise, the children followed his directions.

"I'm Chandler." The boy, wearing tennis shoes that must have cost a fortune, sounded almost more adult than Seth. He extended his hand. Did she see a flicker of approval in those cool eyes?

"Thanks for volunteering for our Easter play, Chandler. In fact, thank you all for helping us out." She didn't know much about kids, but gratitude helped any group grow a positive attitude. She aimed her best smile at Ponytails.

She may as well have tried to impress a gargoyle. Angry eyes raked Chesca from head to foot. The girl turned and wandered away. Chesca felt as if she had failed inspection.

"Stupid weirdo," Chandler muttered.

"You shouldn't call her names." Chesca wouldn't allow this, no matter how rudely the girl acted.

"I know." He grinned. "But Zoe's mean. That's her name, Zoe Eggers."

"You're supposed to say hello to Ms. Appel." A curly haired girl seemed only too happy to yell at Zoe. "Mr. Amundsen won't like it—"

"I won't like what?" Seth, hauling an untidy stack of papers, glanced from Chesca to the children.

"Oh, they get all shook about nothing." Zoe rolled her eyes. Still, at the sight of Seth, her sallow face colored. Her Wild Child hand brushed an escaped strand of hair out of her face. She pasted on a big smile. "I'm glad to meet you, Ms. Appel. My name is Zoe Eggers, and I want to be an actress when I grow up."

You're already quite good. At least, as far as fooling an apparently clueless Seth. He gave Zoe an approving smile as he distributed scripts. For a second, Zoe dropped the facade, her hunger for his attention as obvious as her freckles.

The elaborate hairdo. The gloves. The way her eyes sparkled like rhinestones at his appearance.

Zoe had a huge crush on Seth. Chesca suspected he had no idea.

The girl seared Chesca with a triumphant glare.

We're not dating. She wanted to wipe the smirk off Zoe's face.

But she knew that regardless of the facts, Zoe had just declared WWI—Woman's War I—on her.

Chapter 5

"You want what?" Ryan dropped his greasy bowl of movie-butter popcorn.

Seth grabbed the bowl before much spilled onto his new living room carpet. These football film sessions always got messy. He repeated, "I'd like you to play a disciple."

"You want *him* to be some holy guy in a church play?" Matt stared at Seth as if he'd taken a hard hit to the head.

"I want you in it, too."

Ryan pantomimed laughing himself sick.

Matt, who crunched quarterbacks for exercise during college, looked as if Seth had offered him lace leggings. "No way."

Seth turned back to Ryan, a history nut. "Have you studied the history surrounding Holy Week?"

"No, not that period." Despite himself, Ryan looked interested.

"Roman era, political and religious clashes. . . I could use help in keeping the play authentic."

Ryan wavered. Seth decided to use his trump card. "Zach's gonna to do it."

"Zach?" His friends looked at each other.

"It's not enough the poor guy had to visit his in-laws

tonight." Matt poked Seth in the chest. "No, you have to go behind his back and ruin his reputation."

"Call him if you don't believe me."

Both fell silent. Ryan shook his head. "Why would Zach even think of doing this?"

Seth grinned. "His mother made him promise he would attend church on Easter. He figured he'd rather act in a play than sit in a pew."

"He'd rather wear a dress like guys in religious movies?" Matt rolled his eyes.

"A robe, not a dress." Seth shrugged. "Actually, robes are comfortable. Beats a tight collar and tie every time."

"My wife bugs me to go to church. Acting in an Easter play might keep her off my back awhile." Ryan's eyebrows scrunched low on his forehead. Seth could almost see his friend siphoning information from the Internet into Holy Week history files.

"Forget it." Matt grimaced. "If you think I'm going to be Jesus in your kiddie story, you're psycho."

"Playing Jesus probably wouldn't work for you." Seth kept his face straight. *A Hulk-sized, hairy Jesus with tattoos?* "Peter, maybe. Jesus' friend. Yeah, you'd make a great Peter."

Matt yanked Seth by the collar until their faces almost touched. "What part of 'Do you want your face bashed in?' don't you understand?"

Though Seth knew his friend was kidding—sort of—he didn't particularly like dangling from Matt's giant fists. Throwing up a prayer flare, Seth said, "You owe me, man."

"Aaahhhh!" Matt dropped him.

"I took your sister out. Your sister, who looks and acts like you—only worse. When you begged me to take her out again, you said—"

"No fair." Matt crouched on the floor, rocking as if in pain. "I had to spend a whole week with Mandy. I wasn't myself—"

"You said you'd do anything for me. Anything." Seth crossed his arms.

"I'll wash your car every week." Matt sounded panicky. "I'll grade your students' tests. I'll even go out with *your* relatives—"

"What's the big deal, Matt?" Ryan shrugged. "Zach's going to do this Easter play, so I may as well. It'll keep our women happy." He looked thoughtful. "I haven't acted since high school. I played a Nazi in *The Sound of Music*."

"Now's your chance to be a good guy." Seth offered him a fresh bowl of popcorn.

"Anyway, Seth did you a good turn," Ryan continued. "So bite the bullet, man. Do what you said you would."

Matt dug his fingers into his mop of frizzy black hair.

Lord, Matt needs to be in this cantata. How else will he hear the real story of Jesus?

Matt finally raised his head, glowering. "Okay. But after this, I owe you nothing. For the rest of your life, I owe you nothing, no matter what you do for me. And if either of you mentions this to anyone, I will find you."

"Whatever you say." Seth nodded. *Thanks, Lord.*

☙

No volleyball goddess had ever appeared at choir practice. But, as Chesca's mother said, there was a first time for everything. Chesca tried several times to start rehearsal, but the six-foot blond still stood in the alto section, laughing and chatting. Not that Chesca wanted her to feel out of place. Still, newcomers usually asked her about auditions before they assigned themselves a section—and a choir folder. This woman riffled through the music as though she owned it. How could she catch up? The choir had been rehearsing the cantata music for six weeks.

Great Christian attitude. You had a busy day at the store and no supper, but chill, Chesca. She adjusted her face to match her mental turnabout and welcomed the new singer with a smile. "Hello. Are you interested in joining the choir?"

"I'm Taryn Meister. I'm already a member." She said it with an air of surprise.

The altos echoed enthusiastic assent. "You haven't heard her sing?" "We're lucky she's back." "Taryn's wonderful!"

Now Chesca felt like the newbie. "I don't believe I've seen you—"

"I've sung in choirs here all my life." Taryn waved a hand. "I've just been busy lately."

For two years? Still, Chesca tried to think positive. A person her own age who possessed an excellent voice wanted to participate. "Do you read music?"

"I have a music degree from the UW."

Perhaps Taryn had wanted Chesca's job. Did a challenge gleam in Taryn's perfectly mascaraed green eyes? Chesca decided she was imagining things. "Great. I'm sure you'll learn quickly." She stepped back, tripping over the conductor's stand.

She joined it in a tumble to the floor. Music flew like flapping pigeons. Giggles and cries of dismay mingled. A dozen hands helped her back on her feet and collected music. Cheeks burning, she frantically arranged it on the stand. "Thank you. With your help and God's, I *will* make it through the Easter season. Let's get started."

Once she convinced her choir she hadn't broken every bone, they focused well. She heard Taryn's voice above the other altos, powerful and beautiful. Too loud, as if to showcase her talent. *But, Lord, I've done the same thing to impress new choir directors.* Chesca felt her cheeks redden again. Surely, as Taryn settled into the choir, she would blend better with others. And with Chesca.

She waved the altos in at a tricky entrance. With Taryn's strong voice leading them, they nailed it. Chesca aimed a smile her way.

Taryn smiled back. But that feline gaze—why did Chesca feel like a cornered mouse?

Chapter 6

Early Saturday, the entire cast showed up for their first practice with the choir. On time, yet.

Though he'd arrived at seven, Seth still felt groggy. Had he stepped into a parallel universe?

Nope. Even if he closed his eyes, the long-familiar smell of hymnbooks and lemon oil would assure him he stood in Christ the King's venerable sanctuary. His motley drama crew, segregated by several pews, peered at him and each other as if to say, "So what are we doing here?"

The two church women he'd recruited to play Mary, Jesus' mother, and Mary Magdalene were hitting on all cylinders. But the kids and disciples he'd drafted yawned and gaped as if they'd just rolled out of the sack.

Seth chose Cam, a graduate student, to play Jesus because Cam projected a genuinely caring personality. He also possessed the long brown hair and beard people associated with the Savior. But this morning, Cam, slumping lower in his seat every minute, could use a resurrection.

"Hey, guys." When his actors jumped a foot, Seth realized he'd overdone the reveille voice. "Glad you're here."

Zoe gave him a grin. Her ponytails looked crazier than ever, as if she hadn't taken time to brush them. She made him think of his aunt Phyllis's Pekinese.

"The pleasure's all mine," Matt growled. "How long is this gonna last?"

"Until we get it right." Smiling, Seth threw back the answer Matt yelled at his linemen when they whined about practices. Matt glared at him.

"We're gonna do great." Seth held two thumbs up. "Let's review what we've been practicing down at the Center. Scene one: Where are you?"

"Front door, stage right." Chandler pointed toward the church's platform.

"Back entrance, center," Zoe chirped, not to be outdone. The other girls and women nodded.

Seth eyed his droopy disciples.

"What she said." Matt collapsed backward on the pew, mammoth hairy arms flung wide.

Gagging, Zach and Ryan elbowed him. "Man, did you forget your deodorant?"

"Did you?" Matt shoved back.

Three Stooges, not three disciples. Great examples for the kids. Seth felt like pounding his fellow coaches—until Chesca approached. The headset microphone she wore didn't distract from that black hair rippling down her back. Those big brown eyes almost made him forget why he'd come. He heard the guys in the fourth row inhale in unison. Had he forgotten to tell them about Chesca?

"Hi." She smiled.

"Hey, Miss Chesca." The kids lit up.

One part of Seth melted. The other realized his friends would think he'd drafted them into the cantata to please this hot woman. *Lord, You know the truth. You gave me this idea before I knew Chesca.* "I don't think you've met all the drama team." He introduced them. "And this is Chesca Appel, Christ the King's choir director."

"Welcome." That knockout smile. "Shall we start with Palm Sunday?" When he nodded, she turned back to the group. "Thanks for helping us. I know you will do an amazing job."

Even Matt looked less grouchy. The kids hung on to her words—except Zoe, who had lost her cute puppy face. Instead, she looked ready for a dogfight. What was with that?

Seth ignored the disciples' toothy grins and tried to concentrate on the briefing. Not easy, because he wanted to concentrate on *her*. Chesca handed him a headset, her small fingers brushing his. After testing it with the sound guy, she walked back to the choir with that perfect-posture-yet-totally-feminine stride she had. Shaking Chesca fog from his head, Seth threw out reminders and sent most of the cast to the back of the sanctuary. Turning to two boys, he primed the dramatic pump. "Who are you, Chandler?"

"I'm the paralyzed kid Jesus healed last week." The boy's eyebrows crinkled over cynical eyes. "Did Jesus do that for real?"

"For real. So tell your best bud about it. Both of you, tell the audience the story with your faces." He gave the boys go-team slaps on the back, and they dashed to take their places.

Golden glimmers shone from the choir loft. Seth's stomach lurched, as if he'd eaten too many deep-fried cheese curds for breakfast. He paused, trying to return it to oatmeal equilibrium. Why should stray sunbeams mess with him? A closer look confirmed what his subconscious already recognized.

In the choir loft, a luscious-looking blond raised one blue-nailed finger in a tiny but potent "Hello there."

Taryn.

ꕤ

Had she ever seen Seth without a smile? Chesca, scanning the sanctuary before cuing the organ, paused. He blocked the aisle like a malfunctioning robot, his eyes like unlit lightbulbs. Did she say something wrong?

"Amundsen, ya gonna stand there till Christmas?" Seth's hairy friend wasn't shy.

Seth slowly walked to the back.

Paranoia washed over her. How would he handle that not-ready-for-prime-time cast he'd assembled without his usual savvy? She wanted to dash after him, ask him who or what stole his identity. Instead, she faced the choir and caught the organist's eye. Before Chesca gave the upbeat, she breathed a prayer. *Lord, please help Seth. We need a good first rehearsal.* She let her hands fall, the grand strains of Beethoven's masterpiece swelling from the pipes behind the choir, who undammed flowing harmonies. She lost herself in the glory.

For exactly eleven seconds.

"Heee-hawww!"

Half the choir looked the way she must: eyes bulging like truck-stop plastic fish. The others nearly fell off their seats laughing.

She was not laughing. Not at all.

She'd experienced bizarre cantata dreams before—in fact, every time she'd directed one. Obviously, she'd dozed off over her laptop again—

"Hee-haw! Hee-haw!"

Chesca turned around. Women and children waving imaginary palms halted. With her, they watched the long-haired young man she'd met earlier slide backward off a gray donkey parked on its haunches in the aisle. Disciples pulled on its halter, to no avail.

Not real, said her brain. *This can't be real.*

At least the commotion chased away the robot guy who had freaked her earlier. Seth had indeed morphed back to himself. "I told you about the donkey, didn't I?"

Chapter 7

Did you have a good rehearsal, dear?"

I'm thinking of spending Easter elsewhere. Like maybe Mars. Chesca tried not to slam the old house's front door.

Normally her landlady's milk-and-cookies voice calmed her. And, as a former choir director, Mrs. Metzger understood Chesca's concerns. Today, however, Chesca gripped her tone in a vise of politeness. "We—we have a lot of work to do."

She dragged her briefcase halfway up the stairs before fingers of almond tea fragrance gently tweaked her nose. She turned to see Mrs. Metzger at the foot, holding a steaming teapot. "Would you like to take a cup with you?"

Chesca felt a little ashamed, knowing how much the silver-haired woman enjoyed their chats. A break might ease the knots in her shoulder muscles. Besides, she needed to touch base with her boss about Sweet Sounds business. "Thanks. I'll put this music away then come down."

"Let's toast our toes in the living room."

The thought of a welcoming fire in the marble-mantled fireplace unclenched Chesca's jaws. She disposed of her brief-case then hurried down to the elegant yet cheerful room. Mrs.

Metzger poured tea from her ruby bone china pot and handed a cup to Chesca, who took her usual place on the green settee.

Mmmm. I love being a tea person. Without warning, a cold, clear thought froze her: *Why did I drink coffee at that awful truck stop?*

"Is something wrong with the tea?"

"No—no, it's wonderful, as always." Couldn't she even enjoy a brief repast without a Seth invasion? Chesca quickly returned to smiling and sipping. But her friend's deceptively mild eyes often x-rayed others' thoughts and motives, illuminating their brokenness like fractured bones.

Still, Mrs. Metzger did not probe further. She offered her famous *Schokoladenmakronen*, chocolate macaroons to die for. Munching busied Chesca's mouth so she didn't have to talk. However, even this sweet therapy didn't ease her irritation. She'd discuss Sweet Sounds issues, escape, phone Seth, and tell him exactly what she thought of him.

Chesca and Mrs. Metzger talked about their excellent new part-time employee. Citing superior sales figures for the Peter Rabbit series and Easter egg music boxes, Chesca suggested ordering more.

Mrs. Metzger smiled and agreed.

A few more sips and Chesca could excuse herself, having fulfilled all business, social, and Christian obligations. But she couldn't bring herself to leave, though the fire felt too warm now. Pent-up frustration heated each breath she took. She knew her face was turning red, her cheeks expanding like balloons until she thought they would burst. Finally she blurted, "I just don't think this is going to work."

"More problems with the cantata than you anticipated." A statement, not a question.

Half-annoyed, half-relieved, Chesca nodded. "The worst."

"Oh, I doubt that." The knowing eyes twinkled. "Most choirs and casts save the worst for dress rehearsals."

Chesca gripped her head and groaned. "That's right. Cheer me up."

A crisp note sounded in Mrs. Metzger's voice. "You know this is typical. Keep working, keep praying, and your group will pull it together."

Chesca raised her head. "Please tell that to the donkey."

"Donkey?" Mrs. Metzger's finely shaped brows arched a little more. "Ah, a Palm Sunday scene. So Seth decided to use a real donkey in your cantata."

Chesca nodded and closed her eyes, as if that would chase the nightmare images from her mind. The braying animal, baring its teeth. Jesus, flat on his back, legs wiggling like those of an overturned bug. The decidedly irreligious comments by his disciples as they yanked on the donkey's halter. Especially that big hairy Neanderthal.

"Seth did this without informing you, I suppose?"

Chesca swallowed more tea, trying to extinguish angry flames in her throat. "You suppose correctly." Curiosity prevailed over resentment. "How did you know that?"

"Your reaction." Mrs. Metzger chuckled. "I've also known Seth for years. He always was an idea person. When he was a toddler, I worked in the church nursery. He constantly discovered innovative ways to pile up toys and furniture so he could scale his 'mountain' and jump off."

The picture of a towheaded, miniature Seth was too appealing. Despite herself, Chesca giggled. "He probably didn't inform you of his intentions then, either."

Mrs. Metzger gave a distinct wink. "You suppose correctly."

She set her teacup on a polished walnut table. "It's not easy to work with an unpredictable partner, someone with more vision than precision—"

"That's it." Chesca leaned forward. "That's exactly it."

"Exactly?" Mrs. Metzger's eyes glinted like sunshine on a diamond.

Was Seth's unpredictability the only factor that turned her world upside down? Tiny beads of moisture dampened Chesca's face. Her inner thermostat—something was wrong with it. To her relief, the silver mantel clock struck the hour.

"I had no idea it was so late." Her afternoon posed nothing urgent—other than calling Seth. Nevertheless, she rose.

Mrs. Metzger stood and took Chesca's teacup. "Before you go, may I suggest a possibility that might help you both?"

"Of course." She'd listen, though peace in the Middle East appeared more likely.

Mrs. Metzger put both cups aside and took her hand. "Dear, sometimes God brings two different people together to accomplish a single purpose—"

"Different?" Chesca tried to keep the annoyance out of her voice. "Different, as in living in different solar systems?"

Mrs. Metzger laughed. "Has Seth sprouted antennae yet?"

"Not yet." Chesca tried to quell the smile that pulled at her mouth. "But they'll probably emerge at our next rehearsal."

"The fact that you two complement each other will produce a stronger result."

Complement? She couldn't see it. Not at all. "I'll have to think about that. Maybe while I make *pisanki*."

"Pisanki? Oh, yes. Those Easter eggs you made with your mother and grandmother every year," Mrs. Metzger said.

Despite her angst, Chesca reveled in the memory. "Mom

couldn't wait until Holy Week. We began making them weeks before."

Mrs. Metzger hugged her. "Sounds like an excellent idea."

Chesca clambered up the stairs. One part of her felt better. The other still breathed fire. *Maybe I'd better not call Seth just yet. And Seth, you'd better not call me. Not until I've finished at least two pisanki.*

She entered her apartment, enjoying, as always, her bay window. Instead of placing the sofa against a wall, she used it to separate the galley kitchen and sitting area so she and her guests could drink in crimson maples during autumn or watch silvery snowflakes fall. The trees looked skeletal today. Her first year in Wisconsin, she'd thought spring would never come. But now she knew tiny buds soon would erupt on bare limbs. Squirrels once again would spiral up and down tree trunks. Then the maples would don glorious green mantles of silken leaves that would shade her apartment all summer. Spring arrived fashionably late in Wisconsin, but her arrival made the wait worth it.

Chesca took hard-boiled eggs from the old cream-colored refrigerator whose top only reached her nose. A relic, but it worked well, and she was reminded more than ever of her grandmother's kitchen. For a moment she paused, clutching the bowl, her eyes closed. *Babcia, I miss you so much.*

But Babcia would have wanted her to enjoy their precious family tradition, even alone. Chesca straightened her shoulders and placed the eggs on the counter. While they reached room temperature, she slowly melted beeswax in a small metal lid placed inside a much larger one until the yellow substance turned into a dark liquid. "Now for the secret weapon."

Chesca stuck a straight pin into a pencil's eraser. Taking an egg in her left hand, she dipped the pinhead in the wax and applied rows of feathery strokes as she rolled the egg.

"You've come a long way." She heard her mother's voice. *"When you were three, you thought we were cooking and that you had to crack all the eggs."*

Remembering, Chesca giggled. As a little girl, she'd covered her eggs with hearts, stars, and curlicues that in no way resembled the almost geometric designs her mom used.

"Why do you always do it that way?" Chesca had asked.

"Because for centuries, Babcia's village in Poland decorated their eggs like this. Every village had its own special pattern." Her mother had caressed a shiny finished egg with one finger. *"But they all celebrated the same resurrection—as we do."*

Chesca's eyes moistened. How she missed her parents and grandmother, especially this time of year, which they made so special. For the thousandth time she wondered why a drunk driver had to end their lives too soon. Still, the saber-edged pain she'd suffered as a college freshman now softened into gentle bittersweet moments like these. "Mom, you and Dad and Babcia are celebrating with Jesus now. The very best kind of Easter."

The egg trembled in her fingers, and a tear rested on her flea-market-treasure table. For a long moment, she paused then sat up straight. "I know you'd want me to celebrate, too."

In spite of March weather. In spite of an off-the-wall cantata codirector. She picked up the pencil-pin again and finished the first layer of designs.

Babcia made her reddish dyes from beets, her yellow from onion skins, green from mosses, and black from walnuts.

"Sorry, Babcia. My life is complicated enough." Chesca dissolved Easter kit yellow tablets in one water-filled Cool Whip bowl and purple in another, adding vinegar. She plopped the decorated egg into the yellow one. With several dyeings, the egg would turn gold, and she'd accent the next decorations she drew with purple—an egg fit for a King.

Instead of pencil-pinning traditional patterns on her next egg, however, she drew cartoonlike bunnies. She grinned. Her German-born father, who sometimes felt left out of the annual Polish Women's Eggs-travaganza, would approve. A man of deep faith, he, like many of his countrymen, loved the fun side of Easter. He bought her a big bunny every year, and when she'd completed these eggs, Chesca would display them along with the papier-maché eggs he'd been given as a child. With Cedarburg's German history, she expected to find more. Maybe at the Cedar Creek Settlement Shops?

Lost in yesteryear's glow, she'd almost forgotten Seth's sins. She certainly forgot she'd changed her cell ring tone to the "Hallelujah Chorus"—until it sounded at full volume from her pocket.

The fun bunny egg flipped from her fingers and crunched on the floor.

Chapter 8

Would his call go to Chesca's voice mail again?

Was she really that mad?

He devoured the last bite of Bellyful Burger and gazed around the Hi-De-Ho, hoping somebody would play fish songs and cheer him up. Maybe he'd order another burger.

He'd meant to tell Chesca about the donkey. But he'd only sealed the deal with a farmer friend—for free, yet—three days before, and with parent conferences this week, he'd forgotten.

Okay. Maybe he'd wanted to surprise her. Impress her with the lengths to which he would go to make this cantata the best ever.

Instead, everything went wrong. Stupid—he should have expected trouble when he learned that really was the donkey's name—had acted accordingly. As had Matt. He didn't know which one dug in his heels more.

Even worse: Taryn. Since their breakup, she'd disappeared, spending most of her time in Chicago, he'd heard. God delivered him from what could have proved the worst mistake of his life. But she'd turned up again. In Chesca's choir, of all places.

Janet, beside him, tapped her pad. "You look like you need a big piece of cherry pie, triple-dip à la mode."

Strangely, neither an additional burger nor dessert sounded good. "Nah."

Her jaw dropped to her apron. "You don't want cherry pie? Must be serious. Woman trouble?"

"Not exactly."

"Huh." Her hands went to her hips. "This has something to do with that classy little choir director you brought here." She leaned forward, searching his face. "Or is it that blond again, the one you used to drag here that repolished the silverware and glasses?"

"Um—both, actually."

"*Both?* Son, you don't need cherry pie. You need a passport."

Handel's "Hallelujah Chorus" sounded from his cell. He checked it. Chesca.

"Uh, Janet—"

"Hey, I'm goin'. I don't want to get hit with shrapnel." She bustled back to the kitchen.

Neither did he. Throwing a silent "Help!" to heaven, he held the phone to his ear. "Hi!"

Too loud and cheery. Like a game show host.

Silence.

"I mean, uh, hello, Chesca." Better. He hoped.

"Hello, Seth."

Arctic tone, but at least she called him back. "I wanted to apologize for bringing Stupid to the rehearsal."

A pause. "Look, Seth, I know your friend probably doesn't know how to act in a church, but—"

"Matt? Or the donkey?" His laugh blared into the phone before he could stop it. "The donkey's name is Stupid."

"Oh." One little syllable, lethal as a grenade pin.

He rushed on before she could detonate. "Anyway, I should

have discussed using a live animal with you beforehand. I'm sorry. Really. The next time—"

"*Next* time?" Her tone implied he would include King Kong in the Palm Sunday parade.

"The next time I try something a little unexpected—"

"A little?"

"May I please finish a sentence?" Oops, he'd used Teacher Voice.

Heads turned in neighboring booths. Janet, filling water glasses, shook her head.

Silence again. Then Chesca said, "I'm sorry. I haven't given you much of a chance to explain, have I?"

The answer to that question would be yes, but he knew better than to say it. He cleared his throat. "I should have warned you ahead of time, but I think Stu—er, the donkey—will add authenticity."

"True."

Aha, he'd finally won a point.

"But what if that animal dumps Jesus in the aisle again? It will spoil the whole cantata. Worse yet, what if he kicks somebody? Hurts one of the children?"

"The farmer said he's usually gentle, just gets a little stubborn sometimes. We have to realize he's not a regular churchgoer." No chuckle on the other end. He thought quickly. "We can minimize the kids' contact with him."

"Just how are you going to do that?" She wasn't buying this "we" business. "All they wanted to do today was pet the donkey."

"I'll build a holding stall in the sheltered area near the back of the church where we can keep him before and after his scenes. The kids can visit him only at specified times."

"His own dressing room?" Her voice thawed a little. "Are

you going to paint a star on the gate and send him roses on opening night—er, morning?"

He heard the tiny smile in her voice. "If that's what it takes to keep him happy."

"You'll have to do the same for the church janitor." Her tone tightened again.

Uh-oh. "Did he call you?"

"No. After rehearsal, while you were tugging the donkey back to the trailer, the janitor blocked my side-door getaway and treated me to a half-hour lecture about the sanctity of the church carpets."

Yikes. He hadn't thought about that. "Guess we lucked out today."

"*You* lucked out. But that doesn't mean next rehearsal—"

"I'll take care of it." She still sounded ticked. But she'd referred to their "next rehearsal"—she wasn't going to quit! His heart sang. "I'll figure out some way to protect the carpet."

"Promise?" Still ice in that voice.

He switched to his British accent. "I promise. On my word as a gentleman. Perhaps we should rendezvous to ponder the fine points—and not so fine—of our first rehearsal?"

"I suppose." Her frozen tone softened to ice cream consistency.

Why the accent melted women's angst, he didn't know, but it came in handy. Though she couldn't see him, he gave a slight bow. "Princess, may I have the honor of taking a cup of tea with you after your shift at the Cozy Cuppa Monday next? Or we could go to the truck stop."

"No truck stop. *No* coffee."

"Okay." He blinked, startled out of his English persona. "I'll see you there around five thirty."

He flicked his phone and gave Janet a thumbs-up then pointed at his mouth. She began piling ice cream on his celebration piece of pie.

Whew. Thank You, Lord.

Now all he had to do was figure out how to handle Taryn. And when he might tell Chesca about the lambs.

Chapter 9

Chesca didn't want to meet Stupid. But Seth insisted. "Connecting with cast members ensures their co-operation. You'll like him, I promise."

Their Cozy Cuppa planning session had proved far more productive than she'd imagined—not to mention his occasional intense blue glances that sent a surprise tingle through her even now. . . . So she found herself behind the church, face-to-face with the donkey. He looked even less enthusiastic than she felt.

"Back off." Seth waved a hand at Stupid's fan club. "You can take turns petting him in a minute."

Chandler ducked under Seth's restraining arms. "Scratch him behind the ears, Miss Chesca. He likes that."

"She's a scaredy-cat." Zoe gave her a look of scorn.

Frowning, Seth shook his head at the girl, took Chesca's hand, and guided it toward the donkey's head. Though his touch quickened her pulse, she couldn't help pulling away.

"Does—does he have fleas?" She mentally calculated the number per square inch.

"The farmer said no, but I made a big flea collar, just in case." Seth pointed to the band of smaller ones he'd joined to stretch around Stupid's neck. He took her hand again. "Just pet his nose."

The children watched her. Zoe watched her. Chesca petted the donkey. Much softer than she'd anticipated. He pressed his nose against her fingers. She gave his floppy ear a tentative scratch. Was it her imagination, or did the animal's expression look less wary?

"See? He's a nice guy."

Why Seth's eyes should shine through his glasses with such approval, she didn't know. But she liked it. . . .

"When do we get a turn?" Zoe's snippy voice punctured the magical moment.

"In a sec. I want to show Miss Chesca something." He gestured to Matt, who had just arrived. "Would you hold onto Stupid while we talk?"

"I can't think of anything I'd rather do." Matt gave Seth a fake grin.

"Thanks." Seth handed him the halter, lined up the children, and steered Chesca inside. "See. I told you I would take care of everything."

"What is that? Burlap?" The hallway, sanctuary aisle, and carpet in front of the altar had been covered with coarse brown material.

"My 1970s orange carpet." Seth beamed. "I'd ripped it out of my apartment—my landlord and I worked out a deal to keep costs down for a new rug. I recycled the old one here—just flipped it over. The back's a nice neutral color that, with a little imagination, could be construed as sandy ground, don't you think?"

Yes, she could see that. He must have worked an entire evening doing this. "It looks heavy enough to protect the carpet.

But did you ask Pastor Hoke—?"

"Yep. He might have to coax the decorating committee to leave it there for the next few weeks, but he likes the donkey—and the fact this didn't cost a penny." Seth resembled a little boy who'd scored a hundred on his spelling test.

"Great job." She had to force her eyes away from that smiling, über-handsome face. "But we should get going."

"Yeah." He grinned. "I'd better rescue Matt before he messes with Stupid's good mood."

Her own disposition traveled miles from that initial disastrous rehearsal. Having laughed through the score the previous Saturday, the choir now appeared ready to work. After warm-up, she reviewed the cantata's sticky spots while Seth directed drama traffic. His voice crackled, "Ready!" through his microphone, she waved the organist into "Joyful, Joyful, We Adore Thee," and the choir's symphony of voices commenced.

They actually finished the Palm Sunday scene without incident. She couldn't see how the drama was going behind her, but at least interruptions involved only confusion about who should have done what. No rodeo in the church aisle. No bad language from beast or man. Actually, little language at all. Seth and she had decided that, with little time left before Easter, they would minimize dialogue—and memorization.

They stopped between songs so Seth could coach Jesus and the Three Stooges—er, disciples—for the Gethsemane scene. "Play it as if this is your last night on earth," he told Jesus. "You're thinking the unthinkable for the Son of God—what it's like to die."

His words so moved her that she almost forgot to signal the basses' entrance. Bless them, they came in anyway. Their solo line in " 'Tis Midnight and on Olive's Brow" resonated throughout the sanctuary. Then, as the lights went down, the women began their haunting "ahhhh" as a backdrop for the Gethsemane scene. Lovely. Meanwhile, Jesus and his followers were to pray, illuminated only by a dim spotlight. Keeping the tempo, Chesca glanced behind her. Matt sprawled against the altar rail, his shaggy head propped on one muscled arm. He did resemble a big fisherman, exhausted after a hard day's work. While the other Stooges sacked out with Matt, Jesus—she couldn't remember his real name—looked all the more alone and vulnerable, hands gripping his bowed head in the faux moonlight. Even with characters wearing jeans and sweatshirts, the effect was superb.

Chesca waved in the altos and tenors, their combined sound wringing her heart. Surely it would affect the Easter congregation the same way.... Why had she panicked last week? Mrs. Metzger was right. She and Seth contributed different gifts, but God was weaving them together into something special. Could—could He also be bringing them in sync for other reasons? She spread her hands and pulled them toward her chest in a decrescendo, and her choir softened their tones into achingly beautiful unison. Even in the shadows, her hands looked so small compared to Seth's. She recalled how his big, gentle paw guided hers to pet that absurd donkey, the almost tender look he'd given her through those funny tortoiseshell glasses. Yearning washed over her, nearly as precious and painful as the music the choir was singing...wait a minute. *Which* music were they singing?

Were they on page seventeen or page twenty-one? She tried to keep a steady tempo while frantically searching the score. The repeats, as she warned the choir earlier, could prove tricky. She turned a page. No one in the choir turned one. Odd expressions crept across a few faces. Then more as singers tumbled after each other over the edge, and the song collapsed in a colossal choral train wreck.

"What happened? Did we do an additional repeat?"

"Leave it to the basses. They never know what they're doing—"

"Hey, we were following her—"

Seth's voice joined the confusion as the lights came up. Chesca tried not to flip madly through the music.

Silence fell as a clear, amused voice said, "I don't think Chesca had a clue where we were."

Taryn was smiling, as always. No matter how poignant the song lyrics, she flashed that fake Miss America smile. All she needed was the runway wave. Chesca wished she owned a water pistol like the one her elementary choir camp director used. Chesca's finger fairly itched to squirt that grin off. But why should she feel defensive? *I'm sorry, Lord. I have no defense.* "Taryn's right. I'm sorry. I let myself get distracted, and I lost my place."

She felt the stares of the singers before her, the actors behind her. What was Seth thinking?

"Oooh, shoot her at dawn." Her best tenor grinned. "She actually made a *mistake*."

"No ticket to heaven for you, kiddo." A grandmotherly soprano made a shame-shame gesture.

As the choir giggled, Chesca felt her shoulders unknot. Why did she take herself so seriously? It was no big deal. She threw her hands up. "Okay, okay. You all can excommunicate me—but not until after Easter." She leafed through the score. "Let's start back on page twenty-one."

Behind her, Seth had remained uncharacteristically silent.

She made herself turn around, expecting him to razz her. Instead, he looked at her with that odd robot expression again. What was with that? She prompted him. "I think Jesus and the disciples enter here."

"You mean when the choir does this?" He sang a horrible rendition of the tune, unrecognizable except for the lyrics.

"Yes, yes, that's it." His singing made her teeth hurt. "Let's get back to work so we won't have to stay late."

They did, with reasonably good results. Plenty of stops, starts, and repeat explanations. Spats between the children Seth had to referee. But when they finished on time, Chesca dismissed the choir, feeling cautiously positive. As she chatted with a few and gathered up her music, she watched Seth bump knuckles with the Stooges, congratulating them on their good performance. What a gift he had for drawing people into the church. Without their realizing it, crucial seeds of truth were being sown in their hearts and minds. She decided to pray for Seth's friends each day. As she watched him laugh with the children, she made up her mind. This man, though sometimes certifiable, cared about people and their relationship with God. She could learn much from him. When Seth again asked her to compare notes over tea—or coffee—Chesca would do it. In fact, she would issue the invitation. She started down the platform steps toward him.

And stopped dead in her tracks.

Taryn appeared under Seth's nose. The children scattered as if C. S. Lewis's White Witch had arrived. Taryn lowered her voice, and Chesca couldn't distinguish a word. Seth smiled, but again, Chesca was struck by his unnatural stiffness. What could they be talking about?

None of your business, Chesca. Seth can talk to anyone he wants to.

Still, she lingered, awkward as a prom wallflower, yet unable to leave.

"Good, you're still here." She jumped as a choir member smiled at her apologetically. "Would you play the second soprano part of 'O Sacred Head Now Wounded' for me? My sense of timing isn't good."

You've got that right. Chesca longed to rush over to Seth and. . .and. . .what? Push Taryn away? Smack her with her briefcase? She gave herself a little shake. "I'll be glad to."

A lie. Nevertheless, she pasted on a smile and led the woman to the piano. At least she'd moved closer to the conversation. A sideways glance told her Seth's body language had changed. His arms no longer hung at his sides like metal poles. His hand moved with an authentic Seth gesture.

"Where did you want to start?" Chesca forced herself to focus one eye on the music.

"Page thirty-six. Measure seventy-three."

Now Seth was smiling. Chesca marched through the intro. "One-two-three-four, one-two-three—"

She summoned her voice, but it refused to come.

"Are you all right?" The choir member, sitting beside Chesca on the bench, peered at her.

"A little tired. Rehearsals sometimes strain my voice." Not nearly as much as her emotions. Seth was laughing. And gazing straight into Taryn's eyes.

The woman sent a fond look toward them. "How nice to see Taryn again. The altos really missed her after she and Seth broke up."

"Broke up?"

"They were engaged almost a year." She gave a secretive smile. "Seth looks happy to see her, too."

"Yes," Chesca said. "Yes, he does."

At that moment, Taryn touched Seth's cheek. Her fingers lingered.

The choir member's scrutiny dissolved in a sentimental sigh. "Who knows? Maybe they'll get back together."

Chapter 10

Chesca went for a walk." Mrs. Metzger, manning the counter at Sweet Sounds, gave Seth a Sunday school teacher look.

Why? He fidgeted, though decades had passed since she'd nailed him for shooting spit wads. "Did she say when she'd return? We agreed to meet here to work on the cantata."

Had Chesca forgotten? She'd sounded harried when they touched base between services, but he'd chalked it up to a busy Sunday.

"She mentioned that and said she'd be back soon." Mrs. Metzger gave his shoulder a there-there pat. "Between the sales surge here and the cantata, things are hectic for her. When I came to do inventory, I told her to take off a little early, so she slipped out."

"In this weather?" He'd nearly drowned walking from his car.

"Some ladies are the 'Singing-in-the-Rain' type." Mrs. Metzger's face softened into a smile. "How are things going, Seth?"

"Crazy." He grinned. "But that's me."

"Cantata doing well?"

"Wonderful." He'd felt elated after the last practice—

so positive he could even talk to Taryn without gritting his teeth. "Still plenty of screwups. Even Chesca goofed once." He slapped his forehead in mock horror. "But all kidding aside, God is using this cantata. Chesca's spiritual leadership has blown me out of the water. Every note she directs seems to flow from the Holy Spirit. The music makes an impact on all of us—even the kids and Matt, whose all-time favorite song is 'Who Let the Dogs Out.'"

Chuckling, Mrs. Metzger nodded. "When the choir sings, we all sense God's presence. Our church is blessed to employ Chesca."

To think Taryn almost got that job.

The bells above the door jangled, and Chesca entered, shaking water from a bright plum-colored umbrella.

"Hey." The single word was all he could say. Rain did become her, cheeks like his mom's fresh-picked roses, her dark hair bunched into hundreds of long, tight curls he knew she would label "frizzy."

"Hello." Though her tone sounded neutral, her brown eyes snapped, and as she closed the umbrella, she flourished it almost like a sword.

What is this Zorro thing all about?

Mrs. Metzger to the rescue. "Seth and I were just saying how glad we are that you're directing the choir."

"You are?" The umbrella's point dropped, but Chesca didn't meet his eyes. "Thank you. I—I enjoy working with you, too."

"May I take that for you, Princess?" He held out his hand for the sloppy umbrella.

"No thanks." She stuck her cute little nose in the air and headed for the Cozy Cuppa counter.

He flapped a good-bye wave at Mrs. Metzger and followed,

debating whether to offer to pay for Chesca's chai. Whatever he'd done to annoy her, he hoped to rectify it fast. He'd never felt shy asking women out before, but he'd been practicing in front of his shaving mirror for a week. . . .

She slapped down a few dollars, so he backed off. Before he could mouth the words "butter pecan breve espresso," she'd seated herself at a glass-topped table and opened her briefcase. Now she scratched notes on a legal pad as if preparing for a trial. His?

He asked Charles to pour another chai into a small teapot and ordered cinnamon scones. He folded a paper napkin into a fan—a skill he learned during college while working in a banquet hall—and arranged pats of butter on the scone plate then filled a tray. Hoisting it to his shoulder, he carried it to her table. "Mademoiselle, a fresh cinnamon scone with butter?"

Chesca jumped. Before her startled eyes could translate a "no" to her mouth, he slid the plate before her, slathering a scone with butter, adding fresh chai to her cup with a flourish before sitting down.

"I never know what to expect from you, do I? Donkeys or singing fish or a French waiter?"

Her voice sounded snippy, but she reached for the fragrant treat, a miniscule smile playing about her lips. Her sergeant-straight shoulders relaxed.

Having turned the corner moodwise, maybe she would welcome a hint of romance. As she munched the scone, he held her other hand to his lips. "*Tu es trés belle.*"

Instead of melting, however, her eyes hardened into shiny lumps of coal. She pulled her hand away. "Smooth. Quite the lady-killer, aren't you?"

His jaw must have dropped to his belly button. For once, he

could think of nothing to say. But only for a moment. "And you claim you don't know what to expect from *me*? Most women—"

"I'm sure most women would find this flattering." The coal burst into flame. "Or rather, I'm sure most women *do*."

He threw his hands in the air. "One scone, one kiss on the hand, and I'm a certified womanizer?"

She might kill him with her umbrella before they worked out Jesus' costume changes, but Seth didn't care.

"I—I didn't mean that." The little fire-breathing dragon stared at her teacup. He could almost see the puffs of smoke diminish.

"Then what did you mean?" He'd find out what was bugging her or sit here all night trying.

"I'm sorry. I didn't mean to say. . .those things." She seemed to have doused her own inferno. Now her big, soft eyes entreated him.

He lowered the volume. "Then why did you say them, Chesca?" He heard the pleading note in his own voice. "Do I treat women with disrespect? Have I offended you in any way? If so, I apologize—"

"No, no, no." She said it so vehemently that he stared. "You've done nothing wrong."

"Then why are you mad at me? Did you hear some rumor that I chase women?" He had no idea who would spread such gossip, but he wanted to clear it up now. "I haven't dated anyone since Taryn and I broke up two years ago. You've probably heard we once were engaged—"

Taryn's name acted like kerosene on embers. "You really don't have to explain."

He blinked then leaned across the table until his nose almost touched hers. "I think I do. Did you see her talking to me after practice?"

"I—uh—"Three-alarm fire in her eyes now.

Aha. "I thought Taryn and I were on the same page when actually, we were miles apart. She broke off our engagement a month before our wedding. Some other guy."

"I'm sorry."

He almost grinned. Chesca didn't sound sorry. "I'm not. Bottom line, I was beginning to discover there was more to knowing Christ than just going to church. Much more. Taryn didn't want to discover Him with me. And now. . .she may come to church, but I don't see a change in her."

The fire that had died in Chesca's eyes flamed up in her cheeks. "I overreacted. I'm sure you don't want to talk about this—"

"I'm sure I do." He picked up her hand. Her eyes widened, but she didn't pull away. "Taryn and I are history. I'm much more interested in the present. And the present company. Chesca, you are a beautiful woman of true faith. I want to know you better."

Putting it all on the line, he bent and kissed her hand once more.

Her small fingertip rested on his cheek, so light it felt like a warm breath. Now he was the fuel for spontaneous combustion. He raised his head.

She touched him again. "I want to know you better, too."

Chesca never wasted words. But her eyes—brownie-rich and delicious and infinitely tempting—said it all.

He lost track of how long they sat, saying nothing and saying everything. The door's bells broke the silence as Mrs. Metzger flashed them a sunny smile, tying on her weird polka-dotted rain hat before she exited into the still-pounding rain.

Chapter 11

Why wait?

Chesca knew Cedarburg would blossom when for-real spring arrived. Crab apples, lilacs, and bridal wreath would perfume the air. Joggers and cyclists would appear like magic on the iron footbridge across Cedar Creek, where the Milwaukee Northern Railway once ran. Café owners would set tables, chairs, and pots of yellow-and-blue pansies outside. Townspeople, shedding coats, would take long lunch hours, luxuriating in sunlight.

But would she moan and groan, as she had last year, until the weather cooperated? No way. The calendar had flipped to April, and today, as she exited the Cozy Cuppa after work, the fresh, chilly air made her feel like skipping up Washington Avenue.

First, though, she stopped at Heritage Lighting. Of all the shops in Cedarburg, this was her favorite. She paused on its threshold, already enticed by the illuminated fairyland within. The owner, busy with a paying customer, gave her his usual smile. He never seemed to resent her cashless visits. Perhaps he relished the enjoyment of someone who loved what he loved—a thousand antique lights glowing and twinkling from their raftered heaven. Ornate wrought iron and delicate etched crystal chandeliers, lamps boasting Tiffany coats of many colors, lamps with Chinese scenes painted on translucent globes. . . they all had comforted her on winter evenings when darkness fell early.

Today she felt as if she outshone them all. What a difference a week could make! She waved good-bye and slipped outside again. The Rivoli Theatre's retro Hollywood marquee, with its red neon letters and gold lights, already glittered in the early dusk. A few nights ago, she and Seth had held hands and stolen glances at each other in the screen's flickering light. Finally they gave up all pretense of watching the movie. They bought a tub of steaming popcorn and snuggled on a bench, content to watch traffic together.

Longing for him washed over her like spring rain. *Don't be ridiculous. You don't have to see Seth every day.*

Yes, yes, I do! Part of her wouldn't listen to reason, though she wholly supported Seth's spending the evening with his cousin from California. She paused before the large window that graced Amy's Candy Kitchen, her empty stomach growling.

Trays of huge apples dipped in caramel and Belgian chocolate, many covered with nuts or candies, crowded her view. The seductive fragrance of homemade dips wafted to her nose. She pictured them bubbling in big copper kettles inside.

"Someday." Maybe on her birthday. She turned to go, but sudden darkness—and two strong hands clapped over her eyes—stopped her in her tracks.

"Why not today?"

The scream lodged in her throat dissolved into the familiar double feeling of wanting to kill and kiss him. "Seth Amundsen. You frightened me to death. Aren't you supposed to be visiting with your cousin?"

His hands dropped, but one arm wrapped around her waist. He ducked so his warm, slightly prickly cheek rested against hers. "I couldn't stay away from you."

Too much aftershave, but that didn't keep her from wishing this moment would last forever.

"I don't want to go," he murmured in her ear.

Sixty seconds more, and she'd talk him into truancy. "I don't want you to go, either, but we both know you should. If my family were living, I'd make them a priority."

He gave a reluctant nod. Then he brightened. "Let's do something special tomorrow after rehearsal. I know just the place."

Curiosity dotted her pleasure. "Should I dress up?"

"No, you'll be beautiful in jeans. In the meantime, enjoy this tonight and think of me." Handing her a small white box, he gave her a resounding *mmm-wa* smack and dashed off like a kid late to class.

She sighed, peeked inside the box, and inhaled. The same mouth-watering fragrance that misted the air tickled her nose. She drew out an enormous apple then giggled until she couldn't laugh anymore. Dipped in white chocolate, it featured yellow sprinkles for hair, blue jelly beans for eyes, a red licorice smile, and a pair of glasses perched on a gumdrop nose—Seth!

"Think of me," he'd said. How could she not think of him tonight?

☙

He should have told Chesca about the lambs. Then he wouldn't be hiding behind the church before rehearsal.

The donkey, who seemed to sense his uneasiness, gave Seth

a you-think-*I'm*-stupid? look.

"I know, I know. I forgot."

What a lame line. Who was he kidding? Having won Chesca's heart, he hadn't wanted to mess with the way she looked at him, drain the intensity from her kiss. The memory of their brief, delicious apple encounter last night warmed even his cold toes. But that didn't change the fact he soon would have to face the music. And Chesca wasn't going to sing his favorite song.

"Baaaa." The lambs nosed him through the pen's slats.

Stupid handled the kids pretty well. He hoped these two survived. Seth scratched his head, thinking. Sure, they'd add to the drama. But maybe he should forget about using lambs. Better for them. Definitely better for him—

"Cool! You finally brought 'em!"

"What're their names?"

Small hands pushed past him, around him, reaching for the soft, fuzzy heads.

So much for that option. "They're named Huz and Buz, after guys in the Old Testament." Seth had never heard of them till the theologically inclined farmer informed him. "Don't scare them."

"But I'm gonna lead one, so they'd better get to know me, right?" Chandler always had an angle.

Zoe, elbows flying, dug past him. Seth slid between her and the pen. "No violence, please. Remember the system? We take turns petting the animals. Line up. We don't have much time."

Chandler stroked Huz, the smaller lamb, then let Zoe go next without a fight.

Seth, scanning the group like a security camera, glanced at the boy. Eyes squinted almost shut, he looked like he was thinking hard.

"The choir sings about Jesus being the Lamb of God." Chandler cocked his head. "What's with that?"

Whoa, Seth would answer that one, even if it made them late. "It means Jesus was like a lamb. He didn't hurt anyone. He loved God and people. Yet bad guys nailed Him to a cross."

"I know. That was mean." Chandler's eyes flashed.

A murmur of indignation rippled among the children.

"Not fair!"

"Why did they hurt Him?"

"They thought He was trying to take over. When He told them He was God, they thought He was lying." Seth attached a leash to Huz. "What the bad guys didn't understand was that Jesus *was* God. He told His Father, 'Forgive them, please! They deserve to die for hurting Me, but let Me die instead.' Jesus paid for their sins on that cross. But He didn't just forgive *them*. He paid for all the bad things we do, too."

"Okay." Chandler nodded slowly. "I didn't know why Jesus was a big deal, but I think I get it now."

"Chesca wants to start." A choir member, standing at the back door, waved an arm.

"Why do you always do what *she* says?" Zoe's hands almost stabbed her skinny hips.

Seth blinked at the hatred in her eyes. "Miss Chesca and I work together, Zoe. She's right. We should start rehearsal, or there will be no cantata. Let's go." Seth assigned various children to various leashes, including Zoe, who looked a little less hostile. "Walk slowly. If you're calm, the animals will stay calm." He hoped.

As they trudged to the sanctuary, Seth prayed. And prayed. *God, please help the kids understand what we're doing. Please let Chesca like the lambs. And help us avoid a stampede. Amen.*

ଓ

Late, late, late. Chesca, standing before the chattering choir, tried not to tap her toe. Where were Seth and the children?

The controlled chaos in the back of the sanctuary assured her of their arrival. She simultaneously relaxed and tensed up, but the sight of Seth, his nose wrinkled that cute way, made it all good. Now only Jesus was missing.

"Baaa. Baaa!"

Chesca tore her gaze from Seth. Zoe, ponytails bouncing, skipped down the aisle, yanking a sheep after her. Near the back entrance, another child held the leash of a lamb. Chesca fervently hoped it did not have a nervous bladder.

Zoe pranced madly along the altar rail. The choir exploded with laughter.

Seth's nose wrinkle didn't look nearly so cute as he corralled the obnoxious little actress and the bewildered sheep, sending them to the back again. He turned and approached Chesca as if she wore dynamite.

At the moment, she wished she did. "Quite a barnyard you've gathered, Seth. But didn't you forget the chickens?"

"Oh, I don't use chickens in drama scenes. You have to tie them down, or they'll fly away."

What? She stared.

"I'm sorry." Seth shook his head. "I'm a little rattled."

"That makes two of us. Perhaps you might have told me about the lambs?" Chesca's tone rose with each word.

"Yes. Yes, I really should have."

Seth sounded genuinely sorry. He was looking at her through those adorable tortoiseshell glasses. How she wanted to lose herself in his blue, blue eyes. . . .

A fresh roar of laughter broke the spell. She turned toward the cast again. Seth, wincing, turned, too. What had the sheep done now?

The answer: nothing they hadn't before.

Jesus finally had arrived. Looking more sheepish than the sheep.

He was completely bald.

ଓ

Seth spread a chunk of french bread with creamy cheese from the picnic basket wedged between the front seats of his SUV. He handed it to Chesca then spread the rest of the loaf for himself.

Chesca didn't seem to get the spring-picnic-by-the-covered-bridge idea he found so special. The sleet pecking the windows didn't exactly set the mood.

And their wild rehearsal really drained her. He tried to encourage Chesca by telling her the choir sounded like angels. Which they did, if angels laughed a lot—a reasonable idea, in his opinion. Seth promised to find a wig and beard for their now-hairless Jesus. "You have to understand. It just happens with young guys."

"*What* happens? Pizza overdoses destroy their brain cells?"

"Something like that." He didn't tell her Jesus lost his hair, beard, and mustache because his roommate won their trash can Horse competition. Or that a couple of years ago Seth himself wore pink sequins to school because the Packers blew a game with the Bears. The kids had never let him live that down.

Kids. He frowned. Today his young drama troupe alternately fought over the lambs and let them escape. "I'm sorry the kids were a pain. Especially Zoe." He shook his head. "She was constantly making trouble."

Even Chesca's snort sounded ladylike. "She craves your attention. Zoe's got a huge crush on you."

He had to admit it was true. "She shouldn't be so rude to you."

The snort again. "Get real, Mr. Amundsen. I'm her competition. As long as we're in the same room, she'll go after me."

He wished he could avoid the whole issue with Zoe. And with Taryn. The choir's goofs had distracted Chesca so much she didn't seem to notice Taryn often slipped out of the choir loft during rehearsal to "help" him. Downstairs, where he was directing drama traffic, she descended like a beautiful nightmare. At one point, he hit the guys' restroom to escape her.

No, he wouldn't tell Chesca. Not when she'd finally begun to smile. At least the disastrous rehearsal didn't kill her appetite. Chesca munched bread, cheese, and fruit with almost as much enthusiasm as he did. He especially liked to watch her eat cherries. Stem clasped delicately between thumb and forefinger, she tucked the cherry inside her mouth, her pink lips hardly moving as she ate.

". . .if it's all right with you."

Too late, he realized she'd been talking. He'd listened to exactly six words. "Of course."

A guy couldn't go wrong with that answer.

She gave him her knockout smile but seemed to wait for him to do something. He decided to kiss her. A guy couldn't go wrong with that answer, either. Mmmm. . .

Chesca seemed to like his reply as much as he did. But when he drew back, she wore an odd little smile. "I definitely feel warmer now. But what I asked you to do was to turn on the heater to thaw my feet."

He felt his face redden as he complied. Giggling, she poured them some of Charles's best almond tea from a thermos. He unwrapped chocolate truffles, and their time together began to take on the magic he'd hoped for. Snuggling as best they could in separate seats, they watched the sleet slowly disappear and a hopeful sun throw experimental rays their way.

"Want to take a walk?" He longed to kiss her on the covered bridge, as his parents had, years before. Plus, he really needed to stretch his legs.

She nodded. They exited the SUV and wandered hand in hand around the bare, sodden park.

"It's not pretty, as it will be in only a few weeks, but can't you feel all the green things just aching to shoot out of the ground?"

"Yes. Yes, I can."

Her eyes widened, and he wanted to kiss her before they made it to the bridge. But he wanted to make a point, too. "The park doesn't look like much now, but things are happening underground here. Things we can't see. Just like in the cantata." Finally, he could tell her about the lambs, Chandler's questions, and the children's reaction.

"Thanks. I needed that."

What a smile! He almost pulled his phone out to take a picture.

But it faded. "I'm sorry I get OC about cantata details—"

"And I'm *really* sorry I didn't tell you about the lambs earlier."

"I forgive you." Chesca's finger touched his lips. "But no more big surprises. Please?"

"No more surprises." He touched hers. "Want to cross the covered bridge with me? It's the only one left in Wisconsin, you know."

"I'd love to."

How could a day that began so badly turn out so well? The sun lost its shyness, and a bubbling Cedar Creek laughed to see their happiness. As far as he was concerned, May had arrived. "My parents walked here when they were dating. They'd like you to come for dinner."

"I'd love to." Her eyes sparkled. Then she hesitated. "Maybe after Easter? I'll be a basket case up to and including Easter Sunday."

"No problem." They'd reached the bridge. Its weathered sides, heavy lattice construction, and thick wooden floor always gave him a solid, cross-generation-y feeling, even when he was a little guy, running races with himself from end to end. His parents' dating stories grossed him out then. But now. . . Sunbeams reluctant to release her hair followed them into the dusky interior. He cupped her yielding face in his hands and kissed her as if it would be the only kiss they'd ever share.

Later, he realized his and Taryn's initials were carved near his parents', not far from where they stood. He'd grown up a bit since he carved those. He wouldn't break the law by adding new initials.

But bridge or no bridge, Chesca's name was the one imprinted on his heart. He'd make sure she knew that.

Chapter 12

One perfect yellow crocus. One perfect purple one. Chesca knelt on Mrs. Metzger's front steps to enjoy the brave, delicate petals. She inhaled the spring colors like oxygen. Such a contrast, the two hues, yet perfect together—like Seth and her. She grinned. Everything good reminded her of Seth. Yet two months before, she'd groused and growled her way to a meeting with Pastor Hoke and some unknown drama director who wanted to wreck her Easter cantata.

Chuckling, she rose, deciding to celebrate the sunshine—and the good practices the past week—by walking to the final dress rehearsal.

Since the beginning, she and Seth had reviewed videos of their sessions, brainstorming solutions to help their cast. She agreed with him: the choir sounded wonderful, but their faces looked stiff as those on totem poles. He agreed: none of the male drama members knew how to sit while wearing robes. She had to giggle at Matt's struggles when Stupid, lately cooperative, suddenly parked on his haunches in front of the altar rail. And both she and Seth nearly fell off the sofa laughing when Jesus, amid the tussle with soldiers in Gethsemane, lost his wig.

How could she worry herself sick and laugh herself silly

at the same time?

"Relax," Seth told her. "We'll do our best, pray, and trust God will get His message across."

She'd prayed for other programs. There were no atheists on choir director podiums! But praying with Seth helped her better understand that this production wasn't about them. It was about worshipping God. It was about the needs of their audience and their cast. Now, walking down Washington Avenue, she mused that she'd learned to pray for that scamp Zoe and even for Taryn. Poor girl. She thought she still owned Seth, Christ the King Church, the universe.

Striding past just-budding forsythia bushes, Chesca paused before inserting her key into the church's front doors. *Please, God, give me special patience today.* She asked Him to bless this last rehearsal and to prepare the hearts of those who would experience the cantata the next day.

To her surprise, the door was already unlocked. Seth must have arrived extra early. Her heart danced a springtime jig. Maybe they could steal a few moments together before the gang arrived.

The fragrance of coffee greeted her from the open door of the stairs to the fellowship hall—a sure sign Seth was near, probably in the kitchen, where he sometimes reviewed the drama before practice. She edged downstairs, mischief brewing in her mind. He almost scared her into spasms outside Amy's Candy Kitchen before he gave her that apple. This appeared *the* opportunity for payback. Grinning, she crept toward the open kitchen door, determined to surprise him.

She did.

But a bigger surprise awaited her.

Seth and Taryn. Velcroed together, their lips compressed

in a passionate kiss.

Chesca's playful words strangled in her throat and died.

Seth pulled away from his "ex," his eyes round and blank as blue marbles.

"Well, excuse you." Taryn, pushing a lock of golden hair behind her ear, smiled at Chesca.

Chesca turned and fled up the stairs, Seth's heavy steps behind her. "Chesca!"

A contingent of young actors met them halfway.

"Mr. Amundsen! Stupid's in the library!"

She slipped past them and ran the opposite direction, arrows of Taryn's amusement still lodged in her back, her heart.

ꕥ

"Chesca, the sleet The Weather Channel expected is much worse than predicted." It couldn't be as bad as the storm inside him, but Seth saw from the set of her chin that he'd better stick to the we're-only-codirectors script they adopted during rehearsals. "We'll have to cut practice short—and hope we won't have to cancel the performance tomorrow."

She nodded. Before he could say more, she did a soldierly about-face and marched back down the sanctuary aisle to her podium.

How he wished he could rewind and edit this day. Somehow, some way, he'd corner her before she escaped. They had to talk.

"What's going on, Seth?" Jesus, scratching his chin, had removed his beard. "Problem with the weather?"

"Ice storm. We'll have to cancel the rest of the practice."

"Guess we've got some praying to do." Jesus gave Seth his usual cheerful smile.

Did they ever. "Good idea. Help me gather the gang together. We'll pray before we leave."

He longed to include Chesca and the choir, but as she reviewed tomorrow's schedule with them, her rigid shoulders told him to back off. His group held hands in a circle in the foyer while Jesus prayed. Seth flicked one eye open. The children's heads were bowed, their faces reverent. A miracle. Good. He needed miracles right now.

With the "amen," the kids pulled out cell phones to call for rides. The rest of the cast scattered to restrooms to change from their costumes. All except Matt.

"You're not going to try to take the animals to the farm, are you?" Matt gestured toward the glass back doors, where icy Armageddon raged outside.

"No. I don't trust that trailer out on the roads." He couldn't leave the donkey and lambs in the pen, though, either. A rare headache struck his forehead like a continuous gong.

"I'll call my uncle Fred." Matt yanked his burlap robe up to fish in his jeans pocket for his cell. "He has a barn but lives just on the edge of town. He'll keep the animals."

"Thanks." Seth knocked knuckles with his friend. "I appreciate it. Just give me directions—"

"I'll take care of it. You've got enough to think about."

Did he ever. "Let's just hope this comes off tomorrow."

"Yeah." Matt's voice softened to a seriousness Seth had never heard in it before. "My mom and dad, Uncle Fred and Aunt Celia—man, my whole family is coming to see me in this thing."

Matt turned on his heel, pulling his robe off as he headed for the animal pens.

Seth spotted wadded costumes and tattered palms on the

hall carpet. The ice storm had preempted their cleanup routine. He'd pick up and set up. But first. . .he cracked a sanctuary door, expecting Chesca to have left the state. Instead, she stood on her podium, her head bowed as choir members prayed aloud. At the sight, his chest felt too small to hold his heart.

Then Taryn, eyes wide open in the third row, winked at him.

He felt like covering his face, but Zoe popped up under his nose like a computer ad. "Well, are you going to take me home?"

"Home?" He let the door bang shut. His frazzled brain refused to function.

"You gave me a ride today. Remember?"

Slow as sick software, his mind finally recalled. He'd assured Zoe's mother and stepfather, who went to Milwaukee for a funeral, that the rehearsal would last all day and he could bring her home, too. But Zoe lived in a mansion near Lake Michigan, even farther out of town than the animals. No way could he drive her there. Besides, would her parents make it back home today?

He knew better than to ask her about her absent father. "Zoe, do you have a grandma or aunt here in town?"

"No. All my relatives live in Minnesota. They don't like me." She said this with an air of accomplishment.

He liked her—but right now, he'd rather not deal with her. "Do your folks have friends in Cedarburg?"

"No, mostly out by the lake." Her face fell. "Why are you asking me all these questions? Don't you want to take me home?"

"No—I mean, yes—I mean, I'd be glad to. But the police want people off the roads because of the ice storm. So driving you home isn't an option. Besides, your parents may not make it back to Cedarburg."

"I can take care of myself."

No doubt she could, but— "We need to call them."

Zoe grudgingly pulled out a lime-green iPhone. "Hi, Mom. Yeah, the ice is bad here, too. Mr. Amundsen wants to talk to you."

Zoe's mother sounded as sweetly helpless as Zoe was abrupt. No, they couldn't make it home. Was there a lady or family in the church who would let their little girl stay the night?

He found himself agreeing to work it out. What else could he do?

"Thank you! May I talk to Zoe again?"

Handing the phone to her, he edged to the sanctuary doors, watching as a few remaining choir members held Chesca hostage in the choir loft. Still, he heard the ensuing "Why can't I stay with Mr. Amundsen?" argument and the "No *way*!" that ended the conversation. Zoe stomped back to him, glaring as if he had ordered the storm.

"I'm really sorry, Zoe. But we need to find you a place to stay."

"Mom says I have to stay with a family. Or a lady." Zoe said the word as an epithet. "I don't know anybody here—not enough to stay all night."

This morning, he'd thought the day couldn't get worse. In his misery, he forgot to keep his prayer to himself. "If you think this is funny, God, I'm not laughing."

"Huh?" Her eyes penetrated him like an airport scanner.

"Nothing." He took her hand. Her face lit up. "Zoe, we need to talk to Miss Chesca."

"You want me to stay with *her*?" She threw his hand away.

"Can you think of anyone else?"

A long silence. "She won't want me."

He wasn't going to fib and tell her that wasn't true. "We

haven't asked yet, have we?"

Zoe ducked her chin, glowering at him. But she didn't fight him when he led her to Chesca, who was wearily packing music into her briefcase.

"Chesca."

She turned. He could have sworn two-foot flames shot from her eyes. At the sight of the child beside him, however, she doused them into dark nothingness. "Yes?"

He may as well spit it out. "Zoe's parents are stuck in Milwaukee because of the storm, and she needs to stay here in town. Could she crash at your place?"

For a moment Chesca said nothing as the muscles in her jaw worked. Zoe's pointy little nails dug into his hand like an angry kitten's.

"All right." Chesca zipped her briefcase.

Her bland tone didn't fool him. It said, *If you had any microscopic chance with me, Seth Amundsen, this blew it.*

"Thanks." He forced a smile. "Did you walk today?"

"We'll ride home with Doris. She's checking on the bulletins for tomorrow." Chesca gestured toward the doors. With a glare at Seth, Zoe dropped his hand and followed. The girl and the woman, noses in the air, stalked down the aisle.

"I–I'll call you."

Chesca shot him a final furious glance and banged the door shut.

Taryn emerged from the side, wearing a small, jubilant smile.

Chapter 13

"This is really little." Zoe glanced around Chesca's apartment.

So sorry it doesn't suit you. She fought the temptation to deliver her uninvited guest to Seth's, even if her ancient Ford had to skate there.

Aloud she said, "Yes, it's small."

"What do you do here all day?"

"I'm not here all day. I work at the church—"

"But that's just on Saturday and Sunday, right?"

Chesca gritted her teeth. Zoe wasn't the only one who underestimated her job. "No, I work there almost every day, especially during holidays. Plus, I work at the music box store."

"You own it?"

"No, Mrs. Metzger, who owns this house, also owns the store." Friends with everyone, her landlady would be far more adept at fourth-grade conversation than Chesca. But a note on their message board said Mrs. Metzger, despite her age, was checking on their elderly neighbor. Chesca fought a sudden surge of tears. If only Mrs. Metzger would come home. If only Zoe would disappear. Chesca could cry and cry, and those ample arms would hold her close. She opened a kitchen cabinet so the girl couldn't see her face. "You want some hot chocolate while I make sandwiches?"

"Is it powder or syrup? Do you have marshmallows?"

Chesca held up the packets. "Dutch chocolate or raspberry crème. No marshmallows. Sorry."

Zoe fell back with a sigh of resignation. "Dutch chocolate, I guess."

Chesca shoved mugs of water into her microwave and glanced at the time. One o'clock. Seven, maybe eight hours before this girl's bedtime. Chesca wouldn't ask. She'd just turn off the electricity, if necessary. She slapped turkey sandwiches together. Bananas and granola bars completed the menu. She scanned her shelves. No brownie mix. Chesca didn't like to bake, but it might have kept Zoe occupied.

Thankfully, the girl seemed too hungry to critique their meal.

"You want half of mine?" Chesca's sandwich felt like lead in her stomach.

"Sure." Zoe brightened.

After lunch, however, the interrogation resumed. "You don't have a TV?" She acted as if Chesca had disowned gravity.

"I usually watch television with Mrs. Metzger—when she's home." Chesca emphasized the last word.

"Where's your computer?"

"I use the ones at work."

Zoe rolled her eyes and pulled her iPhone from her red satin jeans pocket. For the first time, Chesca understood why adults let technology babysit their children. But as she cleaned up, nagging empathy reminded her that Zoe hadn't chosen their togetherness, either. This storm had wreaked havoc on everyone.

Her thoughts turned toward her landlady. Even a walk

from next door posed risk of a nasty fall. "I'm going downstairs to see if Mrs. Metzger's home yet."

Zoe nodded, her eyes glued to the phone's screen.

Chesca toured the lower story and peered out windows. No one. She called their neighbor's.

Yes, Mrs. Metzger had decided to stay put. If the storm let up before nightfall, she'd return. Chesca made her promise to call first so she could walk with her.

Chesca hung up, relieved, but a wave of loneliness sent her back upstairs, where Zoe raised a finger in answer to her "hi." Grabbing a library book, Chesca dropped into a chair. She jumped when the "Hallelujah Chorus" reverberated from her pocket.

"So, you *do* have a cell phone." Zoe sounded relieved.

Indoor plumbing, too. Chesca almost said it. Instead, she checked her phone's ID.

Seth.

Zoe's thumbs stopped moving. "I bet that's Mr. Amundsen. He said he would call."

Since Mrs. Metzger might call, Chesca set the phone on vibrate and stuck it back into her pocket.

Zoe resumed tapping.

Ten minutes later, the phone vibrated against Chesca's hip. She checked it. Stuffed it back into her pocket. Ten minutes later, it happened again. Then again.

Seth, leave me alone. If she heard his voice, she would fall apart.

The ice played a mad *rat-a-tat* on the bay window. Zoe's thumbs tapped unmercifully on her iPhone. Chesca's cell buzzed like a hornet. She wanted to grip her head and scream. Instead, she took refuge in her bedroom and tried to think logically.

Sooner or later, she and Seth would have to talk. A

miniscule voice whispered that maybe—just maybe—there might be an explanation for what she saw in the kitchen. But the scene rewound and replayed a hundred times in her head: the traitorous kiss, the shock on Seth's face, the triumph in Taryn's eyes, not only in the kitchen, but throughout the whole tortuous rehearsal. . .an explanation? The meaning seemed all too clear.

Let him suffer her silence awhile. Besides, if they talked, Zoe would hear every word.

How could she make this unbearable day endurable—for her and for Zoe? Her eyes lit on the basket of pisanki on Babcia's sewing machine table. Of course. She rose from the bed.

"Zoe, would you like to color Easter eggs with me?"

☙

A few weeks before, after he surprised her with the donkey, Chesca wore down, finally answering her cell. But today? He could fill up her voice mail, and she wouldn't answer.

The plateful of Cajun shrimp pizza rolls Seth had microwaved steamed invitingly, but for once, he passed on them and his playoff reruns.

Letting things fester between Chesca and him wasn't the answer. And how could the cantata—if it happened—bless his friends and their families, with Chesca wanting to murder him? Not that he was feeling charitable himself. . .

Again he wandered to a window and stared outside. Still the usual streetlights and twinkles from neighboring houses. No power outage. The sleet definitely was dwindling. He checked The Weather Channel. From all indications, the storm was on the wane. He could already hear the rumble of good old Wisconsin snowplows. They'd probably salt the streets all night.

The cantata would happen. He felt it in his bones. Seth re-microwaved and ate the pizza rolls. A man needed a full stomach to be at his best, whether directing a drama, playing football, or fighting with and for the woman he loved.

He bowed his head briefly then went out into the night.

cs

"What a beautiful egg." Mrs. Metzger held Zoe's psychedelic pink-and-turquoise creation with proper reverence.

Zoe's eyes shone. "You can have it. I made a blue-and-yellow one for Mom and Greg."

Chesca, sitting beside her in front of Mrs. Metzger's fireplace, stifled a sigh. Decorating pisanki had transformed the impossible afternoon and helped keep her pain within reasonable bounds. Answering Zoe's questions about egg sessions with her mother and Babcia made Chesca miss them even more, but it somehow soothed the loneliness Easter always brought. And it helped her ignore her quiet phone.

Their truce almost broke that evening when Zoe pronounced Chesca's lentil soup "hot snot." But Mrs. Metzger's phone call and subsequent homecoming—and her chocolate macaroons—apparently made up for the supper.

Mrs. Metzger's mantel clock chimed nine o'clock. Eight whole hours, and neither she nor Zoe had committed homicide. "Time for bed, Zoe. It looks like the cantata will happen tomorrow, so we'll be getting up early."

Joy mingled with annoyance on the girl's face. "But I don't have a toothbrush—"

"I have extras. Tell Mrs. Metzger good night."

To Chesca's surprise, Zoe seemed to like her landlady's hug.

"Come down afterward, Chesca, if you'd like a little

company." Mrs. Metzger's x-ray eyes had missed nothing.

Knowing she wouldn't sleep, Chesca nodded wearily.

Nested in quilts on Chesca's sofa, Zoe resembled a baby bird. "Will you leave a light on? And the door open if you go downstairs?"

So Zoe wasn't a miniature CEO, after all. She needed reassurance. What to do? No, no good-night kiss. They'd achieved semipeaceful coexistence, not warm fuzzies. Chesca patted her back awkwardly. "I'll stay awhile, if you'd like." She sank into a chair.

Whatever other virtues Zoe lacked, she fell asleep fast. Chesca watched the child's even breathing, her cheek pillowed on her hand. For the first time, Chesca wondered what it would be like to watch her own little girl sleep. . . .

But that seemed a remote possibility, especially tonight. The tears she'd fought all day flowed. Chesca made her way downstairs.

Halfway down, she halted. And choked.

By the fireplace, a tall male figure wearing bunny ears wiggled a poofy white tail attached to the posterior of his jeans. He turned around.

Seth.

"Happy Easter!"

"Happy *Easter*?" She almost hissed the last word. "How can you say that after—"

"Care to bunny hop?" He pranced to the foot of the stairs.

They vibrated under Chesca's feet. How could such a big man look so—so ridiculously *cute*? "I certainly do not."

"Then come down and talk to me."

"I don't want to do that, either."

"No matter how you try to get rid of me, I will always be

there." He was grinning, but his jaw set as if he meant it. "In one way or another."

Would he show up at Christmas Eve service in an elf suit? On New Year's in a diaper with a bottle? With infinite possibilities scrolling through her mind, she decided to end the nonsense. "All right. But stop hopping. You'll wake Zoe. And—and—"

"And what?"

"Remove those ears. And that absurd tail."

"Why? I thought I looked rather fetching."

Grrrr. Fighting the impulse to laugh and cry and throw something at him, Chesca descended and sat on Mrs. Metzger's sofa. Where *was* Mrs. Metzger? Chesca heard a few faint bars of Mozart coming from her landlady's bedroom.

Seth wiggled his tail again, and she smothered a traitorous laugh. *Stop it. I want to stay mad at you.* If only she could pretend the scene with Taryn had never happened, snuggle into those strong arms, feel the rumble of his laugh deep in his chest. . .

"Let's cut to the chase, Chesca." Bunny ears flopping with each word, Seth struck a lawyer's stance. "What exactly did you see when you entered the kitchen?"

Fresh anger armed her for battle. "You were kissing your *ex*-fiancée."

"Wrong. *She* was kissing *me*." He glowered. "Which I would have told you, given half a chance."

That brought her to her feet. "Oh, so I'm the bad guy here."

"No, you're not the bad guy." His voice softened. "You're not a guy at all."

"Neither is Taryn." She almost spat the name.

Seth's eyes shot blue sparks. "Yes, Taryn is an attractive

woman. But please give me some credit, Chesca. I want more than looks—"

"So it was my great personality you liked?"

"No. I mean, yes." He threw his hands up. "Why do women always ask impossible questions?"

"Why are you yelling?" Zoe, hugging her pillow and rubbing her eyes, had descended halfway down the stairs. At the sight of Seth, her jaw dropped. She rubbed them again.

Go ahead, Seth. Explain.

"Um, I decided to play Easter Bunny and bring treats for you and Miss Chesca."

Pretty good. Chesca hadn't noticed he'd carried a basket of chocolate eggs.

"I'm too old for the Easter bunny. But thanks, anyway." Zoe gave the candy an affectionate glance, but she repeated her question. "Why were you yelling?"

Shame heated Chesca's cheeks. No doubt, they were keeping Mrs. Metzger awake, too. She walked to the bottom of the staircase. "I'm sorry we woke you, Zoe. We were having a discussion—"

Zoe snorted. "Yeah, my mom and Greg have discussions, too."

"I was yelling. I'm sorry." Seth ducked his head.

Zoe descended until she almost looked Chesca in the eye. "It sounded like you thought Mr. Amundsen kissed that big blond lady in the kitchen. But he didn't."

Their eyes on her, Zoe assumed her stage persona. "I was reading in the corner. The blond lady followed Mr. Amundsen and was all over him before he could say a word." She eyeballed Chesca. "Then *you* showed up. He pushed her away and ran after you."

Blunt Zoe usually told the truth. She certainly wouldn't lie in order to make Chesca feel better. Chesca didn't dare look at Seth. She closed her eyes and wished she could disappear. . . . "It's late. I'll tuck you in again. And I promise we won't have any more loud discussions."

"Why don't you both tuck me in?" Zoe had them where she wanted them. "But Mr. Amundsen?"

"Yes, Zoe?"

"Please take off that stupid bunny outfit."

He complied. Together they ascended the stairs. After requests for drinks of water and stories—stories Zoe wanted to tell—they left the light on, the door open a crack, and headed downstairs. Chesca wondered if Seth would simply walk out. Exhausted, she dropped onto the settee.

After a moment, he sat beside her.

She stared at her hands. "I'm sorry," she whispered. "I'm so, so sorry."

"I accept your apology. I'm sorry I yelled at you." He paused. "Taryn also ambushed me after rehearsal. Do you want to hear what I said?"

She nodded.

"I told her that whatever we shared is ancient history, and that I am in love with you."

In love? With her? After how she'd treated him? The tears flowed again.

His fingers cupped her chin, turning her to look at him.

She burst out laughing then stifled it to keep from waking Zoe again.

Bunny ears flopped on his head once more. And yes, he looked fetching.

Chapter 14

Standing before her choir, drinking in Easter lily fragrance, Chesca knew she wouldn't exchange places with anyone in the world.

She'd passed many unfamiliar faces in the congregation as she led the choir procession down the aisle. Now, as she prepared for the downbeat, she sensed the eagerness of her well-prepared musicians to share their faith. She felt the anticipation of the cast at the sanctuary's door, already raising palms to celebrate the arrival of the King. She rejoiced in the bond between her and the man she loved, both offering their hearts and talents to tell the Savior's story.

She let her hands fall. The pipe organ's first notes swelled and swirled, and the choir breathed as one. "Joyful, joyful, we adore thee. . ."

Easter worship had begun.

☙

Halfway through, Seth exhaled—for the first time since the opening. But things had gone remarkably well. The choir sounded twice its size. The drama troupe surprised even him. Of course, a few glitches occurred. A kid tripped during the

Triumphal Entry, but it hadn't caused a pileup. Stupid balked at leaving the front of the sanctuary, but the lighting guy darkened the stage immediately, and the audience hadn't noticed. The Gethsemane scene had radiated even more pathos than it usually did. Now Matt, pantomiming the disciple Peter's denial of Christ, snarled at the men who pointed at him. When Jesus turned and gazed at him, Matt bent double, clutching his hair with grief. Seth had coached his friend not to over- or underact this scene, but Matt never had gotten it right.

Today, he did. Seth's eyes welled up. Matt understood. Deep inside, he understood what it meant to deny Jesus.

The silhouette of Jesus being beaten made Seth want to tackle his tormentors. The crucifixion took his breath away, though he'd seen it many times. Lights dimmed, and the stark metallic clang of a hammer sounded. Bloodred lights came up on Jesus on a wooden cross, the women clinging to his feet and each other. A nearby spotlight shone on Chandler holding Huz's tether and Zoe, her face buried in Buz's neck. Even from the back, Seth could see tears glistening on Chandler's cheek. They weren't part of the script.

The choir sang "O Sacred Head Now Wounded" and "God So Loved the World" with such subdued power that Seth knelt. The lights faded to black. The silence in the sanctuary resounded with even more meaning than the music.

A minor arrangement of "Christ the Lord Is Risen Today," played by the organ, tiptoed into the room. Section by section, the choir joined in. Chesca had worked hard to capture harmonies that haunted a scene where, at stage right, the women clustered, weeping. Stage left, the disciples formed a hopeless huddle. As the music changed with a dawn-like effect to major chords, a hooded figure entered backstage, speaking first to the women, then the men. As the music swelled, the people's eyes widened, they looked terrified, then ecstatic as the figure threw his hood back.

Jesus.

Peter practically lifted him off the ground as children and animals rushed in from both sides. Jesus swung Zoe, who was the smallest, high in his arms, and to the accompaniment of a majestic chorus of "Christ the Lord Is Risen Today," joined by the audience, the joyous parade wound slowly to the back of the sanctuary.

Seth knew Stupid probably could sing better than he could, but with everyone in the building caught up in worship and the organ shaking the ceiling, he could sing as loud as he wanted. So he did.

ও

"The work you two did was astounding." Pastor Hoke shook Chesca's and Seth's hands. "Have you thought yet about Christmas?"

They groaned in unison then laughed.

"Talk to us in August," Seth said.

Chesca, clasping his arm, felt almost as if she were standing in a wedding receiving line. Her face warmed as people hugged, congratulated, and thanked them.

Mrs. Metzger, dabbing her eyes, told them she'd never been so moved by a production. "I'm thankful you shared this with us—together."

Chesca, noting a twinkle amid the tears, said, "You wouldn't have something to do with that, would you?"

Seth grinned wickedly. "I called her yesterday. She agreed to phone me when you put Zoe to bed."

Chesca tried to look upset. "Then I guess you are to blame for whatever happens—"

"Absolutely." Mrs. Metzger kissed her cheek and moved on to shake Pastor Hoke's hand.

"We appreciate your caring for our daughter." A birdlike woman with Zoe's eyes clasped Chesca's hand.

"Glad we made it back to see her play." Her husband patted Zoe's arm.

Chesca almost missed the small but genuine smile his step-daughter gave him. "I had a good time making Easter eggs with Miss Chesca. And I had fun doing the cantata—except while Jesus was on the cross, Buz peed on my foot."

Chesca giggled hysterically. She pounded Seth on the back so he could speak again.

Finally he cleared his throat. "Think you'd like to do more Bible dramas, Zoe?"

The girl's eyes gleamed, but she kept her expression nonchalant. "Yeah, probably."

After they left, Chesca whispered in his ear, "You'll be coaching her till graduation."

"All part of the plan." He grinned. "If they act out Bible stories, they can't forget them. Chandler wants to do more, too."

Matt, heading up a flock of large, hairy people, gripped Seth's hand. "Thanks, man. This meant a lot to me and"—he gestured toward his entourage—"to my family." He paused. "Might just come to church next Sunday. Got a few questions."

"We can do breakfast beforehand." Seth slapped his back.

"Pancakes at the truck stop? You got it."

Seth, you are an amazing man. Chesca watched him talk football with the group, putting them at ease. *And to think, I could have lost him. . .all because I made an unfounded judgment about him and Taryn.* Chesca still felt her temperature rise at the woman's name. But Taryn's absence this morning spoke only too eloquently of her empty life. Chesca decided to pray daily for her. Who could help Taryn? Not her. Not Seth. Perhaps Pastor Hoke knew who or what could reach her.

The congregation gone, Chesca felt ready to collapse. But she and Seth had music, props, and costumes to put away, old carpet to rip out. . .

"Let's skip it today." Seth touched her cheek. "I just want to celebrate Easter with you."

"And your family." She'd accepted a last-minute invitation when his folks came through the line.

"Mom said dinner would be ready about one. I'll take the animals to the farm. Join me?"

"I can't think of anything I'd rather do." She couldn't believe she meant it, but she did.

" 'Scuse me while I change to jeans." With no one around, he gave her a *mmm-wa* kiss and dashed off.

She dumped her briefcase in her office then headed for the animal pens. Seth had driven the lambs into the trailer. Now he led Stupid in, giving him an affectionate slap on the rump.

"You're an excellent donkey herder. One more of your unique talents."

"Comes in handy when you're a teacher." He slammed the trailer doors shut.

Making a beeline for the truck, Chesca forgot about the ice and danced a wild pirouette across the parking lot. Seth grabbed her before she fell, hugging her to him. "Hey, Princess Chesca, are you trying to relive our history?"

"Only if I could skip the last few days." But she felt like a princess, rescued from danger in his strong arms.

As if cued, he took on his Jingle Bell Prince persona and began to sing, "Jingle bells, jingle all the way." He carried her to the truck. "A little off-key, right?"

"A little." She circled his neck with her arms and laid her cheek against his. "But that's okay. As long as you're not perfect, I'm in tune with you."

Rachael Phillips is a freelance writer in Indiana. She is married with three children.

SILVERY SUMMER

by Eileen Key

Acknowledgments

Thank you to my writing partners, who encouraged me and introduced me to Wisconsin. Thanks, y'all. I appreciate Rebecca Germany and Tamela Hancock Murray for believing in my work. Trevor, Eliana, and Samuel, Nana loves you.

Dedication

For my daughter Rachel, a woman after God's own heart.

"I will refine them like silver and test them like gold."
ZECHARIAH 13:9

Chapter 1

Summer

The young receptionist glanced at the computer and nodded. "Welcome. You're checked in."

"Thank you." Claire Parsons took the room key and exited the back door, the warm summer air a stark contrast to the air-conditioned building. She propped her hands on her hips and surveyed the parking lot of the Washington House Inn, searching for her niece. Melissa clambered out of the van and straightened her shirt. Claire angled toward the middle of the pavement. "I'll help unload suitcases." She noticed a slender young man leaning against the van's bumper.

"Not necessary." Melissa pointed toward the man and flushed. "Brad has offered. He'll help. Why don't you wander memory lane." She smiled. "Seems like that's what you were doing when we drove into town."

Claire trailed behind her. "Um-hmm." She sighed and rotated a ring on her right hand. The broken prong stabbed her palm. "But I'd be glad to help."

"You'll have an opportunity to hawk wares this weekend. Right now I have all the muscles necessary." As they approached the car, Melissa tilted her head. "Aunt Claire, meet Brad Fleming."

So this was Melissa's young man she'd heard so much about—and the real reason her niece wanted to come to Cedarburg. She held out her hand. "It's so nice to finally meet you, Brad. When Melissa told me you were from Cedarburg, I knew you must be special."

Brad shook her hand with slim fingers and a light grip. *Muscles?* Claire's lips twitched and she bit back a chuckle. She shrugged and dangled the extra key toward Melissa. "You win."

Melissa grasped the key, her eyes never leaving Brad's face.

Claire smiled. "I'll meet you for lunch. My treat."

The couple gave no indication they heard, so Claire pulled her purse from the front seat and strolled through the hive of activity on Washington Avenue. Cedarburg's Strawberry Festival weekend drew tourists from all over, eager to purchase unique arts and crafts and sample strawberry delicacies. Her mouth watered at the thought of chocolate-dipped strawberries, strawberry shortcake, strawberry scones, strawberry jam on those strawberry scones. Her stomach rumbled.

A splash of brightly colored purple-and-yellow petunias hung from a wire basket affixed to the streetlight beside her. Looking down the five-block historic district, she stared at the array of shops and ornate cream limestone buildings that had impressed her even when she was sixteen and new to Cedarburg. Across the way, Cedarburg Woolen Mill's display of fabric caught her attention. A sign called children to watch a demonstration of spinning the following day. Claire wished she had the time to watch and explore the cute shops lining the street.

An artist settling in with his easel and paints on the corner nodded a hello. He motioned toward his canvas. "An entry for the Plein Air Painting Event. Wish me luck." The Rivoli

Theatre had been refurbished in black-and-white and neon, and his strokes of paint captured the essence of the building.

"Best of luck."

"Thanks. " He wiped his brush on a rag. "Look forward to selling my pictures every year. But always anticipate winning the competition."

Claire smiled. "I hope to see the finished product."

Stepping around the gentleman, she strolled farther down the street. She looped a strand of hair behind her ear. "Yikes." The ring on her finger caught in her hair. She stopped and gingerly released its hold. She bit her lower lip and stared at the ring. Three storefronts down was the jewelry store. Her heart caught in her throat, and she clenched her fist—the promise ring had been made in that very store. She eyed the sign out front. Different name now.

The broken prong stuck her finger again. Maybe the store had changed hands. "Could be, after all this time." Claire slid her purse strap higher on her shoulder and crossed the street.

A bell tinkled when she shoved the door open. Nothing seemed different in the forty years since she'd last visited. Glass-fronted display cases, warped wooden floor, and a white tin ceiling.

"May I help you?" A stout salesclerk flashed a welcoming smile.

Claire edged closer, glancing at the lovely jewelry in the case. She plopped her purse on the counter and slid the ring from her finger.

"My ring has a broken prong. Would it be possible to have it repaired? I'm only in town through Monday, for the festival."

"Claire?" The woman leaned forward and stared. "Claire Wagner?"

Claire hitched in a breath and gazed at the lady. "I'm Parsons now, but yes, that's my maiden name. I'm sorry, do I know you?"

The clerk chuckled, her chin quivering, green eyes merry. "I was a year behind you, but we shared a homemaking class. I believe you burned the first piecrust we ever made."

Claire laughed. "That's a memory best forgotten." She clasped the woman's hand. "Marie Braun—or is it Marie. . . ?"

Marie smiled. "It's still Braun. And how about you—did your husband come with you?"

"Widowed."

"Oh, I'm sorry."

Thank you seemed an awkward response. "It was a long time ago."

Marie chattered, tales of her parents, their church, and a few close friends triggering warm thoughts for Claire. "And, you know, Eli works most mornings."

A knot formed in Claire's stomach. "Eli?"

"Eli Mueller." Marie lifted the ring, light reflecting from the pyramid-shaped setting with the sapphire set high in the middle. "Didn't he make this ring?" She fingered the slightly bent ivy-shaped prong.

Claire nodded, her mouth dry. He *was* here. She swiped hair from her cheeks. "I had no idea he'd returned to Cedarburg."

"He did. Lived with his folks and farmed, but he's continued as a silversmith. He's highly regarded in the trade." She sighed. "And the Strawberry Festival is a busy season for him." Then she winked. "I'm sure he'll make time for an old friend, though. Can't leave this broken."

"Oh no, no." Claire reached for the ring, her fingers shaking. "This can be done some other time."

"Nonsense." Marie closed her hand, the ring in her palm.

"Where are you staying?" She slid her pen and a notepad across the glass countertop.

"The Washington House. But I don't want to impose, since he's very busy."

Marie dashed Claire's name across a small brown envelope and tucked the ring inside, handing her a receipt. "This should be ready on Monday." She turned and pointed to a bracelet beneath the glass. "That would complement your ring quite nicely."

"I'm sure the lady only wants her ring repaired."

Claire jerked around and faced a broad-shouldered, silver-haired Eli Mueller. Her throat convulsed, rendering her speechless.

"Hello, Claire." He held out a leathery hand and enveloped her fingers. "It's nice to see you again."

Frozen, Claire stared into his hazel eyes. Warmth crept up her neck and flooded her cheeks. "Eli." She jerked her hand away as though burned and punched her fist against her stomach. "Hello, I—I. . . My ring. . ."

He stepped closer.

Claire's tongue stuck to the roof of her mouth. Her lips tugged in a crooked smile. "It's nice to see. . ." She glanced at Marie. "Thank you for your help." She fumbled for the receipt. "I have to. . ." She nodded at Eli and rushed out the door. She circled the end of the block and leaned against a tree to catch her breath. *Eli Mueller.* Her heart pounded. She'd known he might be in Cedarburg, even in the store. She hadn't thought seeing him would be so—painful. She squeezed her eyelids shut, willing memories away.

Pushing from the tree, she tugged at her shirt and straightened her back. Eli was the past. The long-ago past.

She ran her hand through her hair. Too much caffeine and not enough breakfast. That's what caused sixty-year-old heart palpitations. She'd find Melissa. It was time for lunch.

ꕥ

Eli watched Claire round the corner, her silver hair bouncing on her shoulders. On her, the silver seemed elegant. She looked good. Very good. He wanted to follow her, catch up, find out why she'd never—but what words would he use? He shrugged and walked behind the counter. "That was a surprise."

Marie laughed. "Yes, it was." Her eyes probed his face. "She looks lovely."

He ignored the statement. Struggling to contain roiling emotions, he picked up the brown envelope with the words *Claire Parsons*.

"Widowed," Marie said, as if reading his mind.

"This is to be repaired?" He slid the small silver band out. It pinged against the glass, and Eli cupped his hand around it. Claire's promise ring. He had sculpted the trailing leaves around the band and centered sapphire.

His gift to her—before the magic they shared dissipated. She'd kept the ring?

Marie's voice broke the stillness. "I have cookies in the back when you're ready. And I think there's coffee." She laughed. "Might be some milk in the fridge. I know you like to dip chocolate chip cookies."

Eli popped the ring into the envelope. "Maybe later." When he could swallow. "I'll get started on this. Won't take long."

Marie frowned. "You have two orders before hers."

Eli noted the emphasis on the last word. "Yes, I do." He started toward the workroom, his sanctuary. "As I said, this won't take long." Closing the workroom door, he drew the stool in front of his workbench. He sat and dropped his head into his hands. "Claire." He whispered the name which had laced his dreams so many nights. Lovely Claire. How he'd longed to see her again. How many times he had wondered what happened. And here he sat, in a darkened room, a chicken.

He lifted his head. Chicken. His brother's favorite label for Eli. Yet in this instance, Elroy had been so right about him. He'd let her go and never found another.

Claire Wagner was in Cedarburg. He itched to run after her.

Chapter 2

Claire watched Melissa wipe her forehead with a tissue, leaving tiny flecks of white alongside beads of perspiration. She bent forward inside the van and shoved a purple tote box with her shoulder toward the front seat. "This is the last of the pottery. I'm trying to organize so we can set up shop quickly in the morning." She slid her palms down her jeans.

Claire reached over and thumbed away the remaining dots of tissue. Melissa leaned into her hand and smiled. "I'm ready to eat. How about I go get Brad and we meet at that café?" She pointed toward an outdoor seating area.

Claire cast a glance over her shoulder. "Chocolate Factory? Can't go wrong there." She eyed the totes and folding tables. "You sure we don't need to arrange more?"

Melissa nodded. "I'm sure. Forage for food, Auntie."

With a chuckle, Claire said, "I'll snag us a table." She wove her way through a throng of people toward the café. A hostess met her at the entrance of a patio set up for the festival and Claire held up three fingers. A waitress stepped forward and led her to a white table and chairs along the walkway then placed three menus on the table and raised a brow, her pencil and pad ready. "Something to drink?"

"Just water for us at the moment." Claire smiled.

The young lady returned with three yellow plastic tumblers of ice water. Claire relaxed and sipped as she watched passersby.

"Eli." She sighed. Thick silver-white hair—she had once run her fingers through brown hair. He was still handsome. Time had been kind to him. Even though he'd not been kind to her. Her heart picked up a beat. "Cut it out, Claire. You're not here to see him." She set her glass on the place mat.

On Eli's face.

With a yelp, she jerked the glass up. It slipped from her grasp and splashed water down her shirt, across her legs, and into her tennis shoes as it crashed to the ground.

Eli stared at her, his sweet smile—lips turned up more on the left than the right—piercing her heart. Claire used her napkin and dabbed water from his chin.

Silver Line Jewelry's Finest Silversmith, Eli Mueller, Welcomes You to the Strawberry Festival.

The waitress hustled to the table. "Here's an extra, ma'am." She tossed a yellow napkin on the table and collected the tumbler from the ground. "I'll be right back with more water." Claire nodded. Her toes squished inside her tennis shoes. Finest silversmith. Her right thumb tucked inward and automatically touched her ring finger. Empty. As empty as her heart.

"Wow, I'm starving." With a screech of iron against cement, Melissa tugged a chair from the table. "Brad's on his way."

"Here's another glass of water, ma'am." The waitress slid a green tumbler across Eli's forehead.

Melissa leaned forward. "You're all wet." She glanced up at the waitress, an accusing frown crossing her face.

Claire flapped a hand at her niece. "Clumsy me. I dropped the glass." She smiled at the young lady and mumbled her thanks.

"I'll return for your order in a moment." The girl scurried away.

Melissa dabbed at Claire's pant leg with a napkin. "Do you need to change clothes?"

Claire wiggled her toes. "Not yet." She set the menu in front of her, effectively blocking out Eli's smile. Once again.

"What looks good?" Brad's voice broke her reverie.

Claire stared at the menu. Nothing sounded appealing. "A club sandwich." She pushed away from the table. "Would you order for me, Melissa? I'll be right back." She headed toward the ladies' room and a moment of quiet.

Good grief. She'd been in town less than three hours and already the past bombarded her. She scrubbed her hands, grabbed a paper towel, and stared in the mirror. "Lord, I'm going to need help. My heart hurts."

Tiny lines crinkled around her eyes, and her mouth looked like an upside-down parenthesis. She tipped it up. Better. Brushing hair from her face, she leaned closer. Did Eli see an old woman with gray hair?

"Claire," she whispered. "You *are* an old woman with gray hair." She wadded up the paper towel and tossed it into the trash. "Get a grip."

She shoved the restroom door open, barely missing another patron, and wandered back to the table. Melissa and Brad were deep in conversation. A goofy grin spread across Brad's face. He blushed when Claire reached for the back of her chair.

"Mrs. Parsons." He stood and pulled out her chair then immediately turned his attention back to Melissa.

"Thank you." She slid in her seat and gazed over her shoulder at the array of people, trying to ignore the young couple. She glanced toward Melissa. Another goofy grin. She sighed. *Young love.* If they only knew what might happen now that they'd left Purdue. Hearts intertwined as college sweethearts so often drifted apart after graduation.

The waitress placed a sandwich and fruit plate over Eli's advertisement and handed Brad a hamburger and Melissa a salad. Claire wiggled her fingers. "Shall we bless?"

Brad gripped her fingers on one side and Melissa held her other hand. "You pray, Aunt Claire."

Claire offered a blessing and a silent plea of forgiveness for her attitude. She'd allowed old hurts to color their day. She chomped a pickle and determined to cheer up. The Strawberry Festival should signal fun, not gloom.

And she'd known from the get-go that raw memories might crop up. She'd prayed about this trip, and, Eli notwithstanding, she was glad she came.

Brad lifted his glass from the place mat and Eli's grin caught her attention.

A shaft of sadness stabbed her heart.

"Aunt Claire, may I have your room key?" Melissa patted her mouth with a napkin. "I left mine upstairs and need to pick up the tablecloths in a bit."

Claire reached for the purse looped to the back of the chair. Heat rose in her face. She leaned back and looked under the table. "Where's my purse?" She pulled out the extra chair, her pulse racing. "Melissa, I can't find it."

Brad bent over and repeated her search. "Not here."

"You must've left it in the bathroom." Melissa shoved out of her chair. "I'll look." She returned seconds later. "Not there, either." She propped her hands on her hips. "When did you last have it?"

A cold sheen of perspiration coated Claire's face. She

clenched the napkin to her chest. "I had it earlier." A knot formed in her stomach as she pictured plopping it onto the jewelry store counter. She blew out a breath. "At the jewelry store."

Melissa patted her shoulder. "Which one? I'll go with you to find it."

"Are you looking for this?"

Claire swiveled toward the familiar bass voice. Eli dangled her gold Coach purse in the air with one finger and smiled.

"Thank you," Melissa said. "How did you know—" She frowned for a moment then beamed at Eli. "You're Aunt Claire's Eli." Her voice rose an octave. "I've seen your picture."

Flames bit at Claire's cheeks. "Thank you, Eli."

He chuckled. "You're welcome, Aunt Claire." He handed over the purse and stuck his hand out toward her niece. "Aunt Claire's Eli Mueller."

Melissa shook hands with him, a silly grin spreading across her face. "Nice to finally meet you." She introduced Brad. "We were just leaving." Grinning again, she pointed to the purse. "Once I get a room key." Claire fished in the outside pocket and produced a key.

Brad stared at his plate. "I'm not quite finished." Melissa coughed and nodded. He shot to his feet. "I'll save the other half for later." He scooped the remaining hamburger into his napkin, grabbed his water glass, and gripped it in his teeth, mumbling a good-bye around its edge. The couple left.

Leaving Claire with Eli.

ଓଃ

Eli pointed toward an empty chair. "May I join you?" Claire's red cheeks turned rosier.

"Mr. Mueller, may I bring you something to drink?" The waitress stepped closer, bouncing on her tennis-shoe-clad toes.

Eli raised a brow in Claire's direction, and she whispered, "Of course you may."

He ordered a soda and sat across from her.

"Thank you for rescuing my purse." She tucked the large bag in her lap. "It contains—"

"From its weight, probably most of what you own." Eli laughed.

Claire frowned. "I own quite a bit, Mr. Mueller." She slid the purse to the ground then pointed to the place mat. "Though maybe I'm not as famous as this silversmith."

"Ah, product placement. Good idea, according to the Internet." He thanked the waitress when she returned and set the glass on his picture. "I think this is what happens most of the time." He rotated the glass and searched for a topic of conversation. He glanced at Claire. Her back looked stiff, her brow pinched. She was just as uncomfortable with him. He didn't want to cause her pain.

"I suppose I'd better get back to the shop." He rose and tossed a couple of dollar bills beside his untouched drink. "It was nice seeing you. Have a good time." He shoved the chair toward the table. "I'll have that ring repaired in no time."

Claire stared at him, lines around her blue-gray eyes crinkling. "Thank you for returning my purse." Her whispery-sweet voice was music to his ears.

"Maybe we'll cross paths again during the festival." Eli turned and started toward the store. He stepped around a lady with a baby stroller and wandered through the crowd. *You've waited for this moment for years and totally blew it, Mueller.* He pinched the bridge of his nose. *You chicken.*

Chapter 3

A clerk nodded and waved at Claire when she entered the Washington House Inn. The cool, quiet lobby drained tension from her shoulders. The breakfast room was empty at the moment. Her mouth watered at the thought of the inn's award-winning signature scones. Even though she wasn't hungry, she was tempted to ask the cook if any were left.

In her room, she sank into the burgundy paisley wingback chair, slid her wet shoes off, and wiggled her damp toes against the carpet, resisting the urge to crawl under the rose-covered comforter on the bed. A long snuggle with a feather pillow sounded so good.

She leaned against the back of the chair and noted the old stone wall in front of her. According to the inn's history, the mottled cream-and-gray wall had stood since the late 1800s. Old. Like she felt. Fingering the purse strap Eli had held moments before, she closed her eyes.

Knobby knuckles had graced his brown hands. "Silver hair and maybe arthritis?"

Senior citizen or not, Eli Mueller had aged well. A smile teased her lips.

"Aunt Claire?" Melissa's voice jolted the stillness. "Brad's with me. May we come in?"

"Of course." Claire shoved her shoes under the chair and dropped the purse on the floor.

Brad marched in, a red canvas tote in hand. "For you, ma'am." He plopped the bag in Claire's lap.

"What's this?"

Melissa laughed. "Brad said it reminded him of you."

Claire tugged out a sack of jelly beans and three black licorice sticks. She raised a brow. "Why did these make you think of me?"

"Saw 'em in the candy shop. Knew they had 'em in the old days." Brad's face blazed red. "I mean retro. I—I, um. . .wanted to cheer you up." He stared at the floor and shuffled his feet. "Melissa said your Cedarburg boyfriend had jilted you."

Melissa grabbed his arm. "Brad!" she growled. She scooted closer to her aunt. "Are you okay?" She kneeled and placed one hand on Claire's knee. "I know that was a shock, seeing Eli." Tears welled in her blue eyes.

"Honey, I'm fine." Claire stood. "Thank you, Brad. You were very kind to think of me." To tell the young man how she really felt about his gifts *wasn't* kind.

"Whew. I was concerned. That's a relief." Melissa stepped closer to her bed. "Want to do some sightseeing?" She pawed through her suitcase and pulled out a pair of Nikes. "Need these?" She extended them with one hand.

"I'm good." Claire inched her dry big toe along the carpet. "Be glad to go."

Melissa excused herself and dashed into the bathroom. Brad shifted from one foot to the other.

Claire turned and stooped to grab dirty brown clogs from under the bed just as Brad backed up. The two collided, end to end. She pitched forward into Melissa's open suitcase, and a blue bra strap wrapped around her ear.

"Mrs. Parsons. Oh my." Brad grabbed her elbow and tugged. "I'm so—" When he caught sight of the bra, his face mottled purple and he let go. Claire tumbled again.

"Aunt Claire." Melissa rushed to her side. "What happened?"

"Just a little accident, that's all." Claire's words sounded muffled against stacks of clothing. She righted herself.

Consternation shone on Brad's face. "I'm so sorry," he sputtered. "I didn't mean—"

Melissa slid one arm about Claire's waist. "Sit down."

"Seriously, I'm fine." Claire pointed to her shoes. "Hand me those and let's go."

Brad retreated to the door, the back of his neck blotchy red.

"Are you sure?"

Claire glared at her niece. The overprotective attitude had begun to grate on her nerves. "I'm quite sure."

A rap at the doorway interrupted the melee. Brad swung the door open wide. A lady stood in the doorway, a large bouquet in her hands. "Claire Parsons?"

Melissa pointed.

The lady stepped just inside the room and set a vase of daisies on an end table then turned to leave.

"Wait a minute." Claire eyed the vase then the woman. "Where did these come from?"

"The card is tucked inside." She smiled. "Have a nice day."

"Nice day, indeed, when you get flowers." Melissa giggled. She lifted a card from the floral arrangement. "I bet I know who sent them," she singsonged.

Claire's heart pounded against her ribs, and heat rushed up her cheeks. *Daisies.* She blinked hard and stared at the card in Melissa's hand. "Open it."

"Nope." Melissa tapped it with a finger. "Has your name on it." She grinned and handed the card to Claire. "We'll meet you outside." She grasped Brad's elbow and led him out of the room.

Once the door shut, Claire sank onto the bed. Her fingers felt cold and stiff. Daisies. He'd sent daisies before. The day before he left Cedarburg.

She slid a lilac-colored card from the envelope.

Claire, hope you enjoy your return home. Nice to see you. Eli.

Nice? Her hand trembled. Nice to see you? Forty years later and that's all he could think of to say? And how did he know where she was staying? Sure, it was a small town. And he seemed to be pretty important. But how did he find her so quickly? Claire chewed her lower lip.

"Marie." The clerk had her contact information. Anger flashed through her middle. "She had no right to pass on personal information. No right at all."

She scanned the card. "Enjoy my return home." Claire stood and stepped to the window. She caught sight of the edge of a banner down the street.

WELCOME TO THE STRAWBERRY FESTIVAL
SILVER LINE JEWE—

She spun around. Everywhere she turned, Eli Mueller was on display.

Well, he might be important, but Marie certainly hadn't permission to pass on her personal information to him.

Stabbing her hands onto her hips, Claire bumped the telephone perched on the nightstand. She frowned. "I'll report this infraction." She jerked the phone book from a drawer and located the number for the Cedarburg town board. After two rings, a woman answered.

"I'd like to report a—" What was she reporting? "—a poor business practice." Claire swiped dust from around the phone's keypad.

"I'm sorry to hear you're unhappy, ma'am," the lady cooed. "Let me give you a contact number to file a report."

Claire fumbled in her purse for a pen then twirled the florist envelope around, poising her hand to write. "Ready."

"Call Eli Mueller—"

The lady droned on, but nothing computed. Claire dropped the receiver in the cradle and flopped against a pillow.

She would have to complain to Eli about Eli. He'd taken over Cedarburg.

ଓ

"Cookie?" Marie held out a plastic bag.

"No thanks." Eli rubbed his hand down his jeans. Since he'd returned to the shop and ordered flowers, Marie had been unduly attentive. Earlier she'd bristled when asked for the florist's number, her jaw clenched and brow furrowed, clearly annoyed.

Good motivation to get to work. "I'll be in back." Settling on a stool at his workbench, Eli selected a brown envelope and slid out a silver bracelet and charm. He lifted flat-jaw pliers and began to attach the heart-shaped strawberry to a link.

Heaving a sigh, he set the materials down. He leaned one elbow on the wooden table and pinched the bridge of his nose. Daisies. He always thought of Claire when he saw them. Lighthearted flowers. Like she had been.

"Wonder what she's like now?"

"Who?"

Eli jerked around.

Marie stood in the doorway, her arms crossed. "Are you talking about Claire?"

He turned back and picked up the pliers. "Yeah. It's always interesting when you run into old high school friends." He pressed a silver loop onto the charm. "Remember when Cynthia Minto came through town?"

Marie stepped closer and leaned against the workbench. "I do." She toyed with a needle file. "But you didn't send flowers."

Eli straightened, his mouth pressed into a straight line. He faced Marie. Her green eyes probed his face. His ears burned. "You're right." His stomach churned. He'd put this conversation off long enough. "Marie, I appreciate all the help you've given me, all the cookies, the casseroles." He sighed. "But—"

She lowered her gaze. "But I'm not Claire." She wheeled about and shut the workroom door.

"That's correct," Eli whispered. "You're not Claire." He tossed down the pliers and slid the bracelet into the envelope then headed out the back door. A bicycle ride to the covered bridge wouldn't take long.

Sunshine dappled the sidewalk as he rode through town, dodging tourists crossing the way. Flower-scented breezes cooled his cheeks. He nodded at people and laughed at a mother and son rapidly licking strawberry ice cream cones.

Tomorrow he'd busy himself, check out the exhibits, chat with friends and vendors. Today none of those activities interested him.

He rode past the bulk of the residential district and the fire department. The distractions of traffic and tourists slowed. He maneuvered across Highway 60 at Five Corners and kept to the narrow shoulder of the county road, climbing the steeper stretches with more effort than it had taken all those years ago.

More new construction. Big houses. *Wonder how much those cost. And who is going to mow that much lawn?*

The old weathered bridge waited for him at the bottom of the hill. Silent now. Unused for its intended purpose, it no longer sheltered the county road as it had for more than a century but stood beside the new road. Eli nodded to it, a gesture of respect for its faithful service to the community then rolled down the gravel drive into the park.

A breeze lifted his hair. It was several degrees cooler in the shade. He propped his bike against one of the large boulders lining the small parking lot and strolled toward the water. Bypassing picnicking families and couples sneaking kisses, Eli walked along the creek edge, watching the slow pace of the water carry summer's fluff and regret downstream.

He leaned against a weathered post and gazed into the crystal clear water as it eddied about rocks. He'd tossed a good number of those rocks in his youth. He launched a stick in the air and watched it sail downstream. A smile crossed his face. Sadie. The yellow Lab he'd given Claire loved to dash into the water after sticks.

Wonder if she kept Sadie when they left Cedarburg? His thoughts lingered on the past for a moment, and he shook his head. He thrust his hands in his pockets and stirred the ground with the toe of his boot.

"Lord, I've got some making up to do, and I don't know what to say." He shifted his weight and stared at a passing cloud. "Give me the opportunity to talk to Claire." He shoved upright and watched the water a few moments longer. Straightening his shoulders, he turned on his heel and headed back to town.

Chapter 4

Claire aimed the blow-dryer at the steam-covered mirror until a patch cleared. "Can't believe Melissa talked me into this." The Friday night Summer Sounds Concert in the Park did promise to be a fun evening of music. But Eli—

She closed her eyes and waved the dryer across the back of her head then impulsively wrapped her hair over her fingers into a flirty flip. She graduated from high school wearing a flip. Eli had loved the new hairdo and poked her senior picture sporting the new look onto the visor of his car.

But that had been oh, so many years ago. She folded the silver strands under to her usual bob and stared into the mirror. She pressed her lips into a thin line, her pulse throbbing in her throat. "Wonder where that picture went?" she whispered. Her eyes filled with tears. She swiped at them with a tissue and finished with her hair.

"Aunt Claire?" Melissa tapped on the bathroom door. "Are you done?"

Claire swung the door open. "Your turn." The ceiling fan offered a welcome chill of air. "I'll put on makeup at the table. Get a shower before your Brad shows up." She smiled at her brother-in-law's child, the closest thing to a daughter she had. Pulling her makeup case from the bed, she sat down at the table and propped up a gold mirror. The overhead light didn't prove satisfactory, so she slid the curtain away from the window. The jewelry store banner flapped in the breeze. Tears pooled again. "This is his town, and you'll see him whether you like it or not." She glanced at the perky daisies.

She sighed then batted her eyes and applied foundation to her flushed cheeks.

Rising, she riffled through her suitcase. She pulled out a denim skirt and tossed it onto the bed. A bright blue blouse lay folded at the bottom. She snapped the blouse open—not too wrinkled. She stepped in front of the mirror and held it up. "Eli always liked blue."

Eli? She huffed and nearly choked on her breath. Why was she concerned about him? She pulled on the blouse and buttoned it, without looking at her reflection.

Melissa finished dressing quickly, obviously in a hurry to meet Brad. As soon as they stepped outside, the wind tossed Claire's carefully coiffed hair. She gazed at the salmon-pink evening sky. Tourists strolled down the street, most looking spent from their day of shopping and exploring. Brad waited on the sidewalk and tucked Melissa's hand into the crook of his arm. They crossed at the stoplight and meandered down Columbia. In front of them stood the huge Cedarburg Grist Mill and the unusual red-roofed pagoda store—a former service station—which sat near the entrance to lovely Cedar Creek Park.

People lounged on quilts, gathered with their lawn chairs in groups, and perched on picnic tables, chatting. Children climbed on the monkey bars and clambered over a red fire truck slide. Others ran in circles in a game of chase. A quartet played jazz on the stage, strains of a saxophone drifting across the park.

Claire neared the edge of the creek. White water bubbled over driftwood and around rocks. A family of ducks waddled across the streambed, Mama leading her ducklings. Tomorrow they'd be displaced with rubber duckies as children raced theirs downstream in the Cedarquacker 500 Duck Race.

When the music slowed, the gurgle of the water soothed Claire's jitters. She found herself relaxing. After all, she wasn't the only person who'd done dumb things as a teen. Her last dance in this park had been a catastrophe. Whoever brought a greased pig had spoiled all the romance of the evening. She laughed.

"What's so funny?" Melissa tugged on her sleeve.

Claire shook her head. "Memories. Fun times." She pointed at the ducks. "Look at those babies." Anything to distract her niece from probing questions.

Brad flapped the small quilt from his shoulder. "Think I've found a place for us to sit." He pointed to the lawn in front of the stage. "There, away from the playground."

Trekking around people, the three made their way to a comfortable seating area. Brad dropped the quilt, and they settled on its edges. Claire purposefully turned away from the couple. They'd been kind to include her in their evening, but she remembered stolen moments in this very park. She sighed.

If only she hadn't been so adamant—so unbending—hanging on to her father's ideas rather than her own, how different life could've been.

"Good evening."

Eli's voice jolted her from her reverie. Claire's eyes widened, and she gave a jerky nod.

He tapped his forehead in a mock salute. "Enjoy the music." He pressed on through the crowd.

Disappointment enveloped Claire. Eli hadn't stopped. She

brushed grass from her skirt. Why should he?

ᘓ

Eli introduced the second band for the evening. One of his local favorites. His smile felt stiff as cardboard and the words stilted as he spoke. The sentiments were heartfelt, but at the moment his heart *felt. . .sad.* He'd seen her again, looking lovely in blue, and walked on by.

He sat beside the lead guitar's wife at the edge of the crowd, arms clasped across his chest, wondering if Claire was watching him or the band. *Mueller, cut the ego trip. She moved on. Got married. They'd probably had a great life together.* She hadn't even thanked him for the flowers. *Hmph.*

He propped one ankle over the other leg and jerked at a thread on the hem of his jeans. It cut into his finger. A distraction. He hadn't gotten much accomplished today after he'd seen Claire. He sighed, the mellow music dredging up stashed memories.

Her face when he told her he might enlist. Her father's indignation.

Eli blew out an exasperated breath. Mr. Wagner, a conscientious objector, led his daughter away from the high school graduation before he and Claire could talk. Before he could—

"Explain." He shifted on the chair. Gus's pregnant wife lifted a brow. "Oh, sorry, Roxie. Talking to myself."

"Thought you might want to explain where your mind is, Eli." She cocked her head, a gentle smile crossing her face. "Or should I say your heart?"

"Excuse me?"

"Aunt Marie told Mom you had a visitor in the shop today."

Eli's mouth turned down, and he shrugged. "Can't keep anything a secret around here."

Roxie giggled. "Nope. Not for long." She glanced over her shoulder. "Is she here? I'd like to see the mystery woman who captured you so long ago." She clutched her hands over her heart. "Sounds so romantic."

Heat crept up Eli's neck and ears. "You read too many novels, Rox. Real life's nothing like that." He planted both feet on the ground and propped his elbows on his knees. "Real life is working and helping others. Following where God leads." He shoved to his feet. "And He didn't lead me to Claire Wagner."

Roxie's eyes lit up, obviously tickled at his discomfort. "Claire." She rubbed her swollen belly. "Maybe not yet, Eli." She shook a finger at him. "Remember your words of encouragement when Gus and I separated?" She narrowed one eye and mimicked his baritone. "God's not finished with you."

Eli squirmed. The very words he'd used now came back to grab his core. "Want something to drink, Momma-to-be?"

"Thanks. A soda." She fished for her purse. "Then we might continue this line of conversation."

Eli waved her money away and approached a vendor selling sodas. He purchased two and asked a friend to deliver Roxie's. That was a talk he'd just as soon skip.

The cold drink stung his throat, and his eyes watered. He gathered a napkin from the counter and swiped away tears. When his vision cleared, Melissa stood in front of him.

"Hello, Mr. Mueller."

Eli's chest constricted. Would he never escape reminders of Claire?

"Good evening." Muscles worked in his jaw.

Melissa reached for her friend's hand. "Brad and Aunt

Claire and I are seated right over—" She pointed toward the stage.

"I saw your aunt earlier." He sipped on his drink.

"Feel free to join us." Melissa winked at him.

"Thank you." His mouth quirked. "Maybe later. Hope you enjoy the concert." He turned on one heel and walked toward the playground. Children hooted and scooted all over the place.

Children I'll never have. The morose thought caught him off guard. "Shake it off, Mueller."

He watched a boy and girl swing, one after the other, across the monkey bars. His jaw tightened. He'd swung across monkey bars in pursuit of Claire one summer evening, a teenager acting silly. How she had laughed. Until—

A shrill scream split the air. The boy now lay on the ground, blood dripping from his hand. Eli pulled the napkin from his drink, tossed the cup into a trash bin, and sprinted toward him.

"It bit me," the child cried. "Them monkey bars bit me."

Eli scooped him into his arms, knelt, and compressed the cut with the damp napkin.

"Ty! What have you done?" A distraught mom gathered her child and cooed words of comfort. She flashed a smile at Eli. "Thank you."

Eli nodded, adrenaline draining from his body. Claire's finger had been sliced that summer night. He'd blotted the blood from her hand with his shirttail, and his mom had complained about the spot.

He pushed to his feet and mumbled good night. This Friday needed to end.

Now.

Chapter 5

"Tug the covering tighter on the edge." Claire fought the Saturday morning breeze to keep the white pop-up canopy upright. She secured the latch on the aluminum pole and brushed flyaway hair from her face. "Think that'll hold it." She grinned at her niece. Melissa's freckled face glowed from exertion. "Craft shows provide more exercise than I thought."

"You aren't kidding." Melissa knotted a scrunchie around her copper ponytail then looped a nylon rope through a grommet to attach her booth's banner across the front of the canopy.

A sudden gust of wind blasted the lane and wrenched the banner from her hand.

"Ouch!" A skinny gentleman in plaid Bermuda shorts wrestled the sign from his head, arms waving in every direction.

Melissa tucked fabric under her arm, pulling it from his shoulders. Her eager efforts slid the rope from the grommet with enough force to jerk the canopy sideways.

Claire grabbed a corner pole. "Watch it!" The canopy wobbled and tipped over, enveloping the man.

Melissa dropped her banner and scrambled to free him. "Oh my. I'm so sorry."

Red faced and batting at the wind, he emerged. She patted

his shoulder. "Are you okay?"

The balding man grunted affirmatively and snorted his disgust. His Birkenstocks flapped against the asphalt as he stomped away.

Claire stifled a snort, but the look on the man's face as he glared their direction brought it to the surface. She turned on her heel and burst out laughing.

"Thank goodness he wasn't hurt." Melissa frowned. "Aunt Claire. It's not funny." She bit her lower lip. "It really wasn't." After a glance at her aunt she started to giggle. "Help me, please."

Straining to reach the top, Claire righted the canopy and slid her end of the rope through a grommet, forming a knot and straightening the sign. Bright red letters welcomed buyers to Wagner Pottery.

Melissa and Brad used a dolly to unload the boxes of pottery and set them on the display tables. Claire draped fabric up and around small crates to form tiers of shelves and arranged the dishes and vases artfully. Within a few minutes the kiosk was open.

"We're going to grab a cup of coffee. Want anything?" Melissa said.

Claire shook her head and lifted her water bottle. "All set."

"Be right back."

They returned, and the morning passed with a flash. Buyers scooped up pottery pieces and Melissa's face glowed with excitement.

By noon, Melissa decided to go watch Brad participate in the Paint the Festival segment of the Plein Air competition. They had prayed for his nervous fingers. He itched to win.

Claire glanced at her watch. Earlier she'd held her breath

when she saw Eli striding down the street. She hoped—and worried—he would walk toward Melissa's exhibit, but he'd turned away through the crowd.

And she fought disappointment.

A sigh escaped. "It's been two hours." *Such a teenage reaction.* She shook her head and snapped her watchband. "Stop looking." What would she say if he did appear?

Claire adjusted the tops on two cookie jars and added water to the peonies in a hand-painted vase. She'd sold quite a few more pieces in the last hour. Melissa would be thrilled to know a local dignitary bought a set of dinnerware fashioned for the festival with tiny strawberries encircling each plate and the rim of the cups.

People lined the walkway, chattering, shopping, and nibbling various delicacies as they shuffled from exhibit to exhibit. A hum of conversation mingled with jazz music. A hint of barbecue tickled her nose. Next to the table a little girl paused and grinned. A bright blue butterfly decorated her cheek. She bit into a chocolate-covered strawberry.

Claire's mouth watered, but she couldn't leave the stand. She plopped into the lawn chair behind the pottery display. The forecast stated moderate temperatures, but she'd been in the sunshine long enough to feel cooked. In the shade, a breeze cooled her cheeks. Nature's air-conditioning. She bent over and lifted her hair from her collar.

"Claire?"

She jerked to attention.

A portly gentleman in a stretched, stained Strawberry Festival T-shirt leaned over the table. "Are you. . ."

Claire's eyes widened.

George Schiller waved. He slid around a canopy pole and

flapped his chubby hand. "River rats, it's my old girlfriend."

A rush of heat added to the sunburn discomfort. "George." She stood.

He reached sweaty, flabby arms around her shoulders and pulled her against his damp stomach. A musty odor overtook the pleasant barbecue smell.

"My goodness." Claire shrunk away. "It's been a long time." Her lips tipped up in what she hoped was a smile. "What have you been up to?"

George's mud-brown eyes twinkled. "Come to Cedarburg for a week or two every year about this time and keep an eye out for you. Been waiting for you to return." He shook a sausage-sized finger in her face. "You owe me the last dance, young lady." He burst into his signature laugh—a chuckle, a snort, a gasp—and slapped his belly. "Can't fit in that tux anymore, but I can still shake a leg."

The willies-factor crept over Claire. George had followed—stalked—her every summer of high school when he came to visit his grandmother. And all the time in the world couldn't erase the shivers that ran up her spine. She struggled for a smile. "Your family well?" She pictured round little Weebles running behind their daddy.

A cloud passed over his face. "Wife number two just left. Took my only girl." He sighed, then flashed a snaggletoothed smile. "Guess her departure is good timing. My old flame's back in town." His robust laugh burst out.

"Excuse me, ma'am." A lady held up a pitcher. "How much?"

Claire whirled toward the customer then looked back at him. "George, I'm busy at the moment." After she sold the pitcher, she stepped in front of the display table and rearranged the pottery, her mind whirling. George's appearance churned memories—dodging, hiding in the shrubs until he passed her house—and the worst, ducking into the bathroom at church—the men's bathroom! She wanted him gone.

He crunched into the lawn chair and fiddled with his cell phone. "I'm texting my rival." He glanced up. "Eli Mueller needs to know you're around."

"I've seen him." She met his gaze. "We met up yesterday." She started to mention the bouquet. *Fuel the old flame?* Her stomach flip-flopped, and she restrained a shudder.

George wiggled until he freed his body from the chair. "I shot him a text anyway. Told him you're here with *me*." He chortled, scooted closer to Claire, and squeezed her arm. "Don't see no ring on that finger, so let the games begin." He waved thick fingers and stepped into the crowd.

Claire fumbled for her purse and withdrew a sanitizing hand wipe. Swabbing her hands didn't seem to be enough—she wished for a sink and scrub brush. And Eli.

☙

Eli pushed through a crowd watching the bubble-gum blowing contest. Parents called out encouragement to their young contestants. He laughed. Normally they'd be scolding kids for splattering gum all over their faces. Now they cheered them on. All to win a trophy.

He scanned the mass of bodies, watching for silver hair pulled back from a lovely face. He could check the list of participants for the painting competitions. That could narrow down his search.

A stroller bumped into his heel. "I'm so sorry." The woman pushed a baby and carried a toddler on her hip. "It's so hard to manage this crowd." She laughed. "I've misplaced my husband"—she tilted her head—"and am afraid to put this one down."

"Where are you going?"

The woman nodded at the Cedar Creek Café. "Just over there."

Eli hesitated. He wouldn't mind helping her out and carrying the little boy, but he didn't want to send up a "stranger-danger" flag in her mind. "Follow me, I'll run interference."

The lady hitched the boy further up her hip.

Eli bit his lower lip and held out a hand. "Be okay if I push the stroller?" Surely stranger-danger warnings didn't include maneuvering a stroller through a forest of legs.

"I'd be so grateful." The lady swung the stroller handle toward Eli, and the foursome threaded their way through groups of strawberry-smelling patrons.

At the edge of the café, a young man stepped forward. "Babe, where you been? You should've kept up."

The young woman's face flushed beet red. Eli restrained himself from explaining to the dad that *he* should've been responsible for keeping watch over his flock. Instead he settled the stroller so it was in front of him.

"Thank you so much." The young woman's eyes glistened.

"No problem." He backed away from the family, the urge to throttle the dad quelled.

"Mueller."

Eli turned in the direction of the call. He scanned the crowd, looking for the speaker—one he usually heard every summer. George Schiller parted the wave of people, a beefy arm extended in front of him. "Mueller. Did you get my text?"

Tugging his cell phone from the case hooked to his belt, Eli noted a blinking light. "Nope. In this noise, who could hear?"

He rubbed his chin. "What you need?"

A grin crept across George's face, plumping his cheeks and forming his green eyes into slits. "Guess who I saw?" George singsonged then gave his snort-chuckle.

"No clue." Eli hitched a breath. He did have a clue.

"Our one and only love." He clutched his heart. "Claire Wagner is right here in Cedarburg."

Eli frowned. "Yes, I've seen her. She's Claire Parsons now."

George tugged at the waist of his sagging shorts. "She looks pretty good for an old gal. Don't think she's married anymore, though. A-*vail*-able." He snorted.

Eli clenched a fist. The young dad had already fueled his temper, and now George.

"Invited her for the next dance, I did." George belted out his distinctive laugh.

Perspiration dribbled down Eli's back. "Good for you, old man." He clapped George's damp shoulder. "Nice seeing you. Now I'm off to the shop."

"Come on, *old* man. Read the text. Take up the challenge. Probably single, good-looking Claire at the festival." He raised a bushy eyebrow. "Let's see."

"No thanks." Eli forced a smile. "Take care." He spun on his heel and set out to cross the street.

Dodging from one side to another, he glimpsed a canopy lettered WAGNER POTTERY and caught his breath. Claire Parsons. "Must be." He stopped in the center of the street, tourists bobbing from side to side to avoid a collision. Between shoulders, he saw her. Smiling, holding out a pitcher to a customer.

Her wind-tossed bob was swept back by a yellow headband. She wore silver earrings. Pink lipstick. Yellow shirt that highlighted her tanned arms.

Eli watched her converse with the buyer. Another smile, a small laugh. She leaned forward to listen more closely. He recorded her every movement. The crowd noise faded away until he only heard the soft notes of a guitar. They'd listened to the radio while sitting on her front porch, night after night before he'd left Cedarburg.

Eli sighed. He turned to go to his shop then stopped and glanced over his shoulder. "But—" He rubbed his chin. "Can't let George win."

Chapter 6

Where did you go?

Claire saw him. Eli had been standing in the street while she listened to a lady from Milwaukee drone on about her desire to throw pottery on a wheel. She'd restrained herself from throwing the pitcher at the woman and rushing through the throng of people. Her stomach ached and her heart rat-a-tatted against her ribs.

What would she say if she captured him? The most pressing question would be *why?*

She swept her hair from her neck, waiting for the next breeze.

"Aunt Claire." Melissa bounded forward and grabbed her by the shoulders. "Brad placed!"

Brad scuffed his heels against the concrete, a crooked grin plastered on his face. "I didn't win any money, but I did get acknowledged."

"Congratulations, Picasso." Claire gripped his arm. "I was praying for those hands."

Brad ducked his head. "Must've worked." He stuffed his hands in his pockets. "Didn't think I could compete at all."

Melissa laughed. "Smart *and* talented. He's a winner in my book." She glanced at Claire. "We're going to grab a barbecue sandwich before we take over here. Would you like anything?"

"No, honey." Claire dusted her hands together. "I'll grab a bite in a bit. Think I'd like to wash up first." She pointed toward the table. "Notice anything?"

Melissa scanned the area then gasped. "The dishes." Her eyes lit up. "Who bought them?"

"The Milwaukee mayor, no less." Claire laughed.

Melissa grasped her hands and jumped up and down. "What fun." She giggled. "We need to find a list of all the Cedarburg festivals. I might have to come back here." She eyed her aunt. "Bet your boyfriend would know."

A flush crept up Claire's neck. "He's not my boyfriend, Melissa." She attempted a frown, but the girl's enthusiasm seemed contagious. She pointed up the block. "His jewelry shop is just over there. You can ask him."

"That information is online. I'm hungry." Brad toyed with a cookie jar top. "Let's go eat, Mel."

"Fine." Melissa tugged her purse from a plastic bin under the table. She spun and the strap slapped Brad's arm. He jumped, and the cookie jar top flew from his hand.

Melissa lurched forward to catch it. Brad reached over her, and his knee knocked the supporting brace of the canopy. One corner began its descent.

"No, no, no!" Melissa wailed.

Claire stretched and reached the top corner of the canvas. She held it up, away from the tables. "Hurry, Melissa, I can't keep this up for long."

"Let me." A young boy scooted under Claire's arm and popped the brace, straightening the canopy.

Claire rubbed her arms. She was out of shape for that kind of gymnastic routine. She smiled at the boy. Olive skinned, thick black hair and deep brown eyes. Good-looking kid.

"Thanks so much." Melissa squeezed his arm. "You really saved the day." She held out her hand. "I'm Melissa, and this is my aunt Claire." She cocked her head. "You are?"

"Zake Anthony Mery at your service." He bowed. "I'm available to haul packages, get you food and drinks, or help lots of ways." An infectious grin spread across his face.

"Well, you certainly know how to rescue little old ladies in distress." Claire resisted the urge to ruffle his beautiful hair. "Are your parents not in need of your help?"

"Nope. My mom's at her shop—Lorena's Hair Designs"—he shoved his hair away from his eyes—"and knows where I am." He scanned the crowd. "Everybody knows me around here."

A chuckle worked its way up Claire's throat, but she held it in. His brow furrowed. "It's true. I get to run deliveries for lots of storeowners. Mr. Mueller and. . ." He continued to speak but that name drove out any sound. *Eli.* Everywhere she went, Eli. She sighed.

"Zake, I do believe I need a bottle of water, since I'll be the worker bee on duty." Claire nodded at Melissa. "Go eat and I'll mind the store." She fished some ones from her pocket and handed them to the boy.

"Anything else?" He tipped his head. "No shortcake oozing with strawberries and whipped cream? Or chocolate-dipped strawberries? A smoothie?"

Claire gave a half smile. "Water. That's it for now." She secured her hair with the headband. "Then we'll see."

Zake lifted his hand in a wave and trotted down the lane.

Brad shook his head. "That kid's going to take your money and disappear."

"No, he'll be back." Claire dusted her hands on her pant leg and settled into the lawn chair. "I'm pretty sure he'll be back." If Eli trusted him, she would, too.

ଔ

Eli resisted the urge to leave the shop and find Claire before George did. A teenage dream. He slid her ring from the small envelope. A bent prong. Simple enough to fix. He lifted it, and a yearning rippled through his fingers. He tossed the ring onto the counter, and it overshot and pinged on the floor. Bending, he retrieved it and swiveled it on his index finger. He remembered fashioning the strands of ivy, placing that sapphire right in the center. He placed it more carefully on the counter and stepped back. The small silver band of promise shone under his lamp.

Fleeting visions of Vietnam exploded in his thoughts. Sounds, smells long buried surfaced. He sank on his stool. Sweat broke out across his brow. He clutched his shirt and flapped it against his chest to cool off. *No regrets, Mueller. None. You did your duty.*

Whirling around, he crossed the small area to the refrigerator. On the door inside was Marie's bottle of milk. Brought to the shop for him. The plastic wrap on the plate of cookies sparkled.

He'd never seriously considered dating Marie. Why not? He picked up a cookie and the milk, closed the door, and leaned on the fridge. He chewed on the thought as the chocolate chips melted in his mouth. Marie was steady, thoughtful, a woman of strong faith, and widowed. She had no children, so there wouldn't be objections if he asked her out. He bit his cheek.

She wasn't Claire.

He sighed and plopped on the stool. Forty years he'd compared every woman he met and dated a few. But they were never Claire.

"Silly of me. Wishing they were her. " He shoved the last bite in his mouth, and a bout of coughing almost strangled him.

Marie appeared at the door. "Are you okay?"

Eli's watery eyes met hers. "Fine," he croaked. He took a drink of the milk. "Good cookie."

She laughed. "You weren't supposed to inhale them."

Full lips, crooked on one side, but they weren't—

"I'm going to finish up shortly and head back to the festival." He wiped his mouth. "Why don't you close early and enjoy some kind of strawberry concoction?"

"Might just do that." She turned then looked over her shoulder. "We could go together." The longing in her eyes made Eli's stomach clench.

"Thanks. Need to finish up here. I'm not sure how long I'll be."

Marie's face fell. She stared at him for a moment, disappointment etched across her brow, then reached for the doorknob. "See you tomorrow." She jerked the door shut. The slam echoed in the small chamber.

"Case closed." Eli swiveled around and picked up Claire's ring. "Now to close this one, too." He rolled the silver band back and forth. Sliding protective glasses across his eyes, he lifted a sliver of silver from the cabinet drawer and tapped it into a leaf shape. He heated it with the soldering iron then doused it in the pickling compound. Once it was clean he used needle-nose pliers and soldered it to the ring. He gently bent the prong then tightened the other four. Rinsing the ring in clear water, he shook it dry then eyed it with the loupe. Satisfied, he used a generous dollop of jewelry cleaner and polished the ring until it sparkled—sapphire, like Claire's eyes. It looked ready to be completed with—"No, it's complete just as it is."

Unless he could see Claire, talk to her. “Maybe she’d meet me at the park.” Eli reached for the brown envelope and flipped it over. A number. “Bet it’s her cell phone.” He traced the first three digits. “Different area code.”

With a nod, he lifted his phone. After three tries, his large fingers tapped in her phone number on the text message screen. He formed a note, deleted it, and tried again. “Surely she’d be willing to talk.”

☙

Zake sat on a box next to Claire, balancing a plate mounded with a slice of strawberry pie. Her mouth watered.

“Told you I should’ve gotten you something to eat.” He spoke around berries, his wide smile coated with whipped cream. “Want me to go back?” He wiped his chin on the shoulder of his T-shirt. Big brown eyes sparkled.

She shook her head. “Not yet.” A chime sounded.

Zake pointed to her purse with his fork. “Sounds like a text.”

Claire frowned. “Text? On my phone?” She seldom used the feature. Melissa had insisted she add it to her monthly phone plan, but she would rather chat with someone than try to type on tiny letters and remember to punch three times if she wanted the letter *C*.

She rummaged through her purse for the phone, flipped it open, and squinted at the tiny screen. “Who is this?”

“Something wrong?” Zake inched closer.

Claire tipped the cell in his direction.

Zake tapped the screen. “That’s Mr. Mueller’s phone number.”

262-555-9293 WENCH OF CEDARBIRDGH

She drew in a sharp breath. Wench? What?

GYRE U HAIR

"Gyre? Gyre? What? That means spiral. Spiral my hair?" Claire gritted her teeth. A flush crept up her face. Who did this man think he was? Wench? He wanted her hair put up? Maybe in a bun?

"Ohhh." She spun away from Zake's gaze. Everywhere she turned she ran into an Eli reminder. *Now* what was he up to? "If he were in front of me—"

"You okay?" Zake touched her elbow.

Claire drew in a ragged breath and clasped the phone against her chest. "I'm fine." She spit out the words.

"Didn't mean to bother you." Zake slunk to the corner. "Guess I'll go now."

She held out a hand. "No, you aren't a bother. You've been very helpful." Her temples throbbed. "Stay a while longer." His babble of conversation might calm her nerves. Before she did anything rash. Before she went looking for a certain silver-haired man.

Wench, indeed. "Who do you think you are, Mr. Mueller?"

Zake's eyebrows shot up. "Was the text from Mr. Mueller? Does he need something?"

Definitely a loaded question. She patted the boy's shoulder. "Not that I know of." She scanned the words again then studied the keyboard on her flip phone. What letters on a phone would create that weird message?

Zake dumped the Styrofoam plate in the trash, rubbed his hands on his shirt, and grinned. "I'd better check. I'm his number one helper." He darted from under the canopy. "See you later."

Claire wiggled her fingers in his direction. "Tell him I sent my regards." She tossed the phone into her purse and greeted a shopper.

Chapter 7

"Mr. Mueller?" Zake's voice rang through the shop. "Mr. Mueller?"

"Hello, Zake. He's in back." Marie's voice carried to Eli.

The boy slipped into his workshop. "Morning, Zake. What brings you here?"

"Thought you might need me." His mouth slashed a wide white grin.

Eli rubbed his finger across his chin. "Not right now. Looks like you've been enjoying some strawberries." He pointed to Zake's T-shirt.

Zake glanced at the red stain. "Yep. Ate a bunch." His brow furrowed. "Don't tell Mom, though. She'll get ticked off cuz I ate so much sugary stuff." He heaved a great sigh, leaned against the workbench, and toyed with a pair of pliers. "Been helping out, too."

"Good for you, son." Eli soldered a pin against the backing on a brooch.

Zake bent forward for a closer look. "That's pretty."

"Um-hmm." Eli reached for the pliers.

"I met your friend."

Eli glanced up. "Friend?"

"That lady."

"Lady?"

"The one with the white hair." He chuckled. "You texted her."

Eli's breath hitched and he straightened, gazing into the boy's chocolate-brown eyes. "Claire?"

Zake nodded. "She kinda got mad, so I left and came here."

"Mad?" Eli frowned. "Why was she mad?"

The boy shuffled his feet and tilted his head. "Dunno."

Eli touched Zake's arm. "Tell me what happened, please. Why do you think she's mad?"

Zake twirled a file on the bench, sending out a grinding noise much like the one Eli heard in his ears as he ground his teeth. "Zake?"

"Well, she said something right after that text, and I thought she was mad, but she said she wasn't, but then she said your name, grumpy-like."

Eli placed his hand on the twirling file. "Think I'd better go see her?"

Zake chortled. "Not sure if I'd want to, Mr. Mueller. She didn't say your name real nice."

Again? He'd hurt Claire *again*? Eli slumped against the workbench. "You know, son, I think you need to enjoy the festival. Why don't you come in on Monday and work with me?" He reached out his arm, and Zake stepped into his hug. A sweaty-boy smell filled Eli's nose, twisting his heart. How he had wanted a son like Zake.

"Okay. See you later." Zake zipped from the room as quickly as he'd arrived, sucking out the fresh strawberry smell and leaving behind the stench of guilt.

Eli swiveled around and propped his elbows on the bench.

"Lord, how do I fix what I don't even know I messed up this time?"

Face the music.

As clear as a bell, the words chimed in his heart. It was time to talk with Claire.

ଓ

Once Melissa and Brad returned, Claire stomped away from the pottery stand. "Wench of— What would make that man call me a wench?" She shoved her hands in her pockets, clasping her handbag tightly against her side. "Who even uses that word anymore?" She frowned at the Silver Line banner overhead. "Surely Eli could've updated his vocabulary in the last forty years."

Weaving her way in and out of groups of tourists and around strollers and bikes, Claire pounded the pavement. She reached the north end of the festival grounds and realized she hadn't taken in one display or eaten anything. She plopped on a bench and drew in a shaky breath.

"Okay, Claire. You have a choice." She frowned and slapped her tennis shoes on the cement. "Be mad and let Eli ruin this day, or give it up." She leaned against the bench and chewed on her lower lip.

A family stopped in front of her. Angry Daddy bent forward and shook a finger in Little Man's face. "Straighten up and fly right, you hear me?" Tears brimmed over heavy lashes and streaked down the child's face when he nodded. Daddy gently ruffled the boy's hair and pulled him against his leg. "Good boy." Relieved Mom trailed behind the two as they pushed into the crowd.

The scene reminded her of her mama's good conscience/bad

conscience comparisons. She pushed to her feet. "Straighten up and fly right, huh?" She glanced heavenward. "Lord, I'll choose forgiveness. I'm not letting old hurts ruin my short return to Cedarburg."

Tugging her purse strap over her shoulder, she ambled down the street from one exhibit to another. Wind chimes tinkled in the breeze, paintings glistened in the sun, T-shirts hung on display, and everywhere lingered the scent of strawberries. She licked her lips. After lunch, she'd indulge in strawberry shortcake or chocolate-covered berries or—taste everything. She smiled. She'd ramp up her exercise routine when she got home to get rid of the calories. How often did the opportunity arise to sample all these delicacies?

The artist she'd met the day before caught her attention. His face came alive. She stepped near his booth.

"How did you do?"

"I placed." He pointed to a ribbon affixed to the Rivoli Theatre painting. "No money, but I'm excited."

Claire ran her finger across the top of the frame. "Quite a likeness." She smiled. Certainly not her style. "I hope you find a worthy buyer."

"Thank you." He extended his arm in a flourish. "Feel free to browse. We have a nice selection."

The last thing she needed in her home was another painting, but she felt obligated to look at some of the pictures for a few moments. When her new friend turned to an actual buyer, Claire slipped away.

She purchased a barbecue sandwich and a soda then found a table and chair. The first bite transported her back many years. Her dad created a wonderful pulled pork sandwich and used his own sauce. Claire dabbed her lips and chuckled. He'd guarded that concoction's recipe, and only she and her brother had the list of ingredients. She smiled. Her brother had dubbed it "The Recipe" after the Baldwin sisters' "tonic" on the TV show *The Waltons*. Little had those senior citizens known they'd been producing white lightning.

She tilted her head in thought. Maybe she should cook up a batch of barbecue sauce. Would make nice Christmas presents for her niece and nephew. She toyed with the label on the soda bottle. Christmas presents—a shaft of sadness pierced her heart. Every year she spoiled Melissa and Tony, the merry auntie with armloads of gifts. Substitute children since she had none of her own.

Claire shook her head. Melancholy thoughts weren't welcome at the moment. She took another bite and chewed. No place mat on this table. She bit her lip and winced. "No Eli thoughts, either."

She decided to people watch and eat. A harried mother with a sticky set of twins stuck in a double stroller stopped in front of her. The little girl began to wail as Mom scrubbed away strawberry something. Claire smiled at the other toddler. His lower lip stuck out and trembled, and then he joined his sister. Claire chuckled. Not funny for the mother, but certainly a show.

Across the way two teens set up a snare drum and a guitar and amp.

"Oh, time to move on." Music blasting in her face wasn't her idea of relaxation. She took her last bite and tossed away the trash and drink.

She turned to move away from the band.

A familiar voice called her name. She drew in a sharp breath and closed her eyes, feet frozen in place, a sinking feeling in her stomach.

Eli.

Chapter 8

"Claire." Eli inched his hand out and touched her elbow, a tingle shooting up his arm. "May I speak with you for a moment?"

Claire jerked away as though burned. Her eyes flashed and her cheeks reddened. "I don't think we have anything to say to one another, Mr. Mueller." She whirled and rushed off through the throng of people.

"Wait, please." Eli dodged through the crowd, his throat tightening. "Claire, just a second." He sidestepped a child, but not before whipped cream plastered his jeans. He flicked at the glob, pulling away a sticky finger. When he glanced up, he'd lost sight of her.

"Claire?" He raised his voice, but it only added to the din. He clenched his teeth. Zigzagging, he directed his steps toward the Wagner Pottery exhibit. Melissa and her boyfriend were the only two in the booth.

"Excuse me."

"Aunt Claire's Eli." Melissa raised a brow. "Nice to see you. Are you enjoying your festival?"

"Uh, yes." Eli ran his hand down his face, the sticky finger creating a slimy trail. He frowned and swiped at his cheek with his shoulder.

"Are you okay?" Eyes like her aunt's sapphire ones peered into his face.

Eli caught his breath. "Got a bit sticky on the walkway."

"Here." Melissa opened a small package and handed him a moistened wipe. "We're finding these quite useful."

"Thanks." Eli scrubbed his face and fingers. "Actually, Melissa, I'm searching for your aunt." He gave a jerky nod. "Saw her briefly on the street—"

Brad said, "She went to have a late lunch." He reached forward, grabbed a canopy post, and leaned against it.

"Move, Brad!" Melissa's command made Brad jump and release the post. All three watched it sway. As it steadied, they released a collective breath. She plopped her hands on her hips. "We've already avoided disaster once, thanks to Zake."

Eli started. "Zake?"

Melissa smiled. "Your right-hand man. He kept Aunt Claire company."

"So he said." Eli tossed the wipe into a trash bin. "Guess I'll continue my search. When you see her again, let her know I'm looking for her, please."

"She'll be back soon, since we have to close shop in—" Melissa tapped the face of her watch—"an hour and ten minutes." She slipped a bowl into an empty place. "Rules say we have to clear out by six so they can open Washington Avenue."

"Right." A thrill of panic ran through Eli. "Are you going home immediately after?"

"No." Melissa turned toward a customer.

Eli nodded to Brad and trudged toward the nearest coffee stand.

"Hey, Mueller."

Eli groaned. *George?*

The strawberry-stained Strawberry Festival T-shirt George sported now wore barbecue sauce spots. "I'll buy you a cup." He motioned for Eli to join him at the kiosk.

Eli bit his lip. Not wanting to be rude, he ordered a cooling smoothie and joined George at a table.

"Haven't seen you in, what, two years?" George sipped the foam from the top of his drink, a tiny mustache of whipped cream coating his upper lip when he pulled the cup away.

" 'Bout that." Eli twirled a straw.

"Have you spent time with our Claire?"

Eli gritted his teeth. *Our* Claire? "Not much." The orange-flavored drink soothed his throat. Now if it would cool his temper.

"She looked good for an old broad."

Not even an orange smoothie could smother the fury in Eli's chest. He shoved his chair back and leaned forward. He propped his hands on either side of George's coffee cup. "Schiller, I've spent forty years listening to your remarks about Claire Wagner, much of it trash talk. Your total disrespect—" Eli glared into the pudgy man's widened eyes. "Her father told you forty years ago to leave her alone. Now I'm telling you. Leave. Her. Alone." He straightened and spun away, thrusting his hands deeply into his pockets lest one of his fists connect with a bulbous nose.

ꟹ

Claire stepped from the inn onto the busy avenue. Time had slipped away. She needed to help Melissa and Brad close up shop. Turning left, she caught sight of George and Eli at the coffee shop. Ducking her head for fear they'd spot her, she waited for a cluster of people to pass.

"Schiller."

Eli's strident tone carried over the crowd noise. When she heard what he was saying, she clutched her throat, holding back a sob. After all these years, Eli still championed her.

Tears filled her eyes. She rubbed her forehead. A litany of what-ifs spun through her brain. What if her father had allowed them to marry? What if they'd had a family? What if—

Useless thoughts. Kind Eli Mueller, blast from the past, and just that. The past. She didn't want to see George, she didn't want to acknowledge Eli's thoughtfulness. Besides, to him she was the *wench* of Cedarburg. Her chest tightened. She craved the bed upstairs in the inn to hide away and process her mixed emotions.

But Wagner Pottery's wares needed to be stored in the van.

Weaving along the thoroughfare, Claire replayed the scene. Not even Chet had spoken up for her like that in their brief marriage. She tugged her purse closer. No, he'd been too self-centered to pay attention to a young bride.

Claire sighted Melissa, copper ponytail with loose strands flying, hands waving directions. A smile tugged at Claire's lips. She'd poured her life into her niece and nephew, and that had to be enough.

"Mrs. Parsons," Brad called, "would you mind the store while I haul away the goods?" He held the handle of a dolly with four boxes stacked on it. "Melissa, show me how you want these packed."

Melissa swirled toward her aunt, a grin on her face. "I'm a zillionaire!" She laughed. "I did sell a lot of stuff. Can't wait to tell you all about it."

"Can't wait to hear." Claire plopped her purse on the remaining table. "What do you need me to do?"

"Stand here and look beautiful in case someone wants the last of the display." Melissa giggled. "Be right back." She tugged a tote from under a table and followed Brad toward the Washington House parking lot.

Claire watched the weary-worn festival stragglers. Musicians carried their instruments down the street, barbecue pits were loaded onto trailers, sticky, grumpy children hung on to their parents. The takedown happened in a hurry. A police presence seemed to make sure Washington Avenue would be in service at six o'clock.

A box of bubble wrap sat at Claire's feet, so she began to wrap the few remaining pieces and store them.

"Do you have a moment, Claire?"

Claire's back stiffened, and she turned slowly to face Eli. Her heart leaped to her throat, and she struggled to speak. "I'm busy at the moment."

"This won't take long." Eli fixed her with a level stare and muscles worked in his jaw.

"Well, I—"

"Please."

Claire bristled. "Why would you want to speak to a wench?"

"What?" Eli's eyebrows rose. "What are you talking about?"

"The text." Claire turned toward the table and grabbed for a vase and bubble wrap.

Eli stepped inside the kiosk and into her line of vision. "I have no idea what you're talking about. Zake told me you were upset. I only wanted to welcome you home."

"The daisies did that, Mr. Mueller," Claire whispered. "Thank you."

Eli touched her arm. "The text?"

Claire eyed his gnarled fingers. So much time had passed.

"Do you need to see it to remember what you wrote?" She set the covered vase inside a tote and slid her cell phone from her pocket. Flipping it open, she scrolled to Eli's text. "Read."

Eli's large hand engulfed her small phone. His eyes scanned the words. A red flush crept up his cheeks and his lips twisted in a crooked smile. "Claire. I can explain."

She wrapped a bowl, her eyes darting to his face and back to the bowl.

He held out his hands. "Do you see these thumbs? Imagine them punching tiny letters on a screen." He pulled out his phone. "This cell phone has autocorrect. It assumes you aren't spelling a word correctly and, boom, the phone decides what you meant." He bent over, peering into her eyes. "It should've read, 'Welcome to Cedarburg. Glad you are here.'" A chuckle escaped his lips. "This is one for the history books. I truly apologize."

Claire's lips twitched. "Seriously?" She set the bowl inside the tote.

"Truce?" Eli said. "Have dinner with me and we can talk."

Claire studied his face. Ruddy, wrinkles on his brow, silver hair, hazel eyes. "Dinner? Well, I—"

"Aunt Claire!" Melissa shouted. "Come quickly. We need to get Brad to a doctor."

Chapter 9

Melissa tugged Claire along the driveway. "I'm not sure when it started, but he's a mess. I don't know what to do." A whine tinged her words. "You know I'm not good with sick—"

Claire squeezed her niece's fingers. They rounded the Washington House and dashed to the parking spot, Eli fast on their heels. Brad leaned against the back of the van, one arm clutching his middle and the other rubbing his eyes. He looked up and Claire gasped.

Swollen eyes—and a smattering of hives peppered his face. "Allergic reaction!" He wheezed.

Eli stepped forward. "Do you carry an EpiPen?"

Brad shook his head.

"Then we need to get you to the doctor." Eli tugged keys from his pocket and turned to Claire. "I'll take you. Be right back." He dashed down the street.

Brad moaned. "I hate doctors."

Claire murmured words of comfort.

Eli's blue Honda appeared, and he motioned for Brad to get in. "Aunt Claire. . ." Melissa's tear-stained face told it all. She tipped her head. "Please come?"

With a nod, Claire climbed in the backseat. She noted the

pristine condition of the older car. Eli's penchant for tidiness hadn't changed.

"What set off this reaction?" Eli turned left.

"Strawberries." Brad said. "Ask Melissa."

A duo of "*What?*" came from Eli and Claire.

Melissa squirmed in the seat. "Brad's allergic to strawberries."

"I puff up like the Goodyear Blimp."

Eli glanced at him. "But you were fine when I came by the kiosk earlier. And anyway, why would you eat them if you know you're allergic to them?"

Claire's eyebrows rose. He'd come by? While she was gone?

Melissa sniffled. "It's my fault." She swiped at her face. "I never considered—" She bit her lip, and her face turned scarlet.

Claire patted her knee. "Why is this your fault?"

Melissa wouldn't meet her aunt's eyes. She fidgeted and jerked her ponytail tighter.

Brad said, "Tell 'em, Mel. How you almost finished me off." His fingernails raked across his face, and he winced.

The girl released a huff. "I bought chocolate-covered strawberries. And I thought—"

"She'd kill me." Brad looked over the headrest and frowned, hives peppering his eyebrows.

Eli's sudden right-hand turn into the clinic parking lot brought the discussion to a close. He drove under the portico and faced Brad.

"Explain."

"She ate several and then we—kissed." Brad's face flushed, the tips of his ears flamed. "Here I am." He wiggled swollen fingers. "The Michelin Man."

Claire stifled a laugh and took Melissa's hand. "Let's get him inside."

ঔ

Eli nodded to the charge nurse. "Serena, didn't see you at the festival. Working instead?"

"Someone has to stay in the trenches." Serena smiled and tapped Brad's elbow. "Strawberry overdose?"

"How did you know?" Brad mumbled.

"Common occurrence this time of year." She pointed to the triage room. "This way."

"May I come?" Melissa edged closer to Brad.

The nurse hesitated. "Family member?"

Melissa bit her lip. "No."

"Soon she will be." Brad shot the nurse a hangdog look through swollen eyelids. "Please."

Serena grinned. "Come on, then."

A willowy red-haired woman breezed through the sliding glass doors. "Brad, darling."

Brad's eyes lit up. "Aunt Sylvia." He swirled about and grabbed Melissa's hand. "This is my—"

"Your Melissa." Sylvia chucked Melissa under the chin. "Thanks for the text. I'm glad to finally meet you. Let's get our boy some relief." She faced Eli. "Seems I owe you a debt of gratitude for rescuing my nephew." She tucked her arm around Brad's elbow.

Eli nodded. "Glad to help."

Melissa grasped Claire's hand. "This is my aunt Claire."

Claire and Sylvia shook hands.

"No need for you two to wait, Eli. I'll see to them."

Claire lifted a brow in her niece's direction.

"She's right." Melissa glanced at the charge nurse. "May I still go in?"

Serena waved her hand. "Why not? Right this way."

Melissa pecked Claire on the cheek. "I'll see you later." The three followed the nurse down the hall.

"First time I've heard of a kissing allergy." Eli smiled. "Not a bad way to go, I'd think."

A flush painted Claire's cheeks. "Poor boy. I know he's uncomfortable. And embarrassed." She looked at Eli. "I suppose now we can leave."

"Fine with me." He waved a hand in front of his face. "Never have liked the antiseptic smell." He followed Claire to his car.

A gentle wind brushed his face, and he watched Claire's hair loosen from her headband. She looped silver strands behind her ears.

"Think the table and canopy we left will be okay?" Her sapphire eyes probed his face. "I'm not sure I'm able to wrestle it down."

"I can fix that." He pulled his cell from its holster and placed a call to the event director. A short explanation made sure Melissa's items would be stored inside the visitors' center. "And I'll load it for you."

"Keys." Claire released an exasperated huff. "Melissa has the keys to the van."

Eli patted her arm. "We can gather all of it before you leave." *Before you leave.* His gut twisted at the words as they left his lips. He opened the car door for her, and she slid in.

"Thank you." Claire glanced at the clinic. "She'll be worried about her things. I should let her know about your call."

Eli rounded the car and climbed behind the wheel.

She tugged her phone from her purse. "I can text—" She lifted her head and stared at him, a grin crossing her face. "Unless you'd rather."

"Uh-uh." He shook his head. "With these clumsy thumbs, I think you'd better take care of that. I might tell her barbarians absconded with her goods."

She smiled and tapped letters on her phone. A small V formed between her eyes as she concentrated on the text. He noted tiny brown spots on the back of her hands, like the ones he sported. But the years had been kind to her. Very kind. She still had a trim figure, perfectly formed lips.

Wonder if she'd like a chocolate-covered strawberry kiss? He squirmed. *Conversation first, Mueller.* They were finally alone. A knot formed in his stomach. A ticktock of his head popped vertebrae in his neck, and he started the engine.

Eli cleared his throat. "I'd like to take you to dinner."

"Tonight?" She tugged at her capris. "After being outdoors all day?" She shook her head. "I'm too tired. Not tonight."

Was she avoiding a discussion? He chewed his lower lip to keep words of disappointment in check and pulled onto the highway headed toward the Washington House.

"Lunch would be nice."

"Lunch?"

"Maybe tomorrow. After church?" She peered up at him. "Do you still attend Christ the King?"

"Yes." He wiped first one sweaty palm on his jeans and then the other. "Lunch it is."

Claire's phone chimed, and she read the text out loud. "Sylvia says B see doctor Monday. K to stay? Please." Claire drew in a breath. "Guess we are staying until Monday."

Eli looked out the window to hide a grin.

Claire's staying. Two more days.

Chapter 10

Claire shifted on the vanity stool and dabbed her eye with a washcloth to diminish the sting of mascara. Her jittery fingers couldn't hold the wand steady. "Calm down." She peered into the mirror at the reflection of her bloodshot eye. "Aren't you just gorgeous." She puffed out her cheeks, stuck out her tongue at her reflection, and then propped her forehead on her hand. "Lord, I'm so nervous. Settle me down, please."

She'd left Eli the night before with a promise to meet him at church. Just like she'd done so many times before. Sleep had been woven between dreams—holding hands, snuggling into his arms at the movies, sharing a bag of popcorn, lying on the hood of his dad's '59 Chevy, staring at the stars.

Then everything changed.

Claire swiped under her eye with the cold compress and finished her makeup. She slipped into a navy sheath and tucked her toes into red sandals. Standing sideways in front of the floor-length mirror on the bathroom door, she sucked in her tummy then released her breath with a whoosh. "Can't hold my breath all morning." She faced the mirror, hands on her hips. "What happened to girdle days?" A chuckle bubbled up. "No. Can't do a girdle, even for Eli."

"Aunt Claire?" Melissa entered the room.

"Honey, how's Brad?"

Melissa flopped on the bed. "Much better this morning. They discharged him and Aunt Sylvia put him in her guest room. We took turns pampering him all night. He looks less like the Pillsbury Doughboy." She rolled to one side and punched a pillow under her head. "Do you think we can stay a few days?"

"Hmmm?" Claire fiddled with the clasp on her silver cross.

"I want to stay in Cedarburg for the whole week."

Claire wheeled about. "What?"

"Aunt Sylvia's invited us to her cottage on Lake Michigan. Well, not exactly a cottage. It has five bedrooms. Brad's mom and brother are coming—"

Claire lifted a brow.

"To meet me." Melissa drew her knees up. "Aunt Sylvia has plenty of room where we could stay." She tugged on the comforter. "Just until Saturday. Please." She drew out the word.

Claire frowned. "I don't know, sweetie." She searched her mental calendar for a reason to return home and drew a blank. "Let me think about it."

"Great." Melissa yawned. "I'm going to nap. Didn't sleep much, checking on Brad and visiting with Aunt Sylvia."

"Did he need a nurse all night long?"

Melissa laughed. "He thought so." She clutched the comforter under her chin. "He's so sweet. I'm crazy about him." She reached out a hand and grabbed Claire's fingers. "Please consider staying."

Claire nodded. She slung her purse strap over her shoulder. "I'll see you later today." She patted the pocket on her purse. "My cell is charged in case you need me."

"Uh-huh." Melissa closed her eyes and curled under the blanket.

Claire slipped into the hallway and closed the door. "All week in Cedarburg?" She smiled. "I can do that."

☙

Eli knotted his tie again then lifted his suit coat from the hanger. "I hope this day improves quickly, Lord." He'd dodged a river of syrup he'd created on the kitchen counter and endured an army-style cold shower. "Dumb hot water heater."

He folded the coat over his arm and picked up his Bible from the table by his recliner. Pausing in the foyer, he glanced at his reflection in the mirror. He took a deep breath. "This is the moment you've waited for, Mueller. Don't mess it up."

Sunlight filtered through the elm trees on his four-block stroll to the church. He marveled at Caron's full pink hydrangea bushes lining the fence and the bevy of tall purple flowers in Mr. Lee's yard. The peonies and lavender painted a pretty picture. He admired those who could nurture such beauty.

"Claire should see this." He picked up his pace. Claire. She waited for him at church. Like she had so many decades before.

On the short drive back to the Washington House the night before, their stilted conversation stayed on safe topics. He did learn her family had moved to Indianapolis right after he left town, and that her husband had died in a Cessna crash only six months after they'd married.

"I want to know what happened—" He lowered his head, breathing a short prayer. "Today, Lord, give me words to speak."

"Good morning, Eli." Marie climbed from her van, tugging at her skirt, her eyes bright.

Eli nodded. "Morning, Marie."

She smiled and her lips parted to speak. Then her eyes widened. She puffed out one word. "Claire."

Eli turned, and his feet froze to the spot. He met Claire's gaze. *His* Claire stood on the steps of the church. *Their* church. His heart pounded so loudly in his ears he couldn't hear Marie's words. He watched Claire hug a stiff-backed Marie, who then disappeared into the narthex.

"Good morning, Eli." She wore a shy smile.

"Claire." He reached out a hand.

She grasped his fingertips then let go. "Maybe we should go inside."

She turned and walked through the doors, and Eli followed.

"If this is a dream, Lord, don't let me wake up," he whispered.

☙

Claire hadn't been this distracted during church in forty years. Sitting beside Eli, she inhaled his musky scent. When he slid his arm behind her along the back of the pew, her pulse raced. He brushed her side when he crossed his legs. She tracked every movement the man made. Surely it wasn't right to sit in a church service and concentrate on a man. But this was not just any man. This was Eli. *Her* Eli.

Forgive me, Lord. Help me focus on You instead of Eli.

Claire placed her Bible on her lap then let it slide between the two of them. Maybe if the Word of God were between them. . .

The lovely choir director had the congregation stand. Eli held the hymnal for her to read. His fingers brushed hers.

Here I go again, Lord!

Claire sang the song, greeted other parishioners, and listened to the sermon, still in a daze. She sighed, an overwhelming desire for these moments to last. All too soon the closing hymn was sung and the final amen pronounced.

Eli ushered her from the pew, nodding and speaking to those around them. Claire scanned the crowd for anyone she knew. Marie seemed to be the only one she recognized.

"Claire?" A stoop-shouldered gray-haired lady clutched her elbow.

She leaned forward and stared into rheumy green eyes. "Mrs. Griffith?"

The lady squeaked a laugh. "'Tis me, darling girl. Still among the living."

"Oh my word," Claire giggled, instantly transported to girlhood. "It's wonderful to see you." She gently hugged the woman then held her at arm's length. "And I owe you a mountain of apologies for not paying attention during home economics class."

Mrs. Griffith waved a hand, a sweet, flowery scent wafting through the air. "Dear, you were a saint compared to many I taught in thirty years." She tapped gnarled fingers against Claire's cheek then pointed at Eli. "I want you to know something important. Your father was wrong to keep the two of you apart."

The statement took Claire's breath away. She darted a glance at Eli in a conversation with the pastor.

"He always regretted what he did, you know." Mrs. Griffith leaned against her cane.

Claire's face froze.

"Your mother and I talked a good bit about the situation." She wheezed a cough against a lacy handkerchief and peeked at Eli. "Maybe the Lord's giving you a second chance." Her painted-pink lips curved up, and she winked. "I'm listed in the phone book, Claire, if you ever want to chat." She slowly made her way up the aisle.

Her father had regrets? Well, he'd never shown her that side of his nature. An ember of rage against his controlling ways began to burn in her belly.

"You ready for lunch?" Eli said.

She gulped and started to speak then nodded. Tears stung the back of her nose.

You have a choice. Give in to the anger or give it up.

With a glance at the stained-glass window, Jesus the Shepherd, Claire knew she'd give it up. The Lord would help her.

"Yes, Eli, I'm ready for lunch." She slipped her hand into the crook of his arm and walked alongside him out the door.

Chapter 11

Eli followed Claire and the hostess between tables at the Anvil Pub & Grill. The historic building in the Settlement Shops complex echoed with the sounds of Sunday afternoon customers. Mouth-watering aromas filled the air.

The young woman led them upstairs and motioned to a table. Eli shook his head and pointed to one in the far corner. She scooted that direction, placed menus on the table, and returned with glasses of water. "Enjoy your lunch."

Claire sat and sighed. "Smells wonderful. And I'm starving." She scanned the page before her.

Eli forced his gaze from her face and looked at the menu trembling in his hands as though he didn't already know he wanted the Philly cheesesteak.

Claire's delicate hands traced the page. "What's best?" She smiled. His heart hammered in his chest.

"Everything's delicious." Did his voice squeak? He cleared his throat. "Think I'll settle for the cheesesteak." He set the menu to one side. They should definitely eat before a serious discussion. Maybe talk about the weather?

"Sounds wonderful. Think I'll have the same." She unfolded her napkin and placed it in her lap. "Has the summer been nice so far? It's been warm in Indy."

Eli almost laughed out loud. He laid his arm on the table. "Cedarburg's been very pleasant." He tapped his fingers then stopped. *Mueller. Calm down.*

Claire sipped her water. "How many shops are in the Settlement? I was so busy during the Strawberry Festival, I was afraid I'd miss out on them." She toyed with the knife and fork. "Melissa asked if we could stay for a few days, so now I'm sure there will be ample time."

"How many days?"

Claire glanced up. "Until Saturday."

Eli drew in a breath, his heart hammering. "At the inn?"

"No. Sylvia has a very large home on the lake and has invited us to stay. Not far away." Claire leaned back. "Seems awkward to visit someone I don't know, but Melissa was so excited. And I seldom say no to my niece." She shook her head. "I know I spoil her, but she and her brother are my only—"

Children. She'd been about to say children. A pang of loneliness rattled through Eli's middle. He'd missed out, too. *So much to say, Lord.*

"Hello, folks." A perky waitress stepped beside their table and smiled. "I'm Alyce, and I'll be your server." She tugged a pad from her apron.

Claire nodded.

Alyce said, "Have you decided?"

Eli ordered two cheesesteaks and settled in for the conversation he'd avoided for decades.

଄

Claire's first bite of the delicious sandwich melted in her mouth. Tender meat, tangy cheese, fresh bread. But swallowing as she sat with Eli was proving difficult. Stilted conversation, a knot in her stomach, the desire to run, too many ongoing battles to allow easy dining.

Eli swiped his napkin across his mouth. "Great, isn't it?"

"Mr. Mueller, how is everything?" The waitress interrupted their meal again.

"Fine, Alyce."

Claire sipped from the glass the girl had filled moments before and nodded.

He lifted his sandwich. "My favorite restaurant." He'd mentioned that before.

She watched his gaze shift around the room, his jaw twitch. *He's as nervous as I am.*

The realization pulsed through her, and Claire relaxed. Suddenly she was starving and glad for the meat-laden sandwich.

Alyce had buzzed about their table, as welcome as a headache. "Are you ready for dessert?"

Eli frowned. "Alyce, I think we need to finish our meal first."

She blushed. "Sorry."

Claire bit her lip.

"As I live and breathe, Mueller's trying to steal my girl."

A shiver ran through Claire, and she watched Eli's face tighten. She turned toward the voice and forced a smile. "Good afternoon, George."

He puffed his way to the table and dropped a wet kiss on her hand. Claire jerked away and resisted the urge to wipe it against her leg.

"Been hoping to see you again. You staying for Friday's dance, aren't you?" Perspiration dribbled alongside his nose.

Claire shook her head. "I doubt I'll dance anytime soon,

George." She shifted in her seat.

"Don't be too hasty, Miss Wagner."

Eli frowned. "It's Mrs. Parsons," he said, his tone icy. "And you're interrupting our lunch."

George held up his palms. "Okay, Mueller. Round one goes to you." He snorted. "See you soon, Claire."

She lifted the water glass in a mock salute at his retreating form. Not if she could help it.

"Need a dessert menu, Mr. Mueller?"

Eli heaved a sigh. "Alyce, what we really need is a few minutes to quietly enjoy lunch." The girl flushed, turned, and darted away.

He grunted and tossed his napkin on the table. "I'll leave her a good tip." He lowered his gaze and swirled the knife beside his plate. "Claire, I'd like to ask you a question." His eyes roved her face. "Why didn't you answer my letters?"

Chapter 12

Claire stared at him. "Letters?"

Eli caught her hand. "I wrote you every week for months while I was in Vietnam." He squeezed her fingers. "I tried to explain—"

A sharp V formed between her brows. "You wrote me?" Disbelief flashed in her eyes.

He dropped her hand and straightened. "I did."

Color drained from her face, and her lips pulled tight. She took a shaky breath. "Eli, I never received any letters."

He couldn't move. She didn't know. Really didn't know. A rumble of panic laced with something he couldn't explain raced through him. Hope?

Alyce darted beside the table and dropped the check. "Thanks for coming."

"Let's go." Eli fumbled for his wallet, tossed a few bills on the table, and followed Claire downstairs. She reached for the railing beside the creek. A brown dog dashed around a teenager across the way. He stepped closer. "Remember Sadie chasing after sticks we'd throw?" He cleared his throat. "Sweet dog."

"Raised three generations of Labs from your gift." Her voice was husky. She placed one hand on his arm. Tears hung on the edges of her lashes. "Tell me."

Eli tucked her arm in the crook of his. "We'll talk in the park."

Claire gave a jerky nod.

Tourists still streamed up and down the sidewalk, but her presence was all he noted. *She'd never known.* A fierce protectiveness welled in his chest. Her father—

They entered the park and found an empty picnic table. She squeezed his arm for a second before they sat.

"Now tell me," she whispered.

Where to begin? "Claire, you said you couldn't understand how anyone could fight in a war."

"But Eli, I didn't—" Her eyes studied him, a flash of uncertainty on her face. "I wanted to honor my father."

"The promise ring I gave you? I wanted it to be more." He sighed. "I saw your father the afternoon after graduation." He swept a hand over his eyes to wipe away the vision of an angry Henry Wagner. "I told him I wanted to marry you, and he told me to stay away."

She gasped and stilled.

Eli inched closer. Unshed tears made her eyes look darker. His beautiful Claire. "He told me. . . He said my decision to fight in an unnecessary war made me an unworthy choice for his daughter." He struggled for words. "Your father wasn't the only conscientious objector at the time. Even if he didn't respect my position, I had to respect his decision." He picked up her hand. "I sent the daisies with a card, telling you to meet me at the bridge. So I could ask you to wait." He shrugged. "Thought your father might change his mind."

She shook her head. "Mother gave me the flowers. But no card." Her voice rasped the final words as if pushing them from her throat was painful.

"When you didn't show, I didn't know what to think." He paused, his eyes studying her. "I called and your father answered."

She gulped and whispered, "You called?"

He nodded, his thumb tracing circles on her hand. "Then I wrote. Every week for months, I wrote and hoped." He gazed into her eyes. "And when I came home, you were gone." He placed her hand on the table. "But I'm not sure I ever gave up hope."

Claire touched two fingers to her lips. "Oh, Eli. If only I'd known." She sat back.

"Now you do."

ଓ

An ache began under her breastbone. Claire stared into Eli's eyes. He intertwined his fingers with hers. "I came home with so much anger at God over so many things." The muscles in his jaws worked. "It took time and a great deal of prayer, but I've been refined, Claire. Like silver. I try to remember Zechariah 13:9: *'I will refine them like silver and test them like gold.'*" He gently stroked her cheek. "God put me through the fires, and so much dross had to be skimmed away." He propped his chin on his hand. "But there's another part of that verse. *'They will call on my name and I will answer them.'*" His lips curled up. "I've learned to do just that. I call, He answers." He laughed that contagious laugh she'd loved. "Look, you're back in Cedarburg."

"Oh, Eli." A knife of sorrow cut through her middle. "I'm so sorry."

"No need for apologies, Claire." He tucked a strand of hair behind her ear. "I'm just glad you're here."

"After all this time." She sniffled. "I'm truly sorry about the letters, the past. I—I didn't know." The wave of fury at her father crested, and she tamped it down. She'd deal with those thoughts later. Now she understood what Mrs. Griffith meant—her father had regrets. Didn't they all?

Eli leaned forward and brushed his lips across her forehead. Goose bumps ran up her arms. "Oh, Eli," she whispered, her throat tight.

"It's okay." His fingers trailed down her cheek.

She grasped his hand and ran her fingers across calluses on his palm.

He lifted her chin and gazed into her eyes then lowered his head and kissed her. A wave of memories washed through her at the flavor of his lips.

He pulled away. "Waited a long time for that," he said, his voice husky.

Me, too.

"What have we here?"

Claire flinched. George could not, would not, ruin this moment. She whirled about and faced the rotund pest, her lips pressed together.

"Seems you two have been catching up." He smirked and snorted.

"Schiller," Eli snarled.

"George." Claire stood and crossed her arms. "I never had the chance to refuse your dance offer." She placed a hand on Eli's arm. "This is the only dance partner I've ever wanted." She extended her hand to the befuddled man. He gripped her fingers, and she shook his hand. "Glad to have seen you again." She thrust his hand away. "Good-bye."

"If that's the way you feel." George paused then shrugged. "You win, Mueller. You win." He shuffled away, waving one hand over his shoulder.

Eli patted the bench.

Claire sat beside him, her emotions roiling. So much to digest. Her pulse pounded, and a throb began behind her left eye. *A migraine.*

"Did you mean it?"

She massaged her temple.

"Dance partner?"

Her heart raced. "Yes." She smiled. "We could 'cut a rug' as my mama used to say." An aura skip-danced through her field of vision. *Not now, Lord, not now.* A light-headed, too-familiar sensation swirled around her.

Eli pressed her hand to his chest.

"Eli, I—I—" She pulled away and stood. "I have to go."

"No. Not yet."

Claire gulped back nausea and touched a trembling hand to her face. "Will you take me back to the inn?"

"What's wrong?" His eyes narrowed. "You still have headaches?"

She tipped her head. "Not as often, but yes, they catch me." Tears welled in her eyes. "At the worst possible moments."

Eli laced his fingers through hers. Worry crossed his brow. "What can I do?"

She tucked her purse under her arm, her stomach flip-flopping. "I—I—I need to find my migraine medicine." She turned and stumbled on the grass.

"Of course, I understand." Disappointment colored his words. He grasped her elbow and guided her the two blocks to the door of the inn. "Claire." He hesitated. "This has been a shock, I know." His thumb caressed her elbow. "You'll be here for a few days. We'll talk."

She stepped from his tender touch, her head pounding.

"Yes. But not now."

Eli stepped back. "Soon, I hope," he murmured.

The stabbing pain caught her off guard, and a sob caught in the back of her throat. "Yes. Soon." She turned toward the inn, her steps heavy.

Inside the inn's hallway, she fished for the key and entered the cool room.

"Aunt Claire?" Melissa called.

Claire moaned and peered into the dresser mirror, her eyes reflecting the pain—from her head and her heart. Fumbling in her purse, she located her medication.

Melissa came out of the bathroom and motioned toward the closet. "Our suitcases are in the car. Aunt Sylvia has a room for each of us." She leaned forward, a flash of uncertainty on her face. "Although your room won't be inside the main house." She chewed her lower lip. "It's like a gardener's cottage, where she paints."

Alone. Privacy.

"Yes, that's fine." Claire opened a water bottle sitting on the counter and slipped the pill in her mouth. A chime sounded in the depths of her purse. She slid her phone out and read a text. TALK. SOON. STAY. PLEASE STAY.

Claire rubbed her finger over the screen. An intense longing overtook her before a wave of pain swept it away.

Chapter 13

Melissa tapped on the door and entered the gardener's cottage, smiling. "You're looking better this Tuesday morning."

"I should, darling girl, with all your skilled care." Claire lifted her head from the pillow, headache-free for the first time in two days. Despite pain medication, rest, and privacy, a fierce pounding and overwhelming nausea had kept her in bed. "Between Brad and me, you've been quite the Florence Nightingale." She slowly slid from beneath the covers and reached for her robe.

Melissa giggled. "Brad's fine. He just wanted the attention." She cupped Claire's elbow and pulled her into a hug. "I love you."

Claire sniffled. "I love you, too." She held her niece at arm's length and peered into her eyes. "Everything okay?"

"Right as rain." She gave Claire a gentle push. "Get moving and we'll visit with Aunt Sylvia."

"She's been so kind to share her space." Claire looked about the small room, the walls covered with canvases, the corners filled with paints on easels. "I'll be over soon."

Melissa slipped out the door. Claire perched on the edge of the bed. She'd spent her few waking hours in the last two days in tears—her father's betrayal stabbed her heart. How could he have kept Eli from her? She shoved to her feet and paced the room, a deep burning in her middle. Light from the transom filtered into the room, and she centered herself in its beam. "Lord, I need Your help. Forgiveness doesn't come easily to me." She lifted her face to the light. "I choose to forgive my father for deceiving me." She sighed. "Show me the path You would have me follow." A smile flitted across her face. "And bless Eli, dear Lord."

After a shower, Claire dressed and crossed the patio, ready to face Brad's avant-garde relative. She and Sylvia had only shared quick pleasantries Sunday evening before Melissa tucked Claire into bed.

A clunky Schwinn bicycle propped against the garage wall caught her attention. It sported a frayed straw basket on the handlebars. "Just like the one I rode in high school." A rusty silver bell hung beside the basket. Claire pulled the lever, and a tinny ring echoed. She and Eli had ridden the countryside on their bikes, her precious yellow Lab, Sadie, loping alongside. The covered bridge. How many Frisbees had they lost to the sweep of water at that park? Her mouth curved into a smile.

Eli.

Claire touched her lips. The sweet kiss they shared on Sunday seemed a dream. Melissa had roused her Monday morning with news Eli was there, but in her state, she refused to see him. "Today." She smiled. "Today I'll see him."

She grinned and stepped into the kitchen.

Sylvia swept around the end of the counter, silver mules clicking against the tile floor, a gauzy orange cloak fluttering in her wake, and fuzzy red hair caught in a clip at a ninety-degree angle. She air-kissed Claire. "Darling, so glad you've recovered." She tucked a tiny muffin into a napkin and circled the center island. "Once I grab some coffee, I'll be ensconced in your private space for the morning." With a delighted laugh, she filled a cup. "I hate to inconvenience you, but my painting calls." She swirled out of the room.

Brad snorted. "And that's a dose of Aunt Sylvia."

"I'm sorry I kept her room occupied."

"Don't be." Brad shook his head. "She was too involved in closing out the Strawberry Festival to need the space until today." He grasped Melissa's hand. "Tell her yet?" He wiggled his eyebrows.

"Tell me what?" Claire leaned against the granite counter.

Her niece sidled closer, wearing a crooked grin. "Nothing much." She brushed crumbs from the counter. "Except Brad has asked me to marry him."

"What?" Claire squealed and grabbed Melissa. "Oh my."

Red faced, Brad dipped his head. "I called Melissa's parents and they gave their consent."

Openmouthed, Claire plopped on a bar stool and clutched Melissa's and Brad's hands. "Then I consent, too." She squeezed their fingers. "Congratulations."

"My mother is coming tonight." Brad laughed. "She decided not to wait until Saturday."

Melissa slid an arm around Brad's waist. "We're planning a party this weekend."

Claire raised a brow. "So soon?"

"Kind of." Melissa eyed her. "Brad's accepted a position. We'd like to get married in August so we can get settled before the term starts."

"That's wonderful! Where?"

Melissa beamed. "Can you believe it? Stanford!" The light

in her eyes dimmed. "My only regret, Aunt Claire, is leaving you." Melissa touched Claire's arm. "I'll miss you so much."

"Darling girl, I will come visit every chance I get." Claire hugged her niece's shoulders. "You won't get rid of me easily."

Melissa kissed her cheek. "I should hope not." She waved an arm at Brad, who chuckled and joined the group hug.

Claire released them and poured a cup of coffee then sat at the table.

The starry-eyed couple cuddled on the family room sofa. Claire watched them snuggle and kiss, her heart sinking in her chest.

Alone.

Melissa was her only family in Indianapolis now that Tony had moved to Houston. And with the new changes in her church, she'd felt isolated for some time.

Eli's words floated through her mind. *Stay. Please stay.*

"Melissa, where is my cell phone?"

"It's in my room. It needed charging." Melissa shoved from the sofa and returned, waving the phone. "Seems like you have a host of texts. Bet I know who from."

Claire unfolded the phone and tapped the screen's display. She read the first text.

STRAY

A smile crossed her lips, and she scrolled further.

HOPE UR BUTTER. TALL SLOONER?

She slid the display to the last text and giggled.

ELI WOULD LIKE TO TALK WITH CLAIRE.

"Wonder how long that took him?" She sipped her coffee and stared at the colorful display of hydrangeas and petunias in Sylvia's garden. Sunlight glinted from something—

She set her cup on the counter. "Brad, do you think Aunt

Sylvia would mind if I borrowed her bike?"

ଔ

Eli placed the last jewelry order into a brown envelope and slid it into Marie's lockbox. He'd finished the morning's accounts, paid bills, answered e-mail, and chatted with his mother. His cell phone never left his side. Why hadn't he heard from Claire? Tuesday, already. He'd left three messages on her phone and she hadn't called.

His revelation about the letters— "Lord, was it too much too soon?" He settled on the stool and reached for his well-worn Bible. Only time in the Word had gotten him this far, and he needed comfort in its pages. He flopped it on the counter and it spread open. Proverbs 3.

Eli scanned the familiar passage. "Trust in the Lord with all my heart. Isn't that what I've tried to do?" He chuckled. "'And lean not on your own understanding.' Maybe I'm not so good at that part. Yet." He shut the book and replaced it on the shelf.

"Patience." He opened the refrigerator for a bottle of water. A blue plate heaped with cookies sat center stage. "Oh, Marie." Another twinge of guilt pierced his gut. He twisted the bottle cap off and tossed it toward the garbage can. It bounced against a wall calendar and ricocheted to the clock on his desk. Frustration roared through his middle. "Yeah, Lord, the clock's ticking and days are passing." Loneliness enveloped him. It seemed this feeling had been with him for so long. What would he do when Claire left town again?

Eli reached for her ring and slid it on his pinky. The repair done, he needed to return it. He popped the ring inside a special blue velvet box. He'd take it by Sylvia's this afternoon.

He had to see Claire—to know. He raked a hand through his hair. What should he say?

He needed to think. "Bridge time." He opened the workroom door. "I'm leaving for a while."

Marie waved and returned her attention to a customer.

Eli lifted his bicycle from the stand and trundled to the sidewalk. Pushing off, he pedaled down Washington Avenue, a nod or two at friends. He sped up—he had no desire to fraternize at the moment.

Within minutes he reached the park. A silver van and a Mercedes sat in the small parking lot by the covered bridge. Three children lobbed a Frisbee between them while their parents watched. Eli smiled. A pleasant scene. Claire's Lab had fetched quite a few Frisbees in this park.

He propped his bike against a large boulder and meandered to the creek. Soothing burbles began to calm his racing pulse. He squatted and tossed a rock into the water. His knee began to ache. Halfway into a stand, a Frisbee caught him in the back of the neck. He grabbed it just before it flew into the water. He clutched it to his chest, a rumble of laughter rolling out.

"Sorry, mister." A towheaded, wide-eyed youngster stood before him twisting his hands. "Me and my brother didn't mean it."

Eli handed the Frisbee to the boy. "No problem. Enjoy." He rubbed the back of his neck and wandered toward the covered bridge.

It was cool and dim inside, and Eli's steps thunked across the boards. He reached the middle and leaned against the railing. What would've happened if Claire had gotten the note with the daisies? Would she have come to the bridge? Would they have lived happily ever after?

Laughter rang outside. He bent over and peered out a diamond-shaped knothole. He could see the river and edge of the park where the children played.

"Eli?"

He closed his eyes. He *heard* his dreams now?

Footfalls sounded on the bridge. "Eli?"

Eli swung his head around and froze.

Claire.

A flood of love welled up, and he spread his arms wide. When she stepped into his embrace, he bent and grazed her hair with his lips. "You're here." He brushed hair from her forehead and let his hand slide down her cheek. He tilted his head and met her lips. She leaned into his kiss.

"Claire." The word was sweet on his tongue.

She traced his jaw with a finger. His eyes burned with unshed tears. Oh, how he'd ached for this moment. His throat tightened, and he gave her a gentle hug. Releasing her with one arm, he reached for the velvet box in his pocket.

"Your promise ring is repaired," he whispered. He slid it on her finger.

Claire held her hand aloft. A ray of sunlight tapped the silver and glistened atop the sapphire. She looked into his eyes. "Thank you."

Eli smiled. "When I crafted that ring, I made another." He opened his hand, revealing a silver ring guard studded with four diamonds. "This is the seal for the promise ring."

Claire covered her mouth. "Oh, Eli." She clasped his arm and he drew her close, his heart thudding. She ran her fingers across the diamonds glittering in the dappled sunlight. "Eli, you've kept this all these years." It wasn't a question. Her breathless whisper resounded with the realization he'd waited for her.

"I don't need an answer today," he whispered against her hair. "Just hope."

"A hope and a future," Claire drew back, her eyes sparkling. "Isn't that what we're promised?" She gave him a wobbly smile. "Refined silversmith, let's see where the Lord leads us."

He cupped her chin and tipped it up, his heart galloping. "He's led us all these years, and brought us back together." He lowered his lips to hers, pausing a fraction of an inch away. "I believe He's leading us. . .home." His lips captured hers, and warm sweetness twined around and through them like the very breath of God's blessing.

Eileen Key, freelance writer and editor, resides in San Antonio, Texas, near her grown children and three wonderful grandchildren. She's published ten anthology stories and numerous devotionals and articles. Her first mystery novel, *Dog Gone* from Barbour Publishing, released in 2008. Her second book, *Door County Christmas*, released in 2010. Find her on the web: www.eileenkey.com

MAYBE US

by Cynthia Ruchti

Dedication

I wonder if any author has thanked her imaginary characters. I think I should. They always teach me so much about life as I eavesdrop on theirs. Thank you, Beth, Derrick, Oompa, Nicole. . . .

To the very real Clayton: You thought I might forget you, didn't you? How could I forget getting on an airplane and having my Derrick character slide into the seat beside me—all seven feet of him! Thank you for letting me discuss tallness with you and for helping me visualize Derrick as I wrote. You put the delight in him.

Thank you, Becky Germany and the Barbour Publishing staff, for inviting us to tell the stories of these characters. Thank you, Ellen Tarver, for not only editing but enthusing about this book! Wendy Lawton, you and the rest of the Books & Such Literary Agency team infuse joy in every project.

Thank you to my fellow authors for teaching me so much as we wrote. The time we spent together, the reflections we saw in Cedar Creek, will remain with me. It's hard to leave a place like Cedarburg.

And thank you, my dearly loved family, for your joyful tolerance of a wife, mom, sister, aunt, and grammie who writes about people no one's ever met.

A cord of three strands is not quickly broken.
Ecclesiastes 4:12

Chapter 1

Autumn

Beth pushed away from the plate-glass window. With her shirtsleeve over the heel of her hand, she wiped her nose-sized smudge from the glass. The brownie looked smaller now from this distance, but not by much. The single-focus spotlight helped. And the sound of an angel choir. Did anyone else on Washington Avenue hear that?

A brownie frosted with smooth-as-black-ice chocolate ganache. *Thank you, Food Network, for having served as a distraction from college finals.* The Food Network taught her the meaning of the word *ganache*, although cooking and baking might always remain spectator sports for her.

She could smell the culinary masterpieces. How was that possible? Did the shop owner pipe *Eau de Chocolát* through outdoor vents to lure more customers? Her eyes were already in love. Now her nose was, too.

Cedarburg boasted a nice collection of specialty chocolate shops. Fudge. Truffles. Toffee. But a shop dedicated to brownies was a new—and dare she say *glorious*?—addition to downtown.

Beth tore her gaze from the perfect dessert and glanced at the store name arching across the upper third of the front window. LIFE BY CHOCOLATE. Beautiful lettering. Beautiful concept.

The shop was so new the paint could still be wet. This storefront had changed hands twice since Beth came on board with her grandpa's project two doors down. Life by Chocolate was the new kid on the block, from empty to open almost overnight. Buying a brownie or two seemed the neighborly thing to do. Support local businesses.

She pressed her nose against the glass again, grateful for another sleeve to wipe a fresh smudge. Smudge. Fudge. Brownies, brownies, brownies. Gooey and fudgy and probably still warm. Thick and dark and—

Four dollars and fifty cents! Apiece?

Beth touched the window on two points now, leaning her forehead into the glass, too. The owner could afford to hire a professional window washer, at those prices.

The wave of sticker shock retreated, shamed by a stark realization. *At those prices.* That's probably what her customers said when they saw the price tag on the imported, handspun angora two doors down.

Quality costs.

And the brownie with "Beth Schurmer" scrolled invisibly in the ganache sure looked like quality to her.

Decision made. She'd sacrifice the five dollars in the pocket of her jeans to help a new business get off the ground. . .and wear stretchy pants the rest of the day, if she had to.

She pulled the bill from her pocket without losing eye contact with the object of her affection. Who knew a trifolded five could perform like a paper airplane in a Wisconsin early autumn gust? It captured her attention now, soaring on the air currents, a paper/linen version of Forrest Gump's feather.

When it landed on the sidewalk, she trapped it with her foot. A much larger Nike-clad foot smashed her toes like a bully would squash a family of caterpillars.

"Ow!"

"Sorry." The monster foot unstomped itself. "Bad timing. Coach was right."

Beth bent to retrieve her down payment on the world's yummiest looking brownie then looked up. And up. A good twelve inches more vertical than an average guy's head. And topped with glistening corkscrew curls a little redder than caramelized sugar, curls that moved whether his head was in motion or not.

He smiled. "I see you had your tonsils removed as a child."

She lowered her gaze and snapped her gaping mouth shut. He wasn't a freak show. He was. . .

Seven feet tall. With him smiling like that, and his head towering that high above her, she couldn't catch his eye color, but she'd noticed his pale copper eyebrows and a surprisingly toasty complexion.

The scene at her eye level revealed something else. He wore a chef's apron with icing-like swirled embroidery: LIFE BY CHOCOLATE.

She gripped the folded five and shoved her hands into her pockets. "Do you work here?"

He leaned his shoulder against the pale Cream City brick of the storefront as if he were a ladder, a ladder that hadn't planted its legs firmly in the ground. His shoulder slid. He stumbled but recovered quickly, his facial features still locked in an expression of enjoyment of life.

Patting the logo on his chef's apron, he answered, "Work here? Constantly. Too many hours. I'm also part owner of the place."

Whoa. Not what she pictured for a brownie expert. Or a neighbor.

He smiled again. "Why? Do you need a job?"

She improved her posture. "No, thank you. I have more than enough. That's mine," she said, pointing to the limestone building on the other side of the Up the Cedar Creek Without a Paddle lodge-themed gift shop next door. "Well, not mine. It belongs to my grandfather. I manage it for him."

"The Yarn Shop?"

"That's it."

He swiped his hands on his apron and reached his right one toward her. "You must be Beth. I've heard about you. I'm Derrick Hofferman."

He'd heard about her? Well intentioned as they might be, did the whole town have to inform every newcomer about her failure to find a teaching job, her desperate financial picture, having to move in with Oompa, and—

She grasped his hand and shook it. "Nice to meet you."

"They were right." His expression opened wider. "You have the softest hands."

"So do you." She withdrew her hand and oddly missed the warmth. Rubbing the tips of her fingers with her thumb, she said, "It's the lanolin in the wool. A natural skin softener."

He rubbed his together then faced both palms toward her. "Butter."

Beth's mind raced through a menu of replies. *I love butter.* No. *Thanks for your efforts to support the dairy industry.* No. *You're not from around here, are you?* No.

He tapped on the front window with his knuckle. "That'll be two dollars."

Heavenly decadence preened its chocolaty goodness in the

spotlight's glow. "The sign says four fifty."

Copper eyebrows inched above cloud level. "That's for the brownie." He tapped the glass again. "Two bucks to wipe off the imprint of your face." Something caught in his expression as if he'd chomped on a walnut shell. "Not that I'd ever want to get rid of the im— Your face is just fine. Better than fine. It's a nice face. It has some great features. Your nose. I especially like your—"

Beth couldn't help but giggle. Derrick Hofferman's mouth might win the klutzy contest. With that kind of competition, his feet couldn't hope for better than second place.

Chapter 2

"It's wool, not yarn."

Beth took the skein of tightly spun blue-green Shetland wool from Derrick Hofferman's grip. She could like this guy, if he'd start acting normal.

He'd only been in the shop a few minutes, only on the block a few days. But she'd put up with the too-tall-not-to-be-a-basketball-player long enough. Were there no other shopkeepers Derrick Hofferman could bug when his Life by Chocolate business was slow? Or when he needed an opinion about the merits of adding a sprinkling of sea salt to the bubbled surface of his toasted coconut–frosted Covered Bridge Brownie? A mouthful—both the thought and the deliciousness.

The thought of chocolate—never too far from her mind—reminded her of the shipment of hand-dyed black/brown Cotswold sheepswool she'd ordered for the Dolls with Dolls craft guild. From the Internet images she'd seen, the hills of Cotswold, England, looked far different from the rolling green of southeastern Wisconsin. Here, the green was now heavily peppered with leafy fireworks of red, orange, and gold.

Delays in international orders were a given, but the doll makers clamored to get the richly sheened locks on their bald babies in time for pre-Christmas sales. As soon as Derrick wandered back to his own shop, she'd call England.

As natural as you please. She'd call England to check on a wool shipment. How different from the duties she assumed would be part of her career's workday.

Derrick dipped his head toward her as if waiting for a response. To what? Maybe it wasn't the brownie connection. Maybe it was his disturbing mop of corkscrew hair that made her think of the Cotswolds.

Someday she'd have to ask why he chose baking brownies instead of, say, the NBA or life as a gymnasium lightbulb changer or top-of-refrigerator cleaner or outrageous hairstyle magazine model, as if she had any room to talk there. She'd ask about his career choice someday, just to be neighborly. As long as that didn't prompt him to ask about hers.

She readjusted the laceweight infinity scarf at her neck. Right now, his rambling questions kept her from any number of important projects, like knitting more inventory. The surge of customers during Cedarburg's Harvest Festival drained her supply of trademark *moebius* scarves—no beginning and no end. Other knitters tackled a wide variety of creative projects. Beth had one specialty—the math mystery moebius. She itched to get back to the one waiting on her needles—a thick, ribbed moebius too heavy for the early fall temps but perfect for the chill another calendar flip would bring.

"So..." she said.

He didn't take the hint.

At the thought of her work in progress, part of her brain slipped into the soothing rhythm of knitting. It had taken her a month of practice to break the habit of "throwing" the wool with her right hand. Looping wool with the index finger of her left hand changed her three-beat knitting rhythm to a quick, agile two-beat dance step.

And the nosy guy from two shops north was keeping her from the music.

What was she saying? How could a person tire of having a gourmet brownie expert for a neighbor? And a neighbor who liked to share, at that.

His eyebrows arched into the rusty Brillo Pad of his irrational hair.

"Wool," she said, adding extra *o*'s for emphasis. "From sheep, as opposed to a factory. Have you seen an acrylic in the wild?"

"Ah, the wild acrylic." He affected a National Geographic narrator's voice. "Fascinating creatures. Odd mix of warmth and fragility."

The customer's always right. The customer's always right. The customer's sometimes afflicted with altitude sickness because of his height.

"I like that thing around your neck." He bobbed his head toward her.

"It's a moebius."

"'Maybe-Us'?"

"Technically, it's pronounced more like a blend of an *o* sound and an *ay* sound with a little bit of *uh*."

"Moo?"

"Think umlaut. German."

"Like most of Cedarburg." He reached for the skein of Shetland she'd taken from him but not yet returned to its spot in the birch basket. Her grip tightened.

How did he manage that? The skein untwisted between them, no longer tight as a fresh french braid but drooping like loops of overcooked pasta.

His face scrunched into an unspoken apology.

Beth stretched out her hands as if telling a Cedar Creek—or any other location, for that matter—fish story. The loops grew taut. She held the left loop of wool still, flipped the right loop five times, and marveled again that an act like twisting a rubber band toy could restore the too-beautiful-not-to-be-called-art skein.

Derrick grinned. Something in the room brightened. Maybe the ancient electrical system was doing that funny surge thing again. One more item to add to the list of repairs she'd need to tackle.

Historical buildings' virtues sometimes hide behind cracked plaster.

She slipped the tourniquet twist of the right-hand loop of wool into the left. All better. A perfect twisted braid again. With a couple of flicks of her wrist, she had fixed the mess he'd created. The skin at the corners of his eyes crinkled with—

"Your eyes." She stared but couldn't make herself quit. "They're two different colors."

"Recall," he said, emphasizing the first syllable of the word.

"What?"

He closed and opened first one eye then the other. "Tinted contacts. This one"—he pointed toward the Pacific blue rather than the Caribbean blue—"was recalled by the manufacturer."

There was something to be said for both bodies of water. She caught herself debating which was her favorite. Favorite?

He laced his fingers together then pressed his palms in front of him as he stretched outward and up. With a metallic clatter, the tin shade on the ceiling light wobbled. He grabbed the edge of the shade and recoiled. "That's hot!" The light swung wildly. "Sorry." He picked up a Zimmermann knitting book from the stack near him and used it to still the light fixture. . .in more ways than one. With a sizzle and pop, the lightbulb voiced its protest. "Let me change that bulb for you."

"Don't worry about it."

He reminded her of a Great Dane puppy skidding on ice—fun to watch but dangerous to those standing too close to its flailing appendages. Someone might get knocked off her feet.

But who could stay irritated with a man who apologized to light fixtures and made a living as a brownie *artiste*?

Derrick picked another skein from the wooden barrels angled on the display wall. A creamy alpaca. "Wool, huh?"

Nice segue, Derrick.

"Then why is your place called the *Yarn* Shop?" He gestured with the skein toward the logo on the price tags, the information signs, and the checkout counter.

She replaced the alpaca and mentally asked it to forgive Derrick's obvious lack of respect. "Because of the stories."

"What?" His tone revealed a genuine desire to know.

"The stories. The yarns." Beth turned toward the back corner of the shop, where a conversation group of overstuffed worn leather chairs, empty now, encircled an occupied high-backed upholstered rocker. The antique man, as in age rather than interests, lifted a frail hand and waved at Derrick and Beth. That simple gesture would always warm her heart. "His stories bring in more customers than a sidewalk sale. My grandpa—Oompa. He just got back from his army unit's reunion in Janesville. Have you met?"

Derrick's eyes glinted. Warm-water seas do that. In four long strides, he was at the rocker, hand extended. "It's a pleasure, sir."

That familiar lump formed at the base of Beth's throat, the one that reacted when someone treated her grandfather with the respect he deserved.

Derrick crouched at the side of the rocker, which made his face eye level with the rocker's occupant. Resting his forearms on his knees he said, "So, I hear you spin a good yarn."

"Don't get him started," Beth teased. "What he hasn't experienced in eighty-two years of living and working in Cedarburg, he's heard for so long, the lines between 'I was there' and 'I wish I'd been there' aren't as distinct as they once were." She knew Oliver Schurmer would agree with her and retain his sense of humor about it. What a blessing!

Within minutes, Derrick claimed one of the leather chairs, his knees bent almost to his Adam's apple, and his ear bent to Oompa, who started somewhere in the middle of Cedarburg's rich history and wove stories both directions.

England. She could call England with Oompa comfortable and occupied and the brownie guy entertained.

Or. . .she could listen in and let her heart warm to the sound of a creaking rocker, a timeworn voice, and laughter.

When torn between joy and responsibility, why did Beth always cave to responsibility?

☙

Did Life by Chocolate do any business at all? Derrick might as well post a sign on his shop that said, "I'm never in. Check two doors down. If it's a brownie emergency, help yourself and leave the money in the tip jar on the counter."

How was it he could always be underfoot and still have fresh brownies on display every morning when Beth swept the sidewalk and then swept in front of Up the Cedar Creek so she could get close enough to Derrick's shop to check out the specialty of the day?

Oompa was in his element with Derrick so often a fixture in the Yarn Shop. Fresh ears for his stories. "Young man, did I tell you about the time. . . ?"

Without fail, Derrick answered, "No. I'd love to hear about it."

But she had work to do. She couldn't afford the distraction of a man whose morphing facial expressions held such fascination, a man who lit Oompa's countenance when he walked through the door, a man who—

Any man. No time for *any* man other than the fragile, gentle blessing in the rocking chair.

What would she have done if Oompa hadn't taken her in? What if he hadn't loaned her every penny she needed for college? What if he hadn't been willing to wait as long as it took for her to pay him back?

She owed him so much more than however long he needed a caretaker and a manager for the Yarn Shop. Her plans could wait. They had to. He needed her.

Beth arranged her latest half dozen moebius scarves—autumn's best russet, claret, goldenrod, tawny, acorn, and cinnamon—on thick wooden pegs on the wall behind the cash counter then turned to see why the undercurrent of chatter in the back corner stopped.

She'd never seen color drain from someone's face from forehead to chin. Oompa turned from pale to colorless and slumped forward. Derrick caught him before he could tip out of the rocker onto the floor. The older man lay cradled in the younger man's arms.

"Call 911!" she barked.

Derrick looked at her over the limp lump of her grandfather. "*You* call 911! I'm a little busy here." He wrestled the weight to the floor and rested two fingers along the man's carotid artery. "Okay, he has a pulse."

He undid the buttons on Oompa's worn-to-flannel oxford shirt. Was Derrick expecting to perform open-heart surgery or what? She knelt beside the man who'd years ago taught her that love is patient and the man who now tested her patience as a hobby. Derrick took her hand and squeezed.

Without breaking amateur EMT stride, he reached behind him for a thick, oversized skein of wool and tucked it under Oompa's neck. "I'm pretty sure he'll be oka—" Derrick jerked into motion as Oompa's lips turned blue and his breathing stopped. Derrick checked for a pulse again then fist over fist, started chest compressions.

Beth felt her own life draining through her toes. But her heart was still beating, hard enough to make her nauseous.

"Beth! Did you call 911?"

Chapter 3

Derrick watched Beth's soft-as-spun-wool fingers dance with her knitting needles. Such a smooth, graceful motion. Other knitters he knew made great sweeping movements when they twisted the yarn around the needle. Beth's seemed delicately choreographed, an efficiency of energy.

The project in her lap grew as they waited for a doctor's report on Beth's grandfather. What had she called him? Part of a polka. A tuba sound. Ah, Oompa. As in oom-pa-pa.

Derrick's feet formed giant barricades for the others in the waiting area. He tried to keep them tucked in the corner where two vinyl love seats met with an end table between them. He tapped his toes inside his shoes to the steady rhythm of Beth's needles.

Was knitting Beth Schurmer's version of pacing?

He shifted his position, groaned, and arched his back.

Beth half turned, her needles silent.

Nice work. Her grandfather fights for his life down the hall and you have the gall to complain about a tight muscle. "Back labor," he explained, instantly regretting the use of humor.

She moaned and dropped her chin to her chest. Sobs shook her shoulders.

"I'm so sorry, Beth. It's not a time to—" His words were

broken. Maybe an arm around her shoulder would serve as a better apology.

Stirring a whiff of something like lily of the valley, she lifted her head. The grimace he expected was curled on the ends. A smile. She was laughing!

"Thanks, Derrick. I needed the comic relief. Back labor, huh?"

"I'm funnier on paper."

"Seriously?"

"No. Humorously."

She made a face like a pinched cry, but the sound that came out was definitely laughter. It didn't last. Tears took over. "It's because of him."

Derrick snatched a tissue for her from the box on the end table. "What is? And who's the *him*?"

"Oompa. Your back. It's from bending over him all that time doing CPR."

Derrick squirmed, inside and out. "I trained for a while as an EMT."

"So you said."

He palmed his knees. "I normally don't keep going until the victim begs me to stop."

"I figured." That smile again. Like the swirl on a good truffle.

"Your Oompa has a lot of lung power for a man his age."

Beth rolled her knitting project around her needles and tucked it into a bag at her feet. She leaned back, resting her head against the wall. The blond/caramel/cinnamon streaks in her hair fluffed against the bland wall like an expensive work of fiber art. Or a perfectly toasted marshmallow on his S'Mores Brownie.

The shop! How many customers had he lost when they

noticed his BE BACK AT 1:00 sign lied? He glanced at the wall clock. Four thirty. If he were going to pull off this my-reason-for-living-is-to-bake-brownies front, he'd have to at least keep the shop open until—

"Do you think he's still breathing?" Her question was all air, no real sound.

He knew better than to promise the unguaranteeable. "Beth, would it be okay if I prayed with you?"

She looked up at him, an unreadable expression on her face. He'd offended her. Why couldn't he just keep praying for Oompa silently without risking a "don't push your religion on me" or "fine for you, but leave me out of this" debate with a woman who obviously considered him stranger than strange and who, from that angle, could see right up his nose hairs?

"Where two or three are gathered. . ." she said.

Huh. Suh-weet.

If Beth were his sister, he'd reach for her hand to pray. If Nicole were here, she'd sit on the other side of Beth, saying perfectly comforting words and making Beth feel better just by her presence. He'd have to muddle through without Nicole.

Derrick turned his hands palms up on his knees. His eyes hadn't been closed two seconds before he felt a silken hand slip into his.

Silken and sticky. *Sticky?* Un-prayer-like, his eyes popped open.

Beth's hands rested in her lap. The one in his belonged to a pigtailed kidling, a half-eaten Cedarburg caramel apple in her other hand.

"You're my *puzzitt*," the young thing said. Then, without turning, she hollered, "Mommy, I found my puzzitt!"

A woman appeared behind the little girl. "Ella Marie, come

here, please." The mom tilted her head in apology to Derrick and Beth while tugging the child by polka-dot suspenders. "Dad's in radiology. They think he aspirated something. He choked on an apple seed. Not Ella. No, she can handle anything."

Ella took another slurpy bite of her apple, the caramel connecting her to the confection like good pizza cheese. Her mom bent to wipe apple slobber from Ella's chin. "Precocious isn't a strong enough word for my daughter. She—"

"I'm his puzzitt, Mommy. He's a giant." She pointed with her apple.

Beth grinned at him. Derrick concentrated on not looking so giant-like.

"And I'm a dorf."

"That's *dwarf*, honey. And no, you're not." Sighing, the mom continued her cleanup efforts.

Derrick wiped the stickiness onto his jeans—another instant regret. "You just haven't grown all the way yet, Ella."

Beth smacked him on the arm.

"What?"

She leaned toward him and whispered, "Now the poor child will think she's destined to be ten feet tall."

"Opposite!" The "puzzitt" pieces came together for Derrick. "She thinks I'm her *opposite*."

Mom knelt to help steer the remainder of the apple eating. "Preschool. The subject of the week. Next week—rhyming. That should be interesting."

Ella's gaze was locked on Derrick the Giant. "I should marry him."

Beth snickered out loud at that one.

Mom to the rescue. "Honey, he already has a wife."

Derrick shook his head and caught a similar motion

emanating from Beth's direction.

"Sorry. Again," the mom sputtered. "I assumed. . ." She nodded toward Beth's stomach.

It bulged under her shirt.

Ella moved toward Beth. "Will your giant baby have permission hair, too?"

Beth and Derrick both looked to Mom for translation.

"Persimmon. Deluxe pack of Crayolas."

Derrick jumped in. "I don't know. I mean, we're not. . .we're not having a baby. I mean, I don't think she is." He motioned toward Beth, the heat under his collar transforming into a full-blown rash. "But I know I'm not. Not that I could, but even if I could, it wouldn't be with her and I so did not mean it that way and why don't I just stop talking and chew on my shoe?"

Beth reached under the hem of her shirt and removed the bulge from her stomach. Her knitting project. When had she picked it up again?

Ella's eyes widened even more than their previous apricot size. "That's where I keep my babies, too!"

"Beth Schurmer?"

The doctor's inquiry served as a reprieve from the gravitational pull of the conversation with Derrick's puzzitt.

Beth sprang to her feet. Derrick wasn't far behind.

"How is he?"

"Your grandfather's doing very well except for the cracked ribs. They'll give him some serious discomfort after the painkillers wear off."

Derrick turned away and linked his fingers on top of his head. "That's my fault." His stomach soured. His pulses throbbed in his temples like the beater on his industrial-strength mixer at the shop. "My fault."

"Son, you saved his life. Broken ribs are a small price to pay for that, even at his age."

Beth put a hand on his arm without turning from facing the doctor. "Is he going to be okay?"

The doctor looked at Derrick. "The guilt should ease up when you give yourself time to realize—"

"My grandpa! Is Oompa okay?"

"He suffered a pretty significant myocardial infarction. Heart attack."

Derrick turned in time to see her search his face.

The doctor stepped to the side and invited Beth to move down the hall with him. "We can talk in depth in the consult room. Then you can see him. We'll schedule more tests soon."

Derrick felt a tug on his heart. Was it for the older gentleman who'd been given a little more time on earth or for the granddaughter who'd been given back something precious?

Or both?

He knew his place—on the love seat near the end table—explaining to a copper-haired preschooler that as flattering as it was, he couldn't marry her. He had to stay. . .available.

He hadn't made it all the way across the room to the love seat before he heard Beth's voice. "I'm waiting."

Yes. Me, too.

"Aren't you coming?" she asked.

"I didn't know if you'd want me to."

Beth's eyes sparkled with something other than tears. She said, "I don't dare leave you alone with your puzzitt." She winked at the frazzled mom. "I don't have time in my life to attend a wedding right now, especially one that serves juice boxes and Lunchables at the reception."

She turned as if expecting him to follow, a fact confirmed

by the way her pace picked up when he reached her side.

"We didn't get a chance to pray together," she said as they walked toward the consultation room. She lifted her chin a little. "I'm sorry I missed that."

Me, too.

"Rain check?"

Derrick matched his stride to hers. "Anytime."

Chapter 4

Does it hurt, Oompa?" Beth tempered her concern to make the question sound more related to a skinned knee rather than a heart episode with a side of broken ribs.

"Only when I. . .breathe." His grimace proved his point.

"Are you going to be okay here in the shop rather than in bed?" His rocker in the conversation area had an Oompa-shaped depression that seemed to cradle him, but was the strain of sitting and interacting with the Yarn Shop customers going to be too much? What alternative did they have? Neither of them could afford in-home help while he recovered. And he was too alert, too well for nursing home care. Once word got out, all the warmhearted Cedarburg residents would be by to check on him. She supposed this was as good a place as any for her to keep an eye on him and for him to entertain visitors and well-wishers, those he'd been regaling with his stories for decades.

She tucked a stocking stitch lap robe around him.

"Beth, are you trying to help me or make me croak from the heat?" He tore the wool blanket away and tossed it aside.

"Croak? Don't talk like that." She retrieved the blanket, folded it, and laid it over the arm of a chair near him.

"People die, Beth. We all do."

Not you. You're all I have left. "Planning your funeral might be a bit off-putting to customers, Oompa. Could we save that kind of talk for some other time?"

She plumped the throw pillows on the other chairs in the circle, the ones without his shape in them and his spirit giving them life, and fanned the classic children's books she kept on the side table.

He stirred. Leaned forward. Her peripheral vision caught the movement.

"So," he said, his voice weak but his message strong, "we *will* talk about it sometime?"

She let out more rope in her invisible tether to him, venturing as far as the window display and the CLOSED sign she was about to flip to OPEN. "About what?"

"My dying."

The words spun her around and sent a jolt through her nerve endings. "Oompa, think positively."

"I am. I'm positively sure I'm gonna die."

She could threaten to wash his mouth out with soap, but that hardly seemed appropriate. "So, do you hear the death angel knocking at your door?" The nerve jolt exited through her mouth as an artificial chuckle.

"No, that would be your Derrick." He nodded to a spot behind her and to the right. Derrick stood crouched to fit within the boundaries of the entrance door window. With his nose pressed against the glass, he smiled at her and pointed to the small box he carried—dark chocolate brown with a milk chocolate satin ribbon.

She opened the ancient brass lock and let in a whiff of cool October morning air, a smattering of sunbaked leaves, and a "giant" bearing something that smelled divine. Cinnamon? Sugar, definitely. What else?

"If you give me a minute, I'll actually open the box so you don't have to sniff through the lid," he said, dangling the box just above her head.

"Oompa isn't supposed to have chocolate for a while. The caffeine will mess with his heart medications."

Derrick gave the ribbon one tug and it fell away, as did the sides of the box. The chocolate magician. "That's why I made a blond brownie for him. Notice how it's three toned? Like your hair?"

Beth tugged at her feathered bangs.

He spun the now-splayed box like a basketball player might spin a ball. "And for the lady. . ."

"Derrick, it's not even nine in the morning. I may have a soft heart for brownies"—*and those who create them*—"but at this hour I need—"

". . .my latest experiment—Caramel Apple Sour Cream Coffee Cake."

"What? No chocolate?"

His eyes wide—*oh, good, they were the same color today, like gourmet tea steeped a little longer than required*—he laid the confections on the counter and left the building. Dark tea? His real eye color? What happened to the blue?

Beth looked at Oompa across the room. He shrugged.

Within seconds Derrick was back, steadying an egg carton drink holder bearing three pottery mugs. "Hot cider for Mr. Schurmer. Double Dutch Chocolate lattes for Ms. Schurmer and the Crusher." He waited for Beth to take her mug then delivered the cider. On his return toward the front of the shop, he tripped on a wrinkle in the air and toppled forward, his arms extended with the off-balance single mug still lodged in the egg carton holder.

Beth sucked in a breath and reached toward him, not that it would help.

Derrick dipped and swerved, missing the stack of imported wool from Iceland. He twirled past the mosaic of autumn-colored wool she'd so carefully arranged. When he landed—belly down on the floor between display bins—the rust dripped with rich, dark liquid dotted with clouds of cream. The rust of his hair.

Beth exhaled. He lay at her feet, a crown of latte oozing down his face.

He looked up to where she towered over him. "Imagine how hot this would have been without all that extra whipped cream."

Oompa gasped.

Beth stepped over the puddle of Derrick and moved to Oompa's side. He shivered, his face contorted. Beth crouched to look into his down-turned eyes. His eyebrows tilted up in the middle. Gripping the arms of his chair, he opened his mouth and howled.

"That's the—funniest—funniest thing I've—seen—in—a—" He gave up talking and, holding his ribs, let the howls take over again.

Her grandfather risked checking out of life by laughing too hard. Her new friend sat on the heart-pine floor in the middle of her store, leaking an expensive specialty coffee. What was there to do but eat cake?

She sipped her Double Dutch latte between bites, handed Derrick a wet washcloth and a roll of paper towels, and flipped the OPEN sign while the two men dove into conversation as deftly as Derrick dove into foamed coffee.

Ꮘ

"You know why that is, don't you?" Oompa held one arm across his chest as he scooted more upright in his chair.

Derrick felt the wince more than saw it. He should have backed off a little during CPR. Another apology wasn't likely to help matters, though. "No. Why, Mr. Schurmer?"

"To keep the farmers from overloading their hay wagons and the kids from riding on top of the pile." The older man's expression held the twinkle of joy reserved for discovering buried treasure. "The top of the Cedarburg covered bridge opening was squared off so farmers couldn't pile the hay too high and strain the weight limits on the bridge deck."

Derrick jotted the bit of trivia in his virtual notebook. His memory could only hold so much of the great material Oompa fed him like a full-blast fire hydrant. He'd have to sneak away to get this latest batch of stories keyed into his computer. Oh yeah, and bake something. He chanced a glance at Beth, who stood on tiptoes, broom in hand, poking in the general direction of a dark, Idaho-shaped spot in the ceiling. The full length of the broom left her inches shy of reaching the spot.

He excused himself from Oompa midstory, something about a hayride gone awry—*hay gone a' rye*—and crossed the room to where Beth's arm stretched heavenward.

"Can I help?" He reached to take the broom from her. It looked like an ordinary broom—standard, nonelectric model. Must have been static electricity in the air that caused the faint burst of voltage when his hand brushed hers in the exchange.

"I'd appreciate it," she said. "There's such a fine line between antique and old."

"I can *hear* you!" Oompa called from his corner.

Beth grinned. "Not you, Oompa. This building. I think the roof's leaking again."

Derrick brushed a drop of moisture from Beth's blushing cheek. "Either the roof is or you are."

Wrong thing to say. Another gaffe that needed redemption.

She turned away from him, shoulders tilted forward. While she scribbled something on a scrap of paper she'd pulled from a narrow drawer under the cash counter, he turned his attention to the ceiling. Two reserved taps to the Potato State sent the broom handle well past Idaho and on its way to the Balkan Islands. Chunks of damp plaster dandruff floated into his face, hair, head, and shoulders.

He spit one of the smaller flakes out of his mouth. "Tell me—"

Beth followed the trajectory of the plaster snowfall.

"Tell me," he repeated, "this isn't asbestos."

She hugged her arms across her midsection and pressed her left thumb against her closed lips. Her cheeks puffed as if that thumb were the mouthpiece of a trumpet. But the sound she produced was more like wind chimes dancing in a leaf-rattling breeze. Music and laughter in one sweet sound.

"There's a hole in your ceiling," Derrick reminded her.

More music. This time accompanied by a nose-kazoo snort.

"Derrick, you're—" Her sentence died in a choke.

She wouldn't stop breathing, would she? *Breathe, girl. My last attempt at CPR drew mixed reviews.*

Chapter 5

Everywhere she looked, Beth saw color. In the foreground, bright gold and burgundy mums spiked with trios of pumpkins perched against a midground of sandstone, buttermilk brick, and fieldstone buildings. The distant, layered background formed by yards and parks behind the buildings on Washington boasted flame, crimson, squash, paprika. The colors intensified in the saffron light of late afternoon. The air itself seemed to glow gold.

Autumn in Cedarburg. Half her childhood and now half a decade post-college, and she'd still never tire of its exceptional grace. So soon the transition would bring a dusting of snow, brittle ice edging the creek, bare branches, and the reminder of a long winter and the reason God invented wool.

She tipped her watering can over the Yarn Shop's window boxes of tenacious, frost-resistant marigolds, blue fire petunias, and nearly iridescent fuchsia geraniums. The vinca vines had barely peeked over the edge of the bright lavender boxes when planted in mid-May. Now they brushed the sidewalk—a decadent display.

Picture perfect.

She should get her—

Click.

—camera.

"That's magazine-cover worthy." Derrick seemed to admire the scene his camera's viewfinder offered him.

Beth fingered a velvety geranium petal. "They are, aren't they?"

"Oh. The flowers. Right. Yes. Done for the day?" he asked.

"This time of year, midweek, I'd rather close the shop a little early so I can catch up on projects before the next major event and pre-Christmas sales."

"Or. . ."

"Or what?"

Derrick gestured "out there somewhere" with his camera. "I haven't taken time to explore much of Cedarburg."

"You'll enjoy it. Have you been to the gristmill?"

"No."

"You can see it from here."

"Haven't been yet."

"You should stay at the mill until the lights come on. Impressive. The reflection of lights on the surface of Cedar Creek is inspiring."

Derrick's eyes looked as if they were already taking in the scene.

"I think the patio area is still open at the Anvil. They'll turn on the outdoor heaters for these cooler evenings. You might want to have an early dinner out there. With the woolen mill in the background and that elegant sweep of the creek right at your elbow and the food—can't go wrong."

"You'll show me?"

Beth set her watering can on the sidewalk near the shop's door. She pointed east from where they stood. "Gristmill." She pointed a couple of blocks north. "Cedar Creek Settlement

Shops and the Anvil Pub and Grill. You can't get lost. Can't miss the creek. It runs clear through town. Not always in a straight line. It wanders."

"Beth."

"What?"

"Will you go with me?"

"As in. . . ?"

"With. Me. Walking the town. Looking at the lights. Or the moon. Or both. Sharing dinner on a bistro patio beside the creek. Thinking about all the people—ancient and new—who make Cedarburg so unique." His eyes stopped wandering the surroundings and landed on her. "Watching the leaves turn."

Did he mean it as it sounded? Date-like?

A safer idea surfaced. "I know a couple of volunteers from the General Store Museum who give fascinating walking tours of the town. Both are Oompa's friends. They know all the little tidbits of trivia that make a tour interesting. Let me give one of them a call." She grabbed the door handle and thumbed the latch.

"No, thank you."

"You'll enjoy either one of them. Eli's so knowledgeable. He recently got engaged, so you may hear the story of his romance, too. And Charlie—"

Derrick palmed the door and kept it shut. "I'm sure they're great guys." He dipped his head toward hers. "But they're not you."

ଓ

Dumb. Dumb, dumb, dumb, dumb. Unsmooth. As cheesy as the fabulous Brie crepe he'd had at that crepe restaurant in the Settlement Shops two days after he arrived. What a great collection of old buildings—so rich with history, he could almost feel the fingerprints of Cedarburg's forefathers and foremothers in the handrails, sense their pleasure in how the old woolen mill buildings now housed such a variety of interests—vintage shops, artists, the candy shop, the high-end clothing shops for tourists and residents not satisfied with ordinary.

And how convenient of him to let his mind get distracted by a fancy cheese crepe so he didn't have to think about how his less-than-clever closing line drew a curtain over Beth's facial expression.

The delicate skin around her left eye twitched. She opened her mouth as if to speak then closed it. Opened it again. Took a deep breath then exhaled loud enough to pop the windscreen off a microphone. "Okay."

"Okay?"

"I'll take you around to a few places. But I'm taking my knitting, too." She entered the shop, grabbed the ever-present tapestry tote from behind the counter, and took one more glance at where Oompa sat with Sam Ulrich. "Every minute I'm not watching out for Oompa or customers or trying to balance the books and dodge plaster crumbs, I have to work on moebiuses, moebii, moebe—infinity scarves."

"You are obsessed, aren't you. I've heard that about knitters."

"Excuse me?"

Derrick flinched. "Devoted. That's a better word. One would think I'd be more agile with words."

Beth scrunched her face, as if deciding whether to erupt or let it go. Her facial features calmed. Bless her.

"I'm not a knitter." She pulled the door inward and walked into the shiny brass afternoon.

ᴄᴕ

Derrick's footsteps sounded inches behind her, rather than the few feet that would give him enough lead time in case she stopped suddenly. Beth walked at a good clip until she heard him say—loudly enough for all five blocks of Cedarburg's historic downtown district to hear—"Not a knitter?"

She turned to face him, hoping the angle of her head communicated, "Do you mind if I. . .Would you hold it down back there?" A quick glance at passersby showed no one seemed interested in his reaction.

A quartet of retired schoolteachers. She could always tell—they wore little red schoolhouse, ruler, and alphabet sweaters and seemed deliriously happy it was a school day and they were shopping—turned sideways to pass Beth and Derrick. From the other direction, two young moms pushed jogging strollers with cherub children whose outfits probably cost more than Beth's entire wardrobe. Eli and his Claire waved from across the street but made no indication they'd heard Derrick's comment. Beth watched Eli bend to catch something Claire said then break into an expression that looked like a face rumba.

Something tugged at her. Derrick. He held an edge of the robin's egg moebius wrapped around her neck. "You made this, didn't you?"

The way his fingers respected the wool rather than mangled it impressed her, as if he were protective of it. Or protective of her.

"You know I did."

"And you're not a knitter."

"It's not that I *can't* knit."

"Obviously."

"I thought you wanted a tour of the town. The light is perfect. The weather's ideal. There's a lot to see. Let's start at the Settlement Shops in the old woolen mill on the north end of the shopping district. History and charm combined. I'm sure Oompa's told you some of the stories."

Derrick fell into step beside her. His lack of response either meant he was deep in thought or thought little of her lack of response. She'd talk architecture and buildings made of Milwaukee Cream City bricks or limestone slabs and the plethora of historic landmarks and Cedarburg's reputation as a haven for artists and the culturally inclined. Any subject was safer than the inner workings of Beth Schurmer and her too loosely knit life.

"Notice the displays of pumpkins? All from area farms. In the winter, you'll see creative ice sculptures in their place. In summer, profusions of flowers. This downtown district likes to dress up."

Derrick pulled a small leather journal from the pocket of his Columbia vest. His pen scritched as they walked.

A young couple clogged a narrow part of the sidewalk ahead. The pair—Seth and the choir director—refused to stop holding hands. They were, after all, a couple. So Derrick and Beth stepped onto the grass to let them pass.

Beth felt her cheeks warming. The sun showed it still possessed oomph this late in the year. The air hinted at icicles gearing up for their turn, but autumn in Wisconsin showed every petticoat of interest and would once again refuse to stop twirling until the chairs were turned upside down on the tabletops of the season.

Beth slowed her pace. She hadn't soaked in the charm for a long time. She'd only taken quick showers rather than a long, soaking bath in which she could feel every bubble of Cedarburg's effervescence.

Whap! Python thick, a low-hanging branch whacked Derrick across the forehead. He ducked, too late, while the branch rebounded into place.

"Derrick, are you okay?"

He touched the welt tenderly. "Ouch."

"Oh ye of quick reaction time."

"I can see you're broken up over my pain."

"No offense."

"None taken."

"Since I'm decidedly shorter than a refrigerator, I can't imagine living in danger of getting clotheslined by a tree." *Stifle the smile, Beth. Totally inappropriate.*

"And I can't imagine going through life unaware of the dust on top of the refrigerator. You should see me in a ceiling fan store. Saves on trips to the barber shop, I must say."

Derrick's forehead welt formed a capital L. How unfortunate. His comfort with his discomfort was something to admire. If Derrick offered tutoring, she'd probably be smart to sign up.

☙

"Could we eat on the patio?" Derrick's eagerness seemed all the more boyish with that red L on his forehead.

"I believe I suggested it. Right along the creek. One of the best views in town."

A young woman with perfect, satiny chestnut hair, perfect bisque skin, and perfect cocoa bean eyes handed them each a menu as they settled themselves into the wrought iron chairs at the table for two, creekside.

"Nice," Derrick said as the woman left the table.

Beth looked up from the paragraph about her favorite Greek salad, ready to toss pepper in his eyes, when he added, "The way the sun filters through the trees here. It adds even more colors to your hair."

My hair? Did you miss the future Alice in Dairyland or Miss Universe or at the very least the cover girl for the next Cedarburg Chamber of Commerce publication? "Some people think it's a little 'out there.'"

"It's perfect for you."

What word did he use? Perfect? The man's delusional. Must have been the bump on the head. "Thanks."

"You look like my dog."

Derrick Hofferman. Even God won't give you grace to cover that one.

"I mean, my dog is. . .she's a mutt, yes, but. . ."

"A mutt?"

Derrick paused long enough to gulp the hot cider just delivered.

Beth watched his eyes widen. Surprise, surprise. The cider was hot. Tongue-scalding hot. Word-warping hot.

His mug landed on the tabletop with a clunk. "Thee's justh the mosth adorable little puppy you've ever theen."

Beth pushed her untouched glass of ice water toward him.

"Thanksth."

She vowed not to mock an injured man, no matter how comical.

"I have a picthure of her." He dug in his pants pocket and produced his cell phone. "You'll thee. Thee lookth juth like you. I mean. . ."

Beth snatched the phone from His Bumblingness. There on the screen was the canine version of her.

ଔ

“Petite. Like you.”

Beth must have noticed his intentional avoidance of words with an *S*.

“Beautiful fur. Blond and caramel and brown thugar.” Oopth.

“She’s a cute dog. I’m. . .honored you see a resemblance between us.”

Derrick rested his elbows on the table and let his head drop into his hands. Big mistake. The odd-shaped goose egg on his forehead burned.

“Here.” Beth offered her glass of ice water again. He held the glass lightly against the abrasion. The coolness soothed almost as much as the gracefulness of her action compared to the clumsiness of his words.

“I’ve been called a dog before.” Her fingers traced the pattern in the wrought iron scrollwork of the outdoor table.

She glanced over the quiet water of Cedar Creek.

An artist stood on the far bank, the legs of his easel driven into the leaf-strewn lawn in front of the Ozaukee County Arts building. The artist’s high-collared sweater swallowed his neck when he reached to add another stroke to the canvas.

Derrick noted that the artist held up his brush handle against a distant view to gain perspective, just like in the movies. He watched the artist work, fascinated by his *stroke-stroke-stroke-gain perspective-stroke-stroke-stroke-gain perspective* rhythm.

Could Derrick keep a grip on the big picture that way? Here he was, sitting across the table from a woman he found increasingly difficult to deceive.

“I may have a *thcalded* tongue,” he said, exaggerating the lisp no longer necessary, "but my ears work."

"What?" Beth kept her gaze on a trio of leaves chasing each other on the surface of Cedar Creek, riding an unseen current toward the sudden drop a few feet from where they sat. The rush of water over the spillway competed with the light jazz coming from speakers hidden in potted mums.

"Your dog story?"

She fiddled with a corner of her napkin then snapped it open and laid it across her lap. "Oh, you know. Everyone has a sappy story about falling for the wrong person in high school."

"You fell for a dog?"

She flinched. "No. I fell for a jock. He called me a dog to his friends. Behind my back. To the whole school."

"Ouch."

"I was the joke that never failed to get a laugh, the story that came up at every party."

She said it as if it didn't matter anymore. But her eyes reflected something as surely as Cedar Creek reflected the golds and greens along its banks.

☙

"What a cute little dog!" the cover girl waitress said when she delivered their meals. She picked up Derrick's phone. "Do you mind?"

Beth watched Derrick nod that the girl was welcome to admire the photo.

"I love that fringe of bangs over its eyes."

"Her. *Her* eyes." His apple cider scald must have diminished.

Sleek-and-slim smiled. "What's her name?"

Derrick grew an instant sunburn.

An opportunity too good to pass up. Beth prodded. "You

never did say. Her name?"

Whatever he uttered in response started and faded so quickly it seemed a sound only canines could hear.

"What is it?" both women asked in unison.

"Her name's Cuddles."

The two women shared an unexpected moment of connection. Beth wasn't alone in wondering how a guy that tall and that much a guy would purchase a palm-sized puppy and then have the courage to name it Cuddles.

"Well," Sleek said, "that's a pretty successful conversation starter, I'd say. Hey!" She glanced at the phone in her hand and then at Beth. "You two. . .um. . ."

"Yeah. I know. We look a lot alike." *What's a 15 percent tip minus 15 percent?*

The waitress left them to their meals—Derrick's three-cheese burger and Beth's Greek salad. She took the onions he didn't want and he took half her feta, making his a four-cheese burger.

"So," he said, "my dog's name is Cuddles and I miss her."

"Oh. She's. . .departed?"

"Yesterday about nine."

"Your dog died yesterday?"

"Died? No! She departed. On the plane out of General Mitchell. I thought I could run the business and do what else I need to do here while still taking care of her. But, my landlady has a no pet policy, thus no Cuddles. So that sweet dog had to go live with Crazy Aunt Alice in St. Thomas for a while."

Beth set her fork on the edge of her plate. He sent his homeless dog to live with a crazy woman? And the dog flew there? "St. Thomas in the Virgin Islands?" How many connecting flights must that have taken?

"St. Thomas as in the St. Thomas Home for the Perpetually Perplexed. My cousin Tom takes in lovable logic-challenged strays like my great-aunt Alice. Animals, too, sometimes. He comes by the saint nickname honestly, if not papally."

Right there on the banks of Cedar Creek, with too much to do and too much owed, with Oompa's exhales speaking more of heaven every day, with promises unfulfilled and dreams all but abandoned, Beth knew she was blessed. The L on Derrick's forehead stood for laughter.

Chapter 6

History oozed up through the century-and-a-half-smoothed floorboards of the Woolen Mill shops. Pottery stores, gift shops, quirky businesses he wouldn't have noticed if Beth hadn't pointed them out. Others he didn't dare tell her he'd seen before. They lingered for a few extra minutes in a gift shop that played a mutually favorite Chris Tomlin song as background music. They climbed creaky stairs to each level, Beth noting with delight a new business already buzzing with preholiday shoppers in a once empty storefront. She paused at the shop's display of child-sized but sophisticated furniture with high class artwork on the chair backs and headboards.

"Aren't these beautiful?" Her voice had a dreamy quality to it, like pictures drawn in latte foam.

"Did you see the price tag?"

"Can't you picture a table like this with a set of chairs, in lime and plum—oh yes!—as the centerpiece of a shop that sells—?"

She broke off the conversation, halting it with the startle of reverse thrusters on a jet.

"That sells. . . ?"

"I'll come back here sometime when we're not on such a tight schedule."

Derrick, my boy, you have some good qualities. Why is buffoon your dominant trait? If I press her for a direct answer, she may reveal something useful. On the other hand, the question itself might close her down again. We'll be back to talking about pumpkins and bittersweet vines. Bittersweet. There's a connection there, Lord. Isn't there? Something bittersweet holds her from living full-out.

"We have a lot of ground to cover, Derrick. You can keep staring at the 'fur' on my head or we can cross the street to the mural montage on the corner. The heart of Cedarburg captured in one painting. Most of it, anyway."

Derrick followed her down the steps, into the breathtakingly fine autumn air, and across the street to the massive mural that, although stunning, surely missed at least a part of Cedarburg's heart, the one that beat in the woman he trailed.

☙

Beth did her best to retrace the path of the official historic buildings walking tour, pointing out facts she thought might interest someone like Derrick Hofferman. He seemed charmed by everything, taking notes as they walked, which added an occasional point of interest as he discovered the rare uneven spot in the sidewalks.

When a cool breeze kicked up, she undid one of the loops in the robin's egg moebius, let it hang to her waist, and tucked her hands into the soft wool's self-formed pocket.

"That's amazing," he said.

"What?" She glanced around at the vine-covered historic log home on their left, the stone cottage across the street, the flaming maples and muted oaks arching overhead.

"That." He pointed to the moebius.

"The concept has been around for centuries."

"It seems so simple but has so many hidden reasons for being. Like a lot of us, I guess."

Derrick, who are you? And how did a brownie connoisseur from—where's he from?—end up practically next door to mess with my cholesterol and other things related to heart function?

He bent to focus on jotting something in his notebook.

"Can I see what you just wrote?"

His eyes widened like hers must have when she first stood with her nose pressed against the front window of Life by Chocolate. "It's nothing significant."

She took the journal from him. One question filled the page: *She's not a knitter???*

With three question marks at the end.

She flipped to the next clean page, held out her hand for Derrick's pen—*ooh, nice pen*—and wrote a response. She closed the notebook and handed it and the pen to him then resumed her tour guide speech about the wrought iron and picket fences that hemmed so many of the Cedarburg properties. She smiled as she walked and talked, imagining Derrick flipping pages a step or two behind her, looking for the spot where she'd written, *No. And I imagine you don't intend to bake brownies for the rest of your life, do you? No offense to their magnificence.*

He caught up with her two houses later. In one quick move, he wrapped an arm around her shoulders and squeezed. "None taken."

ᘓ

Rooflines and cornerstones, the General Store Museum and the museums-within-the-museum tributes to bygone eras, a quick walk through the latest Cultural Center exhibit—stunning watercolors by an artist Beth said she didn't know but felt she did, a glance through innumerable shop windows, through the narrow panes of the stories-to-tell Stagecoach Inn, an anecdote or two about the Rivoli Theatre and its community effort restoration, some of which he already knew from Mr. Schurmer, and they were back at their starting point.

With one minor difference.

A note on the door of the Yarn Shop read:

Beth, we locked up and took your grandpa to the ER in Mequon. Oh, and the power's out in the shop. No telling why.

Beth's eyes darted. She pointed to him. "You. Can you drive me there? Wait. No. Then you'd be stuck at the hospital, too." She shivered. "I'll call—"

"Where's your car?"

"At Herman's Repair. It spends a lot of time at Herman's. Could we stick with the current crisis?"

"My car's around the corner. I'll drive. You navigate."

"But—"

"Nothing matters more than getting there. We'll worry about the next step later."

She headed toward where he pointed and said, "How about if I just keep my worry file open for frequent updates?"

When a woman could maintain a fingerhold on humor even in the midst of raging panic, that was a good sign. The two bolted around the corner as if training for a Lake Michigan marathon. She sprinted past his lime-green Escalade—a reminder that some bargains just plain aren't.

He waved her back. "Here. Let me get the door for you."

Beth climbed into the passenger seat. "The Realtor lets you

park in the driveway of my dream cottage?"

Derrick didn't have to answer. The way she winced, she must have seen the dog dish on the front porch, the one with Cuddles written in white enamel.

While Derrick clicked his seat belt and turned the key in the ignition, she held her arms toward the admittedly storybook cottage with its hand-chiseled stonework and sweet little porch.

"You bought *my* someday house?"

ꟹ

"Renting. I'm renting. . .temporarily. Hence the landlady with the 'no pets allowed' rule." Derrick pulled to the stop sign on Washington. "Now what?"

Beth's insides twisted. "Well, I have to tolerate you at least until you drop me off at St. Mary's Ozaukee."

"I mean, left or right? Which way do I turn?"

"Right."

"How far?"

"It'll seem like forever. But it's just a minute to Lakefield Road." Beth pulled her cell phone from the outside pocket of her knitting tote. Who was she going to call? Everybody she cared about was either in a hospital bed or in the car beside her and where did she get that crazy idea? She could dial St. Mary's, but she and Derrick would be there before the operator could forward her to the person with information she needed. She repocketed the cell phone and turned to her driver.

"Sorry I was short with you back there. I've always dreamed about that cottage and wondered what it would be like to—" She swallowed the sentence's conclusion.

"You're always short with me. In fact, since I'm a hairbreadth under seven feet tall, pretty much the whole world is short with me."

"You know what I mean, but thanks for not taking it personally. I love my Oompa more than I can express. I shouldn't have—"

Derrick shot her a look. "Resist that thought."

Greek salad bubbled somewhere in her esophagus.

"No should have, shouldn't haves, Elizabeth."

"My name's not Elizabeth. And I should not have left Oompa alone for so long."

"There's a traffic light and an *H* in a square blue sign."

"Oh! Turn here! Left here!"

"Now how far?"

"A ways. It'll look as if we're driving through farmland, but these suburbs of Milwaukee are linked like a pop bead necklace with barns for spacers."

She watched Derrick press his torso deeper into the leather seat.

"You didn't leave him alone, Beth. He was with his friends, very capable friends, it turns out. They recognized something was wrong and got him help. Exactly as you would have."

"If I hadn't been out pretending I had no responsibilities. Kicking at fall leaves and skipping around town as if—"

"As if it were a sterling day and it felt good not to worry about anything for a couple of hours. As if you deserved to be admired by someone other than—" He cleared his throat. "What I mean is that I enjoyed being with you, and it wouldn't have mattered if we were touring this amazing little town or rewiring your shop or dipping brownies in hot fudge fondue."

"You do that?"

"The point is that your grandfather wouldn't want you to

stop living your life while you're trying to help prolong his."

"Right."

"You agree with me? Will wonders never cease?"

"No, turn right! Port Washington Road. St. Mary's is that building down the way with the green glass windows and my dying grandfather inside."

ଓ

"More tea?"

"No. Thanks, Derrick."

"Anything else I can do?"

"You can go home. It sounds as if it will be a while before we know anything."

"All the more reason for me to stay."

Beth attempted a smile. "It must be close to midnight."

Derrick checked his watch. "Nine thirty. We ate a long time ago, Bethany."

She quirked an eyebrow at him. "It's not Bethany, either. Quit digging. And please, go get yourself something to eat."

"I'm on a hunger strike."

"What?"

"It's a matter of principle. I'll only eat if you do."

She sighed. "Clever. Well, I'd hate to see you have to skip a snack, so if you don't mind bringing me an apple or something?"

"Meat. I bring meat. Real men bring meat. Or pizza."

"Nice caveman impersonation." Beth sighed again and leaned her head against the back of the chair in the cardiology waiting room.

Derrick laid his hand on hers. The knitting needles, long silent, clicked together under his grip. "I hereby apologize for any time I choose humor when that's the opposite of what you need. Past, present, and future. One giganto apology."

"Derrick."

"And please know that even when I'm not praying aloud for your Oompa, I'm always praying."

"Derrick."

"If that makes you uncomfortable, you can say so. But you have to know that I'm a hundred percent certain of only a few things in life. How to temper chocolate, why it's not always wise to listen to a car salesman hawking a lime-green Escalade—glows in the dark? And how often will I need that feature?—and the most important one, that God cares about what you're going through."

"I agree, except for tempering chocolate. You're the resident expert there. But Derrick?"

"Yes?"

She laid her hand over his and leaned toward him. "You made me drop a stitch!"

☙

Beth caught the dropped stitch and tore off again at her normal illusionist's speed. What did people do with their worry if they didn't knit? Bite their nails. Shred facial tissues. Sculpt ulcers. Drink copious amounts of—

"Family of Oliver Schurmer?"

Beth tripped over her tote bag in her haste to jump to her feet. "That's me! That is I. I am her. I'm she. I'm Beth Schurmer. His granddaughter. How is he?"

"Recovering well, all things considered. His doctor will have more details for you soon."

"Good. Can I see my grandfather now?"

The nurse raised her overtweezed eyebrows and stole a

quick look at the electronic chart in her hand. "Mr. Schurmer specifically asked to see Derrick. . .Derrick Hoffman?"

"Hofferman."

When had Derrick glued himself to her side? And what was Oompa thinking? Derrick Hofferman hadn't knitted himself three infinities from the worry side of love.

"I think he probably would prefer to see his granddaughter first. I'm just. . .a friend."

I can defend myself, Derrick. Don't go all noble on me. Oh, how incredibly selfish! Oompa has earned the right to request whoever he wants to see first.

"Beth?"

"What?"

"You go ahead. You need to see him. He might be a little, you know, *off* because of the anesthesia or something."

The nurse—maybe a nursing student a few credits short of her degree because of spending too much classroom time plucking eyebrow hairs—slid her weight onto her left hip and said, "Just a few minutes initially, Mr. Hofferman." She looked at Beth and, except for those disturbing brows, seemed genuinely sympathetic. "Then you'll have your turn, Ms. Schurmer."

Yes, let's all share, children. Lord, You don't even have to tell me I'm going to need to apologize to You for that.

ꕤ

Half a moebius later, Derrick emerged through the double doors separating Beth from the world that *wasn't* in solitary confinement like she was. He was engaged in conversation with a thirty-something Michael W. Smith look-alike in scrubs.

Had Derrick been crying? His face was pinched into folds that resembled a pumpkin a week beyond its prime.

MWS-in-scrubs continued a midstream conversation. "So the guy hands me the keys to his Buick and says, 'Do you take Medi-car?"

Real funny, guys.

Derrick caught Beth's gaze and stifled his laughter. "Beth, your grandfather's doing real well. Not a false alarm, exactly, but. . ."

Hope rose, but it might even blossom if she heard something positive from a real doctor's lips.

"He's right. Mr. Schurmer came through the procedure with few complications, considering his weakened condition because of the recent heart episode."

Beth flinched at the memory and the sense of pending doom linked to those words.

"But," the doctor added, "as we've known for a few days now, his heart function is compromised. We were able to open one blockage with a stent. He has a couple of other minor blockages. His main issue right now is the atrial valve. Combined with the damage done by the infarction. . ."

She should have been searching the medical sites on the Internet instead of knitting. Why hadn't she thought to collect a little knowledge that might serve useful in Oompa's care, other than the salt restrictions she had yet to master?

"So, that means surgery?"

Derrick and Dr. Medi-car exchanged glances.

Derrick stepped to Beth's side and put his arm around her.

The doctor softened his facial expression. "Your grandfather would be high risk at best, Ms. Schurmer. Not a strong candidate for surgery, even if he was agreeable to the idea. He's not."

"I don't understand. This is the twenty-first century. There's always something to try." Beth knew her voice sounded strained.

The once empty waiting room grew in population. A family of six entered, huddled en masse like a swarm of bees or those shiny silver fish that swim together in a ball shape to protect themselves from predators.

The doctor motioned Beth toward the private consultation room. The scene was all too familiar. She followed him, Derrick at her side, hope dribbling behind like leaking radiator fluid.

ଓ

"He wants to die?"

Derrick and the doctor each put a hand on one of Beth's knees as the three sat in a semicircle in the small consult room. Dr. Medi spoke. "It's not that he wants to die, Beth. But he will, one way or another. Yes, there are other procedures we can try. But in your grandfather's case, with the growing list of complications and a few underlying conditions he's apparently been keeping from all of us, including his primary care physician with whom I spoke a few minutes ago, those procedures would have a better chance of hastening that moment than postponing it."

"What could I have done differently with his care?"

Derrick watched as Beth's tears trickled a pained acceptance.

"Nothing. From what I've heard, the love and honor you've shown him probably gave him more time than we could measure."

Beth looked from the doctor to Derrick, as if puzzling how this unknown medical practitioner would know anything at all about their relationship.

Derrick angled closer. "I told Dr. Mason a little of what you've meant to your grandfather."

"It's what he's meant to me! Oh, Oompa." She leaned

against Derrick's bicep. "I'll need—" Her voice caught. "I'll need a minute to get used to the idea."

Dr. Mason left the two of them alone in the room.

She's stronger than she looks. Her heart must be breaking. "Beth, he's not afraid to die."

"I know. It's been his life's goal." She shot him a brief, half-formed smile. "Oompa loves this life and has squeezed more joy out of it than most. But he talks about heaven as if he's been planning this trip for a long time and can't wait for the boarding call."

"You'll be okay, Beth."

Her eyes scanned the ceiling. "The God who made Oompa comfortable with the idea of saying good-bye to this life for the joy of eternity is the same One who will hold and love me when he's gone. I know that in theory. I guess it's time to put it into practice."

Beth, I hope you give me the opportunity to get to know you. There's so much more to you than anyone sees on the surface.

She bent to the floor and picked up her wool and needles.

"You're knitting? Now?"

Her fingers followed the edge of one of her finished projects. "No. I'm reminding myself of the mystery of eternity." She traced the moebius in its beautifully confounding, seamless, no beginning and no ending shape. Infinity. "Before long, Oompa will discover—like my parents and Grandma before him—what a wonder it really is."

Chapter 7

October put up a fight but finally acquiesced to November's insistence. Beth stuffed wool batting along the windowsills in the apartment behind the shop to discourage drafts. Out came the quilts, sweaters, turtlenecks, and mittens. She tucked lap robes around Oompa whether he liked it or not. He seldom resisted and always responded, "Dear child."

The stories continued, fragile and breathless. Home health care services brought in a portable oxygen machine with tubing Oompa called his licorice whips.

Cedarburg kept humming with concerts and contests, art events, and the stuff of living. Derrick hired more help for Life by Chocolate. He wouldn't say, but Beth suspected it was so he could spend more time ping-ponging between Oompa's need for a listening ear and hers.

Beth had always wished for a fast-forward she could use to skip most of November and get right to December. Not this year. She savored even the gray days, their solemn brusqueness a reminder that sometimes life is hard and cold and sends shivers through any remaining leaves, any remaining life.

It took a week or two of Oompa's coaxing and Derrick's coaching for Beth to turn her focus from the physical distress her grandfather now felt or would soon experience to the celebration of each moment they had together. The "together" more often than not meant all three.

"Just say the word and I'll back off," Derrick told her one late afternoon when holiday customers were oddly scarce in both shops. "I know this is between the two of you. Your grandfather means a lot to me, too."

"He has that effect on people."

"But I don't have a right to impose myself onto the picture. That's worse than a second cousin twice removed trying to horn in on the family photo." His eyes, still tea colored, couldn't hide their liquid sympathy.

"It's not my call. It's not even Oompa's call. It's God's call. Oompa loves that he can talk to you freely about heaven and his faith without you backing away from even the tough subjects. And I don't know what I'd do without y—"

No. Unfair. Unwise. And unhealthy for her heart. He was a good friend and neighbor willing to help out in a crisis. Oompa deserved her full attention. That's what he'd get.

C3

"I need to get out to the covered bridge one more time."

Beth took a moment to process Oompa's ridiculous request. Her irreverent high school friends would have responded, "Fat chance." She said, "No."

"Yes."

"It's hard enough for you to walk the six-foot hallway from the apartment to the shop. We'll get out Grandma's photo albums later this afternoon, okay? You two took lots of pictures out by that bridge."

"And that's where I met my Joy."

Joy? Grandma's name was AnnaMay.

"She and I had some sweet moments together in that park by the covered bridge."

Beth rose and smoothed the quilt where she'd sat on the edge of Oompa's bed. If only she could smooth her emotions as easily. Who was Joy? And why was her Oompa, a happily married man—meeting some woman for "sweet" moments? It couldn't have been while Grandma was still alive. Not her Oompa.

Who did Beth know in Cedarburg named Joy? Joy Werlitzer? Oompa and Mrs. Werlitzer? Impossible!

Oompa coughed. "Are you going to stand there all day staring at the cobwebs? Or should we get to the shop and see who wanders in needing a little encouragement?"

Lord, do I want to be here if Oompa starts talking out of his head, spilling secrets better left buried?

ଔ

"Try this," Derrick said, extending a plate decked with a thick, round, decadent disk of what looked like a cross-section of a tree. "*Buche de noel.* I'm offering them for the holidays only. See what you think of this."

He forked a generous sample and stuck it too near her mouth to ignore. It smelled divine and melted into wonderfulness as soon as it hit her tongue. "Oh, that's good."

"How's the ratio of pastry cream to cake?"

"You're asking me, the noncook?"

"Asking you, the best taste tester Cedarburg has to offer. And the one whose opinion I most value."

Derrick's attention was so much less irritating than she'd once found it. But something wasn't quite right. His relationship with Oompa had taken on a conspiratorial air. They whispered, and it wasn't just because her grandfather's voice grew weaker by the day. "Speaking of opinions. . ."

With a second fork, Derrick made his own taste comparison. "Could use more vanilla. Ooh! Or almond. No, you have to be careful with almond flavoring. It can get medicinal."

"Which brings us back to what I was trying to ask."

"And maybe a white chocolate drizzle. Just a touch."

"Derrick!" She took the plate from him.

"Hey, don't get greedy. I have more, if you're that desperate."

She handed him the plate and leaned against the cash counter. "I'm desperate for some answers."

Derrick captured crumbs with the back of his fork. "About what?"

With suspicion and incredulity fighting for a chance to speak, Beth eventually said, "Do you know about Joy?"

"Sure."

"You've heard Oompa talk about meeting Joy out at the covered bridge?"

His fork continued to chase fudgy crumbs. "Lots of times."

"And you didn't find that disturbing?"

The customer restroom door creaked open. Oompa was back in hearing range.

"Find what disturbing?" Pushing and leaning on the pull cart that held his oxygen tank, Oompa crossed the room to his rocker. "Oh, child?"

"What is it?"

"I left my reading glasses on the sink in the lavatory. Would you be a dear and—"

"Of course."

She left the men to search the powder room.

No reading glasses. Not on the sink. Not on the back of the tank. She checked the floor, behind the door, on the hook on the wall. Nothing.

When she turned the corner into the body of the shop, she caught Derrick and Oompa deep in conversation, Oompa's glasses perched pertly on his nose.

"Guess they were right here beside my chair," he said. "Good news, though. Your Derrick's come up with the perfect solution."

Quit calling him "my" Derrick, please. He's more yours than mine, for one thing. And for another, I'm beginning to wonder if I have time or energy for either one of you, much less both!

A muscle in her heart twisted.

Time. So little of it left.

Grace. So much of it needed.

"What solution, Oompa?"

"A wheelchair! Why didn't we think of that sooner? Beth, you can wheel me out to the covered bridge. Or a *motorized* wheelchair!" Oompa's plea gained momentum. "I could zoom on down to Herman's and see if his showroom floor is still cleaner than a Lysol convention."

Derrick stepped forward and settled into "his" chair. "How about if we take this one excursion at a time?"

A trio of customers looking for Christmas stocking patterns occupied the next few minutes. Would it be fair to pray for a steady stream of customers from now until Oompa came to his senses?

Holding out his cell phone, Derrick approached. "I have to get back to the store. I'm working on a Thanksgiving brownie with a mocha tuille on top. But here's a number you can call if you want to rent a wheelchair. I'd be happy to pick it up in the Escalade."

Sometimes there's a fine line between accommodating and enabling. Given the circumstances, did she have a choice?

ଓ

The medical rental supply company delivered the wheelchair—a jim-dandy, according to Oompa—the next morning, which was an exceptionally warm day for late November. They test-drove it down the block, Oompa smiling and waving like the grand marshal of a parade. His oxygen tank fit into a clip on the back of the chair. Beth had no excuse but to take the next step—see if it would fit into Derrick's glow-in-the-dark SUV.

It did.

Step two. Could they get Oompa hoisted into the passenger seat?

Derrick pulled a footstool from behind the second seat. It looked like an unpainted version of one she'd seen in that new children's furniture shop in the Settlement. Oompa demonstrated how *easy* that made it for him to climb in and out of the SUV.

Step three. Just do it.

When Derrick insisted on driving and helping with the logistics of getting an old man out of town to an even older bridge, Beth didn't object. She needed all the help she could get. Both emotionally and physically.

She had reluctance to spare, but who was she to deny him a simple joy?

Joy. He'd met the mysterious Joy there on the bridge. Okay, Beth had to admit curiosity served as another motivator.

The leafless trees they passed stood stark against the November sky, like dark veins in marble. The hills seemed eager for a covering of snow. It would come all too soon. At least a dusting by the weekend, the weatherman predicted. Was she ready for the next season?

"Ready?" Derrick rested his hand on her shoulder as he drove but spoke to the passenger in the backseat. She turned to catch her grandfather's reaction, trying hard to ignore the scent of Derrick's unusual aftershave—something between lime and sweet basil.

"Been waiting a lifetime," Oompa said, a smile spreading like warm chocolate.

The county highway, once lined with an occasional farm, now boasted developments of high-end homes among the ancient. New families among the old. New hopes replacing the retired. New seasons.

They topped the final hill and headed down toward the sight that never failed to move her—the long-abandoned covered bridge. Traffic bypassed the bridge with one made of steel and concrete. But a few feet away, standing sentry over the history of the area, over the stories lodged in tree trunks and behind rocks and in the crystal waters of Cedar Creek, was the swaybacked, unpainted, unassuming Cedarburg Covered Bridge. Still standing. Retired from its original use, it still inspired admirers.

What was that sensation stealing her worry? She almost laughed out loud over not recognizing it right away. Peace.

Oompa would be okay, one way or another. And so would she.

cs

Derrick signaled and turned off the county road onto Covered Bridge Park Drive. He drove even slower than necessary, allowing his passengers to drink in everything that made the scene a favorite of photographers and romantics.

He'd seen the park dressed more colorfully just a few weeks ago when he and Beth picnicked in parkas. The chill in the air had worked hard to defy the fireplace flame colors of the autumn leaves. Beth pronounced his latest creation—Chocolate-Covered Donut Brownie—a hit. The colors of the trees sparkled in her glacial blue eyes that day as they talked about things that mattered. Their faith. His appreciation of her.

Derrick now pulled the vehicle to a stop in front of the exercise-ball-sized boulders that bordered the parking area. The arched walking bridge lay to their right, the covered bridge to their left, Cedar Creek in front of them, moving left to right. He exited the Escalade and ran around the back to open Beth's door, then Oompa's, but warned him to stay put until he extricated the wheelchair.

Beth looped a nubby moebius—he'd never get that pronunciation right—around her neck and pulled gloves over her hands before adjusting the oxygen tank onto the back of the chair and draping the tubing over one handle to keep it from getting run over by the chair's wheels or, Derrick assumed, his size fourteen feet.

While Beth guided the operation, Derrick lifted Oompa out of the Escalade and into the waiting chair.

With a quilt wrapped around his legs and a wool scarf around his head and neck, Oompa looked like a toddler bundled up for his first toboggan ride, except for the oxygen tubing peeking out of the scarf wrap.

Brakes disengaged, Derrick pushed the chair forward. "Where to first?"

"Walking bridge, please." Oompa's teeth chattered, more from the bumpy terrain than from the cold.

Derrick caught Beth's gaze. Those compassionate eyes said, "Whatever he wants."

They hung a right. The approach to the arched walking bridge challenged them with end-of-season long grass and cold-crisp leaves. The uneven ground kept Derrick focused on maintaining at least two of the three of them upright. Beth was on her own.

Why did that thought make his throat tighten? More than capable on her own, she stirred in him a longing to be there for her so she wouldn't have to be.

Oompa said little as they pushed on toward the walking bridge. The wheels seemed relieved when they hit the wooden surface and the more rhythmic jostles of the planks. In the middle of the bridge, Derrick turned the wheelchair to face upstream, toward the site of the covered bridge.

"Quite a sight, isn't it?" Oompa's voice registered just a few decibels higher than the sound of the creek gurgling over rocks and hustling toward town. "The last standing original covered bridge in Wisconsin."

Ever the intruder, Derrick was about to step away for a moment when Oompa turned to him and said, "Son, I need a little time with my granddaughter."

"Sure." Derrick locked the brakes and tapped the gauge on the oxygen tank, as if he knew what he was doing. "I'll be over—I'll just—I think I'll—"

"Skip rocks?" Beth volunteered.

"Good idea." He left them and followed the edge of the creek downstream, away from their line of sight. The water fascinated him, but a piece of his heart stayed rooted on the footbridge, wishing it could wrap its arms around the two who remained there.

Chapter 8

"Are you warm enough, Oompa?"

"Cozy as a truffle tucked inside a pocket of cream cheese tucked inside a mound of Double Fudge Delight."

Beth chuckled. "A brownie metaphor? You've been hanging around Derrick too much."

His slight shoulders, padded as they were by the heavy coat she'd insisted he wear, rose then sank lower than before. "Maybe not enough, child. Not enough."

A squirrel rustled leaves nearby, digging for treasure buried beneath their covering.Oompa sat back in the wheelchair. "I wish I'd had the opportunity to get to know him better."

Beth's chest tightened. "He's not going anywhere."

He lifted her hand to his lips and planted a grandfatherly kiss that she felt through her glove. "But I am."

"No pessimistic talk today." She turned her back to the covered bridge and leaned against the modern version's safety railing. "Happy thoughts. Happy thoughts."

"Beth, why would you think talk about heaven is pessimistic? Isn't that the most optimistic thing a person's mind can dwell on?"

He'd put her in her place more than once when she needed it.

"The closer I get, I can almost smell it. I get a whiff of

something that I know isn't blooming now, something like jasmine or. . . What was that fragrance your grandmother always wore?"

"Honeysuckle. Avon."

His head tipped back. "Honeysuckle. Can you smell it?"

Beth closed her eyes. She smelled wool and old leaves and earthiness. How she'd love to take a deep breath of Grandma Schurmer's wide, honeysuckle-scented shoulder, the one she'd often leaned on when life stunk. Maybe Oompa could smell that now, but Beth was still too earthbound.

"Child, things are about to happen."

Beth's heart tumbled. She knelt beside him and gripped the arms of the wheelchair. "Are you okay? Should we get you back to the car? Derrick!"

Oompa frowned and shushed her. "Not this minute. Soon. Good things. Like with the shop."

How could she tell him that when he was gone, she wasn't sure she could keep up the mortgage on the building, much less keep it upright? The repairs and renovations it needed were too much for her. A great old building like that—a great old man like him—and she was helpless to resurrect either one.

She did smell something now. A combination of a familiar fear and a faint scent of basil/lime. Derrick!

Panting, he pounded toward them on the walking bridge. "What is it? Heart? The cold?"

Oompa stretched his neck to look Derrick in the eye. "You came faster than the creek rose the year of the flash flood, back in—"

Derrick knelt opposite Beth and searched her face for an answer she couldn't give. He directed his attention back to Oompa. "Are you in pain?"

"A little," Oompa said. "You're crushing my hand."

Derrick released his vise clamp on the arm of the wheelchair and Oompa's hand that had been resting on it. "Sorry."

Oompa seemed to search for a fitting reply. "Good to know you're responsive," he said, his eyes twinkling. "She calls. You come running. Sounds like the start of a great relationship, if you ask me."

If he hadn't been so frail, and so right, Beth would have slugged him in his bony arm.

ꟹ

"Careful here."

Derrick steered the wheelchair around a low spot and onto the approach to the covered bridge. Once inside the hallowed tunnel of wood and history, the three were out of the wind, light as it was, except for where it stole through the gaps between the boards.

"Never did like all the graffiti," Oompa said, his voice echoing down the bridge's long belly.

As far up as humans could reach, graffiti covered the walls. Oompa motioned toward a spot almost halfway through the bridge, on the wall facing downstream. "No use for graffiti," he repeated, "except this one."

Derrick traced where he pointed. Beth joined him, drawing closer to read the carved inscription. FOUND JOY HERE. The words were low on the wall, near a knothole. Eye level for Oompa in his chair. Stoop level for Beth. Pretzel level for Derrick.

Beth stepped back. "Oompa! You wrote that?"

"I'm pretty sure the statute of limitations has expired on that bit of vandalism." Oompa tucked his neck deeper into his coat collar and scarf.

Derrick's fingers followed the line of the words, worn but clear. Then he traced the knothole. About two inches wide and three inches long, it formed a diamond-shaped window to the world beyond the bridge. He peered through the opening. Cedar Creek glistened in the thin November sunlight. The footbridge downstream stood firm and unweathered, welcoming, but in some strange way storyless. The covered bridge in which the three huddled was bent with the weight of its stories.

"Beth, take a look."

He scooted back so she could crouch in front of the knothole.

"Beautiful. Interesting how such a narrow window can reveal such a wide scene."

Oompa laid a hand on Beth's back. Derrick watched as the knobby gloved fingers traced a sideways figure eight, infinity, across her shoulders. "Child of mine, that's what I've been trying to tell you. It's what this spot taught me."

Derrick stood and stepped away from grandfather and granddaughter. But he couldn't leave altogether. He backed away to the opening of the bridge. Sound carried well enough.

"You and a woman named Joy used to meet here?" Beth said.

"What?"

"Joy. You've mentioned some mysterious woman named Joy. Did. . .did Grandma know about her?"

"Bethlehem Meredith Schurmer! I was entirely and utterly faithful to your grandmother until and every day of the four years since she died!"

She turned toward him. "It's just that you seemed so taken with this Joy person."

"Not a person."

Beth glanced Derrick's direction. He shrugged, at a loss to offer any clarity.

"Oompa." She stood, leaned her back against the wall of the bridge, and sighed. "I want to understand."

"I came here often in my younger days. To think." He sucked in a labored breath. "To sort things out."

His chest rose in another exaggerated inhalation.

"Once, I came a broken man."

ଓ

Broken? When had her grandfather ever been less than monument strong? Before his health failed, that is. When had he not been a rock of faith, confident, in control?

Beth shivered. As soon as the thought occurred to her that she should have worn as heavy a coat as she forced on Oompa, warmth encircled her from behind. Derrick's arms. She leaned into them.

Oompa's face brightened. He pointed at the pillar of strength behind her. "That one. He's good for you, child. You hang on to him."

Beth returned Oompa's smile but added, "That's not the subject we were talking about. Broken?"

"You thought I was handling my grief just fine after your grandma died."

"You kept going." The words squeezed their way past the tension in her throat.

Oompa stared at his feet on the wheelchair's footrests. "On the outside. I kept going on the outside."

Derrick's arms tightened around her.

"You and Grandma were together a long time."

Oompa rubbed his palms on his thighs. "I thought I'd be better prepared to let her go when the time came." He held Beth's gaze. It wasn't hard to decipher the deeper meaning for her.

"'To everything, there is a season and a time for every purpose under heaven,'" Derrick quoted.

Oompa joined in, singing. "Turn, turn, turn."

The two men broke into all-out laughter.

The air chilled by several degrees. "How can you laugh at a time like this? Derrick!" She elbowed him and pulled away. "Oompa! Your heart was broken and you ran to another woman for comfort?"

"Another woman? Oh, Beth. I found *joy* here." He wiped the corners of his eyes and composed himself. "I staggered onto this bridge almost a year after your grandmother died, an inch from wishing my own life had ended. I fell to my knees where you're standing, crying out to God to give me a reason, one reason to believe life was worth living."

Beth's pulse quickened.

"I peered out through that knothole. Until I got up close to it, all I could see was a tiny slice of water and trees, the size of the knothole itself. When I put my eye right up to it, I could see clear downstream, could see that the creek bent and curved and straightened again, that rocks interrupted its flow only temporarily. I hadn't sensed anything more than a distant comfort from the Lord until that moment. I rediscovered joy."

Joy.

"The next day, you called, Beth."

"No job, no place to live, a degree but nothing to show for it except school loans I couldn't repay. Oh, Oompa, if I'd known you were in such a desperate place, I wouldn't have called and added to your grief."

The wheelchair squeaked as he shifted his weight. "Don't you understand? You were my answer. I asked for a reason to live. God gave me more than one, but the primary reason was you. You needed me."

"Yet again. At least as much as I did when you and Grandma took me in when I was just a kid."

"You reminded me that I mattered to someone."

"Oh, Oompa!" She bent to nestle her head on his shoulder and hug as much of him as she could reach. They held each other until Beth heard a ripping sound. Paper, not fabric.

Derrick had ripped a page from his notebook and was making a pencil rubbing of Oompa's inscription: FOUND JOY HERE.

Chapter 9

Did Oompa call you Bethlehem?" Derrick and Beth sat at the two-person round table in the customer area of Life by Chocolate. She sipped a foamed Mexican hot chocolate. He poured himself a clear mug of chilled apple cider. Her Oompa was two doors down, engaged in conversation with one of his buddies, no doubt recounting every sharable detail of his outdoor adventure.

Beth tapped her lips with a brownie-colored napkin, taking much longer than necessary, even if she'd had a hot chocolate mustache.

"Bethlehem?" he repeated. He could see in her eyes a confusing swirl of some emotion that registered as a mix of pride and pain.

"You wanna make something of it?"

"It's not an ordinary name."

She stirred her drink. "It wasn't an ordinary night."

"The night you were born?"

Beth stopped stirring. "Well, that, too, from what I hear. But I meant the night Jesus was born."

He reached across the table and brushed an eyelash from her peach-skin cheek. "It's a beautiful name."

"Bethlehem? It's different. When I was a preteen and

embarrassed about everything in my life, the name felt awkward. But truthfully, it's an honor to be named after the scene of such an important event. Although, I suppose if you took that to its natural conclusion, I could have been named Golgotha."

"That would have been unfortunate."

Her eyebrows rose into her bangs. Then her wind-chime laughter filled the room. He joined in, blessed by her sense of humor once again.

Her strength, her tenacity even when life was tough or short, her *joie de vivre*—hidden sometimes, but there—made him ask, *Lord, maybe us? Is there a future for the two of us?*

Her laughter wound down and left a residue of joy.

"Derrick?"

"Hmm?"

"Can I ask you a personal question?"

What am I doing here? Please don't ask that. Am I really interested in running a brownie shop for the rest of my life? Don't ask. Am I interested in you? Don't ask. . .yet. "Personal question? Sure."

Beth stared into what was left of her hot chocolate. "I might as well just come out with it. I've fallen in love. . ."

He choked on a bubble of saliva.

". . .with your ginger cookie brownies. Yesterday's special. Do you have any left?" Her cinnamon sugar smile told him she was completely serious.

So was he. Different subject.

ঙ

Beth hoped he bought her I'm-so-in-love-with-your-ginger-cookie-brownies save. What she'd really wanted to ask might have sent him running farther than the back room. *Do you see any kind of future for us? Could it be. . .maybe. . .us?*

What had she been thinking? Life was on hold until. . .

That's not a thought Oompa would approve of. One of his themes on the bridge trip was that no matter what the season, life goes on.

But she had a building crumbling faster than Derrick's apple crisp topping. Any breath might be Oompa's last. And then what would she do?

Keep going.

By God's grace, she'd keep going. Maybe with a little help from a new friend as tall as a windmill and as dependable as power outages during ice storms.

Was he making her a fresh batch of ginger cookie brownies? He should have been back already.

She stood and walked to the glass-front display case. "Derrick?"

His recently hired staffers were gone for the day. The mixers and ovens stood silent. He should have heard her, even in the back room.

She leaned over the case. "Derrick?"

No answer.

Life by Chocolate allowed its customers a peek behind the scenes. A large stainless steel table behind the counter served as the cutting and packing table, so people like Beth could watch all the deliciousness in the journey from baking pans to gourmet boxes to her mouth.

What was that three-ring binder on the table's low shelf? Derrick's recipes? Ooh! What a treasure. She skirted around the counter and bent to look, not touch. No, a baker's stash of secret recipes couldn't be more sacred. It wouldn't be right to—

The folder next to it on the shelf looked familiar. She'd seen it often when Derrick sat beside Oompa's rocker. That, and his leather notebook and the comfort-grip pen he carried. If he'd brought the folder to the Yarn Shop with him, it couldn't contain secret recipes.

The folder lay open. She should warn Derrick about how easy it would be for someone to inadvertently discover—

A manuscript? A flash of tightness zinged across the back of her skull. *Yarns from the Yarn Shop by Erik Hoffman.*

Derrick. Erik.

Hoffman. Hofferman.

No wonder the rhythm of his name sounded vaguely familiar! Erik Hoffman had showed up often on recommended reading lists in her creative writing classes at the UW. He wasn't the world's tallest brownie guy. He was the world's sneakiest author!

Oompa's stories! He was using Oompa, using *her* to get to him. What was a nice, godly word for rat fink?

Beth slammed the folder shut without viewing more than the title page. She'd seen enough. Had enough.

She was halfway to the exit when she heard, "Beth?" She turned on her heel, hands on hips.

Derrick stood in the doorway to the back room, plate in hand. "Are you leaving?"

"You could say that."

"Sorry it took so long. I'd frozen the leftover ginger brownies to take to a women's shelter in Milwaukee. I don't have a microwave here in the shop, so I ran down to the café to use theirs. I guess it took longer than I thought, but. . ."

"But you always go the extra mile, right?" The sarcasm in her voice tasted sour in her mouth.

Derrick glanced briefly at the confection in his hands,

frowning as if it had betrayed him somehow. "Did I do something to offend you?"

Beth dropped her hip pose and let her shoulders slump forward. "I'm not going to answer that for fear it will show up in your *book*."

She was within a step or two of the Yarn Shop before the door to Life by Chocolate finished swinging shut.

ଓ

Oompa, he's using you! And me. I know it looked like Derrick or Erik or whatever his name is seemed genuinely interested in us. In you. But he's been pirating your stories like people pirate a WiFi signal!

If she didn't calm down, she could boil dinner without using a stove. And she didn't dare say those words out loud to a man whose heart was as fragile as spun sugar and who could stop breathing by choking on a reply. Her fuming had to stay internal.

Now what?

Lord, now what?

If she tattled on Derrick, the disappointment could spread a pall over Oompa's remaining days. He lit up when Derrick came into the shop. Oompa animated—a heartwarming sight. Like the glow of the Christmas bulbs up and down Washington Avenue.

If she snitched on Derrick, who would suffer? The one man who didn't deserve it, the one who was entitled to all the shiny flecks of joy he could collect this side of glory.

She'd started to hope, these last few weeks. She'd dropped a few pounds of junior high baggage and bad memories. Derrick's attention seemed so real.

Now she knew the answer to her "Maybe us?" question. No.

No way. His interest in her wasn't genuine. And apparently her scars weren't all the way healed. Raw, they stung at the memory of kindness Derrick showed her. His arms around her while they waited for Oompa's doctor. His "Here, taste this" chocolate gifts. The way he made her laugh just by being himself.

Whoever *that* was.

Beth checked on Oompa, who snoozed in his chair, then slipped into the adjoining apartment at the back of the shop. How pathetic! She couldn't find anything to do with her angst except take it out on the dirty dishes in the soapstone sink.

☙

He could see her through the window in the rear door of the apartment, back hunched over her work as if trying to scrub the handles off a spaghetti pot. She deserved an explanation. . . the one he couldn't give her.

Not for a few more weeks.

He leaned his forehead against the door. A little too hard. The clunk made her turn toward the sound, dishwater dripping from her hands and venom dripping from the look in her eyes. No, that wasn't venom. More like liquid pain.

She swiped at her eyes with the back of her hand. Her one-sided squint told him the dishwater still had plenty of suds power, adding insult to injury. Or rather, injury to his insult.

He had to tell her. Both things. About the book and about his true feelings for her, as if she'd believe anything he said now.

"May I come in?" he shouted through the glass.

Squinting and blinking, she mouthed the words, "Go away."

☙

She'd told him to go away. And he *did!*

Beth blinked again. Still gone. What did that say about

him? He didn't even have the courage to defend his actions, to insist, "Hey, Beth, hear me out."

She turned back to the sink, slapped the dishrag on the surface of the water like a beaver might swat his tail, and dodged the tsunami she created.

Splatters of dishwater fell on the devotional book she'd propped on the low shelf above the sink.

Like spit, she thought. She remembered her morning reading, the verse from the book of James, and the punch line author's quote: *Those who receive grace by the bucket and dish it out with an eyedropper fail to understand the vast measure of God's grace.*

Her anger had spit on the page and the concept.

As far as Oompa knew, Derrick was a fine young man who loved to listen to his stories, add a few of his own, and make him laugh. Derrick/Erik Hofferman/Hoffman might have a plan to profit from her grandfather's yarns, but whatever his intentions, he'd blessed Oompa. She could fight that other battle after. . .

"Beth?"

Oompa's voice barely reached her in the apartment, though she'd left the door between it and the shop open. He needed her.

She wiped her hands on the towel lying on the counter and headed toward his voice, knowing she'd keep hers silent rather than risk coloring his final days with the kind of disappointment that now weighed like a millstone on her heart.

Chapter 10

An awkward, Beth-less Thanksgiving—a slow cooker turkey leg and boxed stuffing—bent over his laptop led into three weeks on tiptoes. His arches should be in fine shape by now. Every day he tiptoed around the issue he didn't dare talk about, its pages long edited and fired off to the publisher. Still, they burned an irreparable hole in the fabric of his relationship with Bethlehem Schurmer.

Once the town found out about his buche de noel cakes, he'd been busier than Cedarburg's holiday event calendar. But a tight schedule didn't keep him from wishing things could be different between them, and wishing he could be honest with her without betraying another confidence.

Why she let him continue to visit Oompa, he couldn't say. She kept her distance, that's for sure.

"I tried a new recipe," he said, plate extended toward her. The Christmas log looked so much like birch bark, he half expected it to crinkle when he cut into it.

"No, thank you. I'm not. . .hungry." Beth busied herself arranging moebius scarves on a pegged stand.

Strained, but civil.

"Beth, I think you'll like it. Try just a bite?"

"I'm sorry. I have a customer."

He scanned the Yarn Shop. Oompa's eyes were closed, though his chair rocked as if teased by the gusts of warm air from the temperamental furnace. Shoppers passed on the sidewalk outside the window. Some even stopped to look at Beth's holiday display of knit ornaments.

No one else occupied the shop. She had a customer?

As if knowing his thoughts, she added, "On the Internet."

She wasn't anywhere near her computer. But she also wasn't a liar. That label belonged to him. Temporarily. It hadn't seemed so complicated in its origins; benevolent, even. But now the ruse fed the tension both between them and inside him.

Beth, if you only knew. . .

"I'll leave you to your work, then." He set the plate on the cash counter. She opened her mouth as if to object but didn't.

"Hey!" Oompa hollered from his now stock-still chair. Pointing at the air between the two, he yelled, "Sparks like that could hurt somebody!"

The room fairly crackled with his distress. And it smelled faintly of burnt wiring.

"Get away from there!" Oompa shouted, rising from his chair.

A blue-white spark shot out of the light switch behind the counter, sizzling through the space between Derrick and Beth. They both jumped back. Like frantic synchronized swimmers, they simultaneously pulled out their cell phones, punched a series of three numbers and yelled, "Fire at the Yarn Shop!" as the lights went out.

ↄ

Oompa adjusted the nosepiece of his oxygen tubing. "You know, Cedarburg's first firehouse burned to the ground. Ironic, huh?"

Beth gripped the broom handle tighter and resumed sweeping singed plaster from the floor behind the counter. She should have insisted he stay away from the place. But his insister was stronger than hers. Now that danger of sparks and smoke were gone, he insisted on being in the middle of the action.

"This building is still standing, such as it is," she said, eyeing the thin, smoky shadow that rose a foot and a half above the now defunct light switch. "Once we get the rest of the wiring replaced, we shouldn't have to worry about that, at least."

"Did you call the electrician?"

"Oompa! The firemen just left! Give me a minute."

She dropped the broom and her irritation. "I am so sorry. I shouldn't have groused at you. Sometimes I think this building will be the death of me." She crossed to where Oompa's rocker sat in its current new location, dislodged from its roots by conscientious firemen searching every inch of the shop and the attached apartment for more signs of electrical shorts.

"Oompa, forgive me."

He stroked her hair with more gentleness than frailty. "Oh, child. I'm the one who should ask your forgiveness."

"For what?"

"Saddling you with this building, this shop, with me. That's no life for a young woman like you."

The words forming in Beth's throat got stuck there. She urged them out. "I am so blessed to have had you in my life. I don't know what I would have done without you." That began to sound like a eulogy, so she shifted direction. "You've loved me through some hard years. You've always been there for me."

He leaned his head back. "Did you just say those things to me or to the good Lord?"

A tear traced a Cedar Creek–crooked path down her

cheek. "Both, I guess."

"That's my girl. I wish I could have handed you a building that wasn't so ornery. And a business that stirred your heart."

She drew back. "It's an honor to manage the Yarn Shop."

"But it's not your heart's desire, now, is it?" He tucked his chin to his chest. The oxygen tubing buckled like bent wings at the sides of his throat. She reached to make sure the flow wasn't interrupted.

"Don't think I don't know," he said, "where your heart lies. Just a little while longer, Lord willing, and you'll have a chance to pursue your own dream."

The bell above the door jingled. Derrick walked in with what looked like industrial-strength soot cleaner and a giant-sized sponge. Miserable timing. *He is so not what Oompa meant.*

☙

Erik shook the snowflakes off his built-in wooly cap. "It's snowing."

Beth ignored him, walked to the wide front windows, and peered out into the deepening night. Was she as enamored as he was with the way each snowflake seemed to light up when it drifted past one of the Christmas lights?

"Is it supposed to accumulate?" she asked.

So much for her appreciation of the artistry of it all. He couldn't fault her, though. She'd been through a lot. It probably felt like her life was collapsing around her. Busiest season of the year and her shop was a mess. What might have happened to her inventory if the soot and flames had gone farther than that one wall behind the counter? What if smoke had filled the room rather than just smeared a wall? What if the spark had ignited Oompa's oxygen? What if the short had happened in the middle of the night?

They all had a lot to be thankful for. *They?* Bad habit of his—presuming himself into the scene. Why hadn't he been smart enough to hide the manuscript? So close to the end, so close to success, and he'd ruined what he now knew would have been the greatest reward for his efforts—a chance to win and keep Beth's trust.

"Is it?"

He should have been grateful she was speaking to him. "Is it what?"

"Supposed to accumulate?"

"I'm not sure. Are you two going to be okay tonight?"

What was that expression on her face? Softness. As if she were at least a little grateful he cared.

"We're fine."

Oompa half turned in his rocker. "Erik, put that stuff down and come here. It's time we came clean with Beth. The secret's about to do us both in."

☙

Oompa was in on it? That made no sense. Beth itched to step outside and clear her lungs, her head. Mid-December guaranteed stimulating iciness to the air. Beyond that door, she'd find no smell of soot or secrets.

"Beth, child?"

She rubbed her eyes and pressed her index fingers against her tear ducts. "I'm listening."

As they had so many times in the past months, Beth sat on one side of the rocker and Erik on the other. She rested her hands in her lap and made eye contact with her grandfather. Brief glances at Erik were all she could manage.

Oompa drew a deep, oxygenated breath, smiled, and reached his hand toward Erik. "Beth, meet your new landlord."

"Mr. Schurmer, are you sure this is the time to—?"

"Young man, look at her face. As much as we wanted to wait until Christmas Eve. . ."

She waved her hands in the air between the two men. "I'm here. You could talk to *me* about this whatever it is. Landlord?"

"I've sold the building to Erik. Well, officially to Nicole. She's on her way."

Beth looked from one smiling male to the other, the confusion intensified by their seeming disregard for her distress. "Who's Nicole?"

"That would be me."

The voice came from the entrance. A female version of the man she'd known as Derrick filled the doorway. Copper curls tamed by an updo that made her look even taller than her WNBA height matched Erik's, hair follicle for hair follicle.

Beth sought confirmation from him. "Your sister?"

"*She's* the one who made the basketball team. Hey, Nicole! Let me get that for you."

The woman relinquished the microwave-sized box in her arms. "Somehow I knew I'd find you here." She stripped off her leather gloves, hugged Erik, then rushed to embrace first Beth, then Oompa. "So good to finally meet you two!"

Beth's mouth had hung open so long her tongue bumps dried out.

The box deposited on the counter near the cash register, Erik returned to the circle-of-life-and-confusion. He nudged Nicole toward the chair he'd occupied and drew another closer. "Oliver and Beth Schurmer, I'd like you to meet my much-loved sister, Nicole."

The woman mirrored the same warmth and congeniality as her brother.

"Oompa, good to see you in person," she said, patting his knee. "And Beth." Without taking her gaze from Beth, she said, "Not that you need my opinion, Derrick, but I highly approve."

Beth found her voice. "Okay, what's going on here?"

Butter-smooth hands held hers as if the news about to be broadcast could change her life. "Beth, I make a mean brownie, but my sister and her husband own Life by Chocolate. I'm. . ."

"A writer. I know."

"Nicole owns my building, and now this one, too."

Beth stole a glance at Oompa. Unfazed, he continued grinning as if enjoying a rollicking good movie at the Rivoli.

"Oompa, is that true?" Her substitute career now had more than bad wiring to worry about.

"Hark, the herald angels sing! Glory to the newborn King! Peace on—"

Carolers dressed in heavy coats, some of them sporting Beth's moebius scarves, stood outside the front window, beaming their joy into the shop through the plate glass. Beth considered flinging a shoe at the window in a "not now" gesture, but resisted. The crisis on hold until the song ended, she and the other three turned their full attention to the song. Beth caught the irony that Christmas and chaos collided in her—in Oompa's—shop.

When the singers moved up the street, Beth let the truth of the song, the spirit of the season, unclench her nerve endings. "I don't understand," she said. If Nicole was anything like her brother, she possessed a caring heart and faith to match. How could any of those people not have her best interests in mind? Benefit of the doubt might be the most significant Christmas gift she gave this year.

Oompa's face wore an expression of contentment. He leaned forward to say, "Beth, you've done a fine job taking over your grandmother's wool business."

She looked at the sooted, tangled, plaster-dandruffed shop. *Sure, I have.*

"Any hardships here existed before I made you take over."

Her heart muscle cramped. "Oompa, you didn't force me to manage the shop. I was lost and you. . ." Why couldn't she pry the next word from the hollow in her neck?

"Loved you." Oompa closed then opened his eyes, not a blink but a benediction. "I loved you, and I needed your help."

"Me, too," Erik added. "I mean, needed you. Not that that I don't lo—"

Nicole slapped her brother on the knee. "Erik!" She shot a quick glance at Beth.

"It's okay," he sighed. "She knows I'm Erik Hoffman."

"Does she know everything?"

Beth dragged the conversation back to first person. "I know you're a writer. I know you've been listening to Oompa's stories for a project of yours."

"Of *yours*," Oompa interjected. "It's for you, honey."

Snow swirled in a riot of light-reflecting iced ballerinas in the glow of holiday lights. Her thoughts swirled in a similar tangle, but faster and with less direction. *For me? Oompa sold the shop? Derrick/Erik isn't who he said he was, but it doesn't matter? And now where do I go? And when Oompa's gone. . .* Winter hinted at a grand entrance in more arenas than one.

Her grandfather cleared his throat, which drew her attention back to the indoor scene. "Beth, don't think about your answer. Just say it. The first thing that comes to your mind. If you had the opportunity, and if you didn't feel obligated to do what you thought I wanted, you'd use this shop to sell—"

"Children's books."

"And your Derrick, or rather Erik, writes—"

"Children's b—" Her gasp echoed off the high ceiling.

Nicole left the circle, walked to the counter, and tore the packing tape from the top of the box. She dug inside and returned with a book held against her chest. "Children's books. Like this one." She held the hardcover, half-inch-thick book toward Beth like a Christmas gift.

The smooth cover, the weight of the words tucked inside, the pen-and-ink illustrations reminded her why she loved books. She made a return trip to the cover. *Cedarburg Yarns by Oliver Schurmer as Told to Erik Hoffman*. The room held its breath as she turned to the dedication page and caught sight of her name—Bethlehem Schurmer—and words that made her tear ducts work overtime.

"For me?"

The loose skin under Oompa's arctic gray eyes held crescents of moisture. "I've long known where your heart lay, child. But until Nicole offered to buy this shop as well as her own and I discovered the identity of her famous brother, the one who baked brownies for her between book contracts. . ."

Nicole cringed then smiled. "I may have let that slip."

Oompa took the opportunity to draw a breath. "My bequeathing this building to you would have been a handicap, not a blessing, Beth. For it to stay upright, it needed a face-lift I couldn't afford."

Beth drew a breath of her own.

"Then Erik offered to write my stories to help raise funds for repairs that would have to be done no matter who owned the building. And the sale of the shop will afford you the means to start fresh, following your own dream, not mine or your grandmother's."

"But I. . ." What should she even ask?

Oompa's eyes twinkled. "It sounded like such a good idea to keep it a surprise. My Christmas gift to you. Maybe my last one. Then love made things. . .complicated."

"You can still call it the Yarn Shop," Nicole interjected, "assuming you want to stay in Cedarburg. Stories. Yarns. You've already made the connection in this community. Now, it will be children's stories. A new season for the shop. For you. If you want to stay."

Her pulse pounded. "Will he be here?" She nodded toward the Erik she knew as Derrick.

He crouched to look her in the eye. "I want to be part of this endeavor."

Oh. The children's bookstore. Of course.

"And of your life, Beth. An infinity ending to the question, 'Maybe us?'"

Oompa reached for the book in Beth's hands. "Let me see that thing. Now, turn your head a little to the right."

She obeyed.

"Lift your chin."

"Oompa, what—?"

"Okay, Erik. There's your opportunity."

Beth's breath caught as "her" Erik leaned in, cupped her cheeks in his hands, and planted a brownie-flavored kiss on her waiting lips.

"Sweet," she whispered, when the kiss concluded.

"Sorry. I've been taste testing," he said.

"That's not what I meant."

Nicole punched her brother in the biceps. "About time."

And Oompa, raspy but confident, led in a chorus of "Joy to the World!"

Cynthia Ruchti is a past president of American Christian Fiction Writers and now serves as ACFW's Professional Relations Liaison. For more than thirty-two years, she wrote and produced The Heartbeat of the Home radio broadcast. She speaks and teaches at women's events and writers' conferences. Cynthia and her plot-tweaking husband live in the heart of Wisconsin where she writes stories of hope-that-glows-in-the-dark. You can connect with her at www.cynthiaruchti.com..